To the people of France and to all the brave allies who fought to free them—especially my father, Roscoe Rouse, Jr., who served as a U.S. Army Air Corps B-17 navigator; my father-in-law, Edward Phillips Wells, who served as U.S. Army doctor near the front in France; and to William "Wild Bill" Correll, who served as a first scout with the 100th Infantry division of the U.S. Army in France.

As always, this book is also dedicated to my two wonderful daughters, Taylor and Arden, and the love of my life, my husband, Ken.

THE

French
War Bride

Berkley titles by Robin Wells

THE WEDDING TREE
THE FRENCH WAR BRIDE

THE
French War Bride

ROBIN WELLS

BERKLEY BOOKS, NEW YORK

BERKLEY

An imprint of Penguin Random House LLC
375 Hudson Street, New York, New York 10014

This book is an original publication of Penguin Random House LLC.

Copyright © 2016 by Robin Wells.
Penguin supports copyright. Copyright fuels creativity, encourages diverse voices,
promotes free speech, and creates a vibrant culture. Thank you for buying an authorized
edition of this book and for complying with copyright laws by not reproducing, scanning, or
distributing any part of it in any form without permission. You are supporting writers and
allowing Penguin to continue to publish books for every reader.

BERKLEY® and the "B" design are registered trademarks of Penguin Random House LLC.
For more information, visit penguin.com.

Library of Congress Cataloging-in-Publication Data

Names: Wells, Robin (Robin Rouse), author.
Title: The French war bride / Robin Wells.
Description: Berkley trade paperback edition. | New York : Berkley, 2016. |
Series: Wedding tree ; 2
Identifiers: LCCN 2016014824 (print) | LCCN 2016022549 (ebook) | ISBN
9780425282441 (paperback) | ISBN 9780698405288 ()
Subjects: LCSH: War brides—Fiction. | World War, 1939-1945—Fiction. | World
War, 1939-1945—Underground movements—France—Fiction. |
France—History—German occupation, 1940-1945—Fiction. | BISAC: FICTION /
Contemporary Women. | FICTION / Historical. | GSAFD: Love stories. |
Historical fiction.
Classification: LCC PS3623.E4768 F74 2016 (print) | LCC PS3623.E4768 (ebook)
| DDC 813/.6—dc23
LC record available at https://lccn.loc.gov/2016014824

PUBLISHING HISTORY
Berkley trade paperback edition / August 2016

PRINTED IN THE UNITED STATES OF AMERICA

10   9   8   7   6   5   4   3   2

Cover photos: *Couple* © Collaboration JS/ArcAngel; *Paris background* © Martin Amis/ArcAngel.
Cover design by Sarah Oberrender.
Interior text design by Kelly Lipovich.

Penguin
Random
House

ACKNOWLEDGMENTS

This novel involved a tremendous amount of research. In the process of writing it, I poured through countless old newspaper stories, magazine articles, history books, and personal accounts. Books that were especially helpful included *When Paris Went Dark: The City of Light Under German Occupation 1940–1944* by Ronald C. Rosbottom, *Fleeing Hitler: France 1940* by Hanna Diamond, and *Americans in Paris: Life and Death Under Nazi Occupation* by Charles Glass.

I owe a special debt of gratitude to the National World War II Museum in New Orleans and the American War Bride Experience website: uswarbrides.com.

Heartfelt thanks to William "Wild Bill" Correll of Madison, Mississippi, for his recollection of France during World War II and, most especially, for his service in the cause of freedom. Wild Bill served with the U.S. Army's 100th Infantry and received the French Legion's Medal of Honor for bravery. Thank you, Bill, for your sacrifices, your insights, your memories, and your friendship.

Book
One

AMÉLIE
2016

I never knew what he saw in you."

For a moment, I wonder if I've imagined the woman's voice. *Mon Dieu*, but the words are familiar—I've said them often enough to myself over the last seventy-something years. But when I turn toward the door of my assisted living apartment—I am in the habit of leaving it open, so friends will know when I'm not indisposed—sure enough, there she stands: my husband's scorned fiancée.

She is older, of course—the whole world is, is it not?—and yet, I recognize her. She is still tall, at least compared to me, even though her back is now stooped with age and she walks with the aid of a cane. Her skin is still as pale as milk in a porcelain pitcher, although now it has the crepey texture that is the fate of all *les femmes d'un certain âge*. She still has cornflower eyes, a petite nose, and a way of holding it high as she looks at me, as if she smells something rancid.

I can't say that I blame her. If I'd been Jack's high school sweetheart who had written to him nearly every day while he completed medical school and military service, I, too, would have held a lifelong grudge against the woman he'd jilted me for.

Especially if that woman had been a war bride, and if I'd been wearing his engagement ring, waiting for him to come home and marry me and practice medicine with my father, so that I could live the life of a small-town doctor's wife, just like my mother. And especially, especially—can you do that in English with that word? Double it, like you can with *very* or *really*? I've never known—if I were a tall, gorgeous, smooth-haired blonde who must have had men standing ten deep to dance with me, and the war bride was small, dark, and French.

"Kat," I say, self-conscious of the accent I have tried, but never managed, to lose. "What a surprise."

"I imagine so. Although not as much of one as you gave me."

I laugh, then realize she isn't trying to be amusing. "You're right, of course."

She nods, her mouth a tight, disapproving line.

So. This is not to be an easy visit. I grip the arms of my chair and rise slowly to my feet. "Come in, Kat. Come in and have a seat."

She enters slowly, looking around. I can only imagine how the place looks to her. I moved to the Shady Oaks Assisted Living Center with Jack, when we thought he might recover from his stroke. In trying to make it feel like home, I furnished it with perhaps too many of our belongings. But then, my taste is old-school Parisienne—ornate and layered. I like my surroundings to appeal to all the senses. I watch Kat take in the heavily framed paintings, the large plush sofa, the deeply tufted rose-colored chairs, the fringed drapes. Knickknacks and books and magazines cover practically every surface. It's the kind of room where one can keep discovering things, little treasures like a crystal paperweight shaped like a rose, or the carving of a ship in the corner, or that sketch of a naked woman that she's staring at now, the one that Jack said looked like me. She looks shocked. I wonder if she thinks I posed for it. It pleases me to think she might believe so.

Most likely, however, she's thinking, *How on earth did Jack ever live with all this stuff?*

"Please—take this chair." I gesture to the large, cushioned bergère I've just vacated, the most comfortable seat in the apartment. "Can I offer you tea? Or a coffee?"

"No." Ignoring the chair, she settles heavily onto the sofa, the large gold velvet one that used to be in the formal living room at our home.

"So what brings you back to Wedding Tree?" I ask, retaking my seat as gracefully as my arthritic hips allow.

She fingers the double strand of pearls around her neck. "I have a great-granddaughter who recently moved here. She's with that new computer company in that monstrous building north of town."

"Oh, yes." It is a software firm, and the building is all graceful glass curves, with landscaping that always has something in bloom. I think it is lovely. "So you came to visit her?"

"That is my excuse. I actually came to talk to you." She grips her cane. "I need to know what happened."

"To Jack?" My chest suddenly feels hot and tight. "He had a stroke two years ago." I feel the loss, still, like a physical thing—as if I had lost an arm and a leg and half of my key organs.

"I know, I know. I was sorry to hear about it. Deepest condolences, of course. But that isn't what I meant." She has the grace to look ill at ease. "I meant about . . . earlier. About what happened between you and Jack in France. I want to know the details."

I pull my brows together. "Pardon me, but after all these years, surely it cannot matter?"

Kat's chin rises to an imperious angle. For a moment she looks like a portrait of Louis XVI, where he's wearing one those tight-necked blouses. "It has always mattered."

Oh, la! I cross, then uncross my legs. "Sometimes, Kat, it's best to just let bygones be gones." I realize I didn't say the phrase quite right. "Sometimes one needs to . . ." What is the saying in English for *passer l'éponge*? "To forgive and forget."

"Oh, I've forgiven. At least, I've forgiven Jack."

Et moi?

"I've tried to forgive you, as well," she continues, leaving me unsure if I'd spoken or only thought the question. As my age advances, that happens now and again. "At least as well as is humanly possible, with the little information I have. I forgave Jack right away so I wouldn't live a bitter life. And I haven't." Her chin again tilts up, and her eyes seem to throw down a challenge. "I've had a marvelous life."

"I'm so glad." I am, actually. I have always carried a burden of guilt about the way my actions affected her. "You married, I heard?"

"Oh, yes. A wonderful, wealthy man who adored me. I have four children, nine grandchildren, eighteen great-grandchildren and two great-great-grandchildren."

"What riches."

"Yes." She brushes an invisible piece of lint from her navy skirt. "I met my husband in Dallas when I left Wedding Tree. I've been very blessed. But I have one last item on what my great-grandchildren call my bucket list. You and Jack . . . it's the one thing in my life I have never understood. And . . ." She pauses. "I don't have much time left."

I smile. "At our age, no one does."

"Yes, but I know exactly how little time I have," she says. "You see, I had cancer years ago, and it's . . . well, it's back, and this time it's untreatable. I have no more than six months. Probably less."

My forehead knits. I resist the urge to cross myself. "I'm so, so sorry."

She waves her hand dismissively. "It gives me a framework. I'm carefully choosing how to spend my time."

"And you're choosing to spend some of it with me?" I'm afraid my tone reveals my incredulity. In her shoes, I'm sure I wouldn't have sought out my company.

Her head bobs in a single, somber nod. "I have not been able to understand how I could have been so wrong about Jack. I grew up knowing him, and . . . well, I thought he was an honorable man."

I look down at my wedding ring. The band is worn on the palm side of my finger, so thin it hardly holds together. "He was."

"He went back on his word to me."

"It really wasn't his fault."

"Oh, I know who shoulders most of the blame." The censor in her tone—well, my skin prickles upward, like the ruff of a wolf. "But, still . . . I was just so certain that Jack . . ."

I can't catch what she says next. I lean forward and touch my ear. "Pardon?"

She closes her eyes, her face drawn as if in pain. When she speaks, her voice cracks in a way that strikes the heart. "I thought he loved me."

"Oh, he did!" I say quickly.

"Obviously not enough, or he wouldn't have succumbed to your . . . charms."

The pause in her statement would have been funny if it didn't sting so much. I have always been aware that Kat was a great beauty, whereas I . . . well, no one would ever have described me that way. "I really gave him no choice," I say.

"Unless you drugged him and tied him down, seduction is no excuse for infidelity."

I am startled and amused. I fight to hide both reactions. "No?"

"No. Seduction is only an attempt, a temptation. True love will resist."

Her notion of true love—so naive, so ridiculously American!—makes me smile.

"I fail to see anything funny." Her voice is like needles, prickly and sharp.

"No, no—of course not. It's just that, Kat—it was wartime, and things were not so black and white."

She dismisses my remark with a sweep of her hand. "There are no excuses."

With that mindset, nothing I say will make any difference. "Well, then, why are you here?"

"To hear the truth. My hospice counselor . . . he's been very helpful. He's Jewish, of all things." She leans forward a bit. "You know, Amélie, at your age, you might want to look into consulting one, too."

I think this is a—how do you say it?—a dig, but I can't be sure. "I don't think you can get a hospice counselor if you aren't ill," I say softly, wondering if Kat has some form of dementia. So many of us do as we age.

She shrugs. "Ill, old—it's all the same. Anyway, Jacob suggested that I do whatever I need to do to make peace with the past. And I realized that I needed to come see you and hear the truth."

The truth. Mon Dieu, what a horrifying concept! My heart gives a hard, pointed-toe kick to my ribs. "What did Jack tell you?" I ask, trying to buy some time.

"Very little. Something about you tricking him, but I dismissed it, of course."

"You should have believed him," I say.

Her eyes meet mine directly for the first time since she sat down. "Just how did you trick him? I need to know what happened. Please. I want to hear the full story so I can die in peace."

"What makes you think it will bring you peace? It's likely to anger you."

"Just tell me. Please. It is for the good of my eternal soul."

Oh, my—how does one refuse such a request? My breath hitches.

"I need to know the exact nature of what you did so that I can forgive you fully," she says. "Not for your sake—quite frankly, I couldn't care less about you—but for mine. I understand that God only forgives us as we forgive others." She sits quietly for a moment. "I need to know what you did."

I had believed that the secrets of my early days with Jack would die with me. The notion of dredging them all up, of shining a light on what I had worked so hard to bury, makes my heart both race and stop, although I know this is biologically impossible. "I do not mean to be rude, but this is a private matter. What was between Jack and me is really not your concern."

"Not my concern? Not my *concern*?" She is suddenly a lion—her forehead creased, her mouth large, her voice larger, roaring in a way that is likely to summon an aide. She pounds her cane on the floor to emphasize each word. "You stole my life!"

My upper lip breaks a sweat, while my mouth feels packed with gauze. "You said you had a wonderful life. That you married a wonderful man."

"I did. He was wealthy, handsome, successful, adoring. But . . ."

In that heartbeat of a pause, I know what she is going to say. The words come out barely more than a whisper; the lion is now a wounded lamb. ". . . He wasn't Jack."

No, of course not. No one else in the world was Jack. "I—" I start to say I am sorry, but what good would that do? An apology would bring back nothing, would give her nothing. And I wouldn't mean it, anyway; I would not have given up a single moment with that magnificent man.

"Please," she begs.

I look at her and try to see her objectively. It is what Jack used to do with his patients—to remove assumptions and judgments, to try to see them clearly. She is an old woman, searching for the truth about her life. Ah, *merde.*

"The truth is not likely to bring you the peace you want," I warn again.

In fact, peace is the last thing it's likely to bring. How can she forgive me once she hears the full extent of my deceptions?

How can I forgive myself? I had hoped to die without digging through the graveyard of my past, picking through and laying out all the skeletons of shame and pain—the shame and pain that I'd suffered myself, but far worse, the shame and pain I'd unintentionally inflicted on others.

And yet, what excuse do I have to withhold what she wants to know, aside from pure selfishness? Elise is gone, so I no longer need worry about protecting her. I have lived through the true horror of old age, which is outliving a child.

"I don't even know where you and Jack met," Kat says.

This, at least, I can give her. "It was at a church." It was l'Église Saint-Médard, on the rue Mouffetard in the fifth arrondissement. I can picture it so clearly I might have visited it just yesterday. Jack and I didn't meet there, exactly; one might call it more of an encounter.

"I was kneeling at the end of the altar, sitting back on my heels, my head against the railing, when Jack entered the confessional. He didn't see me—and I didn't look up to see him."

"Wait!" Kat holds up her hand like a traffic cop. "Jack went into a confessional? But he was Baptist!"

I nod. "He was there on behalf of someone else."

Kat sits silently for a moment, apparently digesting this. "And you? You were there because you were religious?"

"No. I was there because I was desperate." Desperate and despairing, with nowhere else to turn.

As I think of it, memories waft in like wisps of fog and cling to each other. "I was . . . how do you say? . . . at the end of my rope. Heartbroken and . . . and . . . just broken. I needed a miracle."

"Why? What had happened?"

"So much. So very, very much." The fog was thickening, coalescing into something with weight and shape.

"I mean with Jack. You said he went into the confessional."

She didn't want information about me—only about Jack. Of course. "Yes. He went in, and I overheard him talking to the priest—he spoke French quite fluently, you know—and what he was saying . . . well, I couldn't help but listen."

"What did he say?"

"He explained that he had been with an evacuation hospital unit in Normandy that was following the First Army on its march through France."

"Yes, yes. He wrote me of that."

"He said he and a young medic were helping a wounded infantryman out of a Jeep when a lone German soldier, dazed and disoriented and probably wounded himself, wandered into the hospital zone. He had a machine gun, and he aimed it at them. The medic had a gun; he knew Jack was not armed. He pushed Jack out of the way and shot the soldier."

I remember how Jack's voice faltered as he told this to the priest. Even now, the memory makes my own throat thicken.

"The medic saved Jack's life, but in the process, the machine gun fired into his chest. As he lay dying, he asked Jack for a priest; he wanted to confess. There was not time to find one. Jack said he would hear his confession, and later relay it to a priest. That was why Jack was at the church that day—to confess by proxy for the medic."

"Catholics can do that?" Kat asks.

What ridiculous details snag this woman's attention! But then, she wouldn't know; like Jack, she, too, was raised Baptist. "No, and the priest told Jack as much. 'Well, I gave my word,' Jack said, 'so I'm going to tell you his confession anyway.'"

"So he did?"

"Yes. Jack said that the medic had been separated from his unit soon after the American landing—what is now called D-day. A young Frenchwoman hid him from the Germans for a few weeks and helped him connect with the American hospital unit. He feared he'd gotten her pregnant. He loved her, and he'd intended to return and marry her.

"The priest replied that he would pray for the young man's soul, and asked his name.

"'Doug Claiborne from Whitefish, Montana,' Jack replied.

"The priest asked if Jack knew the name of the girl or where she was from.

"'No,' Jack said. 'The medic was fighting for his last breath as he told me this. He said he had a note with her address in his coat pocket, but when I looked for it, there was just a hole where the pocket should have been.'

"'Then there is nothing you can do,' the priest said."

I close my eyes, seeing the dimly lit church again in my mind's eye. I can practically smell the wood polish on the altar rail, practically see the flicker of the votive candles.

"It was wrong, but as Jack and the priest talked, their voices grew softer, and I crept closer to better hear. As I neared the confessional, I saw what looked like a doctor's bag outside the curtain. A metal tag was attached to the top. I flipped it over and read his name: Dr. Jack O'Connor.

"'And you, my son?' the priest had asked. 'Do you have something to confess?'

"'Only that I do not deserve to be alive,' Jack said. 'Another man died when it was meant to be me.'

"'Apparently God thinks otherwise. Are you going home soon?'

"'Not yet. I'm stationed at the 365th army station hospital here in Paris—it used to be the American Hospital. I'm here for at least a couple more months, maybe longer.'

"'Ahh,' the priest said. 'Well, I will pray for you.'"

I open my eyes to see Kat frowning at me. Until this moment, I had not realized I had closed them. "Right then and there, I formulated a plan."

Kat's eyebrows rise. "A plan?"

"Yes. But in order to understand, you must know what life was like for me during the war."

Kat waves her hand in that dismissive gesture again. "I don't care about your sufferings. Have you cared about mine all these years?"

"Not as I should have." She does not really want to forgive, I realize. She does not want to let me off the hoof, I think the saying goes. I tamp down my irritation, then force myself to look at her again, as Jack would have done—objectively, without bias or emotion.

Sacré coeur. She is an old woman who is dying. I realize I must grant her wish. But first, I will lay down some rules.

"Some actions only make sense if you know the reasons why. If I am to tell you this story—the whole ugly truth of it all—I insist on telling it at my own pace, in my own way. I will tell it without interruptions or questions, or I won't tell it at all."

She nods, her mouth pinched and tight.

"This might take a while," I warn.

She lifts her shoulders in that stiff little shrug again. "I have nothing to do but hear this and die."

And I have nothing to do but to tell it. I sigh, then draw a deep breath and begin.

2

AMÉLIE
September 1, 1939

For me, the war began with the battle of the zipper.

I was at the dressmaker's shop with my mother on that Friday afternoon, each of us selecting fabric and trim for new winter dresses. Mme Depard's shop always smelled like lavender and face powder, combined with the sharp scent of fabric dye. The scent always filled me with a floaty kind of hopefulness. The dressmakers would conjure up the perfect dress, one that would transform me from a gangly young girl into a beautiful, confident, full-breasted woman. The scent of the shop was a heady promise.

The scent was also an allergen that made my eyes water.

It was after school—fall classes had begun just that week—and I was wearing my uniform: a starched white shirt with a round collar, a shapeless navy pinafore, and oxford shoes. I was sixteen years old and I was, of course, excited at the prospect of a new ensemble. The fabric Maman and I had selected was a green wool jersey, and I'd finally convinced Maman to let me have a fitted waist with a belt—a grown-up silhouette. She had just started allowing me to wear heels and stockings for special occasions.

Maman wanted to pick out buttons for the back, but I desperately wanted my dress to have a zipper. All of the chic girls attending university in the Quartier Latin wore dresses with zippers, and I, still being in lycée, looked up to them. Maman thought zippers looked cheap—which, in truth, they were. They were less expensive to install, and therefore the sign of factory-made clothes.

Papa was a professor, and Maman considered store-bought clothes to be below our station. We did not wear couture, of course, but according to Maman, it would be an insult to Papa's status if we did not wear custom-made.

"Only people who can afford no better wear zippers," she said.

"Movie stars can certainly afford better!" I argued. My best friend Yvette and I adored the movies—especially the American ones. My father said the French ones were better—much more meaningful and artistic. He said that France was the birthplace of *le cinéma*, and that France would still be the moviemaking capital of the world if the Great War had not crippled the industry, as it had crippled all of France.

My father—indeed, all of the adults I knew—talked endlessly about how France had been "before." I knew nothing of "before," since I was born after. All of my life, though, talk of war had been a daily staple. Like bread, it was served up at every meal and gathering. If adults weren't talking about an impending one, they were rehashing the events of the Great One.

Even the French movies were about war. The government insisted that theaters show one French film for every seven American movies in an attempt to get French filmmaking back on its feet. Yvette and I keenly preferred the lighthearted Hollywood movies to the dark, grim, war-themed films in our own language. The newsreels showing German soldiers marching in lockstep provided more than enough military drama for our tastes.

"Katharine Hepburn wears zippers," I told my mother.

"If Katharine Hepburn wore a toilet for a hat, would you want to do that as well?" my mother asked.

We were arguing about this in the back corner when Mme Avant burst into the shop, her umbrella dripping, her face bright pink. Her chest, as large and round as a pigeon's, heaved up and down. Everyone turned toward her.

"The Germans are attacking Poland!" she announced.

It was as if every woman in the store had turned to stone. Maman's face went white. "Oh, no," she murmured, a hand to her chest. She leaned heavily against the display case. "My boys."

My two older brothers were seventeen and eighteen, and they had been champing at the bit to join the French Army for what seemed like forever. Maman had insisted that they wait to be conscripted; Pierre, the oldest, argued that the men who volunteered got the choicest assignments. Papa said it was inevitable that they would serve, but so far, Maman had prevailed.

I largely tuned out talk of war and politics, but even I had been unable to tune out the latest events. Just last week, Germany had signed a nonaggression pact with Russia, and in response, France and Great Britain had signed a pact to defend Poland.

At school just that morning, my friend Lisette, whose father worked at the Louvre, said that the museum was packing up paintings and sculptures to be shipped and hidden in the countryside. Her father had personally helped crate up the Venus de Milo.

There was a heaviness in the air, a sense of something about to happen, like a snow cloud about to drop a blizzard.

"Does this mean we're at war?" I asked.

"If we're not, we're about to be," Mme Avant said.

"We must go home." Maman straightened and collected her purse. "Come."

"What about our dresses?" I asked.

"We'll tend to that later." She turned to the vendeuse, who was holding the bolt of fabric near the trim and buttons. "I'm sure you understand."

"*Bien sûr*," she murmured, her head bent low. "I will set the fabric aside for you."

Maman mumbled her thanks, and clutched my elbow all the way home. We lived in a narrow three-story townhouse, a rarity in the Quartier Latin, where almost everyone lived in flats. It had been in my father's family for generations, and, the year before, Papa had sunk a major chunk of his savings into reinforcing the foundation and modernizing the bathroom and kitchen.

Yvette must have been watching for me from her flat across the street, because she knocked on the door practically as soon as we walked in. "Did you hear?" she whispered.

"Yes," I replied.

We were excited. We knew it was terrible, but we were, in many ways, still children, and we felt as if we were on the brink of a grand adventure. Despite what everyone said, war seemed terribly thrilling and glamorous. All those men in all those handsome uniforms, so brave, so dashing, so ready for love!

Maman turned on the radio. There was no music that night; only newscasters talking, talking, talking.

"We must figure out some hairstyles that will make us look older," Yvette said to me.

We disappeared into my room and stood before the mirror of my bureau, pinning our hair into rolls and updos. Yvette and I were practically sisters; our parents were best friends and we had known each other all our lives. We felt like family, but we couldn't have looked more different. Yvette had blond hair and blue eyes. Her cheeks and lips were always pink, as if she'd just come out of the cold. Her personality was bright and colorful, too.

I, on the other hand, was short and slight, with dark brown hair and light brown eyes.

People would say, "Oh, that Yvette—she's going to be a heartbreaker!" About me, they would seldom say much of anything. I tended to blend into the background, which was fine with me. I preferred being a supportive player to Yvette's plans and schemes rather than hatching my own. I was an introvert; I loved reading and calligraphy. I could have passed my whole life curled up in a corner with a stack of books or with a pen and paper, copying stylistic fonts from magazines and movie posters, while Yvette was always on the lookout for the next adventure.

Yvette left our house when Maman called me to help prepare supper—roast chicken with new potatoes and carrots. Papa came home at his regular time, his face grim. He was alone. My brothers usually accompanied him home from university.

"Where are Pierre and Thomas?" Maman asked.

My father hung up his hat without a word.

"*Non*," Maman breathed, her voice like a prayer. She scurried toward Papa and grabbed the lapels of his coat. "You must stop them!"

"They are men, Marie."

"Not Thomas," Maman insisted. "He is still a boy."

"Seventeen is the age of conscription. And anyway, he will be eighteen in two months. He will be drafted if he does not join with Pierre."

Maman dropped her hands from his jacket. "Still, that could buy some time."

My father loosened his tie and sighed. "Marie, it is important that this be his choice."

"He is too young to make such a choice!"

"It is likely to be the last free choice he can make for a very long time." He took off his coat. "It is a noble thing they are doing. And with any luck, they can serve together, keep an eye on each other. You must not give them trouble."

My mother turned her back to my father, refusing to engage in any further conversation. She banged pot lids and pans on the stove, moving with sharp, jerky movements.

My brothers did not make it home for dinner that night. My father and I ate without them. My mother did not eat. She sat with us, but she only pushed her food around the plate.

As we were clearing the table, my brothers came in.

"Well?" my father asked.

Pierre's back was straight. His chin jutted out at a combative angle, as if he were braced for battle. Beside him, Thomas, too, stood erect, as if he were already a soldier, awaiting orders. They looked at each other, then spoke in what must have been practiced unison. "We have joined."

My mother cried. I think my father did, as well, but he rose and hugged Pierre, then Thomas, so quickly it was hard to tell.

They settled at the table, and Papa poured them stout glasses of wine.

"Are you getting uniforms?" I asked.

"Yes," Thomas replied.

"And guns?"

My mother put her hand to her mouth and whimpered.

"Amélie!" my father reprimanded.

"What? I just want to know if they'll be equipped to defend themselves."

"Yes, little one." Thomas ruffled my hair. I usually hated it when he did that, but I didn't mind so much tonight. Maybe it was just his newly erect posture, but he seemed taller than usual. "We'll be well equipped to defend France."

Pierre picked up his glass. "*Vive la France!*"

Papa, Thomas, and I picked up glasses, as well. "Vive la France!" we chanted.

Papa gestured for Maman to join us. "Come, Marie—you must toast with us." My father poured a little more wine in her glass. When she picked it up, her hand trembled.

"Vive la France!" we all sang out again.

Except for Maman. Under her breath, I distinctly heard her say, "*Vive mes fils.*" Long live my sons.

3

AMÉLIE
September 3–October 29, 1939

Two days later, it was official: France, along with our ally Great Britain, declared war on Germany.

My brothers shipped off to training that very week. They were not alone; all of a sudden, it seemed as if every Parisian male under the age of thirty-five had vacated the city. Yvette and I were devastated; we had envisioned French soldiers swelling the streets of Paris, eating in the cafés, drinking and dancing in the nightclubs we planned to sneak out to. We had not imagined they would all leave!

Most British and American nationals left Paris, as well. Those first few days, the streets were deserted. And then foreigners from other places—Russia, the Ukraine, Belgium, and heaven only knew where else—began pouring in. Many of them were not well dressed, and some of them seemed to have no place to stay. French police began stopping people and checking identification papers—to what end, I have never known.

I do not remember if we did not have school, or if our mothers simply didn't make us go. My father insisted on continuing to tutor Yvette and me in German and English, as he'd been doing for years—but Yvette's father, an engineering professor, was working on a secret government project, so he did not give us our usual extra lessons in higher mathematics.

I was relieved. I hated geometry and algebra and calculus. Papa said knowledge was gold that no one could steal, that I should gladly gather all I could, and that one never knew when one might have need of it. Yvette and I joked that we would slit our wrists if our lives ever became so dull that we had use for mathematics.

The city was so tense it seemed to be suspended on a tightwire. Everyone was hungry for information. Newspapers sold out as fast as they were placed in the kiosks. We listened to the radio constantly in those first days. There was little music; most programming was grim news of Germany overrunning Poland.

The numbers being reported were so enormous that they had no real meaning. How could one even imagine a million and a half German soldiers? How could one fathom thousands of tanks, rolling hundreds of miles through farms and villages, crushing everything in their path? How could one comprehend ten, twenty, fifty, one hundred thousand Polish citizens killed? The numbers fluctuated wildly, but all were astronomical, and the estimates did nothing but climb.

The stories about the German Luftwaffe were the most horrifying of all. According to the news reports, swarms of planes would suddenly darken the skies, then bomb civilian as well as military targets. Railroads, bridges, waterworks, even schools were locked in the bombardiers' cruel crosshairs. Roads crammed with fleeing families were systematically annihilated. German aircraft would suddenly swoop down below the clouds to strafe civilians with machine gunfire in what was called "terror bombing."

As far as we could determine, it was all terror bombing. How much terror could one listen to before one's ears grew calloused? Yvette and I wearied of hearing about it. We would occasionally sneak out—each of us saying we were going to the other one's home—and wander around the Quartier. If we were feeling particularly brave and our parents were preoccupied, we would do this after dinner. One evening we went into a cellar club—a tiny, bare-bones university student hangout with no electricity, just candles stuck in wine bottles. We shared a glass of wine and listened to a middle-aged baritone sing "Begin the Beguine" to the accompaniment of a tinny piano.

The music filled my heart with longing. "How does a woman ever make a man feel that way?" I asked.

"She shows him her breasts," Yvette replied. We giggled like the schoolgirls we were. Under the laughter, I was saddened by the response, because I feared there might be some truth to it. Yvette had an impressive bust, while my chest was as small as the rest of me.

"What if you don't have much for breasts?" I asked.

"Well, then, I think you must flirt. With your eyes and your touch and your body. But beyond that, you must intrigue."

"How?"

She took a thoughtful sip of wine. "I think perhaps you make him a bit uncomfortable. If you can make a man unsettled, you can make him a conquest."

An older man in a tattered jacket was eyeing Yvette in a rather creepy manner from the bar. With most of the students gone, the clientele of the cheap bars in the Quartier were largely middle-aged refugees.

"I think you have made a conquest over there." I nudged her.

She turned, and the man smiled, revealing several missing teeth.

"Merde," she whispered. "Let's go."

We returned to my house, because Maman was a nervous wreck and she liked me to be nearby. Maman wasn't sleeping, and she filled her many waking hours with frenetic activity. She stockpiled dry goods, canned vegetables she bought at market (prior to this, she only canned the vegetables she grew in the summer in the little garden patch behind our townhome), and fitted our windows with ugly blackout curtains. Papa said she was spending money like a drunken sailor on shore leave; Maman said we couldn't eat money if things got scarce.

Papa still went to university every day, but his classes held only one-eighth of the students initially enrolled. Foreign students had gone home, coeds were staying indoors, and young Frenchmen had abandoned school for the military. From what I overheard in hushed, worried conversations with Maman, Papa's pay had been cut in accordance with the diminishment of the student body.

The war news grew more ominous and complicated. At Hitler's apparent urging, Russia invaded Poland on September 17. We waited for word of the British or French entering the fray, but nothing happened. All of France seemed to hold its collective breath.

And then . . . it seemed to be over. On October 1, a month after the invasion had begun, Poland surrendered to Germany. The Germans made no move to invade France. We were still technically at war, but nothing occurred that affected life in Paris.

Yvette and I went back to school. Maman and I went back to the dressmaker, but Maman was so high-strung since my brothers had left that I didn't have the heart to argue about the zipper. I pretended to like the covered buttons she selected.

In mid-October, Germany made an offer of peace. First Great Britain, and then France, rejected it. As with everything, this was great cause for debate. Some thought our leaders were foolish not to accept a peace treaty; others said it was only a German trick.

Most French were relieved that an offer had been rendered. There was much hopeful talk that it meant the Germans would not invade us. Our fortified Maginot Line along the eastern border was too daunting, most people said; the Germans must realize that France was impenetrable. Many hoped that France and Great Britain would broker diplomatic peace, and the state of war would soon be rescinded.

The days wore on. Life returned to normal—or as near normal as it could be at our house, without Pierre and Thomas. The house seemed vast and lonely without them. We heard from them regularly—they were posted together at an undisclosed location in the Alps, at a station of the Maginot Line. Mother and I knitted warm socks and mittens.

Yvette and I were restless. When one of the brasher girls at our school suggested an outing to a jazz club in Montmartre, we eagerly agreed to join in. We would have to sneak behind our parents' backs—they had antiquated ideas about unescorted young women being out at night, and Montmartre was a racy part of town—so we said we were going to Lisette's apartment to listen to records.

Lisette's parents required more of an explanation, so I forged a letter from my mother, inviting Lisette to our place for the evening. (Lisette's parents were sticklers about invitation protocol, and I had a real talent for exactly copying other people's handwriting.)

It was so easy, I felt guilty. Yvette came to my door at seven, and we scampered to the Métro like a couple of thieves, the little money we'd saved from birthday gifts and the occasional babysitting job tucked into our purses. We met up with Lisette and our friend Madeline and rode the train for about twenty minutes, then found our way to the La Grosse Pomme—The Big Apple. The club was founded by the beautiful black jazz singer Adelaide Hall, but Adelaide, like so many Americans in the last few months, had fled France.

As we neared the cabaret, the haunting wail of a saxophone wafted through the closed door. When a doorman in white gloves opened it for us, the music tumbled out, wrapped around us, and pulled us in. We giggled as we stepped inside the crowded club.

It was like entering another world. The decor was luxe—red-flocked wallpaper, crystal chandeliers and sconces, white linen tablecloths. The air was thick with smoke. The mellow tones of Gypsy jazz—a violin wrapping its sweet notes around the bluesy blare of a saxophone, softened by melodic clarinet and a brush-stroked drum—mesmerized us. We hesitated to check our coats—it would cost money to retrieve them, would it not?—but we didn't want to seem simple, so we did.

I looked at the crowd, and immediately felt out of place. Men—many of them our fathers' age—fawned over shockingly younger women. Everyone's dress was far more formal—and far, far more chic—than mine. The men wore suits, and the women wore fitted silk and rayon with low-cut décolletés, their skin aglow in candlelight.

Yvette and my other classmates had somehow managed to get out of their homes wearing dresses, although all of us were sadly mis-attired. In my woolen skirt and round-collared cotton blouse, I felt like a school-girl at a ball.

We were escorted to a table on the far edge the room, away from the stage, and a bored-looking waitress in a scandalously short red frock came to take our order.

We had planned to share drinks to save money, but she wasn't having it. "If you don't drink, you don't sit." Her tone was so like one of our harsh teachers that I whispered to Yvette, "Do you think she works as a nun during the day?" Smothering giggles, we all ordered the cheapest wine available.

No sooner had we settled in than a man in a slick blue suit approached our table. He looked to be in his early twenties—an older man from our perspective. He introduced himself as Herman Beck, and said he was a Swiss banker in town on business. We nodded and smiled. He looked at each of us, one at a time, for several discomfiting moments. And then he bowed before Yvette. It was no surprise; Yvette was stunning. With her impressive bosom and self-possessed bearing, she seemed older than her years—and certainly older than the rest of us. "Would you care to dance?"

Yvette smiled and batted her eyes. "Only if you can provide a partner for my friend, as well." She gestured gracefully to me.

Herman turned, raised his hand, and flicked his forefinger at someone. A young man in a white apron came over. His dark curly hair flopped over his forehead.

"Mademoiselle would like to dance," Herman said, gesturing to me.

"Oh." The young man brushed his hair off his face. He had high cheekbones and a square jawline. It was a nice face. He looked puzzled as to what he was supposed to do.

"Take off your apron and dance with her," Herman said.

"But I—I have to work."

Herman's eyes narrowed. "I am sure your boss would want you to make the customers happy."

The young man shifted from one foot to the other, apparently weighing the consequences of refusing Herman's request against the consequences of acquiescing to it. "Yes, of course."

"Good." Herman took Yvette's elbow and led her out to the dance floor, as if the matter were settled. Yvette smiled back at me over her shoulder. The young man quickly untied and yanked off his apron, then pulled out my chair.

"I don't want to get you into trouble," I said as I awkwardly rose.

He lifted his shoulders. "I will get in trouble either way."

The girls at my table giggled. The young man placed his apron on the back of my chair, took my arm, and led me to the dance floor.

"Will you really get in trouble?" I asked.

"Do not worry yourself about it."

He spoke French with a heavy foreign accent. "Where are you from?"

"Austria."

That was a country the Germans had taken over the year before. I didn't understand all the reasons, but it had something to do with a treaty, and I knew it played a part in France's decision to declare war so quickly when Poland was invaded. "Did you come to France because of the Germans?"

"Yes."

Something in the low, tight way he bit off the word told me further inquiry would not be welcome.

He stiffly held out his arms, and I stepped into them, taking one hand and resting the other on his shoulder. His hand was warm and dry; his shoulder was broader and more muscular than I would have imagined. He placed his other hand on my back, in proper fox-trot fashion. I had danced before with boys from Saint-Julien's, the boys' school in our diocese, and I had, of course, taken ballroom lessons. Never before, however, had I felt dizzy when a hand had touched my back.

I searched for something to say, something to normalize the abnormal way I was feeling, as a low, slow tune began. "What is your job here?"

"I am a busboy. But during the day, I am a student."

"Oh, me, too! What are you studying?"

"Engineering, with an emphasis on physics."

"Is that at all like calculus?"

"Not really, but you must use calculus." He looked down at me. When I met his eyes, he appeared entirely different. My knees suddenly felt wobbly. I had never seen eyes so brown and expressive. They were regarding me with genuine interest. "What do you know of calculus?"

"More than I want. My friend's father is a professor and he tutors us."

"What is his name?"

"Jean-Claude Chaussant."

His eyes widened. "He was my professor!"

"Really?"

"Yes. He is a brilliant man. But he's not teaching this semester."

"I know. He is helping France on some secret project."

He pulled me close to spin me around. "You should not say that," he cautioned in my ear.

"Why?"

"Because the Germans have spies everywhere."

"Here?"

"Everywhere."

I gave him what was meant to be a coy smile. "How do I know that you're not a spy?"

"You don't." His tone was harsh.

I felt my face heat. "Perhaps you should take me back to my table."

"I'm sorry." His hand shifted slightly on my back, stirring up a maelstrom of unfamiliar feelings. "I didn't mean to frighten you. It's just that I've had a bit of experience with the Nazis, and they are . . ." He hesitated, then shook his head. "Do not talk about anyone, especially a man working for your country's defense, if you do not want to make him a target. You must imagine that the walls have ears."

"I will do that. And to help me remember, I will pretend that the sconces are their earrings."

I was rewarded with a grin. "Whatever helps you keep it top of mind."

The song ended. He dropped his hand. I reluctantly stepped back.

"The show is about to begin," he said. "I believe you will enjoy it." He guided me back to my table, took his apron from my chair, and pulled out my seat. He gave a stiff little bow, then headed to the back of the restaurant. Yvette's dance partner soon returned her to our table, as well.

The trumpet player blasted out several notes, like an announcement. A man in a tuxedo stepped into the spotlight. "And now, ladies and gentlemen, I present Miss Marigold Smith!"

Spotlights cut through the smoke, illuminating a tall spiral staircase. A delicate high-heeled foot and a length of leg, sheathed in shiny sheer silk, stepped out of the ceiling. Another leg followed. And then I saw her—a vision of womanliness, wrapped in blue feathers and sequins, climbing down the tight spiral stairs like a goddess descending from heaven. I have never seen anything so glamorous in all my life. She had chocolate skin, smooth as ice cream, and she moved with an exaggerated grace. She was magnificent—and she knew it.

That was the secret, I realized—the knowing. Knowing her own magnificence gave her power. It radiated in her bearing, in the way she played to the spotlight, in her smile. She knew every eye was fixed on her. She knew she had the audience in the palm of her hand. She knew she had every man in the place in her thrall.

The band had begun to play as she glided down the stairs, but I was oblivious to the music until she started to sing. When she did, her sultry voice lifted us all as if we were riding on a magic carpet.

We sat there, that table of girls, watching her as if she were a creature from another planet, completely believing she had lived every lyric that she sang.

At the end of the set, I was emotionally wrung out. Another band took over to play during the intermission. Yvette's admirer, who had gallantly sent our table another round of drinks, returned to take her back to the dance floor. My partner followed in his wake.

"I hope I'm not getting you in trouble with your employer," I said as he moved behind my chair to pull it out.

"It's okay," he said. "Monsieur Beck paid my boss for my time."

"You were ordered to dance with me?"

"Yes."

"That's not very flattering," I said.

Color rose in his cheeks. "I—I don't mind dancing with you. It's better than my regular job."

It might have been the wine—or perhaps I was borrowing a bit from the brash display of female empowerment I had just witnessed. In any event, I couldn't resist teasing him. "So dancing with me is better than picking up dirty plates and glasses? My, how you gush and flatter!"

The pink splotches on his face darkened. "What I mean is, I liked dancing with you. Before, I mean. And . . . and now, too."

I had no response for that. I was glad when the music began. The wine was definitely hitting me. I felt myself leaning against him, drawing close, enjoying the sensation of a masculine body so close to mine. It was all strangely intoxicating.

As the last strains of the song faded, I opened my eyes to see Lisette pointing at her wristwatch.

Oh, la—I had promised Maman I would be home by eleven. I'd lost all track of time. "I have to go," I breathed.

"Yes, that is best. And it would be wise for you not to come back."

"You don't want to see me again?"

"Oh, I would like that very much!" He walked me to my chair, where I picked up my purse. "But it is not safe here."

"Where, then?" When had I gotten so bold?

"At the library at the Sorbonne, in the Saint-Jacques reading room. At four tomorrow afternoon."

"I—I'll try."

He lifted his apron from my chair, then walked me to the coat check, where Yvette's dance partner was bailing out all of our coats. I was aware of his nearness. My body seemed to wear the imprint of his from the dance floor.

He took my coat and held it out for me to slip on. "I don't know your name."

"Amélie. And yours?"

"Joshua. I am Joshua Koper."

"So nice to make your acquaintance."

"Likewise." He smiled at me. The way his brown eyes met mine made my stomach quiver. I noticed another flush of color on his cheeks.

He was older and more worldly, but I had made him blush. Joshua Koper—my first conquest.

I hugged the knowledge to myself like a delicious secret as I buttoned my coat and left the smoky bar for the chilly autumn night, surrounded by giggling companions.

KAT
2016

*T*his is all fascinating, I'm sure, but you've told me nothing about Jack."

Amélie blinks as if she is just waking up from a nap and is surprised to find I am sitting across from her. Her eyes narrow. It seems as if her whole face, which is shaped like a heart, draws in and becomes more pointed. "I said I would tell this story in my own way."

"This is not the story I came to hear."

She lifts her chin. "*Tant pis.*"

Did she just curse at me? I arch one eyebrow. "I beg your pardon?"

"I am sorry to disappoint you."

"That's not what you said."

"No, you are right."

"So what did you say?" My voice comes out a little sharper than I intend, but oh, she is so infuriating!

"I said, 'Too bad.'" She leans back, then gestures with her hands, palms up. "So. Now it is your turn."

"What?"

"It is your turn to talk, since you interrupted my story."

"Me?"

"Yes. I should like to hear about your life with Jack, as well."

I am totally unprepared for this, and more than a little put out. I've traveled all the way here from Dallas to get specific information, and now *she* is making demands on *me*? The nerve of her! But then, she's always been nervy. Apparently that hasn't changed.

And yet . . . I suppose I have some nerve, as well, barging in as I have. I dislike admitting it, but perhaps, as my son once told me, I do have a bit of a Queen Bee complex. I fear it is the result of being an only child and having parents who doted on me.

The truth is, I do feel that others—and life in general—should follow my plans, but that's only because I'm usually right. I'm beginning to suspect, however, that God doesn't always agree with me.

Through the window, I watch a robin poke its beak into the grass and come up with something too tiny for me to see. The little bird probably expected to pull out a big fat worm, and instead only found a seed.

When I first learned that the cancer had returned—the cancer that had claimed a breast a decade earlier—the doctor asked if I wanted to see a hospice chaplain. I hadn't, of course. I'd always hated people who lived one way and then, when confronted with their own mortality, turned cloyingly pious.

But the hospice chaplain had called on me anyway, and I discovered I quite enjoyed his visits. Part of it is the attention—he is very interested in everything I have to say; who wouldn't like that?—and part of it is the broader, kinder, more forgiving perspective he has of God. I don't know how he arrived at the viewpoint—as a Jew, he only has the Old Testament to go by, doesn't he?—and it seems to me that those stories show God at his most judgmental and angry. All the same, Jacob encourages me to explore my own beliefs, both within and without the parameters of my religion.

"Isn't it a little late for that?" I'd asked with more than a hint of sarcasm when he'd first broached the subject.

"No later than it's ever been," he'd replied.

"I only have six months to live," I said.

He shrugged his shoulders. "For all you've ever known, that's all you've ever had."

The thought startled me. "What?"

"You could have been killed by a disease or an accident or a falling meteorite at any point in your life. You have never known that you had more than six months—or six minutes, for that matter."

That shouldn't have been a comforting answer, but oddly enough, it was. And the way he talked about things like self-love and forgiveness and finding peace was comforting, and even refreshingly logical.

Except for that part about expectation. What was it he'd said? Oh, yes. Expectations set us up for disappointment. The wisest course is to take action, but leave the results up to God. I didn't quite get that. How do you have any motivation to live, without expecting things? Aren't expectations simply things you want to happen? If you stop wanting things, don't you stop living?

Oh, this is the frightful thing about knowing my time is coming to an end—the way I keep looking back and questioning everything. I am trying to be brutally honest with myself these days, even though I dislike some of what I see and I don't really have time to change.

Upon reflection, I fear I've lived a self-centered life. I didn't mean to, I truly didn't. But when you're reared to think the sun and moon revolve around you, well, it's only natural to believe so, too. I never quite got the knack of putting myself in other people's shoes—except, perhaps, for my children, and maybe that's because I viewed them as extensions of myself. That's a very unpleasant and unflattering truth, but I fear it's my truth nonetheless.

I've certainly never tried to put myself in Amélie's shoes. The rabbi suggested I do so, and it was his suggestion that spurred this trip. I'm afraid I really didn't come here to empathize, though. I came because it is an excuse to satisfy the questions that have burned in me for decades. The truth is, I fear forgiveness is beyond me; I can't even look at the woman without tasting the green bile of jealousy in the back of my throat.

She is still attractive in a handsome, striking, confident way, even though her hair is too long for her age and completely white. I would rather die than have any gray roots showing—I carefully keep my own hair blond—but on her, the natural hair seems vibrant and carefree and young in attitude—as if it is declaring, *All of me is beautiful, is it not?* That has always been her air. So annoying! Even worse is the way her confidence makes others think she is beautiful, too.

But then, she has the complexion for extreme hair. She has that Mediterranean coloring, like Sophia Loren. It's a look that ages well. Once I'd derisively called her swarthy, but in truth, her skin is pale olive, smooth, and unlined. She's never worn much makeup, but with her dark eyes and dark lashes, she never needed anything beyond lipstick. She wears some now, a bright red shade that would be garish on me but looks vibrant on her.

I resent her for being so effortlessly attractive. I have the kind of looks that need definition and constant vigilance.

I also resent her over-the-top sense of style. She is so needlessly dramatic! The hateful part is, it works. Just look at this apartment! It is just swimming in stuff, and yet, instead of looking cramped and unkempt and cluttered, it looks rich and intriguing and, well . . . inviting. Just look at that carving of a ship on the side table, or that little sketch of a naked woman tucked in the corner. I lean closer to study it again. Heavens to Betsy—is it a drawing of *her*? Do you suppose she took her clothes off to pose for it?

"I'd like to hear about your life here with Jack," she says, pulling my gaze away from the scandalous picture. "I'd like to know what he was like when he was young. What the town was like before the war."

She reaches for a glass of water, her arm as graceful as a ballerina's, her head as regal as any queen's. Her beauty is fluid, I realize. It isn't captured by any of the photographs scattered around the room. It is how she looks in motion—and she always seems to be moving. I watch as she adjusts herself on the chair and tilts her head to an annoyingly imperious angle.

The most aggravating thing about her high-and-mighty demeanor is that it doesn't seem to be deliberate. She isn't trying to be condescending; she is simply being French.

"How did you and Jack meet?" she asks in that enchanting accent. I uncharitably wonder if it is an affect. After seventy years in this country—yes, I still keep count—shouldn't she speak English more clearly?

"I can't remember ever not knowing him," I say a bit stiffly.

Her eyes widen. "Really?" The wistfulness in her gaze disarms me.

"Yes. This was—is—a small town."

"Oh, I know, I know." A quick, rueful smile plays across her face. "He was older than you, was he not?"

"Yes. He was only one year older, but because he had skipped second grade, he was two years ahead of me in school. The summer I was going to be a sophomore and he was going to be a senior . . . that was the year he first noticed me."

"You had noticed him earlier?"

"Oh, of course. All the girls did."

"Yes." Amélie's eyes nearly disappear in laugh lines as she smiles. "Yes, of course they did."

I find myself falling down a rabbit hole of memories. This is happening to me more and more. "By the time he was in high school, we all had crushes on him. I think even some of the teachers had crushes on him."

"I shouldn't be surprised." Amélie tucks a leg under herself, a surprisingly girlish and lithe move for a woman in her nineties, even though she has to use a hand to do it. "Tell me. I want to hear all about it."

The rabbit hole beckons me like a downturned bed. It is not an unappealing prospect, to revisit my younger days. "Up until that summer, I only really saw him at church."

"Church? The Baptist church?" She pronounces it *Bap-tiste*, with the accent on the second syllable. Her expressive eyebrows dart upward. "You went to the same church as Jack?"

"Yes." It is petty, but it pleases me, having known Jack in a context that she did not. It gives me a sense of . . . oh, I don't know. Power. Or ownership, perhaps. Oh, that sounds so ugly and mean-spirited. I am trying to do away with all thoughts that are petty and mean-spirited.

But I can't help it; I had a piece of Jack, too—he hadn't solely belonged to her. He'd been mine first.

"Tell me how your romance started."

Why should I? The thought is not pretty, and neither is the answer: *To get what I want from you.*

But then, that is the motivation for most conversations, isn't it? Getting what one wants. That is what propels people through life. There is really nothing wrong with it.

I hesitate, but it is just for effect. I don't want to acquiesce too quickly, but I will tell her what she wants to know. I might even enjoy the telling.

I sink back into the sumptuous sofa, and let my thoughts sink back into the past. With no effort at all, I find myself talking, and before I know it, it is as if the years roll away and I am once again a girl.

1937

I was fifteen that summer, full of unfamiliar stirrings and romantic long-ings and enormous crushes on movie stars. My friends and I bought into the Hollywood fantasy of a perfect love, and I believed that a Cary Grant look-alike would sweep me off my feet when I was older.

No one in Wedding Tree came close to fulfilling that fantasy, except for Jack O'Connor. Jack and his family had been regulars at church as I was growing up, but after his father died two years before, his attendance had become sporadic. Mother said it was because he was working so hard to keep his family's small dairy and strawberry farm running. Jack had had a girlfriend since junior high—a pretty brunette named Beth Ann Knutson, whose father owned the farm next to Jack's. She was a Lutheran, though, so I seldom saw them together.

All I knew was that on the Sundays he was there, I felt all queasy and hot, just looking at him. He had black, black hair—not brown, but black—and blue, blue eyes, eyes that made me feel kind of hypnotized. He was tall and thin, with wide square shoulders, the kind of shoulders that looked like he was wearing a suit jacket even when he wasn't. He had a straight nose, a cleft chin, and a prominent Adam's apple that made him look mature beyond his years. And I suppose he was; in addition to being a straight A student, he was providing a living for his mother and his sister during the Great Depression.

The Depression didn't mean much to me, because Daddy's business was as good as ever; people fell ill just as often in hard times as in good times. I knew that sometimes Daddy took chickens or eggs instead of money from patients, and my friends all talked about their parents having money problems, but the economic downturn didn't really affect my life.

I didn't know a lot about Jack—back then, ninth grade was still in junior high, so we didn't go to the same school. I only saw him at church—and the prospect of seeing him made attending church a whole lot more appealing.

I wasn't nearly as interested in religion as I was in romance, much to my mother's chagrin. Mother believed that only people who publicly professed Jesus Christ as their personal savior would go to heaven. In the First Baptist Church of Wedding Tree, that meant going down to the altar in front of the entire church during an invitational hymn. Unfortunately, it also meant being completely submerged in the glass-fronted, bathtub-like baptistery by the pastor in front of the whole congregation.

My closest friends had gone through this when they were about twelve, after attending a religious camp the summer before seventh grade. I'd had the chicken pox and been unable to attend camp that summer, or I'm certain I would have taken the plunge along with my classmates.

I balked at doing this on my own; I didn't want to be the only person in the congregation with wet hair. It was a silly, vain reason to risk the wrath of God, or—more important to me at the time—the disappoint-ment of my parents, but the longer I waited, the more impossible getting baptized seemed to become.

I had good reason to be vain. I had a small straight nose, big hazel eyes, a bosom of voluptuous proportions for my age and—most importantly—shoulder-length, golden blond hair. I washed my hair every Saturday night, and my mother helped me roll it up with soft strips of cotton. When I took down the curls Sunday morning, my hair was exactly what every girl wanted. Everywhere I went, everyone complimented me on my beauty, and especially on my hair. I simply couldn't bear to be seen publicly looking like a wet rat, when everyone else's hair was fixed at its Sunday best.

So I postponed going forward during the invitation. A year passed and another group of students went to camp and made their profession—and then yet another. I should have gone up with them, but they were so much younger than me, and I didn't want to look as if I were *slow*.

Every Sunday, I could feel my mother holding her breath and eyeing me hopefully. With each passing Sunday, I felt her increasing disappointment.

This was out of character for me, to not do something I knew my parents wanted. I worked hard at pleasing them, and exceeded their expectations in almost every area. I was pretty. I was personable. I was polite. I did well in school. I was cheerful and neat. I helped with the dishes and went with Mother to visit my grandparents, and, when forced into it, I accompanied her to see some of Daddy's homebound patients.

Perhaps that was why I didn't do it. Maybe I wanted to call the shots in just one private area of my life. Or perhaps I was just an exceedingly vain and shallow girl.

I talked to my friends about it one day after school. We all plopped on my chintz-covered bed, except for Minxy, who sat at my vanity table and played with her hair.

"I think you should just go ahead and do it," Minxy said.

"I don't understand why you're putting it off," Darla said. "Don't you want to be saved?"

I nodded, because that was the only acceptable answer, but the truth was, I wasn't so sure. It didn't sound like any fun.

"What did you feel like afterward?" I asked.

"Drippy," Minxy said.

"And clean," Helen added. "As if everything I'd ever done wrong had been washed away and I had a fresh start."

We were all silent, thinking Helen had depths the rest of us lacked.

"You've got to be saved to go to heaven," Minxy said, brushing her bangs.

"Never mind heaven." Darla leaned toward the mirror and practiced a sultry Scarlett O'Hara pout. "You've got to be saved to go on the high school mission trip this summer."

Minxy, Helen, and I both swung toward her. "There's going to be a trip?"

She nodded. Darla's mother volunteered in the church office, so she often had inside information. "The high school students are going to a small town in Mississippi to help paint the old church, and we're staying at a nearby church camp. And as incoming tenth graders, we'll get to go."

"Whoopee!" Helen jumped beside her on the bed.

"But you have to be a baptized member of the church," Darla said. "That's one of the stipulations."

"Just girls, or boys, too?" Minxy asked.

"Both," Darla replied.

"Oh, wow," Helen breathed. "I wonder if Jack O'Connor will go."

"Ooh, handsome Jack!" I said.

"I doubt it." Minxy patted her hair in the mirror. "My father said their farm is just about to go under."

"Go under what?"

"He means economically. They have a mortgage on the land, and the bank called in the note."

"What does that even mean?" Darla asked.

"It means they have money trouble," Minxy said.

"I'm so sick of hearing about money trouble!" Darla said.

"Me, too." Helen nodded. "It's all my parents talk about. Anyway, Jack is taken."

"Not anymore," Minxy said authoritatively. "Beth Ann and her family moved to Iowa or somewhere a couple of months ago. Maybe he'll go on the church trip to look for a new girlfriend."

My thoughts snagged on this information. Around me, the conversation went on.

"Ooh, what about James? He's going to be the quarterback this year!" Helen said.

"Yeah. And what about Leon?"

"Oooh, long, tall Leon!"

As my friends discussed the merits of all the high school boys in our church, my mind was occupied by one looming thought: it was time to make the walk.

The following Sunday, I headed down the aisle on the first verse of the invitational hymn. Pastor Hasten fairly glowed as he clasped my hand in both of his.

"Brothers and sisters in Christ," he announced to the congregation when the song ended, "the prayers of Katherine Thompson's family and friends have been answered. She has finally accepted Jesus Christ as her personal savior."

Finally? As if I'd lived a long, depraved life! My face burned. Had my holdout caused people to whisper behind my back? I was mortified—and to make my mortification complete, I had to stand at the front of the church after the service while the entire congregation came by and shook my hand, congratulating me on my decision.

The only mitigating circumstance was the fact that the high school students came by, too—including Jack. Good heavens, but he was good-looking! He looked me straight in the eye with a gaze that was like a little piece of sky, and I felt myself go weak in the knees.

"Congratulations," he said. "It was smart of you to wait until you were old enough to be sure of your decision."

I was too stunned to do anything but nod. I must have shaken a dozen more hands after his, but I could still feel the heat of his fingers against mine.

"That was it? That was your romantic moment?" Amélie's expression is incredulous.

"That was the moment it began," I say. "Jack later told me that it was when he first really noticed me. Before that, he'd thought I was just a junior high student who ran in a pack of girls and didn't know my own mind. When I went down the aisle by myself, it showed him I had substance."

"But you didn't." Amélie is nothing if not blunt. "You just said you only did it so you could go on a trip."

I swear, this woman is so tedious! I wave my hand. "What matters, in terms of our romance, is that Jack thought otherwise. And I wanted to live up to what he thought of me." That had been a key part of my relationship with Jack, I thought. He made me want to be a better person, to become the person he thought I was.

"Was Jack there when you were baptized?"

"No, thank heavens. He couldn't attend every Sunday because of his farm. But the Sunday after that, he came up to me after church and said hello. I said hello back. He said he was interested in talking to my father about becoming a doctor, and wondered if I thought he'd mind answering some questions.

"'Oh, no, I'm sure he'd love it,' I said.

"I took Jack right over to my father, and they shook hands. Daddy remembered Jack from an encounter a few years earlier when Jack had helped a sick friend.

"'I'm interested in becoming a doctor, and I'd like to talk to you about it when you have time,' Jack said.

"Just like that"—I snap my fingers—"Daddy invited him to come home with us for Sunday lunch. Unfortunately, Jack couldn't come; he had to take his sister home.

"'Why can't your mother take them?'" I'd asked him.

"'She's at the Methodist church with Mr. Brandon. They're courting.'

"'Your mother and the banker?' It had boggled my mind that people so old would be interested in romance.

"'Well, then, can you come back later this afternoon?' Daddy asked. 'You and I can talk, and then you can join us for supper.'

"'Sure,' Jack said. 'I'd be delighted.'"

1937

Three of my friends came over to my house and helped me prepare for Jack's arrival as if it were a date.

"You need to look older," said Minxy. "Do something different to your hair."

"No," said Helen. "You don't want to look like you're trying to impress him."

"When he talks, you need to ask lots of questions," Carol said. "You should act as if everything he says is absolutely fascinating."

"No," Helen protested. "You need to act bored. He's probably sick of girls fawning all over him."

As it ended up, I stayed dressed in my Sunday best, my hair styled as it had been that morning. After all, that was my finest look.

I sat at the dinner table across from him, my stomach too knotted to eat, while he and my father talked and talked. They talked colleges, they talked specialties, they talked about medical schools. My mother occasionally tried to introduce another topic.

"So, Jack—what is your favorite subject at school?" Mother asked.

"I'd have to say biology," Jack said. "Although I really enjoy chemistry, too."

That was the first—and maybe only—time I'd heard the words *enjoy* and *chemistry* used in a sentence together by a high school student.

"Those were my favorites, too," Daddy said. "Chemistry is the foundation of everything."

"I'm especially intrigued by electrochemistry," Jack said.

"Oh, me, too!" Daddy said. "There's some very exciting work being done with electrophoresis." Then he was off and running on the topic.

Mother ventured to break into the conversation a few minutes later. "Jack, have you seen any movies lately? Kat just saw *Topper* and thought it was wonderful."

"I'm afraid I don't have time for movies," Jack said politely.

"Surely you have *some* spare time. What do you do with it?"

"Well, I read," Jack said.

"Kat loves to read, too," Mother said. Bless her heart, she could tell I was smitten with Jack, and she was trying to help my cause. The truth was, I seldom read anything except magazines. "What type of books do you like?"

"Anything on anatomy, physiology, and medicine," he replied. "But I'm afraid I've exhausted the public library's supply."

"Oh, I have bookshelves full of textbooks and medical journals," Daddy said. "I'll be happy to loan some to you."

After dinner, I helped Mother clean up, while Daddy and Jack went into Daddy's library. After a while, Mother went in and suggested that Jack might like to join me on the porch for lemonade and cookies.

He gladly acquiesced. Together we perused one of the books Daddy had loaned him. Jack exclaimed over a diagram of the nervous system, and I pretended to follow what he was talking about. I was content to just sit beside him and listen.

The following week, Jack returned the books, and Father loaned him more. They spent more than two hours talking, then Jack joined us again for supper. Once again, Mother shooed Jack and me out onto the porch together.

It became a Sunday ritual. He and Daddy would talk medicine for hours, then Jack and I would go to the porch, where we would peruse one of the books.

I knew that Jack was there to see Daddy, but I suspected he liked me a little, too. I caught him gazing at me when he thought I wasn't looking. The problem, I felt, was that he thought I was too young for him.

At the urging of my friends, I finally put him on the spot about it. We were sitting in the porch swing of my parents' home. I held a silk pleated fan. "Next Sunday is the Fourth of July picnic," I said. "Are you taking anyone to it?"

In Wedding Tree, going to a town event with someone was public acknowledgment that you were a couple. I watched the tops of his ears get red.

"I, uh, hadn't really thought about it."

"Well, time is running out."

He looked directly at me. "Are you hinting that I should ask you?"

I glanced away, taken aback by his forthrightness. "Maybe."

"Don't you think you're a little young to be dating a high school senior?"

"You're only going to be a senior because you were skipped ahead in grade school. You're just one year older than me." I waved my fan in front of my face. "My daddy's five years older than Mother."

"Hmm," he said.

"Wasn't your father older than your mother?"

"By eight years." He studied the painted porch floor. "I've wondered if that was part of the reason they didn't get along so well."

This was news to me. "They didn't?"

He shook his head. "They were too different. Mother was used to a refined life in Charleston, and Pop was a farmer always scrambling to make money."

"Sounds more like a difference in ways of life than of age."

"I suppose that was part of it."

"Well, you and I don't have that problem."

His eyes lit with amusement. "No?"

"No. We've grown up in the same town, we go to the same church, and we've gone to the same schools."

"Except I'm in high school and you're in junior high."

"I am not! I'll be a sophomore this fall, which means I'm a high school student, same as you. And I'm very mature for my age. Everyone says so."

"Is that right." He smiled at me, his blue eyes laughing.

"It most certainly is."

"Do your parents think you're old enough to date?"

I had no idea. I'd never been asked on a date before. But I wasn't about to tell him that. "Of course."

"Well, then, seeing as you're so old and mature, would you like to go to the Fourth of July picnic with me?"

I'm sure my smile was ear to ear. I felt as though the sun were shining on my insides. "Why, Jack Bradford O'Connor, I'd be delighted."

"Jack was always direct, yet charming," Amélie says, jarring me out of my reminiscence. "It's interesting that even at sixteen, he was that way."

Isn't it just like her to remind me that she'd had Jack for most of his adult life! I lift my chin. "He later said that asking me to that picnic was the best decision of his life."

At that, Amélie falls silent. She is probably wondering if Jack thought marrying her was even better. I hope not. I hope nothing they ever had together equaled the thrills of first love that Jack and I shared.

But I need to find out. I need to know what happened. "So that's how our romance began. Tell me how yours started."

"I was leading up to it."

I wave my hand. "I really don't need all the background information about you before the war."

"Yes, you do. None of it makes sense without it."

"I'm pretty sure I can figure it out."

She inclines her head. "I will tell it my way, or not at all."

I should have known that she would be difficult. "All right, all right." I sigh. "Continue."

5

AMÉLIE
1939

I was out of breath from rushing when I arrived in the reading room at the Sorbonne library the next afternoon. I paused in the entryway to gather myself. With its soaring ceilings, elaborately carved millwork, and long tables that resembled pews, the room looked more like an ornate church than a study hall. The walls were covered in green silk damask and the ceilings were edged with gold. At the front were three enormous paintings of the world's great thinkers set behind a curved archway that looked like a chancel. Even the silence in the room was church-like. All that was lacking was a cross and an altar table.

I found Joshua sitting at the end of a table by an enormous paned window, backlit by the setting sun.

He was not particularly handsome, and he certainly wasn't well dressed—he wore a hand-knitted sweater in rough, undyed wool, and the cuffs of his shirt were frayed—but something about him—his bearing, his wide shoulders, his thick unruly hair—sent a thrill straight through me.

He rose to his feet when he saw me. "You're here," he said in a hushed tone.

"So are you," I inanely replied, my heart pounding wildly. He pulled out the chair next to his, and I sank into it, grateful to be off my suddenly wobbly legs.

He closed the book he had been reading. "Which school do you go to?"

I was crestfallen that he didn't just assume I went to university. I'd hurried home after class and changed out of my uniform, not wanting him to know I was still in lycée. "I don't think I should tell you," I said in what I hoped was a flirtatious tone. "You warned me to be careful what I said."

"Only if you think it might incriminate someone." His brown eyes were amused. "Do you fear incriminating yourself?"

My face heated. "Of course not."

His gaze stayed on me. "I'm guessing that you don't want me to know how young you are."

"That's not true."

"No? So what's your age?"

"Eighteen."

"You're a terrible liar." He looked me up and down. "I think you're no more than fourteen."

"Fourteen!" The word came out as an outraged squeak, louder than I intended.

"Aha!" He grinned. The expression totally transformed his face. "You just gave yourself away. If you were eighteen, you would be amused that I guessed so low, rather than insulted. My real guess is that you're about sixteen."

So much for appearing worldly and sophisticated. I reluctantly nodded.

"It's okay," he said. "I'm just seventeen, myself."

"Really? You seem a lot older."

His mouth tightened. "I feel older."

"Because of what happened in Austria?"

"That, and what is about to happen here."

"*Taisez-vous!*" ordered the library monitor, a tall, thin whippet of a man who patrolled the room, making sure no one defaced the books or disturbed the tomb-like quiet.

"Let's go get a coffee," Joshua whispered.

"*D'accord.*"

He slung his book bag on his shoulder, then took my elbow and led me to the exit.

I thrilled at the touch of his hand on my arm. It was such a manly, possessive thing to do, to take my elbow. He had the manners of the wellborn, my mother would have said.

Outside, the air was cold. "How did you know I was lying about my age?"

"Aside from how young you look?" He grinned at me as he guided me past a bicyclist.

"Yes."

"You showed all the signs of untruthfulness."

"Like what?"

"Your voice changed. You looked away and no longer met my gaze. You straightened your posture and stuck out your chin."

"How did you know to look for those signs?"

He lifted his shoulders. "Some veterans of the Great War have been teaching me things that will be useful if the Germans invade."

"But why . . ."

"So many questions! It's my turn to ask about you," he said with a smile.

"Okay," I said, realizing I had done nothing but quiz him since we'd left the library. "What would you like to know?"

"Well, first of all, how have you been lucky enough to have Professor Chaussant for a tutor?"

Lucky wasn't the word I would have used to have described the grueling twice-weekly tutoring sessions, but I wasn't about to tell him that. "His family and my family are very good friends. We live across the street from each other, and my father is also a professor at the Sorbonne. So my father tutors Yvette Chaussant and my brothers and me in English and German, and Professor Chaussant tutors us in higher mathematics. This has been going on for years."

"So you speak German? That will come in very handy if they overtake this country."

"Oh, that won't happen," I said. "Hitler offered us peace."

He made a derisive sound. "He only wants France off high alert so he can catch you unawares. They will attack, you can be sure."

Our conversation paused as we entered a shabby café. We sat at a small table by the window and ordered two coffees. "How come you're so certain Germany will attack?"

"Because Hitler is ruthless. He wants to conquer the whole world."

"No one can conquer the whole world!"

"Ah, but he thinks he can. That's what makes him so dangerous. He's a madman—brilliant, but mad. And because he believes it is doable, he will stop at nothing."

It was easy to believe that Hitler could, indeed, be crazy. But that didn't explain the German army. "How has one madman gotten his entire country to go mad along with him?"

"It happened slowly, over many years. Germany had a very hard time after the Great War. The Germans were beaten down, defeated, humiliated. He's offering them a sense of pride and purpose. After years of being the underdog, the Germans are eager to buy the message he's selling."

"Which is?"

"That they are conquerors, rather than the conquered. That they deserve to be in charge."

"Even if they attack, everyone says there's no way the Germans can get through the Maginot Line," I said. "France has been fortifying it since the Great War."

"I hope you are right, but I fear you are not."

"Then why did you come to Paris, if you think France will also be invaded?"

He took a sip of coffee. "We had nowhere else to go."

"Who is we?"

"My mother and myself. The Germans murdered my father as we were about to leave."

It sounded like something that happened in a movie, not something that happened to someone I knew. "Oh, I am so sorry! Why did they kill him?"

"We are Jewish."

He looked at me with those clear, brown eyes, and I sensed he was reading how this news would affect me. I knew little about the Jewish people, other than that the Germans hated them and that my parents sympathized with their plight.

"So was Jesus," I said.

He laughed. "Quite so. The Germans seem to have forgotten that."

"Were you there? When your father . . ."

"Please." He raised his hand, interrupting me. "I don't want to discuss this."

This was one of the great mysteries that Yvette and I had pondered over and over—what should a girl talk about with boys? Apparently, one shouldn't pry into sore subjects.

"I'm sorry," I said, sincerely chagrined. "I didn't mean to make you feel bad."

"It's okay." He took a sip of coffee. "So—tell me about your family and your friendship with the Chaussants."

So I did. I talked about my mother, my father, and my brothers, and I babbled about my close friendship with Yvette.

He leaned forward. "Yvette was the one dancing with Herman Beck?"

"Yes."

"I hope she has the sense not to see him again."

I set down my coffee, rattling the saucer. "Why? Is he one of the spies you warned me about?"

He spoke in a low tone. "I only know he's connected to all kinds of unsavory men, and many of them will sell anything—information, stolen goods, people—for the right amount of money."

"What do you mean, they will sell people?"

"Prostitutes. Unsuspecting women. Young girls such as yourself. Sometimes children."

"Why?"

He frowned at me. "You have to ask?"

I hesitated, not wanting to appear naive, but honestly not sure.

His mouth tightened. He leaned closer to me and spoke barely above a whisper. "There are men who enjoy inflicting pain, or worse. There are men who want to do depraved things to children."

"No," I breathed. To say I was shocked would be an understatement. I had never heard, never thought of such things.

"I am afraid it is true." He looked at me. "I can tell from your face that Yvette is planning to meet him. When?"

"Tonight," I found myself confessing. "He's—he's sending a car for her."

"Does she want to have sex with him?"

Sex? "Of course not!" My face heated. "She wants to dance and flirt and . . . and maybe share a kiss." Just saying the word *kiss* embarrassed me.

"He is not a man to just flirt and kiss. You must tell her not to go."

My skin felt as if a cockroach had crawled over it. "But he seemed so nice, so respectful . . ."

"What do you think evil people look like? They don't have horns, like devils. They look perfectly normal, perfectly nice—maybe even nicer than average."

"Are you certain Herman is evil?"

He lifted his shoulders. "I only know there are many rumors about him. In my experience, rumors are like flies; whenever they're buzzing around, they're usually circling something rotten."

"I'll warn her to stay home tonight."

"Do more than warn," Joshua said. "You must stop her."

We quickly finished our coffees, and he walked me to the corner. "This is where I turn."

"Can I see you again?" he asked.

"I would like that very much."

"I have class tomorrow afternoon, but the day after, I am free until five. Can you meet me again at the same place, same time?"

I nodded and leaned in for *la bise*, but he just stood there awkwardly. I straightened and waggled my fingers. "*À bientôt*," I said, and hurried away.

I went straight to Yvette's flat. Her mother let me in, and I headed to Yvette's bedroom, where she was fixing her hair for her rendezvous.

I quickly told her what Joshua had said.

She fell on her bed, clutching a pillow to her chest. "Oh, mon Dieu!"

"You can't go."

"But—how do we know Joshua's right? Maybe he's just being melodramatic."

"Yvette, you can't risk it. You can't go off in a car with a man who may be mixed up in prostitution or worse."

"But he seemed so nice!"

"Yvette, think about it. What does a man his age want with a young girl like you?"

"I don't look that all that young. I told him I'm twenty-two."

"I doubt he believes that. You were with a table of girls who look like me."

She gazed at me for a long moment, then exhaled a resigned sigh. "I suppose you're right." She plopped down across her mattress. "But I was so excited about going!"

"I know, Yvette, but you can't."

She stared up at the ceiling. "I am just so bored! I would almost rather get into trouble than be so bored!"

"Not this kind of trouble, Yvette."

"No." She blew out another sigh and rolled over on her stomach. "No, you are right."

I rolled over beside her. "Do you want me to see if Joshua knows some other boys?"

She shook her head. "I have no real interest in boys. Herman intrigued me because he is a fully grown man." She plucked at a thread on her bedspread, then cast me a sidelong glance. "Do you know who I really wish was here?"

"Who?"

"Pierre."

"My brother Pierre?" My eyebrows flew upward.

She seemed fascinated by a thread on her coverlet. "Yes."

Surprise and dismay swept through me.

"I've been writing him," she said.

"You have?"

She nodded. "And he's writing back. Two letters this week."

"Two letters! That's one more than he sent us!"

She smiled and lifted her shoulders.

"What does he say?"

"The same things he writes to your family." She kept her gaze fixed on her coverlet. "Plus he tells me his thoughts and feelings."

"Pierre has thoughts and feelings?"

"Of course he does. He's a very sensitive man."

A man? Since when was Pierre a man? "So you . . . like him?"

"Yes. Yes, I believe I do."

This turn of events stunned me, and not in a happy way. "Was something going on before he left?"

"No." Her voice held a tentative quality that made me push for more information.

"No, but . . . ?"

She still wouldn't meet my eyes. "Well, the last few months before he left, I developed a little crush on him."

Why didn't I know this? Maybe because I didn't want to know. I didn't like the idea of my best friend and my brother. And she must have sensed that, because she hadn't told me.

"So . . . is something going on now?"

"No. Maybe. Sort of." She smiled. "He says he thinks I'm pretty, but he hasn't really thought of me as girlfriend material because I'm your friend and so much younger."

Right, I thought.

"I wrote him there's only two years' age difference between us, which isn't very much. And just because I'm your friend is no reason I can't be his friend, too." She twirled a strand of hair. "I told him you wouldn't mind. You don't, do you?"

I did, but I couldn't say why. "It—it's odd, is all." I didn't know how I felt. Strangely pushed aside, mostly. Maybe displaced. Definitely off-balance.

Another thought occurred to me. "Do you write him about me? Did you write about the other night?"

"No, of course not! I can't risk him telling your mother."

Thank heavens she hadn't completely lost her head. "Please, please, please don't tell him about Joshua!"

"Oh, I won't. Don't worry." She grinned. "Your secrets are safe with me. And I hope mine still are with you?"

"Yes, of course. It's just . . ."

"What?"

"Well, I would hate for you to lead him on and break his heart."

She laughed as if this were wildly funny. "As if I could!"

"Well, I don't think you should try."

"I wouldn't! It's nothing like that. It's just a little long-distance flirtation, that is all. So tell me about your date with Joshua."

"It wasn't really a date. We met at the library and went for coffee."

"Did he pay for your coffee?"

"Yes, of course."

"Then it was a date! Tell me all about it."

So I did.

"Do you think you will introduce him to your parents so you can truly date?"

"I don't know. What do you think they will say?"

She gazed thoughtfully at the wall. "Your mother will not like that he's an immigrant."

It was worse than that. I was fairly certain my mother would not take kindly to me seeing someone who wasn't our religion. "My father would not think it matters. He would be impressed that Joshua speaks French very well even though Yiddish and German are his native languages. I think he would be impressed that Joshua is an engineering student with a bright future."

"Yes, but your mother will want to know all about his family." She gave me a wry grin. "You have met your mother, haven't you?"

"Yes." I sighed. Yvette was right; my mother could be a snob.

I sneaked out and met Joshua two days later—and continued to meet him two or three times a week as the winter wore on. We fell into a pattern of walking and talking. He would hold my hand and he would give a quick peck on the cheek hello and good-bye, but he never really kissed me.

Yvette peppered me about it after every outing. "Did it happen?"

"No. But he gazes at my lips, and he smells my hair."

"Oh, that's so romantic! He must be shy, though. You need to prompt him to make the first move."

After a couple of months of this, I made sure we were on a deserted side street when it was time to say good-bye, and I turned my face toward him as he went to kiss my cheek. His lips met mine. He stiffened, and I thought I had made a terrible miscalculation—but then his mouth moved over mine with an ardor that left me breathless. It was everything I had dreamed of, and more. It was a chocolate soufflé of a kiss—hot and melting and sweet.

Too soon, Joshua groaned and pulled away.

"Don't stop," I whispered.

"I don't want to start down a path where I may disrespect you."

"You wouldn't!"

"I will probably try. A man's desires—they are not honorable. It will become more and more difficult to stop, and before I know it, I might compromise you."

"You wouldn't," I repeated.

"You might want me to."

"I just want you to kiss me again," I murmured.

I watched his Adam's apple move. "I want that, too. You have no idea how much. Sometimes at night, I think about you, and . . ." He blew out a harsh breath. A thrill chased through me.

But his next words were like a bucket of cold water. "Romance is not something we should even consider in a time of war."

"We're not really at war," I said. "There's no actual fighting." Everyone called it *la drôle de guerre*—the joke of war. The Americans called it "the phony war."

"It will come," he said, "and when it does, it will be brutal. It is best for us just to stay friends for now."

The thought of being something more in the future emboldened me.
I stepped closer and put my hands on his chest. "Our friendship would
be more special if you would kiss me again."

He took my hands, removed them from his chest, and stepped back. "Do
not persist in tempting my baser nature, or I will not see you anymore."

"You would quit seeing me rather than kiss me?"

"Yes. I do not want to ever harm you."

If his kisses were a prelude to how it would feel, I very much longed
to be harmed.

—

I did not want him to stop seeing me, so I followed his rules. Rather than
kissing, we talked at great length about politics, about Hitler, about the
impending German attack. I asked about his family, and learned that he
had distant aunts and uncles and cousins flooding into Paris, and that many
of them were temporarily staying with him and his mother. I also learned
that he'd had a younger sister who had died. He would not tell me how.
Every time I broached the subject, he would come up with a reason to leave.

I did learn that his father had owned a fine leather-goods store. The
family had lived in a lovely house in Vienna, but now lived in a squalid
apartment in the eleventh arrondissement. His mother took in ironing
to help pay the rent, much to his shame and chagrin.

"She says she does not mind, but it is probably a good thing my father
is dead," he said bitterly. "It would kill him to see her reduced to this. I
want to quit school and fully support her, but she says my education is
the key to the future, and hope for the future is all she has to cling to."

—

On my own, I learned all that I could about what had happened in Austria
in 1938—mainly by questioning my father. He was delighted that I was
taking such interest in world affairs, and would give long, boring expla-
nations involving Poland and other countries I didn't care about, talking
in such detail that my eyes glazed like a Christmas ham.

As for Joshua, I learned that if I asked about political history, he would talk freely. If I asked about his personal history, he would shut down. Little by little, though, I broke through his defenses.

We were at a deserted student café on a cold afternoon, sitting at a table by the fireplace, when he finally told me what happened.

"I know that Germany annexed Austria a year and a half ago," I said. "Why didn't Austria fight the takeover?"

"We had a very weak leader. The Nazis presented annexation as a wonderful thing for our country, and most Austrians did not mind. But the Jewish population . . . oh, that is another story."

"What happened?"

"The Nazis started a hate campaign against us almost immediately. Posters went up on every lamppost, along with awful comics in the newspapers calling us thieves and crooks and the scourge of the world. They made it difficult for Jews to travel or operate businesses. But it became untenable after Kristallnacht."

"'The night of broken glass.' My father told me about this. It was started by a murder here in Paris, right?"

He nodded. "A German diplomat was assassinated. The Nazis claimed it was conspiracy masterminded by Jews. They used it as a reason to attack Jews in Austria and Germany. The windows at our home, at my father's business, at our neighbors' homes were all broken that night. And afterward, the military relentlessly preyed on the Jewish community. They would stop us and make us do stupid things."

"Like what?"

"They made an elderly woman who lived across the street hop on one leg while carrying water. They made an old man crawl down the street."

I put my hand over my mouth.

"They repeatedly vandalized our property and looted my father's store. They confiscated insurance payments for the damage they had inflicted, saying we were responsible for the destruction. We decided to emigrate. Father thought Paris would be the best location to open another store. But the Germans did not make it easy for Jews to travel. We had to get a visa and have documents approved, and to do so, we had to pay bribe after bribe. Delay piled upon delay."

Joshua's hand curled tight around his coffee cup. "In order to emigrate, we had to agree to leave everything behind and to pay extraordinarily high 'taxes.' In the end, we had only a little money—maybe enough for a few weeks of food, but not enough to start over. But by then, it didn't matter. The situation was so bad that it was impossible to stay. We were so glad that at last we had all the required papers."

I barely dared to breathe. His eyes had a faraway look, and I was afraid that if I interrupted, he would end the conversation as he always had before. This time, he kept talking.

"The night before we left, I went to say good-bye to a girl. She and I . . . well, we were romantically involved. It is a mistake I will regret all of my life. I should not have left my family."

"Why?" I gently prodded.

"When I got back, my mother was hysterical, and my sister . . ." He put his hand to his forehead and rubbed between his eyes. "She was catatonic. My father—he was lying in the hallway, on what looked like a red carpet. It took me a moment to realize it was a pool of blood, and he was dead."

"Mon Dieu! What had happened?"

"Three German soldiers had come to check our house, supposedly to see what goods we were leaving behind. The real reason, I believe, is that they were looking for me. That night, they rounded up all young Jewish men in our neighborhood and sent them to concentration camps."

I reflexively started to make the sign of the cross, then stopped myself.

"My father didn't want to let the soldiers in. This, of course, angered them. They forced the door, then saw my sister. My father tried to get her to run. This infuriated them more. They tied my sister to the bed, strapped my parents to chairs and then, they . . ." He ran his hand down his face. "They raped her. All three of them, one after the other, like dogs, while my parents watched. My father broke free—how he managed, my mother says she does not know; outrage and courage must have given him supernatural strength. He charged—Mama said he was like a bull. They shot him, then they left.

"An elderly neighbor came over as soon as I arrived home. He had been watching the house from across the street. He's the one who told us the Nazis were rounding up young Jewish men that very night. I wanted stay and bury my father, but my sister was out of her mind with terror and shock, and my mother was hysterical, and the neighbor insisted we go. We took only what we could carry. We walked and walked and walked until we reached a train station in the suburbs of Vienna, a neighborhood where no one expected to see a Jew, so no one was looking—and with our papers, the papers we had given everything for— well, we were able to catch a train to Paris."

He looked up at me. "So. That is my story. That is how I came to be here. That is how I know the Nazis are brutal beyond belief."

"Your sister—you told me she had died?"

"My mother found her in the bathroom two weeks later, at the apartment where we stayed with some other refugees when we first arrived in Paris. She had slit her wrists." He lowered his head, but not before I saw that his eyes were swimming. "She found it impossible to live with the shame."

I put my hand on his arm.

"I failed her. I failed my father, my mother—my whole family. I should have been home. If I'd been with them, this would not have happened."

"No." I desperately wanted to lighten his burden of guilt. "If you had been home, you, too, would be dead."

"At least that would have been honorable. If I had been there, they would have just taken me and left my sister alone."

"You cannot know that."

He buried his eyes in his hands.

"The important thing now is that you stay alive and try to provide a future for your mother," I said.

He rubbed his eyes, then reached for his coffee. "That is not what I think in the dark of night. I fear that is not what my mother thinks, either."

I reached for his hand. He squeezed it. I leaned in to kiss him, but, as always, he turned away.

AMÉLIE
1940

The joke of war stopped being funny on May 10. That was when Yvette and I came home from school to find Maman wringing her hands as she listened to the radio. Yvette's mother stood beside her.

"What has happened?"

"Germany has invaded Belgium," Maman said.

"And Luxembourg and Holland," Yvette's mother added. "It's a blitzkrieg."

It was the first time either Yvette or I had heard the word. I thought it sounded like a pastry. "What's that?"

"It means lightning war," Yvette's mother said. "Planes suddenly appear and drop bomb after bomb. And then panzer tanks move in and destroy everything in their path."

A shiver ran up my spine. "Why are they attacking those countries? Has Germany declared war on them?" I asked.

"Nothing was declared. They just started bombing and invading."

If they were doing that to countries that they weren't even officially at war with, what would they do to us?

When I voiced my concerns at dinner, Papa was quick to reassure me. Or maybe it was my mother he wanted to reassure. She seemed to be falling apart. Her hair was unkempt, her dress was wrinkled, and her face had taken on an unhealthy pall.

"We have defenses in place," he said, "and we have allies. There are more than three hundred thousand British troops—the great British Expeditionary Force—in our country to shore up our army."

The British had a new prime minister, a man named Winston Churchill. No one seemed to know anything about him, except that he had never advocated trying to make peace with the Nazis, as the previous English prime minister had.

We heard that the British and French military were moving toward the Dyle River. Were Thomas and Pierre on the move, as well?

Over the next few days, life in Paris went on as usual, except for the fact that the radio played more news than music. Yvette and I went to school. Father continued to teach at university. France had become so inured to a war that wasn't really a war that it was hard to realize how much the situation had changed. Everyone still believed the impregnable Maginot Line would hold.

Joshua was the one who told me the news when I met him at the Jardin des Plantes, in the Allée Becquerel. We had taken to meeting there now that the weather was warm. "The Germans are in France. They invaded through the Ardennes."

"The Ardennes forest?" I had studied French geography just last year. "That is supposed to be impenetrable."

He nodded grimly. "Which is why it was virtually undefended. No army in the history of the world has ever been able to get through." He shook his head. "No one has ever seen warfare like this before. The Germans are using tanks and the Luftwaffe in a new way. No one could have even imagined the things they are doing."

"What will happen?"

"We have no way of knowing. We must hope the English will save us." He thrust his hands in his pockets. "I long to join the French Foreign Legion, but I can't leave my mother. She says she can't make it without me." He blew out a sigh. "I fear it is so."

"I don't want you to leave, either."

He placed his hand over mine. "It may be best that we all leave."

"Where would we go?"

"Ah, that is the question," he said. "That is why we stay." His mouth took on a determined set. "But that does not mean I will not fight. The front line is not the only place to battle the enemy."

―――――――

The days went by. The radio told us very little—Joshua said it was propaganda to keep us calm—but we learned from travelers flooding in and from radio programs from London that Holland had surrendered.

Even after the surrender, the Germans continued their cruel assault. We heard they'd bombed Rotterdam, killing more than a thousand civilians and leaving more than 85,000 homeless. We heard that more than 10,000 French soldiers were captured in a single day.

And then we heard that the Germans were bombing northern France; the roads were jammed with millions of northern French inhabitants who'd either been bombed out of their homes or feared it was about to happen. The French and British armies, who had believed the Germans were coming through Belgium, found themselves trapped as the Germans rolled through the forest and lowlands, backing them against the sea.

I did not understand all that was happening, but I understood that the British had retreated along the English Channel and were arranging for ships to pick up their soldiers.

"What are they doing?" Papa railed. "Everyone knows that the channel is no place for military maneuvers. It will never work."

We later heard that it had—that the British had evacuated 300,000 British troops. "They've abandoned us," Papa moaned.

Joshua saw it differently. "The British were wise to withdraw so they can come back and help France fight another way."

We heard that tens of thousands of French soldiers had run or surrendered. Were Pierre and Thomas among them? I prayed it was so, for then they would not be among the 100,000 French soldiers rumored to already be dead.

Along with Maman, I went to mass and lit candles for them every day. We heard that nearly 150,000 French troops had been rescued by the British ships. I prayed that Pierre and Thomas were among them, that they were safely in England.

Paris was suddenly very crowded. The city streets teemed with refugees—from Belgium, from Holland, from northern France. My private school was abruptly dismissed for the summer, three weeks early, because so many students' families were fleeing Paris.

At first, Papa said we would stay. "Leaving shows a lack of faith in France and in our military. The Germans won't make it to Paris. We will stop them, just as we did in the Great War."

Yvette's mother arrived at our door with somber news otherwise.

"The Germans are on the way," she murmured in a low voice. "I received word from Jean-Claude."

"French troops will intervene before they enter Paris," Papa insisted.

"He says there are no French troops to defend us. Those who haven't been captured or killed were stationed along the Maginot Line and can't get into position to halt the advance. Yvette and I are leaving tomorrow for my father's farm."

I had gone there with Yvette for several summers. It was near Dijon, in a beautiful part of the country. Her widowed grandfather was a dear man who insisted I, too, call him *Grand-père*. I fell into her arms. "Oh, Yvette—you can't leave Paris!"

"I must," she said. "And you must, too."

Even Joshua, who thought there was no safe place to flee, thought we should leave Paris.

"Well, then, you and your mother should leave as well," I told him two nights later when we met.

"We have no money and nowhere to go," Joshua said grimly. "Besides, we are hosting many, many distant relatives who have lost their homes and are in worse shape than us. But you and your family— it would be best if you leave."

Maman and Papa argued that night. After learning that Professor Chaussant thought Paris was unsafe and discovering that most of his colleagues were fleeing, Papa had reversed his opinion. He now insisted that we leave immediately. "We have no choice."

"But this is our home," Maman argued. "How will our boys find us if we leave?"

"They are not coming home anytime soon," Papa said grimly.

"You don't know that!"

"I do, Marie. And so do you. Our soldiers will be fighting a long, long time."

7

AMÉLIE
1940

*M*aman and Papa continued to exchange sharp words, late into the night. The next day, the radio aired French Prime Minister Reynaud's speech to the Senate that included the ominous phrase, "The country is in danger."

"Did you hear that, Marie?" Papa demanded. "We are putting Amélie in danger."

That set Maman to packing. I was told to fill a suitcase with all the clothes that I could carry. Papa sent a telegraph to his brother Roland in Marseilles to tell him we were coming. *Mon oncle* lived with his wife and my paternal grand-père in a small but lovely apartment with large windows, iron balconies, and a breathtaking view of the port.

"I don't want to go there," Maman grumbled. I didn't blame her; my uncle's wife, Margaux, was a harsh and disagreeable woman. "If we must leave home, let's leave Europe altogether. Let's go to America."

"With what?" Papa was clearly losing patience. "We spent the bulk of our savings renovating the house. We do not have enough money for a long journey to another continent."

I packed my clothing. The radio blathered more and more bad news, couching it in such transparently foolish optimism that even I, who secretly believed that everything would work out like a magazine short story, knew it was a lie. Out the window, all of Paris—indeed, all of France!—seemed to be flowing through the streets. I have never seen the roads so congested, never seen so many faces so grim and distressed. My stomach balled into a hard knot.

Maman insisted on taking sausage, bread, and a couple of jars of canned food. She left a note for Thomas and Pierre, in case they came home before us. She washed every dish and dusted every surface.

"What are you doing?" Papa demanded when he returned from the telegraph office. "If the city is bombed, the entire place will be covered with dust, if anything is left standing."

"Ah, but if there is no bombing—and I pray to God there won't be— then I want everything clean and sparkling to welcome us home."

Papa threw up his hands and murmured something under his breath about the irrationality of women. "You have thirty minutes." At the end of that time period, he turned off all the lights, put all our suitcases outside on the stoop, then took Maman's elbow and firmly escorted her outside. He locked the door behind us. We climbed down the four steps to the street and were swept into the wave of humanity slowly surging forward, the crowd so thick everyone was forced to go in a single direction.

We headed toward the Gare d'Austerlitz, which is close to the Jardin des Plantes, where Joshua and I had been meeting. I kept my eye out for Joshua, but he was nowhere to be seen.

The train station was so packed you could hardly edge sideways toward the ticket office.

"They are overselling the tickets," a woman complained to Maman as Papa got in line to handle our ticket purchase. "They are selling with no seats. And people are disregarding the dates and times. They are climbing onto the first train they can elbow their way onto."

Maman relayed this to Papa when he finally returned with tickets for the next day. "We must board the very next train," she insisted.

Papa, being Papa, refused to break the rules. "I will not participate in anarchy."

Maman plucked two tickets from his hand. "Suit yourself, Alphonse. Come, Amélie." Taking my elbow, she started pushing through the crowd toward the tracks, where a train had just arrived.

"This is not right!" Papa sputtered. "It is not fair to the people who purchased tickets for this train."

"Those people already left on an earlier one," Maman said over her shoulder.

"I can't believe you would do such a thing!"

"If the situation is so dire that we must leave our home to protect our child, then it is dire enough to do whatever else it takes."

"But all these people . . ." Papa waved his hand. "They have children, too."

"You love to quote that English saying, 'all is fair in love and war.' Well, Alphonse, this is a matter of both."

"But, Marie . . ."

My mother's face took on a look I recognized from battles at the dressmaker's. When her mouth flattened into that pinched set and her chin tilted to that rigid angle, there was no changing her mind. "You can come with us, or you can stay," Maman said. "Either way, Amélie and I are boarding this train."

It was a hot, crowded, exhausting nightmare of a trip. It took five hours, and we stood the entire time, squashed beside a family of Belgians that included a crying toddler, an old toothless woman, and a man with one eye. The scent of sweating bodies, dirty diapers, and day-old garlic breath kept me from feeling any hunger, despite not having eaten since breakfast.

The train stopped in Lyon, and the conductor unexpectedly called out, "*Tout le monde débarquent.*"

Papa grabbed his arm. "Pardon, monsieur. We have tickets to Marseilles."

"The army has requisitioned this train to carry troops. Everyone must get off here."

"When can we catch another train south?"

"I do not know. You will have to talk to the ticket agent."

Apparently most of the train's occupants also needed to talk to the ticket agent. We stood in line for nearly four hours. When we finally got to the window, we learned that the next train to Marseilles would not come until two days later.

"That is ridiculous!" Papa sputtered.

"It is the best we can do," the agent said.

The hotels were overflowing. Along with many other travelers, we ended up taking refuge in a church for two nights. Maman and I slept on the pews, and Papa slept on the floor beneath. The church was hot and airless, and a child with a horrible hacking cough kept us awake most of the night.

We spent much of the next day in line—to buy bread, to buy cheese, to use a toilet. The toilet situation was the worst! At one point, I had to pee in an alley as Maman stood guarding my privacy. I thought I would die of embarrassment.

After another torturously crowded train trip, we finally made it to Marseilles. The streets were jammed with motorcars, horse- and ox-drawn carts, buses, trucks, and many, many people like us—on foot, carrying baggage, looking tired and bedraggled and displaced. My feet throbbed as we walked more than three kilometers on the cobblestone streets to my uncle's apartment. I was hungry and tired and my shoulders ached from carrying my suitcase. I would have sold my soul for a warm bath.

We climbed three flights of stairs and knocked. My *tante* Margaux opened the door, her eyes red-rimmed, the bags beneath them more creased and puffy than the last time I'd seen her. She wore an apron over a black dress that accentuated her gaunt frame.

"You are too late." She folded her arms across her chest.

Maman and Papa looked as bewildered as I felt. "Too late for what?" Papa asked.

"The funerals. We buried them yesterday."

"What?" Maman gasped.

My father's face went white. "Who?"

"Roland and your father." Margaux frowned with irritation, her tone terse. "Didn't you get the telegram?"

Papa staggered backward.

Mama dropped her bag and put her arm around him to steady him. "This is the first we've heard of this," she said. "He needs to sit down."

Margaux stepped aside to allow us into the parlor. Maman and I helped Papa to a sofa.

Papa's face was pale and waxy-looking, his voice was a low croak. "My father. My brother. Both . . . gone?"

"If you did not know, why are you here?"

Maman answered for him. "Everyone is fleeing Paris ahead of the Wehrmacht."

"What happened?" Papa asked.

"Roland was taking your father to the barber. Your father fell in the street—no one knows why. Perhaps it was his heart, perhaps he stumbled. Roland bent down to help him, and a truck hit them both."

"Mon Dieu, mon Dieu!" Papa's face was white. He suddenly looked very frail and ill. It rattled me to my core, seeing my strong papa in such a state.

"The doctor said death was instantaneous for them both," Margaux said.

"So there was no pain," Maman stroked Papa's arm. "They did not suffer."

I went into the kitchen and found a decanter of brandy and a glass. I carried both to the living room and poured Papa a drink. His hand was shaking, so Maman helped him tilt the glass to his mouth. Tante Margaux moved to take the decanter away from me. In my first act of open rebellion against an adult, I refused to let her. Instead I refilled the glass and handed it to Maman, who took a tiny sip herself, then helped Papa down the rest. Margaux frowned at me. I cast her a mutinous look and refilled the glass yet again.

"If you came to stay here, I am afraid I have no room," Tante Margaux said. "My parents, my sister and her family, our daughter and her children are here. My two sons' wives and children are staying in your father's apartment."

"I—I see." Papa rubbed his eyes.

"You cannot throw us on the street, Margaux." Maman's voice was like sharpened steel. "We spent two nights sleeping in a church in Lyon, and Marseilles seems just as crowded. You have just dealt Alphonse a terrible shock."

"Yes, but I only have limited beds, and . . ."

"We will sleep on the floor tonight and tomorrow." Maman spoke as if it were already settled. "That will give us time to make other arrangements. I am sure Alphonse's father and brother would not want you to turn us away at such a time."

"No! No, of course not." She gave an insincere smile. "You are welcome here."

———

We did not feel welcome. We slept on pallets in the kitchen. I listened to my father and mother talk softly. I heard Papa's muffled sobs. I cannot tell you what that did to my heart, to hear my father cry.

I was too young to fully comprehend the depth of despair he must have been feeling—to have lost his last living parent and only sibling, to have fled his home against his wife's objections, to not be welcome at the place of refuge he'd counted on. I was also, blessedly, too young to understand the direness of our situation.

I remember thinking, *How can an old man fall in the street when the Nazis are invading? How can everyday tragedies still happen, while our country is under attack?* The very least God could do, it seemed, was to grant a reprieve on non-war disasters.

8

AMÉLIE
1940

*T*he next day, we bought flowers and went to the church grave-yard. I did not have a close relationship with either my uncle or grandfather—I hadn't seen them in several years—but Papa's grief was a noose around my heart.

After talking with the priest, Papa wanted to visit the graves alone. Maman and I stayed in the church and said prayers for their souls and the safety of Thomas and Pierre. I prayed for Joshua, as well—as well as for comfort for Papa.

Maman encouraged Papa to call a professor he knew at the university at Aix-en-Provence, about thirty miles away. There was no work for Papa, but the professor arranged for us to stay in a dormitory.

Once there, I thought I would go crazy; I was living quite literally on top of my parents in a bunk bed. There was no kitchen; we ate fruit and vegetables we purchased in town, and had one meal a day at a pension for the elderly. It was hot, it was miserable, and I thought things couldn't get any worse.

In about a week, they did. On June 10, as Maman and I were coming out of a patisserie, we heard planes overhead. A few minutes later, we heard several distant blasts.

A crowd gathered on the street to stare at the sky. Several separate plumes of smoke were spiraling upward from the direction of Marseilles.

"What is happening?" Maman asked.

"It looks like Marseilles has been bombed," responded a woman in a blue and white dress.

"It's further east," said a man in a stylish suit. "Looks like Hyères."

We hurried back to the dorm and waited for Papa to come home from the library. Maman grabbed him the moment he entered the room. "The Germans are bombing us!"

"No." Papa sank heavily on the bed. Fatigue and grief were etched on his face. He looked, I realized with alarm, like an old man. "The Italians are."

Maman and I gaped like a couple of fishes.

"That makes no sense," Maman said.

Papa heaved a sigh. "Mussolini has been waiting to attack a weakened country. Everyone thought it would be Yugoslavia, but he is an opportunist, and . . . well, France is about to fall."

"Has the whole world gone mad?" Mama wailed.

"So it seems."

"I told you we should have stayed in Paris!"

"Alas, Marie—the Wehrmacht are advancing on the city even faster than anyone feared."

"Well, we can't remain here. We must join the Chaussants in the country. We were invited, and they have plenty of room."

Papa nodded. I don't know if he really agreed or just conceded. This was the first time I had seen grief up close. On Papa, it looked like a serious illness.

And so we began another long and arduous train journey, this time toward Dijon. Since we were now heading north, the crowding was not as bad.

As the train rattled down the track, we learned from the gentleman seated next to us that the French government had fled Paris for Tours.

The *government* had fled? I could scarcely take it in. All of my life, I had believed that my country was an immutable force—one of those things that was absolute, that could not fail, that was the bedrock of existence. God and country—the words went together. And now . . . the government, the very heart of my country, was running? I felt as if the sky were falling.

We were bone-tired when we pulled into the station at Dijon. M. Chaussant's farm was several miles beyond the city, near the small town of Arcy-sur-Cure. Papa found a taxi driver who had just relocated from Paris to give us a ride. On the drive, he told us about *l'exode.*

"You were fortunate to travel out of Paris by train," he said. "The roads were virtually impassable. Not only Parisians, but refugees from northern France and Belgium, people with terrible stories of bombed-out homes— many on foot, others in trucks or cars or on bicycles, or carts pulled by horses and mules and even oxen. People ran out of gas and just abandoned their vehicles. My taxi, fortunately, has two gasoline tanks.

"The first day, it took fifteen hours to travel five kilometers. A regiment of French troops was trying to move north, and we couldn't even clear the road to let them pass."

"Mon Dieu," Maman murmured.

"Many of the travelers were French soldiers heading home, some wounded, others full of despair. Oh, the tales they told!" He lifted his hands from the steering wheel and clasped his cheeks until I feared he was about to veer off the road. "It was enough to raise the hairs on your head."

Maman leaned forward, her eyes anxious. "What did they say?"

"They said that the Germans are fighting with weapons that we're not prepared to defend against. Their tanks are unassailable. And the airplanes . . . the German Luftwaffe flies very high, then suddenly swoops low, many planes darkening the sky all at once. They are bombing the roads without regard for civilians. *C'est terrible. C'est vraiment terrible!*"

Maman kept wadding up the fabric on her dress, leaving big blotches of wrinkles. It was so unlike her that I feared she was losing her mind.

It was dusk when we pulled up to the farm. Yvette was working in the garden when the taxi squealed to a stop. I jumped out of the vehicle and flew toward her. She shaded her eyes, then started running toward me. We fairly crashed into each other's arms.

"Is Pierre with you?" she asked when we pulled apart.

"Non." The question hurt my feelings—or maybe it was the way her face fell at my answer that crushed my heart. It was probably both. I feared that she would have preferred to see Pierre instead of me.

"We haven't heard from him," I said. "Have you?"

"Non. But then, the mail is not getting through very well."

Neither were telegrams. Nothing seemed to work as it was supposed to. So many people had fled their homes, leaving their jobs unattended.

I tried to push aside my dismay about Yvette's greeting. I did not want to let Yvette's infatuation with my brother ruin our reunion. "Pierre will know to look here for us," I said.

We linked arms and walked toward the farmhouse.

At dinner, the war was all anyone could talk about. "The BBC says Paris has been declared an open city," Yvette's father said.

"What does that mean?" Yvette asked.

"It means that an enemy can just walk in and no one will lift a finger in defense." Papa's voice was bitter.

Yvette's father took a gentler tone. "It is saying to the Germans, 'Don't bomb us. We won't fight you.'"

Yvette and I looked at each other. "So now France will be part of Germany?"

"Never!" Her grandfather's eyes blazed out of his weathered, sunken face. "France will never cease to be France."

"But . . . what does this mean? Will the soldiers still fight?"

"Not in Paris," Yvette's father said.

"Elsewhere?"

There was a long silence. "We do not know," M. Chaussant said softly.

"So . . . if the army stops fighting, will Pierre and Thomas come home?" Yvette asked.

"How can they?" Maman asked. "They can't go to Paris if it's occupied."

"If Paris falls, all of France falls," Papa announced.

"Is that true?" Yvette asked.

She was looking at her father, but Grand-père's hand banged hard on the wooden table. "France will fight. We always have, we always will." His tone was stern, the kind of tone that said, *Do not dispute my word.*

No one did.

The next morning, a family—a large blond man, his dark-haired wife, and their two sweet-faced daughters, aged seven and nine—stopped and asked for water. They introduced themselves as the Morans. They had owned a *boulangerie* in the seventh arrondissement, and they had fled Paris just two days before. They were traveling the back roads when their car had broken down. They were now afoot, trying to get to a family member's home in Dijon.

Maman and Mme Chaussant insisted that they join us for lunch. As they ate, M. Moran told us what had been happening in Paris.

"We could hear bombings as early as June third—Orly, Bourget, and even some buildings in the fifteenth and sixteenth arrondissements. The newspapers and French radio said we should stay and wait, that if an evacuation was necessary, we would be told to leave. I believed them." His voice trembled. "I figured, the girls' public school was still in session. Surely the government would not still hold school if it were unsafe." He shook his head, his mouth tight, his eyes bitter. "I was such a fool."

His wife covered his hand with her own. "You only did what you thought was right."

"I was a fool! On June eighth, with no notice, the schools closed. That evening, the BBC said the Germans were just 122 kilometers north of Paris. The *Boches* were at our very door, yet French radio said everything was fine! On June tenth, we learned that the government had fled the day before."

Grand-père uttered a low oath.

M. Moran's eyes blazed with outrage. "When I learned that the government had run away like cowards in the night, I felt so betrayed!"

"You were," Grand-père said bluntly. "We were all betrayed."

The roads were so congested that it had taken the Morans two days to travel a distance that normally would have taken two hours. To conserve gasoline, M. Moran turned off the engine whenever traffic hit a standstill. He had prudently brought extra gas cans and they might have made it to their destination, but the engine had stalled and would not restart.

After lunch—and after offering them an opportunity to clean up and change clothes—Grand-père gave them a ride in his old truck into Arcy-sur-Cure, where they could telephone their relatives for a ride into Dijon.

That night, French radio announced that all men aged eighteen to fifty should leave Paris immediately to keep from being forced to labor for the Germans. I wondered, of course, about Joshua. At every turn, I wondered about him.

9

AMÉLIE
1940

On June 14, the radio announced that Paris had been occupied by German troops. What had been inconceivable a few short weeks ago had come to pass.

The reaction of our parents was, to Yvette and I, more terrifying than the actual news. Both of our fathers shed tears. Even steely, bristly Grand-père wiped his face with a handkerchief, then harrumphed and muttered about catching a cold. Maman bawled like a baby. Even Yvette's mother, the calmest, most stoic woman I had ever known, cried.

We remained glued to the radio, eager for details, although we could hardly bear to hear them. The next day, the BBC aired a Parisian's first-hand report. It went something like this:

Early yesterday morning, I was awakened by a German-accented voice on a loudspeaker. It said that the Wehrmacht were moving in and occupying Paris, and announced an eight o'clock curfew for the evening. Most of the stores were boarded up and closed. The streets were largely deserted. The Wehrmacht marched in, in formation—a frightening sight. We'd been told that the German soldiers were skinny and scrawny and malnourished, but that wasn't true.

They were well fed, both taller and brawnier than our French troops. Nothing about them appeared to be weak or sickly. They had sturdy boots, and they were all clean-shaven. They marched in to the music of a Nazi band. We heard they had stopped their advance outside the city to shave and shine their boots before entering Paris.

Next came the tanks and trucks and cannons—big and ominous, thundering on the pavement. The Nazis hung a flag with a swastika from the Arc de Triomphe. Throughout Paris, swastikas replaced French flags—on government buildings, on monuments, in front of the large hotels. Signs were posted throughout the city saying that Paris was now under the "protection" of the German army.

"Protection!" Papa scoffed.

We have heard that the French government relocated first to Tours, then to Bordeaux, then to Clermont-Ferrand, and is now at Vichy. All is quiet now in Paris, although reportedly fighting continues south of Paris.

On June 17, we learned that Prime Minister Paul Reynaud had resigned, and that Marshal Philippe Pétain, a French hero from the Great War, had taken his place. Petain immediately made an announcement that was carried over and over on all radio channels. *"It is with a heavy heart that I tell you today that you must stop fighting,"* he said. *"The French government calls on the German government for an armistice."*

"What is an armistice? What does this mean?" I asked.

Maman looked at Papa. "Is an armistice the same as a surrender?"

"Yes," Grand-père answered bitterly. "It is the word 'surrender' wearing lipstick and high heels."

———

We soon learned that France had, indeed, completely surrendered. We heard that Hitler had demanded that the armistice be signed in the same railroad car where Germany was forced to surrender at the end of the Great War.

On June 18, we gathered around the radio for the BBC broadcast. General Charles De Gaulle addressed France from London.

As he began speaking, my skin tingled and my very bones vibrated.

I knew in my heart that this was something to capture, to remember. I grabbed a piece of paper and, in my fastest shorthand, jotted down the key parts in his exact words, which I then committed to memory.

It is true we were, we are, overwhelmed by the mechanical, ground, and air forces of the enemy. Infinitely more than their number, it is the tanks, the aeroplanes, the tactics of the Germans which are causing us to retreat. It was the tanks, the aeroplanes, the tactics of the Germans that surprised our leaders to the point of bringing them to where they are today.

But has the last word been said? Must hope disappear? Is defeat final? No!

The same means that overcame us can bring us victory one day. For France is not alone! She is not alone! She is not alone! She has a vast empire behind her. She can align with the British Empire that holds the sea and continues the fight. She can, like England, use without limit the immense industry of the United States.

Whatever happens, the flame of the French Resistance must not be extinguished, and will not be extinguished.

"We are to fight," M. Chaussant said. "He is calling for resistance. That means we are to fight."

"Well, I am good and ready," said Grand-père.

Four days later, the radio reported that the armistice papers had been signed. The French army was, shockingly, disbanded.

"What will happen to Pierre and Thomas?" Maman asked.

"Aside from whatever has already happened?" Papa said.

Mama's face lost color. "Alphonse!"

"I did not mean to upset you, Marie—but the truth is, we do not know. I well imagine that any French soldiers they capture now will be sent to work camps in Germany."

"Perhaps they will go to England to join General De Gaulle," I said.

"Yes. Or come back to France and join the Resistance inside the country," M. Chaussant said.

According to radio reports, we learned that France was now divided into two zones: *Zone occupée*, which included Paris and northern France, including Grand-père's farm; and *Zone libre*, which was under the control of the new French government at Vichy.

"The Free Zone." Papa spat out the words as if they were tainted sausage. "What a joke! The new government of France is nothing but a German puppet! They are using French politicians and police to carry out German oppression, while they save their men for warfare."

"It is an attempt to deceive our very souls," Grand-père agreed. "They are trying to make us think we want to do as they want us to do. They are trying to turn us against our own."

"Which will be worse off?" I asked. "Occupied France or Free France?"

"Only time will tell," answered Yvette's father, "but I suspect it will all be the same."

That night, General De Gaulle again spoke in French on the BBC. We all clung to his every word, as if his remarks were lifesavers thrown off a sinking ship. Once more, I grabbed a pencil to record the key parts, word for word:

> It is absurd to consider the fight as over. Yes, we have been heavily defeated. A bad military system, the mistakes made in leading the operations, the government's spirit of abandon have all made us lose the Battle of France. But we still have a large empire, an intact fleet, a lot of gold, and allies with immense resources.
>
> If the forces of freedom finally prevail over those of slavery, what would be the fate of a France which submitted to the enemy? Honor, common sense, and the superior interests of the nation command to all the free French to continue fighting wherever they are and however they can.
>
> I, General De Gaulle, am starting this national task here in England . . .
>
> I invite all the French who want to remain free to listen to me and to follow me. Long live a free and independent France!

"We must resist," Papa said.

"Yes, but we must be smart about it," M. Chaussant said. "We can't just start shooting at Nazis, or we will be murdered ourselves, and that will not help France. We must organize. We must work together. We must form an underground network to thwart their efforts and undermine their every move."

"Amélie and I can help," Yvette said.

"You are girls." Maman flapped her hand, as if the suggestion were a fly. "Stay out of it and leave the war to the men."

But when we went to bed that night, Yvette and I whispered together eagerly.

"Surely there are things we could do to help France," I said. "We speak German."

"Yes. We may be girls, but we can find ways to help fight. We can be a distraction to the Nazis, if nothing else. We can divert their attention while French operatives steal their weapons."

I rolled my eyes. "You and your cleavage can be a distraction."

"You can distract, as well! You can show your legs and give that sensual little smile."

"I don't have a sensual smile," I said dismissively—and then a hopeful little spark flickered in my chest. "Do I?"

"Oh, yes! I have seen you use it on Joshua. You have a way of turning on your womanliness that is quite devastating."

"Do you know what I do? I pretend I am the chanteuse at that club."

"Non! Vraiment?" Yvette giggled. "Well, it is your secret weapon."

A secret weapon, I thought as I drifted off to sleep. It was probably a good thing to have, if I were to be part of a secret war.

10

AMÉLIE
1940

*T*wo weeks later, Yvette and I were helping Maman and Mme Chaussant in the kitchen when a German truck rolled up in front of the farmhouse and four German soldiers climbed out.

We all froze and stared out the window. "Mon Dieu," Maman gasped. She started flapping around like a startled chicken, pulling off her apple-printed cotton apron as if company had arrived.

"Go and fetch your grand-père," Mme Chaussant ordered Yvette.

Grand-père had prepared for this moment. He had hidden every weapon on the property except for a rusty musket, an old pistol, and a bayonet that had belonged to his grandfather. He'd left those weapons in the house because, he'd said, the Nazis needed to find something. He'd also hidden the family silver, canned food, and two smoked hams.

He had warned us all, with his scariest, squintiest glower, that when the soldiers came—and he was certain they would come—we were to keep quiet and let him do the talking, regardless of what happened. He did not want them to know that any of us spoke or understood German, because they might press us into some kind of service for them. He had given my father a steely look until Papa had reluctantly nodded.

Yvette ran out the back door to the garden and called her grandfather, who was securing tomato plants with stakes.

I continued to stare out the window. One of the soldiers was older, maybe thirty-five. The other three were young, only a little older than

Pierre, and shockingly good-looking. It was disconcerting to discover that this horrible enemy could be handsome.

Mme Chaussant crossed to the dining room to look out the window facing the fields. My father was returning to the house; Yvette's father had pulled down a large hat to shade his face and was shuffling toward the far field, walking with the stooped shoulders and slowed gait of a much older man.

The Nazis rapped on the door.

Grand-père opened it. The rest of us crowded behind him. "Yes?"

"Good day, sir." It was the older soldier who spoke, in halting, polite, but very rudimentary French. "We are in need of information."

"What kind of information?"

"We need the names, ages, and occupations of all inhabitants of this house."

Grand-père told him our names, one by one. A young soldier with wavy blond hair and blue eyes wrote it all down. The three other soldiers stood in the doorway, their hands clasped behind their backs, and surreptitiously eyed Yvette and me—mostly Yvette. One of them smiled at her. She started to smile back—it is a reflex for a girl to smile at an attractive boy, is it not?—but her mother pinched her arm. Yvette ducked behind her and kept her eyes down. I poked her in the side and we exchanged a secret amused glance.

Grand-père told the soldiers that M. Chaussant was his widowed younger brother, used his middle name and added twenty years to his age. He gave my age as twelve and Yvette's as thirteen. (We were terribly indignant until he explained, after the Nazis left, that growing children would get more in food rations and that if the Nazis thought we were too young, we wouldn't be taken to work camps in Germany. It was the first time we had heard that girls might be shipped off to Germany. Yvette and I were appalled and terrified.)

Grand-père told the soldiers that my family were friends from Paris and that Papa was a teacher—but he added in an aside that my father had recently suffered a blow to the head and was now a little slow because of it. (He later explained that the Germans would be likely to press Papa into service for their cause or send him to a work camp; they disliked having able-bodied men among the civilian population, because they posed a threat.)

The older German, apparently the only one who spoke French, said we needed to go to the town hall to register; from now on, he said, food would be rationed. He then asked us to surrender all of our weapons. Grand-père gave them the pistol and the rifle.

"May we search your house?"

Grand-père lifted his shoulders. "I have no way of stopping you."

The soldiers paired off and set about looking through every room. They searched under mattresses and pillows, peered into closets, rifled through drawers. They seized Grand-père's bayonet from under his bed. As they went through the bureau in the room Yvette and I shared, one of the young soldiers held up one of Yvette's bras.

"The thirteen-year-old has big bouncy breasts," he said in German.

The other soldier chortled. "Imagine what she'll look like when she's sixteen."

They both laughed. Grand-père came to the door and glared. Chastened, they closed the lingerie drawer and resumed their search of the room.

They made copious notes about everything. They listed things that made no sense to us—family portraits on the wall, the number of bedrooms, the cookware in the kitchen.

They took all the potatoes, turnips, and onions from the root cellar. Outside, they plucked the fruit from the trees in the orchard and took all the ripe vegetables from the garden. They then gathered up all but four of our chickens. "I am sorry for any inconvenience," the oldest German said. "The führer requires food for the troops who are keeping your peace."

I thought Grand-père would choke on that. His left eye twitched.

"One last thing," the soldier said. "We must take your radio."

Grand-père's face turned purple. "The radio? Non."

"It is the order of the führer that all radios be confiscated."

"*Il y a une couille dans le potage*," Grand-père muttered.

The older German frowned.

"What did he say?" asked the shortest German in his native tongue.

He put his hand on his hip, frighteningly near his holstered pistol. "Did he insult the führer?"

"I think he said there's a testicle in the soup," replied the older soldier in German, looking clearly puzzled.

Two of the young Germans grinned. One actually laughed aloud.

"It poses a problem," Grand-père said, rephrasing the more colorful expression he had just used. "Without the radio, we will have no way to know what is going on."

"Ah. Let me put your mind at ease. We will keep the citizenry informed of all that you need to know."

"I'll just bet," Grand-père muttered, as they hauled the radio—it was large; it took two men to carry it—out to their truck.

"I hope the chickens crap all over the wires and render it unusable," Grand-père said as they drove off.

Papa was spitting mad. Only Maman's hand on his arm had kept him from jumping into the conversation—or trying to throttle the Germans. His face was red and contorted in anger. He let out a string of curses in German, using words I didn't know but could easily guess at, as the truck kicked up a rooster tail of dust on the dirt road.

When M. Chaussant returned from the field and heard what had happened, he was more philosophical. "I can build a radio. All in all, this could have been much worse."

"I hardly see how," Papa responded.

Grand-père looked at him, and for the first time, I wondered if he believed that Papa was, in fact, a little damaged in the head. The shock of discovering his father and brother dead, his worries over the fates of his sons, and his inability to provide shelter for his wife and daughter had perhaps caused something within him to snap. "Don't tempt the Fates, Alphonse, or they will show you."

Grand-père was right. In late August, Yvette's aunt, along with her husband, two daughters, and three large teenage sons, arrived from Alsace-Lorraine. Their home had been destroyed in an air raid when the

Wehrmacht first invaded France. They had been staying with her husband's family near Tours, but the Germans there had begun rounding up men between the ages of fourteen and fifty and shipping them to labor camps in Germany, so they came seeking refuge here.

The house was now too crowded. We were also low on food.

"It is not right that we take up resources the Chaussants need for blood relatives," Maman said.

Papa gazed at her wearily. "What do you propose we do?"

Mama gave him a wistful, sidelong glance. "From the reports, it sounds as if everything is quiet in Paris."

Indeed, from all accounts, it sounded as if life in Paris was almost back normal. "*Eh, bien*," Papa sighed. "We will go home."

I was thrilled to be going back to the city—back to Joshua!—but heartbroken to be leaving Yvette.

"You should come back to Paris, too," I urged Yvette's mother.

"Non, *chérie*. Our family must stay here. The Boches would love to use my husband to help them develop deadly weapons, and if he refused— as he would—they would kill him."

"Can't they find him here?"

"Yes, but they would have to be actively searching for him. From what we hear, they are rounding up French scientists if they are easy to find, but they are not seeking them out. Our family is safer here."

I could mount no argument against that. Besides, although he had been very secretive about it, Yvette and I knew that M. Chaussant had met with several local men to organize resistance activities against the Germans. I also knew that he had installed a false wall in the attic and hidden a new radio set there, and that he and Papa had dug a wide new cellar in the barn and hidden it under a pile of hay.

Maman, Papa, and I made plans to depart. Travel—like everything since the Germans had taken over—required time and paperwork. We had already gone to town and registered to get our ration cards and identity papers; now we went back for travel permits. We then went to the train station to buy tickets. The cost was three times more than it had been just a few months earlier, and the earliest departure date was two days away. Apparently the German army had first use of the trains, and the citizens were relegated to just a few cars.

Back at the farm, we gathered our belongings and prepared to leave. The night before our departure, Maman brought me a shapeless dress belonging to Yvette's deceased *grand-mère* and told me to wear it on the train.

I held up the worn gray dress in abject dismay. "Why?"

"Grand-père and Papa think it best if the German soldiers don't find you attractive."

As if that would be a problem! I was both embarrassed and outraged. Yvette thought it was hysterical.

"You needn't worry," I told Maman. "Men do not find me so irresistible that we must hide my charms."

Yvette rolled on the bed, laughing.

"You have no idea how lovely you are," Maman said.

"That is true, Amélie." Yvette sat up and nodded.

"You will wear the dress, and you will pull your hair back in a tight chignon," Maman decreed.

I held the dress up in front of me. "Are you sure this is ugly enough to downplay my exquisite beauty? Perhaps I should wear Papa's britches and M. Chaussant's work shirt and pretend to be a boy."

"And we can put dirt on your face and a cap on your head," Yvette added. "And you can wear Grand-père's work shoes, with manure on the soles so your smell will keep the men away!"

Maman refused to back down.

"I will wear it for the trip," I finally conceded, "but I will wear my own clothes when we get home. I refuse to dress like a babushka in Paris."

The next morning, I donned the hateful dress and put my hair in a bun.

When it was time to say good-bye, I hugged Yvette, and we both cried. "I will miss you so!" she said.

"And I, you! Who will I laugh with? How will I make it through this war?"

"You are stronger than you know, *ma petite*," she said. "And don't forget—you have a secret weapon."

"And you have two, but you must keep them hidden unless a big diversion is called for."

We giggled and hugged good-bye again, and then Grand-père drove my parents and me to the station.

————

Our train was on time, but even the cars reserved for the French were crowded with Germans. I began to see the wisdom of wearing the ugly dress as soldier after soldier boldly sized me up.

Three young Frenchwomen boarded our train car at the next stop. They wore dresses and heels and lipstick, and made me feel like a frumpy old nun. The German soldiers practically fell all over themselves to dance attendance upon them. They helped the women stow their luggage, they bent to light their cigarettes, and they bought them drinks in the dining car. The women flirted back, as if the soldiers were just ordinary attractive men instead of enemy occupiers.

"Disgraceful," Papa muttered. He passed me part of the newspaper. "Read this," he said. "You will be less noticeable."

"I couldn't be less noticeable if I were invisible," I whispered back.

"Let's keep it that way."

Papa, I noticed, was agitated; his mouth was tight, his face red. He tapped his foot constantly. He looked as if he were about to explode.

"Are you all right?" I asked.

"It makes me angry, seeing the Wehrmacht riding our trains through our country, their bellies full of our food," he whispered.

"Alphonse, do not think about it," Maman said.

"What else am I to think about?"

"Whatever you thought about before."

"I cannot even remember what that was."

"Look at the scenery, then."

I decided to take Maman's advice and turned my attention from the inside of the railcar to the passing scenery. The countryside was unchanged, but at each station, the military presence of the Germans was inescapable. The boarding platforms were a sea of gray-green uniforms with bottle green collars and epaulets. The sight of the Nazi flag flying where the French flag should have been made my chest feel tight and hot.

AMÉLIE
1940

*I*t was late afternoon by the time we got to Paris. The first thing I noticed was the swastika hanging in the station where the French flag should have been. As we stepped out onto the street, though, I was struck by how unchanged the city looked. More stores were open than closed, which surprised me. I had thought that most of the city would be shut down.

We hailed a taxi. The driver told us that the city was peaceful enough, but that the Nazis watched everything and everybody. He said there was a shortage of everything from shoestrings to lumber, but especially a shortage of food.

"The Boches have enormous appetites," he said. "They eat like great beasts, leaving little for the rest of us."

It was early evening, and we were exhausted and hungry. "I am so glad I canned extra food," Maman was saying as the taxi turned into our neighborhood. "I can heat up some vegetables for dinner. And won't it be wonderful to sleep in our own beds!"

I peered eagerly out the window as the cab turned onto our street. My first thought was how lovely and welcoming the house looked, with the lights shining through the windows.

"Why are the lights on?" Maman asked.

Papa was busy paying the cabdriver and perhaps did not hear. He pulled out his keys as we walked up the steps to the door.

He had no sooner fit the key in the door than it jerked opened. A tall German in evening dress—he wore black tie—loomed in the doorway.

Papa gasped. I don't know who looked more surprised—Papa or the tall German.

"May I help you?" he asked in stilted French.

Papa blinked and sputtered. "Who are you, and what are you doing in my house?"

"Your house?" the man echoed.

"Yes. My house." Papa strode angrily into the entry. Maman and I meekly followed.

Once in the foyer, we noticed a group of ten or twelve men gathered around our dining table. Music poured from the living room. The scent of roast meat—so delicious and heady that my mouth watered—filled the air.

"You are mistaken. This is the residence of Colonel Schiltzen."

"I am not mistaken." Papa pointed. "That is my piano, and my table that your friends are sitting at—and that glass you're holding is my wife's wedding crystal."

Maman pulled on Papa's arm, her face pale and alarmed. The dining room chairs all scraped on the floor as the men scooted backward and rose.

"What's going on out there?" a man called.

"Nothing," replied the German. "Just someone at the wrong address." He took a slow, impudent sip from Mama's glass.

Papa reached out and snatched it from his hand, sloshing wine on the entry hall rug.

"Alphonse!" Maman stepped forward to tug on Papa's arm, just as the German slapped Papa across the face. Maman fell back, as if she, too, had been struck.

Papa lunged, knocking the man off his feet. I think Maman screamed—or maybe it was me. I huddled against the wall, my heart in my throat. Papa knelt on top of the German and began choking him. All of a sudden, we were surrounded by Germans in evening attire or dress uniforms, and a gun exploded.

Papa went limp. His hands fell from the German's neck, and his arms dropped to his side like rags. He slumped forward as the tall German scrambled out from under him. Papa's legs collapsed as if they were boneless. His blood poured out on the Aubusson rug that had graced the entry hall for at least a century.

"Alphonse!" Maman knelt down and turned him over. His eyes were open, full of shock and pain. A sickening hole was in the center of his once white, now red shirt. Maman cradled his face in her hands, then turned imploring eyes up to the Germans. "You must take him to a hospital!"

"Get him out of here," ordered one of the Germans in a uniform with braided shoulder boards and several medals, a squat man with a ruddy complexion. He made a flicking motion with his hand. "Be sure to put a blanket in the car so he won't get blood everywhere."

Two men in uniforms picked him up by the armpits and dragged him toward the door. Maman scrambled to her feet and started to follow.

A third uniformed German barred her way. "You cannot go."

Maman's eyes were wild and unfocused. "But I must accompany him to the hospital."

Two officers in the foyer laughed.

"No need, madame. They will take good care of him," one of them said in French.

As the officers pulled Papa out the door, his head was limp and lolling forward, and his eyes were closed. He was unconscious—or worse. A few moments later, a car engine roared. I heard tires squeal, and I knew Papa was gone.

I reached for Maman and put my arms around her. I must have been in shock, because my brain registered what was happening, but my emotions were numb.

"What are we to do with the woman and the girl?" one of the officers in the foyer asked in German. "They are witnesses."

"So? They can warn others what happens to brash Frenchmen."

"But you know our orders. We are not to create any incidents to outrage the public."

"Those are old orders. They are about to change."

"Yes. We will soon outrage plenty." The men laughed.

"Still, they saw me shoot him," said a stocky German. Until he spoke, I had not known who had pulled the weapon. I studied his face. The image of it burned into my memory, into a hot, dark part of my soul I never knew I had, a part where hate dwelled.

"He deserved to die," said the man with the braided shoulder boards, whom I assumed to be the colonel. "He was attacking a German officer."

A man in white tie turned to Maman and spoke in crude French. "Madame, you must leave now and you must not ever come back. Furthermore, if you speak of this, things could go very badly for you. Very badly indeed, I am afraid."

"But my husband . . ."

"He assaulted a German officer. He was restrained." He opened the door. "I am so sorry that you stumbled upon the wrong residence."

"This isn't wrong," I said.

The soldiers looked at me.

I was surprised to find that I had spoken. My mouth was like cotton, yet I knew I must try. "This is our home. We left before the invasion, but we are back now."

"I am sorry, mademoiselle, but the house has been requisitioned for an officer. It now belongs to the führer."

"Please . . . just tell me, where have you taken my husband?" Maman persisted.

"You do not want to be where he is." The man in white tie was edging us out the door.

"But—but where are we to go?" I asked. "Where are we to live?"

"That is not our concern. Perhaps wherever you have lived until now." He stepped forward, forcing us onto the stoop. "Now go."

As the door closed behind us with a heart-wrenchingly familiar thud, I realized that life as I had known it was over forever.

12

AMÉLIE
1940

*M*aman was a sobbing mess, insistent on finding Papa. She refused to believe he was dead, or soon would be; she was convinced we needed to check the hospitals.

I did not think, for even a moment, that the Nazis intended to get medical help for Papa. Even if they did, I knew it would be no use. You could not save a man who had been shot in the heart at such close range.

Maman wandered into the street and wailed. For the first time—but not the last—our roles were reversed. I was the adult, and she was the child. Her need was my call to action. It was, oddly, a blessing; it gave me something concrete upon which to focus.

I felt strangely detached and bloodless—as if my veins had emptied onto the carpet along with Papa's. My whole body felt numb, the way a leg can get when you sit with it tucked under. That night, and for the next several weeks, my brain operated like a clock. It clicked forward to the next minute, to the next task—and then to the one after that. It did not pause. It did not reflect.

"Let's go see Mme LeMans," I said. I led Maman to our neighbor's door. We knocked, but the apartment was dark and abandoned.

"Perhaps we can stay at Yvette's apartment," I suggested next. "Yvette mentioned that her bedroom window is loose." She used to sneak out of it and come visit me in the dead of night. We had enjoyed doing things that were daring and dangerous just for the thrill of it. How childish that seemed now!

I went around to the window and cupped my hands to the pane. There was just enough light left to see that everything inside was topsy-turvy. Someone had tossed the apartment like a salad.

Maman looked inside, as well. "Oh, mon Dieu!"

"They were looking for M. Chaussant," I said. "It would not be safe to stay there."

"What are we doing anyway, looking for a place to stay? We cannot rest. We must go to the hospitals to find your papa!"

"Maman." I took her by the shoulders and looked into her eyes. They were strangely blank, as if she could not see. "They weren't going to take Papa to a hospital."

"They must! They must!" Her voice grew shriller and louder.

"Let's try the Lauries," I proposed, desperate to quiet her. I led her to our next-door neighbors' house and knocked. The lights were on, but no one came to the door. I rapped louder, again and again.

At length, the door opened a fraction of an inch. "We cannot help you. You must leave us alone."

"But, Mme Laurie—it's Amélie and Maman."

"I know. I heard the gunshot and the loud voices."

"Then you know we need help!"

"I'm very sorry, but they told you to go."

"They just meant we couldn't stay at our home! I'm sure they didn't mean . . ."

She held up her hand. "They watch everything that goes on in the neighborhood. I cannot risk helping."

Maman pressed her face to the crack in the door. "Lorraine, how can you turn us away?"

"I—I have to take care of my own. My uncle and aunt are here from Poland, and . . . we cannot be under scrutiny."

"But surely . . ."

"No. I am sorry." She closed the door with a terrifying finality.

Maman sat on the stoop and started wailing again—a wild, loud, animal sound.

I grabbed her arm and pulled her to her feet, as if she were a toddler having a tantrum. "You must stop that." My voice was fierce, a tone I didn't recognize as my own. "The Nazis will hear, and they will kill us."

"I don't care."

"Well, I do."

Her eyes seemed, finally, to focus. She looked at me, and it was if she just remembered I was her daughter. "Yes. Oh, Amélie, yes, you must live. But what are we to do? Papa had all our money. I have only a few sous."

It is impossible to say that my heart sank, because it was already at the bottom of the deepest pit. The news of money trouble paled beside the immediate problem: where were we to go?

We knew many people in Paris, but none better than the neighbor who had just turned us away.

"We will go see Joshua. He will know what to do."

"Joshua? Who is that?"

"A young man I sometimes studied with."

"You never mentioned him."

"He was part of a group Yvette and I sometimes joined," I said vaguely. "Do you know where he lives?"

"I know where he works," I said. "We'll go there and find out his address."

"This is a terrible part of town," Maman grumbled as we hauled our suitcases through Montmartre. "Why, this is a red-light district!"

I did not know what that meant, but the neighborhood seemed more dangerous than it had before the occupation. A woman in a low-cut blouse stood on the corner, a cigarette in one hand and an open bottle in the other. Down the alleyway, I saw two cigarettes glowing down in the dark. My skin prickled as a German soldier looked at us. I was relieved when we turned the corner to see the lighted sign of the La Grosse Pomme. Good. It was still open.

"What kind of place is this?"

"A club for live music."

"But . . ."

No doorman stood outside to assist with the heavy brass door. I pushed it open. A different band was on the stage, playing a French ballad. No more jazz or Dixieland. No more Negro faces. The musicians were all Caucasian, and the music was as bland as vanilla pudding.

"Is Joshua working tonight?" I asked the maître d'hotel.

He looked from me to Maman. He did not recognize me.

"Joshua Koper," I clarified.

He arched his eyebrows. "The busboy?"

I tilted my head and channeled the confident attitude of the chanteuse. "Yes. Can you please tell him Amélie is here to see him?"

I kept my gaze boldly locked on his until he nodded. "Wait here."

Maman and I sat in the entry. I am sure Maman was in shock. Under normal circumstances, she would never have entered such an establishment, much less have sat down. Under normal circumstances, she would have riddled me about how I knew of such a place and what I was doing consorting with someone employed there.

The maître d' returned. "He says he will meet you around back."

"Thank you," I said. I touched Maman's arm. "Wait here. I will only be a few moments."

Joshua was waiting for me in the alley. At first, his face lit with a smile. "Amélie! You're back!"

His expression quickly changed as his eyes searched my face. "What's wrong?"

I told him what had happened. The words seemed to cut my throat, as though they were made of broken glass. It hurt to get them out. My face was wet when I finished.

He pulled a scrap of paper out of his pocket and jotted something down. "Go to this address and give this to the woman who answers the door. That will be my mother. She only speaks Yiddish, but she will help you. We are sheltering many friends and distant relatives, but she will put you up for tonight."

"Thank you. Oh, thank you!" I gave him a kiss on the cheek. He held me close for just a moment and the warmth of him, the solid comfort of his chest . . . well, I started to cry. *No. I must not feel anything.* If I started to feel, I could not function. I straightened, took the paper, and walked away. After a few steps, I paused and turned back.

"I don't know if Maman will come with me. She wants to go to the hospitals to look for Papa."

"Tell her I'll check them for you. Tomorrow will be soon enough for her to face the truth."

AMÉLIE
1940

*T*he apartment was in a run-down, unkempt neighborhood, in a building so crude it didn't have a concierge. It didn't even have indoor stairs. Maman and I climbed up two rickety sets of steps on the outside of the building and knocked on a grimy door.

As promised, Joshua's mother welcomed us after reading his hastily scrawled note. She could speak no French—nor English, nor barely any German. She waved us inside. Paint peeled from the chipped plaster walls, and the ceilings were stained and sagging. Each of the three forlorn little rooms—there was a tiny kitchen, a combination living room and dining room, and a bedroom—were lit by a solitary lightbulb dangling from a frayed wire. The leaky, smelly bathroom was down the hall, and shared by all residents on the floor.

She indicated we were to take her bed. I started to refuse, but Maman was in such bad shape that I conceded simply so she would lie down. By now Maman was shaking, the color from her face completely gone. She had not said a word as I led her from the club to the apartment. Mme Koper heated some thin soup and offered us each a cup, with no spoon. I held the cup to Maman's lips and forced her to sip some.

I'm not sure how many people were lodged in the apartment—at least ten when we first arrived; maybe fifteen or even twenty later. People kept coming in after we were in bed, and four that I counted—maybe more—bunked down on the floor of our room.

I was exhausted, but my nerves were spooled tight. Every time I closed my eyes, I saw the hole in Papa's chest. It looked like a weird red cave. I did not emotionally connect the vision etched on the inside of my eyelids with my father. There was a disassociation between my head and my heart.

I was sure I would never fall asleep. I held my mother and stroked her hair, as if she were a child. Her trembling stopped at length and her breathing grew slow and steady. I said a prayer thanking God for the small mercy of unconsciousness. I lay awake and listened for Joshua to come home, but at some point, fatigue overtook me.

I awoke early, when the sun was but a promise on the horizon, and sat up in bed. The memory of the day before seemed like a bad dream. When I realized it wasn't, grief and despair and panic flashed through me, so hard and rough that I was thrown back on the pillow—but then the steel door that separated my head from my heart banged shut again, and I arose to address the day.

It was early, but there was already a line to the bathroom. Maman was sitting up when I came back to the bedroom. She had used a chamber pot in the room, which I now had to find a way to empty.

She looked at me eagerly. "Did your friend find Alphonse?"

"I—I don't know," I said, feeling cowardly.

Joshua was in the kitchen, and he was more blunt. He pulled out a chair for Maman and indicated she should sit. "I hate to tell you, madame, but your husband is dead."

Tears sprang to Maman's eyes. Her lips pressed together hard, and then her eyes did the same. She opened them and wiped her face. "I must arrange his funeral. Where is his body?"

"The Nazis have disposed of it, and they will not reveal where."

Maman's face crumpled like wadded-up paper. I held her as she sobbed for a long while. I wasn't sure if my neck was wet with her tears or mine.

Joshua spoke in a language I didn't understand to people as they shuffled into the kitchen—explaining, I assumed, why we were grieving. A gray-haired woman put mugs of tea in front of Maman and me, and rested a sympathetic hand on my shoulder.

"I am so sorry, madame," Joshua said to Maman. "This is war, and I'm afraid your husband is a casualty."

I didn't know exactly what to do, but I did know this: we needed a place to stay and we needed food. For both of those things, we needed money. "Maman—where did Papa bank?"

"On rue des Écoles, near rue Monge."

"We have to go there."

I put on my nicest dress, and helped Maman to do the same. I put on Maman's lipstick—her hand was shaking—and I put some on myself, even though up until now, she had forbidden me from wearing it. We left our bags at Joshua's place.

We walked to the bank and went in. I asked to speak to an officer.

We were guided to a desk, where a thin man with oiled salt-and-pepper hair greeted us and pulled out chairs for us. He looked at Maman, waiting for her to speak, but she sat silently, like an obedient child. I briefly explained the situation.

He folded his hands on the desk. I noticed his nails were clean and neatly trimmed. "I am very sorry for your loss, Mme Michaud." His eyes were warm with sympathy as he addressed Maman. "Do you have identification papers?"

Maman rallied to respond. "My—my husband had them in his pocket. We were traveling, and . . ."

"I am sorry," said the banker, "but I need some form of identification."

I took Maman's purse and rummaged through her wallet. My heart sank. I pulled out a snapshot of Papa and handed it to the banker. "This is my father. Do you know him?"

He looked at the photo, then glanced at my mother, who was now unabashedly crying. I thought of Joshua's words. "My father was a casualty of war," I said. "Surely there are exceptions to your rules in such a case?"

The man ran his hand down his face and sighed heavily. "Let me see if there's anything I can do." He took the photo and disappeared into the back.

I opened Maman's purse again and took out her rosary beads. I pressed them into her hand, and together we mumbled prayers.

At length, a tall gentleman with a nose like a hawk's beak approached and bowed before Maman. "Madame, let me express my deepest sympathies. I knew M. Michaud and thought he was an exceptional man. I am very sorry for your loss."

His stately bearing revived some of Maman's usual manners. She dabbed at her eyes and managed a nod.

He sat down across from her. "As a financial institution, we are bound by certain procedures and protocols. The law and our clients expect it of us. Before turning the account of a deceased client over to his family, we must have proper identification, a marriage certificate and a death certificate. "

"We do not have those," I said.

"I understand. Unfortunately, without them I cannot give you access to the funds in your husband's account."

"But . . ." I began.

He raised his hand to me, and continued talking to Maman. "I can, however, authorize a small loan against the account to help tide you over. And later, when you can get the proper documents, you can come back for the rest."

"You don't understand. It is unlikely we'll ever be able to get the proper documents," I said.

"I do understand." He leaned forward and spoke very softly, as if not wanting to be overheard. "But Germans are here at the bank, watching all that we do. I dare not deviate much from standard procedures. And if M. Michaud was killed for attacking a German officer, they will undoubtedly declare him a criminal and seize all of his holdings. I am offering more help to you than I should."

And so it was that Maman was given the equivalent of about two months of Papa's wages. I watched her tuck it carefully into her wallet.

We checked into a hotel—it cost a small fortune in francs—and I put her to bed. I pulled down the covers, fluffed the pillow, even helped her take off her shoes, as I had a toddler I had once babysat. Everything was difficult for her. She suddenly seemed very old.

The money from the bank seemed an enormous sum to me, but when I considered the cost of the hotel, I realized we could only stay there for three weeks. And that was without factoring in the cost of food. The cost of food, I realized when I went to buy us croissants and coffee, was ridiculous.

"It is high because it is scarce," Joshua told me when I went back to his apartment for our bags. "To make things worse, the Germans have raised the exchange rate in their favor, so that the reichsmark is worth many francs. They pay far less than we do for essentials."

"What are we to do?"

"You must find an inexpensive place to live and a way to support yourselves."

It was not enough that I was now Maman's mother; now I must become my own father. I needed to become a wage earner.

I needed to find a paying job.

AMÉLIE
1940

I left Maman asleep and went to look for work. I had hoped to find something at a seamstress shop or a department store, but there was nothing. The next day I tried hotels and restaurants, all to no avail. At the end of two days' searching, I had nothing to show but sore feet.

Maman was gone when I returned to the room the second afternoon. She came back around dusk, and she looked better. Her face was still lined with grief, but some of the color had returned.

"Where have you been?" I asked.

"To talk to a priest." She set down her purse and took off her gloves. "Papa will soon be at rest."

"What do you mean?"

She sat on the bed and smoothed her skirt. "I paid an indulgence."

"What?"

"The priest will say thirty prayers. If Papa died without any mortal sins against him, that should be enough to get his soul out of purgatory."

My heart felt like a sack of stones. "How much?"

The amount she named made me sink onto bed beside her. "I can't believe a priest asked that of you!"

"There is no price you can put on your father's soul."

"But that is half of all the money we have in the world!"

"I had to do it. We didn't give him last rites or a proper burial. It was essential."

I rested my head in my hand, suddenly sick with worry. I was more practical than devout. It seemed to me that God would want us to eat and have a place to stay. But Maman . . . well, Maman was Maman.

"Did you ask the priest if he knew of a place we could get work?"

"No, of course not."

"Maman, we must find a way to support ourselves. And we must find a place to stay."

"Perhaps Cousin Hildie can take us in."

Hildie—the eldest daughter of Papa's late older sister! I had completely forgotten about her—but then, I hadn't seen her since I was about nine years old. As I recalled, she was a dour spinster who worked as a concierge at a small apartment building.

Maman said she had never been warm toward us, and that didn't change when we showed up at her door that evening.

"I can't let you stay," she said. "This is a tiny apartment, and I don't have room."

"As I recall, Papa helped you get this job," I said. "And I believe he paid to bury your parents."

"Amélie!" Maman looked at me, shocked that I would so rudely bring up a such a delicate matter.

It had the desired effect on Hildie. She uncrossed her arms and sighed. "I don't see how I can put up two people in this tiny place."

"Well, let Maman live here. I will stay for only a night or two."

"But, Amélie," Maman asked, her face creased with worry, "where will you go?"

"I will figure something out."

"You cannot stay with that young man's family!"

"No, of course not."

"And I don't think you should see him again."

I stared at her, incredulous. "Maman, he took us in. He looked for Papa. He helped us when no one else would!"

"Yes, but he is a foreigner. I don't even know what language they were all speaking. He does not come from our kind of people."

Indignation rose in my throat. How could she be so prejudiced?

"Besides," Maman added, as if she had not said enough, "they're very poor."

"You and I are now very poor."

"Nonsense. Once we get our house back, we will be fine."

She wasn't in her right mind. There was no point in arguing with her. I took the money from her purse, leaving her only a little, so she couldn't think of some other cause to pay the priest to pray for.

I went to Joshua's apartment to enlist his help in finding a job. "Are there any openings at the club?"

"No. And if there were, it is no place for you."

"But . . ."

"No." His expression grew hard. "You must consider all of Montmartre off-limits, unless you want to be raped or forced into prostitution. It was not safe for a young girl before, but it is extremely dangerous now. You must never come to the club again."

I thought of Maman's reaction to the area. I remembered how my skin had prickled at the sight of women in low-cut blouses and slit skirts, at the cigarettes glowing in the dark alleyways. I reluctantly nodded. "But I must find work. I can speak German. Surely that must have some value."

"Yes." Joshua looked at me thoughtfully. "Yes, it does. Maybe more than you know."

"I will do whatever I must to take care of Maman. I am a hard worker. I am strong and I am brave."

"I see that. It worries me." He blew out a sigh and rubbed his jaw. "Meet me at the sciences building at the Sorbonne. Seven o'clock, class-room 129—and do not tell anyone where you are going. I think I know someone who can help."

———

At seven, I found Joshua sitting in a small classroom with a bearded, middle-aged man in a jacket who looked like a professor. Perhaps he actually was.

A stack of papers lay on the desk at the front of the room, as well as a French textbook on calculus. Two chairs were pulled up to the professor's desk. It looked as if Joshua was being tutored or was possibly helping grade papers.

Both men politely stood as I approached. "Amélie, this is M. Henri."

We shook hands, then Joshua pulled out a chair and placed a paper in front of me. "If anyone comes in, pretend that we are discussing a class project on calculus," he murmured.

I nodded.

"I understand that you read and speak German and English?" M. Henri asked.

He spoke French, I noted, with an English accent. "Yes."

"Then your country has need of you, if you are willing to take some risks."

My heart leapt. I nodded eagerly, longing for a chance to fight the Nazis. "What do you want me to do?"

"First we must lay out what you must not do." He leaned forward. "You must not tell anyone—and I mean *anyone*—that you are working for our cause. You cannot tell your mother, your closest friend, your brothers, or any coworkers. You must be the very soul of discretion. And if you are caught, you must do your best not to tell the Boches anything for at least three days."

"I promise."

"Ah, yes. We all promise at first. And it is important to have good intentions. However, if you are caught, you will spill everything you know. They will make you."

"No."

"Yes. There is no question of it. Therefore, we will give you no information that you do not absolutely need—and you will only be told what you need to know right before you need to know it."

"That is reasonable."

"It is important that you understand the danger you are putting yourself and your loved ones in. You need to understand that the Boches will kill anyone they catch working against them." He looked at Joshua. "You know she puts you and your family in the gravest danger."

He lifted his shoulders. "We are Jews; we are in danger anyway. I trust her."

"Hmm." He looked at Joshua for a long moment, then turned his attention to me.

"Are you willing to do demeaning work?"

Here I hesitated. "What do you mean by demeaning? If you ask if I am willing to violate my morals, then . . ."

"No, no, he is not asking that," Josh interrupted.

"Not yet, anyway," M. Henri said.

"Not ever." Joshua glared at him.

The Englishman gave a slight smile. "I was making a joke."

"It was not funny."

"Perhaps not." He turned to me. "*Pardonnez-moi*. But you need to know, mademoiselle, that if you are caught, you are unlikely to emerge with your life—much less your virtue. Or even your teeth."

"I was wrong to suggest she could help." Joshua started to stand. "This is a bad idea."

I put my hand on his arm, restraining him. "I am the one who gets to decide."

We locked eyes. I channeled that chanteuse's self-assurance. It wasn't sexuality that was my secret weapon, I realized; it was the conveyance of confidence. I wanted—no, I *needed*—to work against the Boches who had so brutally killed my father—and who, for all I knew, had wounded, killed, or captured my brothers, as well.

Joshua sat back down. I looked at M. Henri. "What kind of job would I do?"

"We need eyes and ears in places where officers gather, let down their guard, and speak freely to one another. We will put you to work someplace you might overhear or see something useful. You look very young, so you will have to be placed in a menial job where you will not stand out." His eyes seemed to issue a challenge. "When I say menial, I mean you will have to clean bathrooms and chamber pots or scrub pots and pans."

"All right."

"We can get you a job as a maid—perhaps at a hotel. The one I am thinking of has a dormitory for some of its full-time help."

A dormitory would get me away from Hildie's. "That would be perfect for my situation."

"If we can get you on, you will have to work exceedingly hard. No one on staff at the hotel will know you also work for us. You will start with the lowliest jobs and work your way up to cleaning guest rooms or public spaces, where you will be of value to our cause."

"I am a hard worker."

He scribbled something on a sheet of paper. "Go fill out an application for employment here."

I glanced at the name of a hotel. "I already tried there. I was told there were no positions."

"One will become available tomorrow." He steepled his fingers on the desk. "There is one other condition. This one is very important—extremely important."

"What?"

"No one must know that you understand German or English. If anyone talks to you in either language, aside from a greeting or a basic phrase that any schoolchild would know, you must act as if you don't understand. It is harder than you imagine."

"I can do that."

"Can you?" he said in English.

"Of course," I replied.

He quirked up an eyebrow. I put my hand over my mouth, realizing my error.

Joshua touched my hand. "You will do better with practice."

I stared at him. "You speak English?"

His head bobbed.

"Why didn't you tell me?"

M. Henri looked at me as if I were a dimwit, then turned to Joshua. "You two cannot be seen together. It could compromise our work." Joshua nodded.

"You cannot go to the hotel to see her," he told Joshua. He then looked at me. "And you cannot go to his family's apartment or his place of work, not ever again. In fact, for the next few months, you are not to see each other at all. Is that understood?"

I looked at Joshua. His eyes were sad, but his gaze was sure and steady. "It is for the best," he told me.

My throat was thick. I was still emotionally numb from my father's death. Being around Joshua made me feel things, and feeling things hurt. Perhaps it was for the best, for the short term, at least. I nodded.

M. Henri turned back to me. "We will try it and see. You will be watched. If our evaluator does not think you can handle it, you will be let go."

"But I need the job!"

"And France needs information. But even more importantly, we need to maintain secrecy." He turned to Joshua. "She must have training."

"Yes. She is not a good liar, and she cannot tell when someone is lying to her."

M. Henri jotted something down on a slip of paper and slid it across the table to me. "Go to this address every Thursday night at seven. You will say you are visiting your elderly aunt, Mme Dupard. Thursday will be your evening off at the hotel." He regarded me somberly. "I am worried that you are too young, and that your emotions are too transparent. We will give this a try, but I have my doubts."

"Amélie is very smart and brave," Joshua said. "I believe in her."

Joshua's words echoed in my mind frequently in the months ahead. I was installed at the Hotel Palais, in a tiny bunk bed in a room with twelve other women. I was given a uniform—a black dress with a white apron and cap—and told to provide my own black shoes and stockings. At first, as I worked solely in *les arrières-salles*, I wore a plain apron and cap with no frills; later on, when I was promoted to chambermaid, my apron and cap had ruffles, which were excruciatingly difficult to iron.

As promised, as the newest hire, I had the worst jobs. I worked incredibly long hours, sweeping and mopping and scouring the kitchen and employee areas. At first I seldom came into contact with hotel guests. I was friendly with my bunkmates and coworkers, but I did not grow close to them.

On my first day off, I took Maman to sign up for a ration card at the local police prefecture. The Nazis had instituted rationing for food as well as clothes, shoes, and just about everything else in September. My ration card was stamped at the hotel, where I ate at the employee cafeteria.

I saw Maman briefly three times a week—on Sundays, Tuesdays, and Fridays—and I gave her half my salary. At Hildie's urging, she started taking in mending for the building's tenants. From what Maman told me, she was making enough cash to pay for her own groceries, but she never seemed to have enough money. I feared that Hildie was taking advantage of her, eating up everything that Maman bought, because Maman was losing weight. She didn't style her hair or press her clothes or take any of her usual care about her appearance. She'd lost all interest in life since Papa had died. She went to church and prayed for Thomas and Pierre. That seemed to be all she cared about—her sons coming home safely.

I, too, prayed for them, although my faith no longer felt strong. I prayed for Papa's soul, Maman's health, for Yvette and her family, for the war to end, and for Joshua's safety. I did not really believe that my prayers did any good, but I feared that not praying might cause harm. I prayed as if prayers were a magical incantation that held up the sky, as if it were my responsibility to continue shouldering my part.

Every Thursday night, I went to the address M. Henri had given to me, about fifteen blocks from the hotel. Mme Dupard was an attractive woman who arranged her silver hair in a well-styled chignon and always wore the same black sweater. Her apartment was large but sparsely appointed.

My training was varied. At first she talked to me. She was very interested in my calligraphy skills, and gave me samples of handwriting to imitate. Then she made me walk across the room. She taught me to hunch my shoulders and make no eye contact so as to appear nonthreatening and invisible; she also taught me how to command a room, with my shoulders held back, my head high, my eyes flashing.

"You will need this someday," she said with a smile.

I particularly liked that lesson, because it strengthened my secret weapon.

Most evenings, though, she made me sit in her kitchen and listen to a story, which I then had to repeat to another person in the living room. That person would be playing a role—a hotel manager, a Nazi officer, a friend, a coworker . . . even my own mother. I then had to endure an inquisition about the story, making up parts that were lacking to make it sound credible. I was critiqued on things like eye contact, hand gestures, even the rate of my breathing. Then I was sent to the bedroom to tell the story to yet another person all over again. Sometimes I had to repeat it once more. I never knew if the people at the apartment were trainers or fellow trainees.

I could not understand how so many people could gather in Mme Dupard's apartment without being noticed by the Nazis. Later, I realized she had two secret doors connecting her apartment to adjacent ones. She even had a hidden opening in a closet ceiling that led to the apartment on the upper story. People appeared to be coming and going from several apartments in the same building.

During some of my early training sessions, I simply listened to conversations. I was supposed to detect who was telling the truth, and who was lying. I was told to take notes and write a report in English.

I became, over several months, very good at dissembling—and even better at determining when someone was lying to me. I also became proficient at summarizing conversations, picking up important nuances, and conveying the information in concise, correct reports.

The interest in my calligraphy skills intensified. A man with a heavy mustache gave me lessons and helped me refine my skills. I wrote the name of a police *prefecture* official over and over, and was finally entrusted to write it on travel documents. Every week thereafter, I spent at least half an hour of every session forging signatures on official papers.

After a few weeks at the hotel, my responsibilities—but not my pay—increased. I still worked all day, but now I was also on call at night to tend to emergencies for hotel guests.

I was awakened from a deep sleep to clean up the vomit of drunken German officers or their whores. I was called to clean up bloody and urine-soaked sheets or carpets. I was called to sit at the bedside of an ill fräulein's child, to wash and press Nazi uniforms, to bring ice, to polish Nazi boots. I cleaned up dog feces and once, I removed a strangled cat from a room.

I nodded and smiled and mimed, pretending not to understand when I was spoken to in German. M. Henri was right; it was very difficult not to respond, especially when the Boches made rude comments and conjectures.

I kept my expression vacant when they guessed what I was wearing under my skirt, commented on my small breasts or made lewd comments about my backside. I pretended to be oblivious when they wagered about whether or not I sucked men's organs like my little rug vacuum, or if I rode my boyfriend like a horse. I kept my hair pulled tightly back in a severe bun and I kept my shoulders hunched up, my eyes downcast. I thanked God for my olive complexion, which helped disguise the flames that licked my cheeks.

As the weeks went by, my training at Mme Dupard's shifted along with my responsibilities at the hotel. As I started cleaning officers' bedrooms during the day, the lessons at Mme Dupard's began focusing on searching for information. I was taught to look through papers that were openly lying about, and to search for papers that were concealed in officers' clothing and bags or stealthily hidden in the room, behind baseboards or loosened floorboards. I learned to pick locks on briefcases and luggage. I learned to search under rugs, under mattresses, under shoe insoles, and in the lining of jackets. The Nazis, I learned, were very fond of hiding papers in the lining of their jackets. Some even had zippers installed for that purpose.

I was trained to pay special attention to maps, engineering plans, notes in pockets, and scrawls on matchbooks. I was taught to look for things like hairs or threads placed over papers or briefcases so that the owner could detect if anything had been moved. I learned to put things back exactly as I found them.

I was finally deemed fit to be fully deployed into action, and at last I received my instructions—as well as a small camera and a roll of tape. I was to summarize everything found onto onionskin paper, then fold it into quarters and tuck it into my brassiere. If I ran across maps or engineering plans, I was to take a photograph. And every time I went to see my mother, I was to stop at a church on rue des Gallois, where I knelt in the fifth row on the left and taped my paper—and the roll of film, if I had taken any photos—to the bottom of the pew in front of me.

I had some close calls. One afternoon I was in the middle of searching a briefcase when I heard a key in the door. I quickly shoved the contents back inside and locked it, just as the door opened and the officer walked in, accompanied by a prostitute.

Another time I was going through a jacket, and the room's occupant actually caught me. I said I was checking to see which clothes needed to be pressed. The end result was that I had to iron his clothing every day for the rest of his stay at the hotel.

I dutifully recorded everything I found. I wrote reports on things that seemed of no consequence, because I'd been told that I had no way of knowing what was important.

Apparently that was true. I reported a hand-scrawled note: *7 p.m., Café du Bois, rue de Charonne.* I thought it was a reservation for dinner; it turned out to be a meeting of Nazi intelligentsia.

I was thrilled when Mme Dupard told me that. It was the only inkling I ever received that what I was doing had any merit. I can only assume she was allowed to tell me because I had been complaining that my efforts were of no account.

———

Fall stretched into winter. Since we had fled Paris in late spring, all of the clothes in my and Maman's suitcases were lightweight; I spent a fortune buying each of us winter coats. It was ironic that as the weather grew cold, the numbness that had protected me from the pain of Papa's death began to melt away. I awoke at night, sobbing, the blast of the Nazi's gun echoing in my head. I cried when I entered the church to leave my messages. Music of any sort would cause tears to flow down my cheeks. More than once I had to pretend I had a cold when a song on the radio caused me to dissolve into tears while working at the hotel.

I grieved Papa. I grieved the life I used to have and the things I had taken for granted—a full stomach, warm socks, a hot bath, privacy. I missed my brothers, Yvette and her family, and Maman as she used to be.

And I missed Joshua. When I learned in November that one of the bellboys ran a personal courier service on the side—for a few centimes and Métro passage, he would deliver notes or packages anywhere—I sent a note to Joshua, asking to see him. My heart leapt when he sent word back that I should meet him at our old spot in the Jardin des Plantes by the river, before the nine o'clock curfew.

We embraced. He did not kiss me, but his eyes caressed my face, and it was nearly the same.

"I have missed you," I told him.

"And I, you," he said. "But we must not make a habit of this."

His face looked thinner, older. I dared not ask what he had been doing—Mme Dupard and the others had drilled into me the importance of ignorance; what I did not know, I could not betray.

We walked away from the Seine—the wind off the water was like a knife—deep into the garden. Joshua talked about the Nazis. He saw ominous patterns and purpose in German behavior.

"They started out treating the citizens of Paris relatively gently, to suppress our desire to rebel. Besides, they want Paris to continue to be Paris, to be the ultimate R & R center for the Wehrmacht. They even have a slogan for their soldiers: *Everyone gets a day in Paris.* That's why they encourage French citizens to go about their business as usual."

That did, indeed, seem to be the case. Stores, pubs, and restaurants reopened—but they had little business from Parisians. French citizens had no money.

Joshua told me about the increasingly harsh treatment of the Jews.

Much of this I did not know, although I had seen anti-Semitic articles in the newspapers.

He told me that in October, a census had been taken of the Jews. The Schutzstaffel, or SS, had visited Joshua's apartment and demanded to see passports and papers of everyone there. Joshua, I was relieved to hear, had not been at home—but the Nazis had taken his mother's name, and the names of everyone staying there.

"Why did they not lie about being Jewish?" I asked.

"You have met my mother," Joshua said. "She speaks only Yiddish."

I felt very foolish. "Of course."

"Besides, practically everyone in our neighborhood is Jewish, and the Nazis know this. They try to bribe us to report on our neighbors."

"How horrible!"

"Yes. They want to turn us against each other. And it will be the same here as in Austria; some will betray their neighbor if they think it will help their own family."

And that was not all. Jews were now prohibited from working in certain professions, such as banking or law or civil service. Jewish-owned businesses were forced to place a placard in the window, stating:

THIS BUSINESS IS MANAGED BY AN ARYAN STEWARD APPOINTED
IN ACCORDANCE TO THE TERMS OF THE GERMAN ORDINANCE OF
OCTOBER 18, 1940.

"The stewards pocket all the money," Joshua said bitterly. "It is like Austria all over again."

He abruptly grabbed me and drew me into a kiss. I was bewildered by the timing and the force of it, but I melted against him, savoring the warmth of his lips on mine, the strength of his arms around me. I hated that we wore coats; I ached to feel more of his body against mine.

Just as suddenly as it began, he pulled away. "I am sorry," he murmured. "Two Boches were walking by, and I thought it would be less suspicious if we were kissing instead of talking." His breathing was harsh, and his voice sounded like sandpaper.

"I didn't mind," I said. "In fact, I wish they would come back."

"Oh, Amélie, Amélie—how you torture me!"

"In a good way, I hope."

"Oh, it is an exquisite torture, to be sure—but it is torture all the same." Something close to despair darkened his eyes. "It is not wise for you to see me. You would be punished if you were caught with a Jew."

"I do not care."

"Well, then, I must care for both of us. You would lose your job if either *la Résistance* or the Nazis discovered us—and I might lose my life. Go—it is getting late."

"When can I see you again?"

"I do not know. Do not ask. Do not send me messages. We must not meet again for at least several months."

"But . . ."

"If you care for me, you must abide by this."

"I must know that I will see you again, Joshua. I must have something to live for."

It took a moment, but then he sighed. "I, too, need a light in the dark. You are that light to me. We will meet again after the first of the year. I will contact you."

The holidays were abysmal. I had to work on Christmas Day. I saw Germans eating Christmas goose and stuffing and giving each other holiday greetings, while my stomach rumbled with hunger. The sight fueled that bitter, black part of me, the part that felt like the dark center of Papa's gunshot wound. Surely Christ had not come and died so that such men could feast while the rest of us starved. Surely God would not allow this to continue.

But he did. It continued, and it grew worse. The winter was the coldest in Paris's history, as far as anyone could remember. It snowed six inches on New Year's Day. Food became even scarcer, because supplies were cut off due to the road conditions. The soup that was a staple for the employees at the hotel became thinner and thinner.

So, alas, did all the hungry residents of Paris.

15

KAT
2016

*A*mélie pauses for a moment, and I can't resist speaking up. "I have been here for hours, and your story is still years away from the time you met Jack."

"*Eh, alors.*"

I don't know what that means, but from her expression, I guess it is, *So what?* Irritation rises in my chest. "So when will you get to the part I care about?"

"After I get through telling you the part you need to hear."

"Well it's certainly taking a while. I need to use your ladies' room."

"Of course. It is the door on the left."

I could hardly miss it in such a tiny apartment. I rise from the couch less gracefully than I want, then use my cane as I make my way to the bathroom. I close and lock the door, and then, of course, I snoop. I look in the drawers, expecting them to be bulging with makeup and beauty creams. To my surprise, I find only a good dermatologist-grade skin cream, an inexpensive eye cream, and three lipsticks. I open each one. There is a coral, a bright pink, and a blue-red. Really? This is all of her beauty products?

Her medicine chest strikes me as ridiculously spare, as well. There is dental floss, mouthwash, and three extra toothbrushes. Who are they for? Gentlemen callers who stay the night?

Or maybe family; I know that she and Jack had two other children, a boy and a girl. Both of them became doctors, and they each have families of their own. Amélie has a slew of grandchildren and great-grandchildren.

She has very few medicines for a woman her age—only some Tylenol, a blood pressure medication, and prescription sleeping pills. I shake out three of the Ambien and put them in my pocket. She owes me at least a few nights' good sleep.

I use the toilet, flush, and wash my hands.

"Find everything okay?"

I don't know if she asks because she knows I have looked through her things or not. Her smile is pleasant and unruffled. Her face never gives away a thing. "Yes, thank you." I resume my seat.

"Would you like some lunch?"

"Why, yes, I would."

"We can order something in or we can go to the dining room," she says.

"Here, please. I would like to continue our talk."

"Of course." She pulls a menu from a drawer and hands it to me. I expect to see hospital-type fare, but the choices are those one might find in a nice restaurant.

"The quiche is always good. It comes with fresh fruit."

"That's fine," I say.

She picks up the phone and calls in an order.

"Now." She folds her hands in her lap and looks at me. "Tell me how your romance developed with Jack."

"I told you how it began."

"Yes, but I want to know the course of it. Was your first kiss at the picnic?"

I am about to say that is none of her business, but she stops me with a pointed look.

"I assume you will want to know the same from me."

Of course I do. And while I resent her not-too-subtle attempt at coercion, I want her to burn with the same jealousy I feel. I will take my time telling her, so she can experience some of my irritation, as well. "We went to the Fourth of July celebration together."

"Oh, yes. America's Independence Day." She shifts in her chair in that annoyingly graceful way and gives an amused smile. "I suppose there were fireworks."

Is she trying to be funny?

"Actually, there were. Of more than one kind."

"Of course." There is that little wry smile again. "With Jack, how could there not be?"

1937

It so happened that the Fourth fell on a Sunday. Instead of the usual parade, the town elders decided to have the celebration at the town square that evening. Jack came to the house Sunday afternoon and spent a couple of hours with my father. We followed the usual routine, only instead of going to the supper table, Jack and I headed to the town park. He carried the heavy wicker basket Mother had helped me pack with cold fried chicken, potato salad, coleslaw, and brownies, along with mason jars filled with iced tea. I carried a blanket along with a tote bag filled with real plates, silverware, and cloth napkins.

We spread our blanket in the shade of the park lawn, in view of the cupola-covered stage where local musicians took turns playing guitar, banjo, and fiddle. After staking our space, we sauntered around, talking to friends. I was fairly bursting with pride at being with handsome Jack. We watched the kids' three-legged race, looked at the Ladies Guild's patriotic-themed quilt display, and cast votes for the best patriotic bike decorations. The high school band performed patriotic songs, and all of the town's veterans, including my father, marched across the stage as the rest of us applauded.

As the sun sank over the treetops, we settled back and ate our dinner. (Back in those days, people figured you could safely leave food out for three hours before it went bad. So funny how I remember that detail!)

The junior high music teacher, who could reach very high notes but sang a little off-key, belted out an odd selection of songs—hymns, show tunes, love ballads, and patriotic songs. In the distance, we saw my parents standing and talking with a group of adults. Daddy's arm looped around Mother's waist.

"Your parents have a good life," Jack observed.

I nodded.

"Your father asked me what kind of practice I have in mind. I told him I'd like to be a small-town doctor, like him."

"I'd love to be a small-town doctor's wife, like my mother." The moment I said it, I realized how it sounded. I hadn't meant to be so bold; I was just stating fact. "I—I didn't mean . . . that is to say, I wasn't implying . . . I didn't mean you and I should . . ." I felt my cheeks burn.

He glanced at me, his eyes twinkling. "Well, sounds like we have our futures all planned out."

The heat in my cheeks spread from my head to my toes. I tried to imagine what Barbara Stanwyck would do in a movie. I longed to say something flip and breezy, but nothing came to mind. "You weren't even sure you wanted to take me on a date," I finally said.

"Oh, I was sure, all right. I was just trying to figure out how to pace things."

"Pace things?"

"Well, I have about eight years' worth of college to get through before I'll be able to support a wife, so it seems wise to take things slow." He lifted a ringlet of my hair. "You're not the kind of girl a guy just dallies with."

My chest felt as if someone were standing on it. I couldn't breathe. "What about Beth Ann?"

"Oh, she wasn't, either. She was a fine girl—really fine. I didn't mean to imply that."

"So what did you mean?"

"Well, dating her taught me that I don't want to date someone just as a lark. It's time consuming and if things don't pan out, people get hurt."

"How romantic."

He laughed. "That's my point. It's not."

"So your point is, romance is not romantic?"

"It's not like in the movies, that's for sure. My parents had a big dramatic movie-style romance, where everything was fast-paced and passionate, and in the end, they were miserable together."

"But couples need some romance. There has to be a spark."

"Oh, yes. I agree," Jack said.

"So . . ."

He looked at me. "Are you asking if I feel a spark with you?"

I nodded. Overhead, the fireworks were starting.

"Oh, yeah," he said. "You make me feel like the sky looks right now."

I looked up and saw an explosion of red lights. Satisfaction spread through my chest. "Good."

"And you?" He leaned in close. "Do you reciprocate the feeling?"

I batted my eyes at him. "I won't know until I kiss you."

He smiled. "Well, then, we'll have something to look forward to."

"So he didn't kiss you?"

Amélie's words pull me back to the present. "Not that night. Not until the homecoming dance. He respected me too much, he said."

As he must never have respected you. She looks so somber that I think, for half a moment, I had said the cruel words aloud.

"It is true. He did respect you, Kat," Amélie says at length. "He always talked of you and your family with the highest esteem."

"He talked of me?" My heart dances.

"Oh, yes. He was quite devastated over what he did to you. And your family."

So why did he do it? That is the reason I am here, to finally learn the truth. "So how did things start between the two of you?"

"I'm getting to that, Kat. I'm getting to that. But first you have to hear all the background information for it to make sense."

I sink back on the sofa and sigh. It is going to be a long afternoon.

16

AMÉLIE
1941-1942

*O*ver most of the next year, I kept my head down and focused on whatever task was directly in front of me. It seemed as though the news went from bad to worse. The British could not conquer the Wehrmacht, the Germans were getting the upper hand, and the Americans still would not enter the war. Shortages worsened. There were long lines for everything. We suffered power outages caused by ice and floods. In the summer, the city sweltered and stewed. It seemed as though God himself had set his face against France.

A few bright spots were scattered throughout that hard year. In January, I heard from Joshua. We began meeting once a month at a cobbler's shop that belonged to one of his friends. The shop owner would step out when I entered, and Joshua would enfold me in a hug. I wished he would never let me go, but he soon pulled back. He refused to let our romance escalate.

"If the Boches come in, pretend that I work here and I am helping you with a shoe," he said. We only had a few moments each month to hold hands and talk, but I lived for those minutes, when I was close to him.

Joshua told me of the increasing hostilities of the Nazis against the Jews. In May, four thousand Jewish men were called to the police prefecture to check on their "civilian status"; they were all arrested and shipped off to German camps. Jews in Paris were now forbidden to own bicycles, radios, or telephones. They could not go to restaurants, clubs, movies, or concerts, and they were forbidden to use public telephones.

"Are you sure you want to keep seeing me?" he asked. "I can offer you nothing."

"You offer me a reason to keep going," I said, and meant it with all my heart.

———

In October, I finally got a letter from Yvette! One of the many letters I had sent to her had made it through the egregiously bad postal system. She had my address, and now, one of her letters had made it through to me—and she had the most wonderful news! She had heard from my brother Pierre.

I jumped with joy as I read the news. He had made it through the war, and he was, in fact, in Paris! He had gotten at job with the police at a prefecture in the eleventh arrondissement.

My heart stuttered at that news. Pierre was working for the police? The French police served under the Nazis!

But then, what job could a young, able-bodied Frenchman possibly hold in Paris during the occupation? All of the young men who didn't work under the Germans in some sort of civil service job had been sent to work camps. Pierre was lucky to have a job at all. Perhaps he, too, was working subversively to help France's cause.

At the first opportunity, I went to his prefecture and asked for Pierre. He was out, but I left a note with my address.

The next day, my worried supervisor told me a policeman was asking for me in the lobby.

It was Pierre! I ran into his arms, and he swung me around. He was thinner and older. He looked like he'd aged ten years in two.

We kept hugging each other. The front desk supervisor came up, tapped me on the shoulder, and chastised me; it was unseemly for a chambermaid to have any personal interaction in public. I explained that it was my brother, that I hadn't seen him since before the war. He relented and offered to let me talk with Pierre in his office. Neither of us sat.

"Where have you been?"

"In a work camp in Germany." He and several other former French soldiers had escaped while working on road repairs. "How are you? Where are Maman and Papa? I went to the house and learned that a German officer had requisitioned it. What happened?"

I told him, first, that Maman was living with Hildie—and then I explained what had happened to Papa. He turned away, his face to the wall. His shoulders shook, and I knew he was sobbing.

"I cannot believe Papa is gone," he said at length. "Our family is falling like dominoes."

My heart stuttered. I feared I had become all too adept at reading between the lines. "Do you mean . . . Thomas?"

He nodded. I sank into his arms, and we both wept. At length, he told me what had happened. They had served together. During the Battle of Dunkirk, Thomas had been directly ahead of him during an advance. Thomas had taken a bullet to the face during a barrage of German fire. Pierre had tried to carry him to safety, but Thomas died in his arms. Pierre had been forced to leave him beneath an oak tree.

"Oh, Pierre! This will devastate Maman. She will be so happy to see you, and then . . ."

We both cried some more.

The next day, I went with him to see her. Maman opened the door. Her hands flew over her mouth as if she were seeing a ghost—then she crossed herself and drew Pierre into a fierce hug. "*Mon fils*," she murmured, over and over. She pulled back to look him in the face. Her knuckles caressed his cheek, her eyes filled with tears. "Mon fils!"

Her joy soon turned to wails of deepest grief, however, when, seated at Hildie's kitchen table, he gave her the news about Thomas. At first, Maman refused to believe it. "It might have been someone else. All soldiers wear helmets and the same uniform, so they all look alike. You said his face was hit. He might still be alive."

"Maman, it was Thomas. I took his wallet from his pocket."

"Somebody could have stolen it."

"No, Maman. It was he. He was right in front of me."

"No." She shook her head. "I would know if my son were dead."

When I went back to see her three days later, Hildie tipped me off that Maman had quit buying groceries. Up until now, Maman had borne the burden of spending hours in line to buy rations for them both.

"Is she eating your rations?" I asked.

I wouldn't have put it past Hildie to lie so that I would give her money, but she shook her head. "I don't think she's eating at all."

I found Maman hunched in the bedroom, repairing a seam on a white shirt. "What's going on, Maman?"

I finally pried it out of her. She'd gone back to that unscrupulous priest. She'd spent all of her money on an indulgence to get Thomas out of purgatory, even as she continued to believe he might still be alive.

And she was fasting. She thought that fasting might bring about a miracle. At the very least, she believed it would be good for Thomas's soul.

I told Pierre. He muttered a foul curse, then took Maman to a restaurant and insisted she eat. She complied so that Pierre did not waste his money.

I am sure she went on other fasts, however, because over the course of the next few months, she continued to lose weight at an alarming pace.

The holiday season of 1941 was bleak. The only good news was that the Americans were joining the Allies, because, tragically, Japan had bombed them. This left many of us baffled. Japan? What did Japan have to do with Hitler? Apparently the Japanese and Germans had formed an unholy alliance. The world had, indeed, gone crazy.

Many Parisians were encouraged. "The Americans made short work of the Germans in the Great War," said a middle-aged doorman in the employee lunchroom. "I'm sure they'll do the same this time."

If only it were that simple. The winter, again, was unusually harsh. Maman developed a bad cough. Hildie complained that she couldn't sleep with Maman's constant hacking. She muttered vague threats about evicting her; Pierre responded by sending by a uniformed friend who knocked on the door, and told her that they'd had a report she lived alone. All women living alone were subject to housing and serving a Nazi officer. That quickly put an end to Hildie's complaints about Maman.

Pierre took Maman to a doctor. He gave her cough medicine, but he said her heart was bad.

Maman took to her bed. I went every day to see her. She quit coughing, but she weakened at an alarming rate. Ten days after she took to bed, she lapsed into unconsciousness. She roused one evening and feebly grasped my hand. "I need a priest."

I didn't want to call one. I knew Maman would fight death if she knew she had not been given last rites.

Hildie sent for a priest anyway, then went and fetched Pierre. It shocked me, how quickly Maman's condition deteriorated. We stood on either side of her, each holding a hand, both of us crying, as Maman's chest rattled with every labored breath.

And then, exactly six months to the day after she'd learned she'd lost her youngest son, Maman breathed her last.

We buried her in a plain pine box. Buying it took the last of the cash Maman and I had gotten from the bank. Pierre, Hildie, and I were the only ones who attended her funeral mass. Maman was laid to rest in the family plot of the church cemetery, without her husband or son beside her.

Six months, I thought. That is how long it takes for a person to die of grief.

In another six months, would it be my turn? How could anyone hurt this badly and not die?

I was wrong. I did not die. I worked, I ate, I fell into bed and into exhausted slumber.

I would awaken in the night. In that darkened room, amid the snoring of eleven other women, I would see images of Papa being shot, and of my mother breathing her last. I pictured Thomas without a face. I wished I could remember them in happier times, but my mind seemed stuck in a ditch.

I was constantly exhausted. It was hard to say if it was because I was working two jobs—cleaning the rooms and copying everything I could find, my chest tight with fear, my fingers aching from writing—or because I was carrying around a millstone of grief.

The grayness of those days was lightened by my meetings with Joshua. We would cling to each other. He would tell me I was precious and beautiful and that he dreamed of me at night. I would tell him he was brave and handsome and that when the war was over, we would go dancing together and stay out until dawn.

"Staying out until dawn is overrated," he said with a smile.

"I would not know, since the curfew for French citizens is nine," I said dryly.

"I have a special permit, since I serve the Boches at the nightclub."

"Surely you don't work until dawn!"

"Not at the club. But I often see dawn in Neuilly."

I frowned. "Neuilly? That's miles away—at the very end of the Métro line. What are you doing there?"

His eyes grew somber. "I cannot tell you, just as you cannot tell me what you do at the hotel."

I nodded slowly, disliking the distance our secrets created between us.

He turned my hand over and embraced it with both of his. "I will say this—I believe I am doing what I was sent to earth to do."

"How lucky you are to feel that! I sometimes wonder if I'm serving any purpose at all."

"You are. You are helping to save lives and shorten the war," Joshua said. "Information is crucial, and it is becoming more crucial all the time."

"I don't think I'm supplying good information."

"That is not for you to know. Believe you are helping and just keep going."

"Even if I feel like I'm stumbling around in the dark?"

"Especially then. Keep going forward and look for the light."

"What if I see no light?"

"Keep going anyway, and trust it will appear."

"What if it does not?"

"Do not ask that question. Ask only, 'What do I need to do today to move forward?'"

His words replayed often in my mind. I trudged through my days, and finally received another letter from Yvette. She wanted to come to Paris, but her mother forbade it. She wrote me of life on the farm, of chores, and of things she could not wait to tell me in person. Her letters, I suspected, were deliberately vague and upbeat so they wouldn't be intercepted. The Nazis were overseeing everything, and only a fraction of the mail—Joshua estimated twenty percent or less—was getting through.

And then, early one evening in April, one of my roommates—an older woman named Rose—tracked me down as I finished cleaning the last of my rooms for the day. "Someone is waiting for you by the back service door."

I signed out for the day and hurried to the back door. My heart soared when I saw a woman with hair the color of sunshine. "Yvette!" I hugged her tight. Her clothing smelled like smoke. "What are you doing here?"

She clung to me. "Waiting for you."

"This is no place to wait!"

"I have nowhere to go. My . . . my mother . . . and my grandfather . . ." She collapsed into sobs. "All gone, Amélie. They are gone. And I—I fear the Nazis are looking for me, too, and I have n-no papers . . ."

I held her close and let her sob into my neck. I, too, cried. "Come inside," I said at length.

I pulled her through the doorway and into the corridor, then into a closet where we stored the cleaning supplies.

"Tell me what happened."

She drew a deep breath, and began. "It was the middle of the night at the farmhouse. I awoke to the sound of the door being crashed."

"The Wehrmacht?"

She nodded.

"Were they trying to get your father?"

"Non." Her voice was low. "They already have him."

"Oh, Yvette!"

"They came and took him three months ago. And I think they were watching us afterward. And . . . well, you know, of course, we were working for the Resistance."

I remembered how our fathers had dug an extra cellar and hidden the crude radio in the attic. I nodded.

"A few weeks ago, a British fighter plane crash-landed a couple of miles away." She drew a breath. "We helped smuggle the surviving airmen to the coast."

"And the Nazis discovered this?"

"Not right away. Two weeks later, the airmen were caught near Brittany—just when they were nearly free. One of them talked, and apparently he described me." Her lower jaw trembled, the way it had when she was a child and learned her grand-mère had died. "I heard the Nazis question my grand-père. They asked where I was. I wish now that I had just gone downstairs, but I climbed out onto the roof and into the branch of a tree, as Grand-père had instructed me to in an emergency. I dropped to the ground, ran to the large oak by the fence, and climbed to the middle branches. I stayed there, hidden." She shivered.

"They thought I was in the attic. It was too dark to find me, so they set fire to the house. But first they shot my grand-père and my mother." She buried her face in her hands. "I heard the shots. Oh, Amélie, the guilt is killing me! I wish I, too, had died."

"Oh, no," I said, hugging her and rubbing her back. "No. Your mother and your grandfather and your father—they wouldn't have wanted that. You know they wouldn't! You did exactly the right thing, exactly what your grandfather had told you to do."

"Yes, but I was the one the airman described, the one who led them to us. It is my fault."

"You cannot think that way."

"I cannot help it. I—I flirted with him."

"So? That is not a crime. You probably lifted his spirits."

"Oh, I feel so guilty! And now . . . now I don't know what to do. The Nazis think I am dead. If they discover I am not, they will kill me."

"It's going to be all right," I said.

"No, it's not! My family is gone, and I have no papers. A person cannot roam Paris or even eat without papers. And I cannot apply for new papers without the Nazis discovering I am alive."

"You need a new identity." I had forged signatures on official papers at Mme Dupard's; I knew it could be done. "We will handle it."

She turned pleading eyes to me. "Can you contact Pierre? I don't dare go near a police prefecture without papers—the police are always stopping and asking to see them!—but I know he will help me."

I considered the situation. Joshua or Mme Dupard would be more likely to know how to get false papers, but I couldn't do anything that might compromise them. I certainly couldn't bring either of them to the attention of my brother. Besides, I was sure Pierre would do all he could to help Yvette.

"Yes," I said. "I will go get Pierre. Wait here while I change out of my uniform."

I first took Yvette to Hildie's home. As I expected, Hildie protested, but I reminded her of the Nazi edict about women living alone.

Fortunately, Pierre was at the police prefecture when I arrived. He immediately grabbed his coat and came with me. The prospect of seeing Yvette set his face aglow. *He loves her*, I thought. I had trouble keeping up with him, he walked so fast. I breathlessly explained the situation to him as we walked.

He embraced Yvette like a long-lost lover, then sent Hildie on an errand. We all settled at the kitchen table. His eyes never left Yvette's face. "I know a way to get you new papers," he told her. "Amélie and I will say you are our sister."

"What?" Yvette and I said the word together.

"I believe it will work." He leaned forward. "An officer in our arrondissement had to get new papers for his cousin after he lost them. He found a magistrate who agreed to issue the papers if the cousin brought two witnesses who could testify as to his identity. He quizzed them separately about personal matters—the color of the kitchen in the house he grew up in, for example, or the meal their mother prepared when he was sick. When the answers matched up, he was satisfied that the man was who he said he was."

"We can do that!" I exclaimed. "Yvette knows everything about our home!"

"But . . . won't they look up your family records and see there is no accounting of me?" Yvette asked.

Pierre lifted his shoulders. "The Germans say that French records are notoriously incomplete, misfiled, or full of mistakes. They will accept a notarized paper from a magistrate. We will simply say you lost your papers on the Métro."

And so it was that Pierre and I went with Yvette down to the magistrate's office the following week. We swore that she was our sister. We were each separately questioned about our childhood—where the linens were stored, our mother's maiden name, the names of pets, our father's job. We all answered the same. It was a piece of cake, since we had known each other since childhood, and since Yvette had spent so much time at our house. Yvette was photographed and issued papers.

"And now, I need a job," Yvette said. "I want something where I can help the Résistance."

Pierre stopped walking and turned toward her. "No. There is no sense in putting yourself at useless risk."

Yvette lifted her shoulders. "To live is to be at risk. To be of service to France is not useless."

Oh, she had such a bold way of speaking!

"You do not want to get on the bad side of the Nazis," Pierre said.

"I would not, if I didn't get caught."

"But you are likely to get caught. They are smart. They are everywhere. And they are winning this war."

"We must not let them win!" I said.

"You both are very naive. What you must not do is to put yourselves in harm's way." Pierre's eyes were steely as he looked from Yvette to me and back again. "Have we not all lost too many loved ones already?"

Yvette fell silent, but I knew her. Pierre's argument would not have changed her mind.

"Are there any jobs at your hotel?" she asked me.

"I don't think so, but I will ask."

I would not ask the hotel personnel, I decided. I would ask Mme
Dupard.

———————

"She understands German and English, as well as French," I said several
nights later. I had sent word to Mme Dupard, and received a message to
meet M. Henri at the back of a patisserie near the Sorbonne. He had
brought a heavyset woman with him. "Yvette could make a valuable
asset."

M. Henri looked at me closely. "Have you told her you are working
with us?"

"No."

"You must not, under any circumstances. You must not say anything
to your brother, either."

"Of course not. He works for the police."

"Exactly. And you know who the police work for."

"But Pierre also speaks German and English," I said. "He, too, could
be an asset."

This was met with silence.

"You will be tempted to talk to them, especially to Yvette," the woman
said. "You will think you can trust her, but you must not say anything.
To speak would be to compromise the entire operation at the Hotel Palais.
I know how hard it is to keep a secret from a friend who is as close as a
sister, but you must."

"Yes, yes, of course. I will say nothing. But Yvette has already worked
for the Résistance. She is loyal to the cause."

"More loyal to the cause than she is to your brother?" the woman asked.

"I think she would understand the importance of keeping the two
loyalties separate."

M. Henri looked at his compatriot. I had a feeling they had already
discussed this. "We will approach her via a stranger. You are never to
discuss this with her. It is best for you not to know if she works for the
cause or not. And, of course, she is not to know that you do, either."

"I understand."

AMÉLIE
1942

The following week, Yvette got a job working as a waitress in a restaurant. I did not know if M. Henri had helped her secure the position or not. She continued to live with Hildie, who charged her rent.

We mourned each other's parents nearly as much as our own. The first few months she was in Paris, Yvette was in the hard, raw stages of grief; she never went through a period of numbness, as I had. Instead, her *douleur* turned almost immediately to anger, an anger that demanded action.

The Germans were a clear target of hatred. "The Boches act as if waitresses are invisible," she said one evening, when I had stopped by her place of work to walk with her back to Hildie's. "They think we are too dumb to know their language."

I did not ask why she did not let them know she understood what they were saying. I hoped it meant she was working for the Resistance again.

"What sorts of things do they say?" I asked instead.

She lifted her shoulders. "Rude things, sexual things. Often about me."

I nodded. I endured the same, but with her voluptuous body, she must receive ten times as many comments. "How do you keep from blushing?"

"I wear rouge. It looks like I am always blushing, so they cannot tell a real one from the phony."

I laughed.

She looked at me directly. "They also say things about meetings and plans. It is amazing, the information they convey without giving a single thought that I am right there." She drew a drag from a cigarette and angled a cagey look at me. "I imagine you have the same situation at the hotel."

I couldn't tell if she was trying to draft me into service, or trying to get me to confess that I, too, was working for the Résistance. In either case, I would not bite at the bait. "They are not really around when I am working." I decided to turn to a topic that had been bothering me. "Are you worried about Pierre? I fear he is becoming a Nazi himself."

"Oh, no," she said quickly. "No, you are wrong."

"He works for the police, and they are Nazi puppets. And he was quite adamant that you and I should not have anything to do with the Resistance."

"He was only trying to protect us."

I took it further. "I know that you and Pierre are getting very close."

"There are boundaries to our closeness. Well, maybe not physically." She giggled.

"Yvette!"

"Well, he and I are lovers—you might as well know."

Under other circumstances, I would have wanted details—but considering that this was my brother, I did not pry.

"There are boundaries to closeness between anyone and everyone these days—even lovers. Even the dearest and oldest of friends." Yvette's eyes were somber. "It is safer for others not to know certain things. It frees the mind from worry."

"Yes."

"We must protect those we love by not telling them too much."

"Yes, you are so right." My heart lightened; I had a comrade-in-arms.

"It can be hard, though, not talking about things that are so important."

"It can be very hard," I agreed.

"Compared to the other hardships of war, however, it is a light burden to bear."

Having Yvette back in Paris brightened my life considerably, especially as she regained much of her old optimism and energy. Yvette and I did our laundry together on Sunday afternoons at Hildie's—we had to boil water and scrub our clothes in the sink on a washboard, and it was much more pleasant to have company during the tiresome task. As we worked, Yvette told me more than I wanted to hear about her love life with Pierre.

"Please," I finally said, putting my hands over my ears. "I do not want to know all of this about my brother."

"Oh, you are such a prude!"

"You are both in love. You should just get married."

"We want to."

"He has asked you?"

She nodded.

I clapped my hands together. At first I had been very conflicted about Yvette's romantic involvement with my brother, but they obviously adored each other. "Was he terribly romantic about it?"

"Oh, not at all. He was very matter-of-fact. He said, 'I want us to marry, but your papers say we are brother and sister.'"

"Oh, mon Dieu!" It was a ramification that had not even crossed my mind when we had testified to get her new papers. Apparently none of us had had the foresight to think it through.

"If it weren't so annoying, it would be quite comical. Everyone Pierre works with thinks I am his sister, because that is how he introduced me when I first came to Paris. So now it is necessary that we act like siblings in public, because police are everywhere, and we never know who knows whom from different prefectures."

What a situation! I shook my head and laughed. "Anyone who sees you together would think you are a pair of perverts, the way you look at each other."

She dunked a white slip into the bucket of clear water. "What is funny is that some of his friends have asked me out."

"Oh, no! What do you say?"

"That I have a fiancé in the south of France."

"Where do you and Pierre meet?"

"Here, when Hildie is out. She does her shopping in the mornings."

"I will be sure to never come visit then!"

Yvette sighed dreamily. "I wish we could go out dancing, but that is not what brothers and sisters do."

"No. Pierre has never taken me dancing."

We giggled as we used to. It was so good to laugh together again.

"Just think—if Pierre and I marry when the war is over, you and I will be sisters for real."

"According to your papers, we already are."

"Yes, the same papers that are preventing it." She wrung out her slip. "Oh, this whole war is so troublesome. So many, many lies and secrets!"

"Yes."

We looked at each other for a long moment. Each of us, I am sure, was thinking of all that we wanted to say but could not.

"What is happening with you and Joshua? Romantically, I mean."

"Not much." Not nearly as much as I wanted. "A few hugs, a few kisses—that is all he will allow."

"So what do you do when you meet?"

"We are not together very often or for very long. Mostly, we talk. He tells me what is happening in the Jewish community. Yvette, he has heard horrible, unspeakable things about the Nazi camps."

"I have heard rumors, as well. Pierre says it can't be true."

"Perhaps he doesn't want to believe it's true, since the police enforce the Nazi laws."

"Pierre is just trying to earn a living. He is hoping to get a promotion." She soaped a white blouse and rubbed it on the washboard. "If he is promoted, he would be able to transfer to another arrondissement, perhaps even to Neuilly-sur-Seine. If that happens, hopefully we can live together."

"Neuilly! Joshua told me he is doing some work there."

"Oh, really?"

Too late, I realized I should not have spoken. "Forget I said anything."

"It is already forgotten." Yvette smiled at me. "If Pierre and I move to Neuilly, you will have to move with us."

"No, no, no," I said, shaking my head. "I would not want to live with lovebirds. I could not bear to hear your shrieks of passion in the night."

Yvette laughed. "We would find a place with very thick walls."

"They do not make walls thick enough! No, I will stay in Paris and visit you on the weekends."

AMÉLIE
1942

I heard the Jews are all going to have to wear stars on the left
side of their coats," said a maid about ten years older than
me, a woman named Mathilde with reddish hair and a sharp nose. It
was late May, and we were seated at a table in the employee dining room
with a group of fellow hotel workers, eating our soup.

"I heard that, too. They'll be yellow with black outlines, with the word
'*Juif*' in black letters," said Geraldine, a laundress with dark brown hair.
"And they'll be as big as the palm of their hand."

"Are they supposed to make them themselves?" asked a doorman.

"No. They're supposed to report to their local police prefecture according to the first letter of their last name and to surrender one textile point."

"They have to pay to get a star?" I asked, incredulous.

"Yes." Mathilde dipped her spoon in the thin broth. "But then, they
can afford it. The Jews have all the money."

I wanted to protest that this was not so—that many Jews were even
worse off than most French citizens. Jews were prohibited from working
in many jobs, and they had to pay all sorts of unfair taxes and tariffs.
Most stores refused to sell them food, and the few that did, charged them
more. But Mathilde, like so many other Parisians, lapped up the lies the
Boches were serving.

"That's right," agreed Geraldine. "The exposition explained all that."

She was talking about the huge free exhibition called "The Jews and

France," which had run for months at the Palais Berlitz on l'avenue de l'Opéra. The exhibition depicted the Jews as a criminal race responsible for everything that was wrong with France. It was all evil propaganda, but many people—too many people—were ignorant, and ignorance made for gullibility.

I wanted to protest, but a huge part of my training had been about the importance of keeping my mouth shut. The best course of action would be to keep my head down and finish my soup without a comment.

I tried, I really did, but I couldn't quite manage it—not when Mathilde added, "If it weren't for the Jews, we wouldn't have all the food shortages."

"You don't really believe that, do you?" I asked. "That's just Nazi propaganda."

"No, it's not! If you saw the exhibition, you'd understand how it's all their fault."

"Besides, if the Nazis weren't here, we wouldn't have a job," said another maid. "They're the only ones who have the money to stay in the hotel."

I nearly choked on my soup. *If it weren't for the Nazis, my parents wouldn't be dead and I wouldn't need a job*, I was tempted to reply—but then a humbling thought stopped me in my tracks. Most of these women would have needed a job, war or no war. I had been so blessed my whole life, coming from a well-to-do family, and I had absolutely, positively taken it for granted.

"I think I would prefer cleaning up after tourists instead of soldiers," I said.

"They're no better, believe you me," said Geraldine.

"Well, I'm just grateful to have a job," said my friend Daphne.

"Me, too," I agreed. "It gives me a roof over my head and food in my belly—such as it is."

And for that, we were most fortunate. The Palais was one of the few hotels that provided maids' quarters and three meals a day. True, we had to surrender our ration stamps, and true, the food was fairly awful—it was said that our meals were made from the table scraps of Germans dining at the hotel. Still, it was enough to keep us from starving, although we all grew thinner and thinner, week after week.

The workers with families who didn't board at the hotel had it far worse. The bellman told me his wife stood for hours in line to get food every day, and all too often when she reached the front of the line, nothing was left to buy.

"I wonder why the Germans want the Jews to wear a star?" Daphne asked.

"So we don't accidentally fraternize with them," Mathilde said. "Can you imagine, if you ended up having one as a friend?"

"Or taking one as a lover." Geraldine tittered, and the whole table joined her. Everyone, that was, but me.

When I went to the cobbler's shop the following week, I was horrified to see that it was closed. Plywood was nailed over the window. Joshua stepped out of the store next to it—apparently he'd been waiting for me—and I was horrified all over again.

On the left side of his jacket was a large yellow star-shaped patch with *Juif* written in black letters inside.

"You cannot wear that star," I said.

"I have no choice."

"You do, too! No one knows you're Jewish."

"Are you kidding? Everyone in this neighborhood is Jewish." He gestured to the cobbler's shop. "Why do you think this happened?"

"But you work outside this neighborhood. No one knows you are Jewish when you are out and about unless you tell them."

"You are naive to think that."

"I am not naive!" Not anymore. I was a woman who had seen her father shot, who had held her dying mother, who had just that morning cleaned a vast amount of blood from the carpet of a Nazi-occupied hotel room.

"It would be more terrible if I pretended not to be who and what I am," Joshua said. "The Nazis want to shame us. And they cannot, for we are not ashamed of who we are."

"But it makes you conspicuous. You will become a target."

"I am already," he said sadly. "So are my mother and the other Jews we shelter. There are too many of us to hide. Besides, Amélie—there are Jews who would turn me in if I did not comply."

With no place to meet, we walked around, then sat at the back table at a small café. The waitress stared at the patch on Joshua's jacket and hesitated. I thought she was going to refuse to serve him. An ordinance had been passed that Jews were forbidden in cafés and restaurants.

He looked her in the eye. "My money is as good as anyone's." He reached in his pocket and placed some coins on the table.

She reluctantly took our order and returned with two small glasses of wine.

I leaned toward him, aching for a kiss, but a kiss did not come. He kept his distance from me. Under the tablecloth, however, he held my hand. I took it and pressed it between my knees. I longed for his hand to move higher. It did not.

Joshua had said that we couldn't get things started, that if we started the fire, it would blaze out of control. The fact I did not get the caresses or kisses I wanted made me crave them all the more.

Instead of kisses, he bared his heart. He talked of the importance of his work, and I knew he was not talking about bussing tables. He told me that he conjured faces in his mind when he was in danger or despair. He would picture the faces of his father and his sister and his mother. He would picture the faces of those he was helping. But mostly, he said, he would picture my face.

The waitress stopped again at our table. "I am sorry, but my manager says I must ask you to leave."

"It's all right." Joshua left the coins on the table, even though they surely exceeded what two drinks would cost. I started to rise. He put out his hand, stopping me. "Please—stay a few moments more. It is best if we don't leave together."

My heart was heavy. That horrid star on his jacket was changing everything. "When and where will we meet again?" I asked.

"It is time we stop meeting, Amélie."

"No!"

"My heart does not want to give you up, but we are putting each other in danger."

His yellow star hovered over the table as he leaned forward. "We must both continue our work. We will help no one if we are killed or imprisoned. So for now, this is good-bye. You must not try to contact me."

"But . . ." I clutched at his jacket.

He gently removed my hands. "It could cause me and my loved ones great harm if you do."

He could not have said anything more persuasive, and he knew it. I watched him go, my heart going with him.

The next week, Pierre sent word for me to meet him in the evening, after my day shift ended. It was unusual; since Yvette had arrived in Paris, he spent all his spare time with her. In fact, I had not seen much of him since our mother's death.

I met him at the corner café. Handsome in his dark blue uniform, he was already seated at a central table. He rose, greeted me with la bise and ordered two coffees. When our drinks arrived—horrible, bitter coffee, thinned with roasted acorns—he took a sip, grimaced, then wasted no time on small talk.

"Who is this young man you are seeing?"

My heart skipped several beats. "I do not know what you mean."

"Don't pretend, Amélie. You were seen with a young man not far from my prefecture."

My pulse pounded like the hooves of a runaway horse. I weighed the wisdom of feigning ignorance against the reality that Pierre already knew. "He is just a friend—someone I recently met at the hotel."

"My source said you seemed to know each other very well."

"Who is your source?" Dread filled my throat. Had Yvette betrayed me?

"Another policeman saw you." He took another punishing sip of coffee. "I asked Yvette about this before I called you."

"And what did she say?"

"She acted like she knew nothing, but I could tell she was covering for you. I can tell when she lies. Besides, something she wrote me when

I first joined the army now makes sense. She said you were pining for a foreign student you'd had a romance with."

My palms were sweating. "It is not a romance. It is simply a friendship."

"I heard he looked at you like a lover."

My heart battered against my ribs. "That is ridiculous."

"Your blush says otherwise. Do you know his nationality?"

"He is Austrian."

"He is Jewish." Pierre said the word as if it were a nasty oath.

"So?"

"So? That is all you have to say?" His eyes burned. "Are you *fou*?"

"No." I tilted up my chin. "I simply don't see what difference it makes."

"The Jews—they are not like us, Amélie. You cannot get involved with a Jew."

"I can do as I wish."

"I forbid it."

"You can forbid nothing. You are not my father!"

"Listen to me, Amélie. It is dangerous."

"I don't care."

"You will care if you are caught. Besides, it is beneath you."

I stiffened as if I'd been slapped. "In what way? Joshua is one of the smartest, kindest, most loyal, self-disciplined people I have ever met."

"He is Jewish. He has bad blood."

"You sound like a Nazi."

"The Nazis are right about many things."

I gazed at him, horrified. "How can you say that? They killed Papa. They killed Thomas. And they killed Maman, just as surely as if they'd put a knife to her throat."

Pierre drained his cup. "What they did to Papa—that was not right. But Thomas . . ." He ran a hand down his face. "It was war. We were trying to kill them. You need to understand, little one—the old France we knew is gone. There is a new regime, a regime that will last beyond the war. The Nazis are in power, and they will stay in power. When this war is over, you want to be on the side of the winner."

"No. I want to be on the side that is right."

His sigh was long and weary, like a wind that had blown across an entire continent. "Who can say what is right?"

"Even a child knows that brutality and prejudice and greed is wrong," I said hotly.

"Oh, Am—you sound like *une Américaine*."

I tilted my head up. "And what is wrong with that?"

"They are ridiculously idealistic. They don't face facts."

"Yes, they do. And the facts are, the Nazis are brutal and vicious and selfish and cruel."

He leaned forward. "The facts are, from the beginning of time, some people have ruled and others have obeyed."

"It is not fair."

"No, it is not, but life is not fair. Realistic people accept that, then try to make their own situation better, not worse." He put his cup down so hard it rattled the saucer. "You are to stay away from this Jew, do you hear? I am up for a promotion, and I will not let your dalliance ruin my chances."

So there it was—the real reason! I would not give him the satisfaction of telling him Joshua had already ended things between us. "He is my friend. It is nothing more."

"Then it should be easy for you to stop seeing him." He wagged a finger at me. "If you do not, I will see to it that he disappears."

"No! You leave him alone!"

"If you leave him alone, so will I. Otherwise . . ." He shrugged. His mouth was set in a hard line. He looked cold and uncaring, completely unwilling to compromise. It struck me that I really did not know Pierre anymore.

"I cannot believe you would be so cruel." I rose to my feet.

"I am watching out for your best interests."

I picked up my purse. "My interests, or your own?"

19

AMÉLIE
1942

The summer of 1942 was as hot as the winter was cold. My work at the hotel was grueling. I cleaned from six in the morning until seven in the evening, and those were just my official hours. When they needed extra hands to help clean up after banquets or parties, I was drafted to help. My more senior position meant that most nights, I slept without being called for nighttime duty.

I was now trusted to work in the finer hotel rooms, the rooms occupied by the more senior Nazi officers, many of whom were transient guests rather than officers with regular quarters. Every day it was someone new, someone who may or may not have important papers I needed to find.

One day I found a map. The last roll of film would not advance in my camera, so I did not know if I had taken a photo or not. I tried to make a crude copy—I put a piece of paper over the map and traced it the best I could, but I did not have time for the details.

I dropped the film and my map at the church, then dropped a note in Mme Dupard's mailbox with the predetermined message for camera problems: *Estelle is out of socks.*

Later than afternoon, I found a note on my maid's cart, hidden between the sheets:

M. Estelle, Parc Monceau; 15h00, par la pyramide.

I hurried out after work and took the Métro to the Monceau stop.

I walked toward the pyramid. "Do you think we'll see the moon this evening?" asked a woman wearing a black hat, who was gazing up at the sky.

I drew closer. It was Yvette! My courier was Yvette!

"I think the clouds will cover it," I replied, according to the script I had been given by Mme Dupard.

Yvette opened her arms, and we shared la bise.

"So now we are in the open," I said, holding her at arm's length. "Are you surprised?"

"I suspected from the very beginning. I knew you had a great, brave heart."

I knew the same about her. However, I was worried about Pierre. "You will keep my secret?"

"Of course. Pierre knows nothing of this—nor will he ever." She pressed my arm. "Come quickly. I do not have much time." I followed her into a tailor's shop.

Inside, the store was empty. She turned the sign on the door from *Ouvert* to *Fermé*, then led me to the dressing room and untied a small cloth roll from around her waist. She unfolded the cloth.

"What in the world . . ." I looked at the small, flat object she handed me. "Is that a camera?"

She nodded. "We could not tell if your camera was broken or just the film, so now you have a better one, flat enough to tie around your waist. And here." She handed me four rolls of film. "Put these in your brassiere."

I unbuttoned my blouse and did as she said.

"You are to put the map in the brightest light possible and photograph it from different angles and distances. Then tape the film under the pew in front of you when you kneel at mass tomorrow."

"I am nearly out of tape."

"We thought of that, as well." She lifted some tape from the cloth roll. "I will show you how to refold and tie the packet."

She did just that, then handed it to me. "Now—put it around your waist."

"Very clever." I put it on, then rebuttoned my shirt.

She retucked her blouse. I saw her rib bones protruding. "Mon Dieu, Yvette—you have gotten so thin!"

"So have you."

"Not as thin as you. You are nothing but skin and bones!"

"I swear, I am hungry all the time," she admitted.

"Does Hildie eat all your food?"

"No, but our rations do not buy much. Most of the time, I feel as if I have a howling wolf in my stomach. The worst part is serving food at the restaurant and not being able to eat any."

"Can't you sneak a few bites in the kitchen?"

"If I did, I could be arrested for stealing. They made an example of a kitchen helper last month, and it scared the rest of us out of our minds."

"That's horrible!"

"Yes. Yes, it is. The Boches do not want the French to eat their food unless they are *collaborateurs*." She said the word as if it tasted foul. "Oh, how I hate serving the French girls who consort with the Nazis! How can they betray their fellow countrymen like that, without helping the cause? I resent it so! I resent that they have full bellies and clothes and heat in the winter—and wine and shampoo and shoes that don't have holes in the soles—and here we are, so very, very hungry, working our fingers to the bone."

"We are helping to win the war."

"I have often thought I could do more valuable work for France if I were the mistress of a top officer. As it is, I get to listen to tidbits of conversation, but then I must leave for another table. I cannot linger too long without looking suspicious. If I were sitting at the table, as some of those girls do . . . Well, they're in a position to really give us information, if any of them understood a lick of German."

"Surely some of them speak German."

"A few have rudimentary knowledge. I actually talked to M. Henri about recruiting one of them."

"And?"

"He says we cannot trust anyone who is not already on our side before they begin an alliance."

"You mean dalliance."

Yvette gave a dry laugh. "Exactly. He said we cannot trust someone who is already in the enemy's bed." She leaned close. "And then he asked if I were interested in such an assignment! Can you imagine?"

"No!" I was appalled. "I think I would have slapped him."

"He could tell I was insulted. He said he did not mean to disrespect me in anyway. He said in war we must use everything we have at our disposal, that nothing done to save France would be unholy."

"He used that word?"

"He did."

"So if one were to turn it around, *la collaboration horizontale* is a holy pursuit."

"If undertaken for the right reasons, yes."

"You would not seriously consider such a thing!"

"No, no, no. I adore Pierre, and I could never be unfaithful."

"But otherwise?"

She lifted her shoulders. "They killed my family. They destroyed my home. Why should I care what they do to my body?"

20

AMÉLIE
1942

*W*hen I awoke on the morning of July 16, it seemed like just another day. Bastille Day—the French national holiday of freedom—had been two days before. That was a day that was supposed to be special, but the Germans had forbidden any type of celebration.

I did not learn that this day was different until lunch. I sat down at the table next to Isolde, one of my roommates.

"Isn't it horrible?" she whispered.

I looked at my bowl, thinking she was talking about the soup. It actually looked quite good today—it had small but identifiable pieces of potato, and even held the promise of meat.

My blank look must have tipped her off. "You haven't heard?"

"Heard what?"

"About the *rafle*."

It meant raid—or roundup. The word made my stomach curl. "What rafle?"

"It started in the dead of night. Around four this morning. The police are rounding up all the Jews. Thousands and thousands and thousands."

"The police? But the police are French. The Nazis are the ones who hate the Jews."

Isolde lifted her shoulders. "I guess the Nazis told them to."

Geraldine leaned across the table. "They're sending them to the camps."

My stomach sank like a stone at the bottom of a pond. We had all heard of the camps. We knew they were horrible places, but exactly why was a mystery, because no Jew ever escaped and came back to tell us.

Some said they were work camps, where the prisoners were forced to quarry stone or pave roads or do some other type of grueling labor for hours and hours, with not enough food or water. Aside from the lack of water, it didn't sound all that different from the life of the typical Parisian. This was the experience Pierre described when he talked about the prisoner-of-war camp where he'd been held.

There were rumors, of course . . . whispered, bloodcurdling tales of cruelty and torture and murder. They seemed like ghost stories—too outlandish and awful to be real.

"They're even gathering up women and children," Isolde whispered. "They're taking them to the Vel' d'Hiv."

The Vel' d'Hiv was what the locals called the Vélodrome d'Hiver—the winter racetrack. It was a large indoor cycle track with a glass roof, not too far from the Eiffel Tower. The roof had been painted dark blue to keep it from being a target for aircraft attack.

"I heard that the police have arrested nearly the entire eleventh arrondissement," Geraldine said.

That is where Joshua lived. That is also where Pierre worked. I could not eat, but I could not just get up and leave. I sat there, nauseous. I needed to see if Joshua and his mother were all right.

When the girls cleared their plates, I stood. I could not stay at work any more than I could stop my heart from beating.

I hurried to my room and quickly changed into street clothes. All hotel personnel were forbidden from wearing their uniforms outside—plus I had to have my papers. One could not go anywhere without papers.

One of my roommates was passing in the stairwell, her arms laden with linens. "I just got word that my aunt is very sick," I said. "Please tell Supervisor Leharte that I've had to rush off to tend to her."

———————

I didn't wait for her response. I hurried down the stairs and outside. It was hot, the kind of hot that makes your clothes stick to your skin and causes sweat to trickle down the inside of your brassiere.

I headed to the Métro. I had to show my papers to no less than three German soldiers. I finally disembarked at Le Marais and climbed the stairs out of the Métro to see three policemen hustling two women and five children into the back of a truck. Their loud, frightened, heartbroken sobs tore the air.

I scurried down a side street toward Joshua's apartment. The street was alarmingly empty. The building, usually swarming with people, was silent. I raced up the rickety stairs to the third floor and found the door standing open, hanging from just one hinge. The apartment was in chaos. Furniture was toppled, clothing was strewn all over, and the kitchen counters were bare. The cabinets hung open. Every crumb of food, every teaspoon of flour, was gone. Nothing remained on the walls but a broken mirror.

I hardly recognized myself in it. My eyes were wild, my mouth red from where I had been biting my lips. I had been crying, and hadn't even realized it.

Out the open window, I heard a scream. I turned to see a woman holding a baby, struggling with a policeman. He was dragging her to a truck, and she was resisting. As I watched, another police officer hit her with the butt of a rifle.

The smack of the gun against her skull reverberated in the eerily quiet air. I gasped and watched her fall. The first policeman grabbed her baby as it tumbled from her arms, then loaded it into the truck as if it were a bag of beans. The two officers then seized the unconscious woman and tossed her into the truck beside him.

I closed my eyes and slumped to the floor. I must have sat there for some time, trying to think what to do.

I had no idea where to find Joshua. I could only pray that he had gotten word and taken his family out of there. If not . . . if they were at the Vel' d'Hiv . . . well, I had to find a way to get them out.

Yvette. She always seemed to know what to do. I would go find Yvette, and she would help.

21

AMÉLIE
1942

*O*h, my God." Yvette's hand flew to her mouth as we rounded the corner and saw the Vel' d'Hiv. A crowd of buses, lorries, and military trucks were parked in front. French police in their dashing blue uniforms were escorting what looked like entire families—men, women, children, the elderly—into the building.

Nausea rose in my throat.

"Do you think they're here?" Yvette asked.

"I hope not, but I fear they are."

Yvette looped her arm through mine. "Come on."

"Do you think we can just charge in there?"

"I don't see why not. They seem to have no problem with women going inside." Her mouth took on a grim set, and her eyes narrowed with anger. Yvette's anger was a terrifying force, because anger made her fearless.

She marched me up to the door, where two policemen stood guard. "We're looking for our brother, Pierre Michaud."

"I don't know him," said the shorter one.

"He's a policeman with the second sous-prefecture, eleventh arrondissement."

"Well, he's either here, or out in the trucks. All police are on this task today."

"All of them?"

Both men nodded.

"Why are these people being arrested? What crime have they committed?" I asked.

"They are Jews."

My temper flashed. "I thought the police were to keep the peace, not do the Nazis' dirty work."

Yvette elbowed me sharply.

"We're just following orders," said the taller officer.

"Could you please let us in so we can look for our brother?" Yvette batted her eyes at the younger man. "Our aunt is very ill, the ambulances are not working, and we need his help getting her to a hospital."

"I have orders to keep this door secure."

"And so you are. You are letting no one out. But surely no one would mind a couple of French girls going inside."

"I cannot."

Yvette pulled a stub of pencil out of her purse. I gasped as she slowly, deliberately unbuttoned the top button on her blouse, her eyes on the officer the whole time, and pulled a piece of paper from her brassiere.

The policeman's eyes ate her up. His mouth opened; he licked his lips.

"Perhaps you could just look the other way for a few moments while we go in," she suggested. Using the back of her purse as a hard surface, she scribbled something down. "And then perhaps I won't look the other way if you come to visit me tonight." She dangled the address in front of him.

"If he won't do it, I will," said the taller policeman beside him, reaching for her address.

Yvette shifted her winsome smile.

With a muttered oath, the first policeman plucked the piece of paper from her fingers. "Very well. But be quick about it. And if you're caught, I had nothing to do with it."

She blew him a kiss and pulled me along inside.

"What on earth are you going to do when he shows up tonight?" I asked her.

"If he goes to that address, he'll find himself at a butcher shop across town. Come."

We walked into the dome. It was dim despite the strong sunlight outside; the painted glass roof let in a little light, but not much. The stench of urine and sweaty bodies was overpowering.

"Good heavens! Don't they have any restrooms?"

"No. They closed them off," a thin woman next to us said. "Apparently they have windows in them, and they're afraid we'll escape."

"This is horrible," Yvette said. We worked our way through the standing crush of people, looking for Joshua, for his mother, for Pierre. It was so crowded, it was impossible for me to see much more than the shoulders in front of me. Yvette was taller, but her view was impeded nearly as much as mine.

The track was a steep, paved slant, meant for bicyclists racing laps. A few cots had been set up on the slant. Very old, very ill, and very pregnant women lay on them. Everywhere, children were crying.

"Mademoiselle, avez-vous de l'eau?"

I turned to see a woman holding the hands of two small girls. "There is nothing to drink, and they are very thirsty."

"I will see what we can do," I promised.

I went up to a police officer standing off to the side. Yvette tagged along. "Excuse me. My sister and I are looking for our brother, a policeman from the eleventh arrondissement named Pierre Michaud. Do you know him?"

"No, I do not. And you should not be here."

"Yes, yes, we know," Yvette said. "Can you tell me where we can get water?"

"There is none."

"None at all?"

"No."

"No water, and no restrooms?" I could barely contain my indignation. "How long do you intend to hold these people here in these conditions?"

He lifted his shoulders. "We were ordered to bring them here and guard them. That is all I know."

We spent hours in the Vel' d'Hiv, going round and round the track and the seats, looking high and low, questioning every policeman we encountered. At last, in early evening, I finally spotted Joshua's mother sitting on a pile of blankets and coats in the middle of the track. I leaned down toward her. "Mrs. Koper?" I said.

Recognition flashed in her eyes. She clutched at me, sobbing.

I bent down and hugged her. "What happened?" I spoke in German, hoping she could understand that language a little.

A woman beside her with a blue scarf over her head answered me in German. "Around four this morning, there was a hard knock on the door. Before we could answer it, the French police kicked it open. They pulled us out of bed and told us to pack a change of clothes. One asked where we kept our valuables. We have no valuables. We gave him what little we had—a few centimes, a candlestick. They took us to a truck, then brought us here."

Beside her, a little boy about two years of age started to cry. The woman pulled him on her lap. The child's pants were wet. I watched a wet spot grow on the woman's brown skirt, as well.

My heart sank. "Is Joshua here?"

"No. He was not at home. But the police asked for him by name."

Joshua's mother grabbed my arm and said something I could not understand. I looked to the other woman. "She says that you must find him and warn him to leave France."

Joshua's mother said something else. The woman listened to her for a moment, then leaned close. "She believes he is at the railroad yard in Neuilly, in an abandoned boxcar."

My throat was almost too tight to talk. "I will do what I can."

"Come with us," Yvette urged. "We will try to get you out of here."

The woman translated. Joshua's mother looked around her at the people with her huddled on ragtag blankets beside her, and said something in Yiddish.

The woman looked up at us. "She says, 'No. I will not leave my family. My family is my fate.'"

"How about you?" I asked.

The woman forlornly shook her head. "I have three other children— and my sisters are here. How can I leave without them?"

Joshua's mother put her hand on mine. It was large-knuckled and dry, with skin the texture of a withered apple. She looked at me with eyes that were very much like Joshua's and spoke in Yiddish.

"She says, 'I have lived my life,'" translated the woman. "'But Joshua is young, and you must help him survive. Find him and convince him to leave France.'"

I nodded, my eyes full of tears. "We will go look for him now."

We started for the door. We had only gone a few steps when a hand gripped my arm. "What are you two doing here?" demanded a familiar male voice.

Pierre! Why, oh why did we have to run into him now? "I could ask you the very same thing."

"I am doing my job."

"Rounding up defenseless women and children?" I asked.

Pierre's scowl deepened. "This is not the time or place for such a discussion." He looked from me to Yvette. "I asked what you two are doing here, in a place where you clearly should not be. What were you discussing with those two women?"

"We are looking for the children of a friend," Yvette said. To my surprise, Yvette pulled a photo of two young towheaded children from her pocket. "We asked if they had seen them. Unfortunately, they hadn't. But then they wanted to know if we could help them get out of here."

Pierre gazed at the photo, his attention diverted. "Whose children are these?"

"They belong to the night janitor at the restaurant where I work." Oh, Yvette was smooth! I envied her facile tongue. "Her name is Bernice Austin, and her husband was a French soldier. Like Thomas, he was killed during the invasion. She came home from work this morning to discover her children and the babysitter were gone. She came back to the restaurant, frantic."

"Is she or the babysitter Jewish?"

"Non, but they live in the eleventh arrondissement, because it was all they can afford, and she fears they were picked up in the rafle. We have been looking for you, because we knew you could help."

Oh, mon Dieu! I could not believe how effectively Yvette worked Pierre. She gave him a gaze so trusting and adoring it would have melted a heart of stone. "Can you check and see if they are here?"

He blew out a hard sigh. "All the names have not yet been compiled into one list. It is an impossible task. But what is the name of the babysitter?"

"Anna Mireaux."

"And the children's last name is Austin?"

"Yes."

"I will make a note of those names and give it to the person compiling the master list. It is the best I can do."

"Thank you, Pierre." She batted her eyes at him. "Is there somewhere besides here that they're gathering Jews?"

"Some have been sent to Drancy. But there is no point in your going there. Let your friend look for her own children."

"She is beside herself, and she has no one to help."

Pierre gave a deep sigh. "Go home, both of you, and stay away from this affair."

"You cannot tell us what to do," I told him.

He glared at me. "I suppose you came to look for your Jewish boyfriend."

"Non! That is over."

"You were talking to those Jewesses as if you knew them."

I gave him my most scornful look. "You are too coldhearted to understand simple human empathy." I grabbed Yvette's arm. "Let's go and leave him to his dirty Nazi work."

Yvette went along with me, although I saw her cast a longing gaze over her shoulder.

"Where did you get that photo of the children?" I asked Yvette.

"Off the body of a dead German soldier."

I gasped. "Where?"

Her head inclined. "I cannot say, but I will tell you that it is very handy to have. It's an acceptable excuse for almost anything." She tapped the photo before putting it back in her pocket. "I suggest you get one yourself."

"Yes, well, unfortunately, I do not see a lot of dead Nazis." I looked around the Vélodrome, at the miserable mass of humanity huddled there. A wave of anger swept over me, so sudden and fierce that it left me breathless. How could they possibly gather up women and children and the elderly and crowd them into a building with no water, no bathrooms, no food? The rumors of what else awaited them made my stomach churn.

Getting out of the Vélodrome was not as easy as getting in. We had to show our papers to no less than five different guards, show the photograph three times, and use Pierre's name twice.

We took the Métro to the Pont de Neuilly, all the way at the end of the line. It was nearly dark by the time we arrived. Train tracks ran beside the Métro stop. We followed the tracks some distance away, and finally found an area where a side track branched off. Four boxcars sat apart, unattached to each other or a train.

"Do you think he's in one of those?"

"There's only one way to find out," Yvette said. She reached up and knocked on the door of the first one.

"Joshua?" I called. "Joshua, are you there?"

No answer. We went to the second and repeated the same drill. At the third one, the door slid slowly open.

"Joshua!"

"Mon Dieu—Amélie! And Yvette! What on earth are you two doing here?"

"We went to the Vélodrome, and your mother said we should come warn you."

"My mother is at the Vel' d'Hiv?"

"Yes, with all your aunts and cousins. There has been a huge rafle."

"Oh, dear God." He hung his head, then ran a hand across his face. "So now they're gathering up women and children?"

"Thousands of them," Yvette said grimly.

A scuffling sound came from inside the boxcar.

"Is someone with you?" I asked.

He looked both ways, then reached down to help us up. "Yes. Come in. You mustn't stand outside."

He pulled first Yvette, then me inside, then slid the door closed, leaving it open only a crack for air.

It took a moment for my eyes to adjust to the darkness—but soon I could make out five children sitting against the wall. The oldest looked to be only nine or ten; the youngest was probably three or four.

"Who are these children?" I knelt down beside a girl who was maybe eight, holding a child aged four or five on her lap.

"Polish orphans. I'm trying to get them to Switzerland."

"You've been doing this all along?"

He nodded. "Many Jewish children were brought to France by friends and family after their parents died or were imprisoned—children from Poland or Austria or Germany or Romania. They came thinking France would be safe, but now . . ." He shrugged his shoulders, not needing to say anything further.

"How will you transport them?"

"There is a network—*L'Oeuvre de Secours aux Enfants*. We use trains and cars and trucks—whatever means we can find. It's nearly impossible to get papers that would allow them to stay here, even if we could find people who will take them in, so we smuggle them to safe houses or convents, or across the border."

"When will you leave?" Yvette asked.

"Tonight, if we are lucky. There is supposed to be a truck. But it might not come until tomorrow night—or the night after. We must wait for the transportation."

"You and the children could be stuck here for two days? In this boxcar, in the heat?"

"We have no choice." He suddenly held up his hand. "Shhh! Someone is outside."

I heard the sound of a vehicle door closing. *The transportation has arrived*, I thought. I heard the rumble of low, murmured voices, and then the door to the boxcar abruptly slid open. A bright light shone into the dark car, blinding me.

"I knew it!" shouted a familiar voice.

"Pierre!" Yvette gasped.

"I knew it," Pierre's voice snapped like a trap. His flashlight glared at me. "I could tell you knew those Jewish women. So this is your boy-friend, eh?"

Before I knew what was happening, Joshua rushed forward, tackling Pierre's knees. Pierre crashed hard onto the metal floor. I heard the sickening thud of fists on flesh—over and over and over, as the two men rolled. In the dark, it was hard to see who was on top of whom.

And then, abruptly, the boxcar rocked as more men climbed in with more flashlights. I could make out the black of three SS officers' uniforms in the flashlight beams that glared every which way in the boxcar. One of the officers picked up Joshua and threw him against the metal wall. His head hit hard, like a hammer on an anvil.

Pierre staggered to his feet. Joshua lay crumpled on the floor, not moving. The young girl behind me screamed. I hauled her and a younger child onto my lap. Yvette gathered the other three children in her arms.

"Stop!" I pleaded. "Please!"

Pierre walked over to Joshua and gave him a kick. "Filthy Jewish swine."

Joshua groaned. At least he was still alive.

"Please! Please don't hurt him any more," I begged.

The SS officer yanked the child from my lap. She flailed at him with her arms and legs. He slapped her hard, full across the cheek. Her head twisted to the side as another German carried her outside like a sack of potatoes.

"Go! Run!" Yvette urged the children in her arms toward the door. Pierre roughly grabbed two of them, slinging them to the floor. The boy rose, and Pierre hit him—hard, with his fist, in his stomach. The boy flew across the railcar and hit the metal wall with a sickening thud.

Yvette and I both rushed toward the child. The back of the boy's head had a deep gash. His blood pooled on my skirt. He was breathing, but just barely.

Yvette looked up at Pierre, her eyes angry blue lightning. "I can't believe you hit a child like that!"

"He's a Jew—the source of our ills, the reason for this war," Pierre snarled. "Baby rats might be cute, but they grow up to be rats all the same."

The boy was limp, his eyes closed.

Two SS officers grabbed Joshua and yanked him to his feet.

Yvette whirled on Pierre. "You have let them poison your mind!"

"We should take the women as well," one of the SS officers said in German.

"You can stop the act now," Pierre said to us. His eyes held a weird expression, a look I recognized as a warning. "We have them in custody."

I didn't know what he was implying until Joshua looked at me.

"Act? That's what it was, all this time?" His eyes were a hot glare. "You betrayed me!"

"No," I said, shaking my head, devastated that he would think that. "No!"

"Betrayer!" Joshua yelled, as he was dragged out. "Traitor!"

I stared, my mouth not working.

"Are we taking the women or not?" A French police officer asked the last remaining SS officer.

"No. They are my sisters," Pierre said in German, talking to the SS officer. "They knew the Jew from the university, that is all. Like all women, they have a soft spot for children and underdogs. That is why they talk so insolently. But they are on our side. After all, they led us here. They are responsible for this capture."

"We are not—" I protested.

Yvette's elbow knifed into my side, cutting me off.

The SS officer seemed to weigh the matter. "Let me see your papers."

Yvette pulled hers from her pocket. When I didn't move, she pulled mine out of my pocket, as well.

The SS officer looked at them, then thrust them back at us.

"Go." He waved his fingers in a dismissive gesture, then turned to another officer. "Keep someone posted here to arrest whoever was coming to meet them."

"I'll see my sisters home," Pierre said.

"Don't bother." I'd never before heard Yvette's voice, usually so warm and vibrant, sound like a block of ice. "We will go on our own, the same as we came."

I was inconsolable on the Métro ride home, although Yvette tried. She sat beside me, her arm around my shoulders as if I were a child. I leaned against the window and cried. Fortunately the subway car was empty. "I can't believe Joshua thought I betrayed him," I moaned.

"He didn't," she said. "He only said that to save us."

"He looked so angry! So bitter!"

"He was angry at Pierre." She gazed out the window as the Métro clanged around a corner. "Pierre tried to save us, too, you know. And he succeeded." The subway swayed and rattled. "We were saved by the lies of the men we love."

"But Joshua—and those children! Pierre turned them over, knowing they would be . . ." My mouth could not say any of the words that formed in my mind.

"I know, I know. I will never forgive Pierre. It is over between us."

I glanced at Yvette, aware, for the first time, of how the events of the night had affected her, as well. "Oh, Vettie! You have lost as much as me, and yet you're so strong!"

"The man I love is not being dragged off to a camp." The Métro took a sharp turn, throwing us against the window. "Although, after what he did to that boy, I wish he were."

My feelings about Pierre were too raw and jumbled to untangle. He had saved us from being captured by the SS—but he had followed us from the Vélodrome. He had used us to capture Joshua.

But I was the one who was most at fault. My tears fell afresh.

"I should have done as Joshua wanted and stayed away," I sobbed. "If I hadn't tried to help him, I wouldn't have harmed him."

"No. The fault is Pierre's. He is trying to curry favor with the Nazis to advance his career." She shook her head, her mouth bitter. "I could never marry a man who could do the things he did—who thinks the way he thinks. I cannot believe he hit that child, and then acted as if it were nothing." Tears tracked down her face. She angrily brushed them away. "I did not know him."

"The war has changed him."

"It has changed us all."

Her voice was angry—angry and hard. "Without Pierre, there is no reason I can't get more and better information to help the cause."

"What do you mean?"

"I told you before. There are officers at the restaurant—high-ranking officers—who would love to have me as their mistress."

"Oh, Yvette—you did not mean that."

"Why not? I would have access to their pockets, to their files, to their conversations. I could gain entrée to dinner parties with other officers. We already know that when they think we don't understand their language, they talk freely in front of us. I could do a lot of good for the Resistance. And I wouldn't have to starve, either. I could be well fed. I could even bring you food. Maybe even get food for the orphans."

"Yvette, do not talk this way!"

"Why not? I have been giving my love to a man who is cruel, who could smack a child across a boxcar, knocking him unconscious, maybe even killing him." The Métro rocked hard around a corner. "Not only is Pierre cruel, he is weak and spineless; he let himself be brainwashed by propaganda. He has no principles aside from pursuing his own good. I think it is worse to sleep with a Nazi who is French than a Nazi who is German. At least the Germans are loyal to their own country." She shook her head. "Your parents would be devastated at what Pierre has become."

"You don't need to compromise yourself just because Pierre is corrupt."

"Compromise myself? I was compromising myself with Pierre and I didn't even know I was doing so. No." She shook her head, her chin resolute. "I am through being emotional and stupid. The next time I take a lover, I will know exactly who he is and what I can get from the situation.

No more sentimental foolishness for me; I will carefully select a man who can give me access to important information that the Resistance needs."

"Don't do anything impetuous," I begged Yvette. "Promise me that you will think this through."

"I will be as cold-blooded about this decision as Pierre was about his decision to let us lead him to Joshua."

"It is my fault," I whispered. "It is all my fault."

"No. No, it is not, and I will not listen to such talk." She smoothed my hair back from my brow, the way my mother would when I was ill. "You have done nothing wrong. You have nothing to be ashamed of, and no reason to feel guilty."

"I do feel guilty, though."

"We all do." Yvette blew out a hard breath. "It is the price we pay for being alive during this terrible time."

22

AMÉLIE
1942

I continued to suffer over Joshua. I awoke in sweats from dreams of him. I dreamed that we were trying to reach each other, but the ground stretched and cracked into a ravine that swallowed him up. I dreamed that I was about to eat a thick, juicy steak; my mouth salivated as I drew the knife through the rare meat—and then I realized it was Joshua's thigh. I awoke from that dream screaming, much to the annoyance of the other women in my hotel dormitory.

I dreamed, too, of Pierre—strange, rambling dreams that intertwined images of him as a boy with a monster. He had multiple grabbing arms, like an octopus; he was suddenly three times larger than his real size; he would smile, and his teeth would become razors. The heart-wrenching thunk of the child hitting the side of the boxcar would make me awaken with my heart pounding and my face stained with tears.

Pierre came to see me in August. I was at work at the hotel; I had just finished cleaning my last bedroom, and was pushing my cart down the back hallway when Isolde bustled up. "A policeman is in the lobby asking to see you."

"What does he look like?"

"Handsome. Tall. He has a romantic little scar on his jaw."

Romantic—bah! Pierre had gotten the scar from a backstreet boxing match when he was thirteen and I was eleven. My mother took him to get it stitched up by the doctor, and when she brought him home, my father had whipped him for fighting for sport. Pierre had muttered a violent curse against Papa behind his back. The incident had confused and frightened me. Even as a child, it had made no sense that men would use violence to encourage peace. Where was it all to end?

"That is my brother," I explained.

"He said it was urgent and most important." Isolde was nearly breathless with the drama of it all.

I rolled my eyes. "Pierre is prone to exaggeration. He probably wants me to sew buttons on his coat."

Isolde giggled. "Tell him I will gladly sew on his buttons."

I could not, of course, simply refuse to see him; Pierre was the police. Whispers swirled around me as I made my way through the hall to my supervisor. I explained that Pierre was my brother, that he had requested to talk to me, that he probably had news about someone in my family. She let me go, but insisted I follow the rules and first change out of my hotel uniform—to avoid, I am sure, bringing the slightest hint of scandal to the hotel.

I sent word that I would meet him at the employee exit, and then changed into one of my two summer dresses. It was hot and humid, but it was not the heat that made my palms sweat as I walked toward him. The very thought of Pierre made my insides boil with anger—anger and guilt and self-loathing.

Despite what Isolde had said, I thought he looked terrible. He had lost weight, and his skin had a sallow look. I was glad to see it.

I held myself at my most rigid as he gave me la bise. "Have you brought word of Joshua?" I asked.

"You know that is not possible."

"I know no such thing. I did not know that my brother would arrest a man trying to help innocent children—nor that he would kill a child so casually."

Pierre's back stiffened. "I did not kill that boy."

"No? He was barely breathing when last I saw him. What is his current state of health?"

"I have no way of knowing."

"Of course you don't, because the Nazis took him. But I'm sure he's just fine, because nothing is better for a severely wounded child than being dragged to a Nazi camp."

His brow furrowed. "This sarcasm, this bitterness—it is most unbecoming."

"Is that so? Well, then, perhaps you should throw me against a wall and call the SS to arrest me."

He looked at me, and for a moment his eyes were those of the Pierre of my youth, the brother who longed for affirmation from our father for his athletic abilities, but only got criticism for his poor grades. His eyes begged for acceptance. "The boy only had the wind knocked out of him."

"Is that what you tell yourself in order to sleep at night?"

"I did not come to see you to be berated."

"Too bad. So why did you come? To ask me to help you win back Yvette?"

His lack of an immediate response told me I had hit the nail on the head. I knew that she had refused to see him since that fateful night. I knew that he had repeatedly gone to the café where she worked, and that each time he sat down in her section, she arranged for another waitress to serve him. I knew that one time she had told a Nazi customer that he was her brother, that he was trying to shake her down to pay off his gambling debts, and that she was afraid of him. The Nazi and two of his cronies had thrown Pierre out of the café and escorted her home.

"She will not see me. I cannot explain myself to her if she will not listen."

"There is no explaining away your behavior, Pierre."

"I wait outside her apartment, but she is never alone."

"I know this about Yvette: you cannot forcibly change her mind. Any efforts you make to coerce her will backfire."

"I know, I know. But I cannot live without her."

"You must, because she is done with you."

"Do you think that, in time, she might change her mind?"

I did not, but I could see that was not an answer he would accept. "I do not know. But right now you are doing more harm than good, trying to force your attentions on her. Perhaps after the war is over, if you show proper remorse . . ."

He scowled. "When the war is over, she will be the remorseful one."

"Ah. Well, then, you have your answer."

He looked at me, unsure what I meant. "Can you talk to her?"

"And say what? That you are sorry?"

"Yes. Tell her anything that you think will help. Tell me what to say to her, and I will say it."

"But would you mean any of it?"

The tight set of his mouth, the impatience in his eyes told me he saw no reason that should matter. I held up my hand before he could form a lie or excuse. "You know what, Pierre? There is truly nothing to be done."

"I cannot accept that."

I could see that I would never extract myself from this conversation without giving him some course of hopeful action. "Well, then, if you must do something, do this: give her some time. Because one thing is certain—the more you push her right now, the more you push her away."

"I am doing that, aren't I? I am pushing her away." He gazed down, blinking hard. He truly loved her; it was clear to see. "Yes, yes, I know I am, but I can't seem to help myself." He blew out a long sigh, looked up at the sky, turned away from me, then turned back. "How long must I wait?"

"At least six months."

"Six months! That is a lifetime."

In this war, it well could be. "You asked me what I thought, Pierre. I cannot help it if you don't like the answer." I rose. "I need to get back to the hotel."

He started to walk with me.

"I can make it on my own," I said. "Good-bye, Pierre. Don't contact me again."

"You don't mean that."

"Oh, but I do. I do." I turned on my heel and walked away.

23

AMÉLIE
1942–43

*O*ver the next year, the German stranglehold on Paris tightened. At the same time, the caliber of soldiers guarding the city declined; the strapping blond warriors who had initially invaded Paris were replaced by older reservists or soldiers with limps or eye patches. Germany was calling up all able-bodied soldiers to fight the Allies on the front.

This did not mean that their rule over Parisians was less harsh. Quite the opposite; citizens were stopped more and more frequently for no reason at all and forced to show their papers. Food, already scarce, became even scarcer. Leather was practically impossible to find, which was a serious issue to me when my shoes wore through the soles. I stuffed cardboard in the bottoms, but it did a poor job in the snow.

Even the weather was brutal. The winter was, again, bone-chillingly cold, with record amounts of snow in Paris.

The worst of it, however, were the reports of what had happened to those captured in the Vel' d'Hiv roundup. All of them had been sent to Auschwitz. Little was actually known about this camp, but it was rumored to be a place of death and horror—the most terrible of the terrible. Yvette consoled me that the stories about the camp were too outlandish to be credible. I could not sleep for thoughts of Joshua suffering or being tortured. I wondered if he were still alive. If he were not, I did not want to be alive, either.

Yvette took up with an officer in the Wehrmacht in late October. Gerhard was highly positioned and clearly smitten with her. He installed her in his rooms at a luxury hotel and he bought her new clothes. She gave me her old shoes, which were a godsend. They were too large, but they tied on top, thank God, which helped me to keep them on my feet. With three pairs of heavy woolen socks—she gave me thick socks for Christmas, which were very dear and hard to find—the shoes actually fit.

In November, the Germans occupied the Zone libre, doing away with the Vichy government and any illusion that France was determining its own fate. Free France had never been truly free, anyway, so there wasn't much difference to the average French citizen. It did mean, however, that there were more soldiers in southern France, and that they kept a tighter eye on the populace. This made things a little more difficult for resistance workers—including me, because I had finally convinced M. Henri to let me serve as a transport.

I had first contacted him and asked to help transport Jewish children to safety. This, I thought, was the only way I could make amends to Joshua.

"The Children's Aid Society is not part of our program," he said. "We assist them when we can, but we are not directly involved." He had given me a very serious look. "You are needed where you are, Amélie. You have moved up at the hotel and it would take us years to replace you. And your calligraphy skills—do you know how many people you have helped?"

I was now spending two hours every Wednesday evening at a convent, forging signatures on identification papers, ration coupons, and travel papers.

"Every time you write the name of an official, you are aiding the cause."

"But I want to do more!" I said. "I now have an entire day off twice a month. I want to use it to help the cause. I can serve as a courier."

"That is dangerous."

"I have no fear." And I didn't, because I felt I had nothing to live for. I was in a depression so deep that everything was colored in shades of gray.

"Alas, that might be a problem." He sighed and rubbed his jaw. "Lack of fear makes one reckless."

I persisted, however, and when they fell into desperate need of a courier—the last one had been caught, the one before had just mysteriously disappeared—they turned to me.

I began traveling, once a month, to Tours, taking information and film. My alibi was that I was visiting my ailing elderly aunt, Tante Beatrice.

Yvette's beau, ironically, helped secure my travel papers. Yvette and I, after all, were legally sisters, so it was a natural favor for him to grant. Indeed, it would have seemed strange for me not to ask him.

There was a problem with that, though: I had to use my real name. Most couriers—indeed, almost everyone working for the underground— used phony names, to prevent those that were captured from turning in other resistance members. I lacked that extra layer of protection.

"It isn't a matter of if, but a matter of when, you will spill information if you are caught," M. Henri told me. He held up his hand as I started to protest. "Do not be insulted by this; professional spies, clergymen, people of the highest training and character . . . they all break under enough pressure. There is only so much a human being can take. God knows this, and so do the Nazis."

"Then I must be extra cautious."

"Yes. You must agree to take no chances."

I agreed, but in those dark days in France, life itself was a chance.

My "aunt," Beatrice Zouet, was far from infirm. She was elderly, to be sure, but she was a lively sprite of a woman who ran a safe house in the country for Resistance workers, occasional downed Allied airmen, and, to my great satisfaction, Jewish children being smuggled to the border of Switzerland.

I was always met at the station by a middle-aged widow, Mme Molin, who gave me a ride in a donkey cart to Mme Zouet's run-down farmhouse, four miles out of town. Mme Molin was the neighbor of my "aunt," and her caretaker—and, if rumors could be believed, her sometimes lover.

"Bonjour, Mme Molin," I greeted her in January. "It is wonderful to see you."

"You too, my dear." We exchanged la bise, and put on a little act for the soldiers and passersby at the station.

"How is Tante Beatrice?"

"Oh, she has been under the weather, I am afraid. But she is slightly better. The doctor came by this morning."

"Her heart again?"

"Yes. And she has a little cold."

"I brought her a poultice for her arthritis." I lifted the large basket I carried. Inside was, indeed, a very smelly concoction—smelly enough to discourage too much investigation by soldiers. Underneath, among the cloths that padded the covered bowl, were the papers I was smuggling.

"How very thoughtful." I climbed into the cart and set the basket on the floor by my feet. The pouch belt hiding the film under my dress rubbed against the hard backboard as I sat down. I leaned forward to ease the pressure as Mme Molin flicked the reins.

Once we were out of town, we could talk more freely.

"Did the doctor really come?" I asked.

"Yes. He was treating a mother and child who jumped off a train headed for the camps. The mother broke her arm. The child just got some cuts and scrapes."

"They're staying at Tante Beatrice's?"

"They were, but it was too dangerous. We transported them to an abandoned house this morning. We'll pass it on the way." The mule turned off the main road, onto a dirt path through a copse of trees. The snow from the last storm had largely melted, but occasional large drifts remained, and the clouds threatened more snow before the day was out. "The SS are looking for her."

"Why?"

"She was a renowned forger. She made excellent papers for many, many Jews, helping them to sneak out of the country. Her escape embarrasses them."

"Eh, bien." The news that the SS were so keen to capture a forger made me squirm on the wooden seat.

"The Nazis have vowed harsh retribution to anyone who helps them. Did you know that they shot four Resistance workers last week?"

"I heard that. I am so sorry."

"They are very intent on finding this woman. They have searched Mme Zouet's farm and been back twice. We are trying to keep a very low profile."

"Perhaps I shouldn't have come today."

"Your visit is expected. If you had not, that would have created suspicion."

As we turned the corner, I heard large dogs barking.

"This is not good," Mme Molin muttered. "The Boches have their dogs out searching. And the house where the woman and child are staying is right ahead."

A low-flying airplane roared overhead.

I gazed up and Mme Molin's weathered forehead creased in a frown as the mule clopped slowly around the bend. As we turned the corner, a woman with her arm in a sling came out of the outhouse.

"Oh, mon Dieu!" Mme Molin gasped. "I told her to stay inside!"

The plane apparently had spotted the woman, as well. It turned and circled back toward us. Mme Molin yanked the mule to a stop under a tree. She tossed the reins to me.

"Wrap these around the tree branch!"

I did as she ordered.

"Get down. Get down!"

I dove to the floor of the cart. Machine gun fire strafed the ground. A loud explosion rocked the cart, causing a flash of red I could see through my closed eyelids.

"Mon Dieu, mon Dieu!" Mme Molin muttered. The donkey was trying to buck, but his tethers to the cart prevented him from rearing, and the reins wrapped around the branch held.

I raised my head. The roof of the house was an orange and yellow blaze.

"My baby! My baby is in the house!" wailed the woman, flapping her good arm. The dried grass around her, as well as her skirt, was on fire.

Mme Molin clamored down from the cart and raced for the house, her black skirt billowing against the snow drifts on the roadside like the wings of a crow. At the same time, a man darted from the woods and knocked the woman to the ground. I first thought he was a Nazi trying to harm her, and then I realized he was putting out her flaming clothes by rolling her.

"My baby! My baby!" the woman cried as the man helped her to her feet.

"What room is she in?" Mme Molin called, peeling off her coat.

"The front."

Mme Molin dipped her coat into a snowdrift by the firewood. Yanking it over her head, she dashed through the front door. A long moment later, she emerged—a screaming child in her arms, under the coat.

The house exploded behind her, throwing them to the ground. My legs shook as I climbed down from the cart to go help them. By the time my foot hit the snow the man had seized the child, grabbed the woman's arm, and hustled them to the woods. I hurried toward Mme Molin and helped her to her feet.

"Are there others in the house?" I asked.

"Perhaps, but it is too late to help now."

"But . . ."

Mme Molin shook out her coat. "We must get back in the cart. The plane will be back and the Boches are undoubtedly in the woods. We must not be spotted here."

"But what about the woman and her child?"

"Leave it to our men. They will hide them. It is best that we do not know anything further."

She was right, of course. We piled back into the cart. I pulled the reins from the branch as Mme Molin yanked on her coat. The donkey raced down the path. Mme Molin let him have his head. He carried us from the burning house as fast as his legs and lungs would let him, racing as if he wished he had wings.

I hung onto the side of the cart, stunned by what I had seen. So quickly things could change! So quickly one must decide to act! And I had sat there like a stone, while Mme Molin and a Resistance worker hiding in the woods had sprung into action.

"Was the woman badly burned?"

"I do not think so."

"The child?"

"No. She was unconscious from the smoke, but quickly found her lungs—as you heard."

We rocked wildly for a while as the mule sped down the road.

"How did the man know to put out the fire on the woman's clothes like that?"

"The local firefighters taught us after the first bombings. If you are on fire, the best thing to do is roll on the ground."

"I never knew that."

"Yes, well . . . war has taught us many things we never thought we would need to know."

Too many, I thought. I had always wondered how I would react in an emergency if someone needed to be saved. There were two types of people, I had always thought—those who jumped into action and those who froze. I was chagrined to learn that I was one of the frozen. "How did you have the presence of mind to take off your coat and put it over your head before you went into the house?"

"Again, it is something I was taught. If I perish of smoke or fire before I save someone else, I will help not the cause. Plus a wet coat is a protection from the fire."

"I was paralyzed by fear."

"It is just as well. Unless you know how to properly assist, you only become one more person who needs to be saved."

I vowed, then and there, that I would not be paralyzed again. If war was a fast teacher, I intended to be a fast learner.

We had to go past the burned house again on the way back to the train station. Thanks to fresh snow, the fire was extinguished, but a cloud of smoke still hovered. The mule balked as we neared it; we had to get down out of the cart and lead him past.

A crowd of townspeople had gathered to gawk at the destruction. One couple, a man with a beard and a woman with a long, gaunt face, greeted Mme Molin, who introduced me as Mme Zouet's niece.

"The Germans are saying that the woman they were hunting was killed," said the woman, in a low voice. "I don't believe it. There were two bodies inside, but they were both men."

"Oh, no," I gasped.

"I think one was René Foret," the man said. "It looked like his boots."

"Oh, poor Hélène." Mme Molin crossed herself. I did the same. "And the other victim?"

"No one yet knows," the woman said.

"Do you think the woman made it to the border?" the man asked.

"I think she made it away from here," Mme Molin said. "That in and of itself is a victory. Only God knows how it will end for her."

Only God knew how it would end for any of us, I thought. I sometimes wondered if anyone would be left alive from this war, or if we would all just kill each other.

AMÉLIE
1943

*T*he train ride home seemed extra long. I leaned against the window, my head bouncing against the glass. Every time I closed my eyes, I saw fire rain down from heaven. I thought of Mme Molin's words, of how we should count any escape a victory, but the math didn't work. Two lives had been lost in the saving of two. And we were by no means certain that the two we'd tried to save were still alive—or, if alive, would make it through the following day.

My heart was heavy. The train was delayed at two stops along the way, and it was very late—well after the nine o'clock civilian curfew—when I arrived in Paris. I stepped out of the train station onto a dark street and headed down the rue Aignon toward the hotel. Three drunk German soldiers staggered out of a tavern.

I tried to walk around them, but they deliberately blocked my path. "Oho! What have we here?" asked one in slurred German.

"Let's see if we can get an evening's pleasure without having to pay anything," said a second. They all laughed raucously, insolently certain I couldn't understand their language.

My heart pattered hard in my chest. The first soldier grabbed my sleeve and leered, his beer breath steaming in the cold night. "Want to have a little fun, mademoiselle?" he asked in heavily accented French.

"No, thank you," I responded.

"That is not how you get cooperation," the tallest soldier said in

German to his peers. "I'll show you how it's done." He turned to me, straightened his cap, and addressed me in bad French. "You are out after curfew, mademoiselle. You are breaking the law."

"I—I just got off the train. Would you like to see my travel papers?"

"No, we want to see your cootch," said the second soldier in German.

They all laughed uproariously.

Fear welled up in my chest. I pretended not to understand. "I am heading back to my residence."

"And where is that?"

"The Hotel Palais."

"Oh, you live at a hotel?" Their eyebrows shot up. They looked at each other and laughed.

"I work as a maid there," I said, wanting to shoot down any ideas that I was a hooker or kept woman.

"Oh, a maid, eh?" The tall one leered. "So you make all the beds? Want to straighten my sheets?"

The other soldiers laughed and elbowed each other.

"Please—I just want to go home," I said.

"Well, then, you need to be very nice to us."

My mouth went dry. "I—I am being nice."

"No, you're aloof. What are you carrying in the basket?"

"I took a poultice to my great aunt for her arthritis."

"Arthritis?"

Apparently he didn't understand the French word for it. "She has aches and pains."

"I have an ache you can treat," said one of the other soldiers in German.

They all laughed. I edged away.

"Hey, hey, hey—come back here," said the tall soldier. "No need to be so standoffish." He pulled me roughly toward him. "Let us see what you're wearing under that coat." He pried at my top button. His finger touched my neck.

I don't know what came over me. I didn't think; I just acted. I jerked up my leg and kneed him in the groin.

"Ow!" He released me to grab his crotch. As the other two soldiers laughed, I turned and started to run, but I wasn't quick enough. The soldier I'd hurt snatched my arm and spun me around. The next thing I knew, I felt cold metal on the back of my head.

"You little whore," he snarled.

The gun cocked. I closed my eyes and thought of Maman.

"Wait, Kyler," said one of the other soldiers in German. "If you kill her, we'll have to file a report. We don't want to mess with that this late."

"Yeah." The second soldier lurched on the pavement. "Let's just go have another drink."

For a long moment, my life hung in the balance, as Kyler weighed the merits of revenge for his sore crotch versus the inconvenience of paperwork. Apparently I wasn't worth killing, because at length he hurled me from him.

I fell to the pavement, breaking my pot and skinning my knee.

"This is your lucky night, you French slut," he growled. "But I'll be watching for you, and you won't get off so lightly next time."

I scurried down the dark street toward the hotel, holding my breath that I wouldn't encounter any more soldiers. I let myself into the side door, then stood in the hallway, catching my breath.

Isolde came by, carrying her soap and shampoo out of the bathroom.

"There you are! I was beginning to wonder if something had happened to you."

"No," I replied. "Just a long train ride."

"How was your aunt?"

"A little under the weather. The poultice seemed to help a bit."

"Good. Well, nothing much happened here, either."

"Just another boring day for both of us," I said.

The irony, of course, was lost on her. I followed her to our dormitory, feeling very much alone in the crowded room of women.

25

AMÉLIE
1943

*M*y God, Amélie—you could have been raped or killed!" Yvette said a week later when I told her my tale of the encounter with the German soldiers.

I was lounging in a chaise in the hotel suite where Yvette now lived, drinking real coffee. I don't know when I'd last had real coffee. Her hotel was very swank and served only the extremely wealthy or extremely high-ranking Wehrmacht officers.

Yvette's German *protecteur* was both. She routinely gave me food left over from her sumptuous meals with him, food that she rolled into napkins and stuffed in her handbag.

"Have another cookie, ma petite. You are so very skinny!"

"I know, I know." I looked down at my rail-thin frame. "At least it's not much of a change for me. But you—you looked ill when you lost so much weight."

"It is good to not be hungry. But sometimes I think I'd rather chew off my arm than spend another night doing some of the things that Gerhard . . ." She broke off her words and lit a cigarette.

"Tell me," I urged.

"I find it hard not to recoil when he touches me," she confided. "And when he kisses me or asks me to do certain things, I fight the urge to retch. And sometimes, he ties me to the bed, and . . ." She inhaled a puff of smoke, then waved her hand. "But it does not matter. I am providing the Résistance with important information. I remind myself of that every day. And the war is turning in our favor."

"Really?"

"Yes. The Boches won't admit it, of course, but the battle of Stalingrad was a major defeat. And the Allies are bombing the hell out of Germany."

"France, too."

"*Oui.*" We sat there, somber. The hard truth was that the British and the Americans—the very armies trying to save us—were bombing German targets in France, but there was often collateral damage. It was a horrible fact of war. Paris itself was spared, but nighttime strikes sometimes hit the suburbs.

"So." Yvette tapped her cigarette on the side of an ashtray. "How is work at Hotel Palais?"

"Much the same as ever, except the soup is even thinner. And one of my roommates disappeared."

"What do you mean, disappeared?"

"Just that. She went out on her day off, and she did not come back."

"Was she working for the Resistance?"

"No. At least, I can't imagine that she was."

"Was she Jewish?"

"Again, I think not, but who can be sure of anything these days? She was supposedly from Lyon. I have wondered if she ran into the same soldiers I ran into, with a different result."

"There are many things that could have happened to her."

"All of them bad."

"Perhaps not. Perhaps she escaped to America."

"Ha!"

Yvette took a drag from her cigarette. "That is what we should do when the war ends."

"Go to America?"

"Yes! It is the land of opportunity. France will be poor for a long time to come."

"Oh, don't say that! When we are liberated . . ."

"We will still be poor and hungry. All of France will be poor and hungry for many years. That is what happened after the Great War. Besides, where are we to live after the war?"

"I have no idea."

"I have been thinking about it a great deal." Yvette exhaled a puff of smoke. "You and I need to go to America and make a fresh start."

"How will we get there?"

"We will save our money and buy tickets. Or we will fall in love with American soldiers and marry them."

"My heart will always belong Joshua."

"That is what you think now. Once I thought that of Pierre."

"And now?"

"He is dead to me." She took a long pull from her cigarette. "He came to see me last week."

"And?"

"I told him if he didn't leave, I would tell Gerhard and have him arrested." She flicked her cigarette over an ashtray. "He asked about you, Amélie. He still loves you."

"He loves no one but himself."

"Perhaps. But, still, Amélie . . . he is your only family."

"No." I reached and out gripped her hand. "I have you."

"Yes." She smiled as she squeezed my fingers. "We are sisters—and we have the papers to prove it. But you must go. Gerhard will be here soon."

"And he won't like to find me here?"

"*Au contraire*. He would like it too much. He wants you to join us in a ménage à trois."

"Very funny!" I stopped short at the look on her face. "Mon Dieu. You aren't kidding!"

She tilted her head. "He has some very odd ideas about lovemaking."

My chest tightened. "Oh, Yvette! Does he—does he hurt you?"

"Not too much." She looked away. "Not too often, anyway. And I have learned much valuable information."

My expression must have conveyed my alarm, because she smiled.

"It is okay. He is leaving next week. He does not know I know, but of course, I do."

"What will you do?"

"I have met another officer who can greatly help our cause. He and I have already talked."

"Is this someone you could love?"

She gave a wry grin. "I hope not; he is already married. Besides, love has nothing to do with it. He holds a very strategic position. It will be a bonus if he is kind." She ground out her cigarette and rose. "But enough. You must leave."

She wrapped the extra cookies in a handkerchief, tucked them in my purse, and walked me to the door. "Take care, *ma soeur.*"

We exchanged la bise. I walked away, my eyes strangely wet. Regardless of outside appearances, Yvette was sacrificing as much for France as the men fighting in the trenches. The difference was, they were lauded, while she was scorned.

26

AMÉLIE
1943–mid-1944

*O*ver the next year and a half, life in Paris became grimmer, harder, hungrier. The people of Paris were gaunt, beaten down, fatigued, and ill. Resentment bubbled up in small ways that the increasingly harsh occupiers crushed with unreasonable cruelty. Not only were Jews, Gypsies, and other "undesirables" rounded up and carted away; so were ordinary French citizens, often for acts of rebellion as benign as singing "La Marseillaise."

The winter was, again, desperately cold. Coal and wood were next to impossible to find. At my hotel, the servant quarters of the hotel were no longer heated. All warmth was saved for the paying guests.

It seemed as though there were two Parises: the gray, miserable, oppressed one of the ordinary citizen, and the beautiful bright one filled with gaiety and music and delicious food, the Paris now almost exclusively inhabited by German officers and their collaborateurs. It was a cruel trick of fate that those living in the first Paris had to catch frequent glimpses of those in the second. Anger seethed—especially when they saw the enemy eating more food in one meal than their entire family had for a week—building like black jealousy in a lover's heart.

Yvette, alas, inhabited the Paris of plenty—and even I, who knew her motivations and how she hated it, at times found myself resentful. On the surface, it seemed a world of privilege, but I knew that she, too, had problems, problems too dark and tormenting for her to fully tell me.

She did, indeed, seem much happier with her new "beau"—although she found it difficult to hold her tongue.

"I swear, Amélie, sometimes I just want to scream when his officer buddies are gabbing away. I hate the way they talk about us, as if the French are inferior to the almighty German, as if our only purpose is to serve them. As a Frenchwoman, they think I should just look nice and give them compliments and be sexy in bed." She waved her cigarette. "I remind myself often that my real role is to gather information about their plans and movements. But I have nearly given myself away half a dozen times just because they make me so angry."

I'd had another close call, myself. I'd been photographing a map when I heard the key fit into the door. I managed—just barely!—to put the map away before the door opened, but all I could do with the camera was tuck it under the bed. To my dismay, the officer was drunk and very amorous. I pretended to go along—I actually let him kiss me!—then told him I needed to use the restroom before we made love. I retrieved the camera from under the bed and carried in my palm as if it were a little clutch, mimicking the way I'd see Yvette coyly leave a table to go touch up her lipstick. The officer was too inebriated to realize that a maid wouldn't carry a purse—or to realize that the door I exited led not to the bathroom, but to my escape down the hall.

27

KAT
2016

*A*ll of your adventures were very exciting, I'm sure, but when will we get to the part where you met Jack?" The day is wearing on. So is my patience.

"Adventures? You think I'm relating adventures?" Amélie leans forward, her eyes sharp and flashing. "You think that starving, freezing, working my fingers to the bone, always in danger, sleeping in a room like a cell, trying to just stay *alive*, for God's sake—was an *adventure*? You think that living under the thumb of *les Boches*, seeing people treated with unbelievable cruelty, mourning my loved ones, and standing in endless lines for everything was an *adventure*?"

There she goes again, with her Gallic overexaggeration. I sigh and put down my coffee cup. "Well, you certainly make it all sound very . . . dramatic."

"Really? You think scrubbing toilets is dramatic?"

I shrug. "I would like for you to get to the point."

"We will get there at my speed, in my way. Since you again interrupted, it is your turn to talk. So tell me . . . what were you doing in 1943?"

Nineteen forty-three, nineteen forty-three . . . that was the year after the U.S. entered the war. I search through the archives of my memory. "I was in college."

"College! Oh, you were very fortunate. Where did you go?"

"To LSU in Baton Rouge. Daddy insisted I go to his alma mater, although I wanted to go to Newcomb, because by then, Jack was in medical school in New Orleans." The wheels of time seem to be spinning backward.

"Were you in a sorority?"

"Yes, but it wasn't all fun and games as you probably suppose. We did a lot of work for the war effort. We raised money and collected rubber and tin, and we tended a victory garden."

"That was very noble of you."

I am not certain if she is sneering at me, or if *noble* is just the odd word choice of a foreigner. I suspect the former. "My war experience was very different than yours," I concede. "America wasn't invaded or occupied, but we were fighting the Japanese as well as the Germans, and we were very worried about the future. Our men were on both sides of the globe, and we had shortages and rationing, too."

"Yes, but your rationing still allowed a family to be fed. There was milk for the children."

"We were in better shape than you, but we were still sacrificing."

"You know nothing about sacrifice."

"Oh, no?" Anger flashes through me, hot and fast as lightning. "We sacrificed our sweethearts and husbands and sons to save your sorry French asses."

"I beg your pardon?"

Oh, dear, I shouldn't have said that. Sometimes words come out that I only mean to think. And yet I am furious. "It makes me angry to think of red-blooded Americans dying to help you people with your slatternly morals."

"What?"

"Well, let's face it. There was a lot of loose living in France."

"Why on earth would you think that?"

"From what you've told me. And from what everyone knows about life in Paris. And from what happened with you and Jack."

She sits up as if the back of her chair has sprouted spikes. "I'll have you know I was a virgin when I met Jack."

I flick my wrist dismissively. "Oh, maybe you convinced him you were."

"He was a doctor! He knew about these things."

"Oh, please. I've heard of the tricks you continental women used—tightening powders and chicken blood and such."

"What?" Her eyes are round with incredulity, her face so surprised, it surprises me. And then she tosses back her head and laughs. "Good heavens! Is that what you think?"

Yes, it is exactly what I think—what I've always thought. I am certain Amélie was an experienced seductress who lured Jack into her bed. But I am angry, and I am saying things best kept to myself. I force myself to take a deep breath. "I am sorry. I am probably speaking out of turn."

"I would say so!"

"I find . . . I don't always think before I speak these days."

"Yes, well, that can be understood."

We sit there for a moment, silently acknowledging the indignities of advanced age. It is a strangely unifying common denominator between us.

"Let's begin again," she says. "You were telling me about 1943."

"Yes." I draw another calming breath, and just as quickly as it hit, the fury leaves. "I was in college, and Jack was in a special expedited education program sponsored by the army. The military was desperate for doctors. They paid for all his schooling and sped everything up. Jack finished his undergraduate degree in two and half years, going year-round with hardly any breaks, and medical school in about the same. It was very difficult, very intense." I could see him in his uniform, so tall, so handsome.

"He was due to graduate May 1944. He proposed the Christmas of 1943."

Amélie's poised expression seems to crumble a little bit. "How did he propose?"

I have always wondered the same thing about Jack with her. If I tell her what she wants to know, hopefully she will tell me. If, that is, she ever gets around to talking about Jack.

"He wrote to my father and asked for my hand." I have sometimes wondered if he and my father weren't closer than he and I. Jack would often write one letter to the two of us, and most of the information would be aimed at my father. But that is not the story I am telling.

Daddy kept it secret, of course, but I had an inkling. My mother couldn't help from dropping little hints. It was on Christmas Eve. We had been to a party at the mayor's house, and Jack had accompanied us back to my parents' home. He told my parents he wanted to give me my Christmas present early. My parents left us alone in the parlor.

"'Let me get your gift,' I said to Jack, thinking this was to be our gift exchange.

"'That can wait.' He took my hand and pulled me to the settee. I sat down. And he got down on one knee and asked if I would do him the favor of becoming his wife." I giggle at the memory. The favor! As if he were asking to borrow a cup of sugar. I had thought it was so funny.

"Well of course, I was so happy, I couldn't speak. I just nodded with a big lump in my throat. And then I threw my arms around his neck and he kissed me, and then I dashed out of the parlor, nearly banging into Mother and Daddy—I think they'd been listening at the door. 'Guess what?' I told them. 'I'm engaged!'"

"I assume that meant Jack was, as well," Amélie interrupts.

"What? Of course."

"You said *you* were engaged."

"Well, they were *my* parents."

"I see." She gives a dry smile that can't mean anything good.

I feel the bile of resentment and dislike flood my mouth. She is trying to imply that I made it all about me. Oh, dear—had I? The question briefly flickers in my mind before I dismiss it.

"They were very happy about it, I am sure," she says.

"They were thrilled. Daddy already had champagne chilling—as Baptists, we hardly ever drank, but this was a very special occasion. Daddy popped the cork, and it flew across the room. And Daddy toasted to our wonderful lives together, and Jack toasted me, saying he was the luckiest man ever, to be getting such a beautiful bride and marrying into such a wonderful family."

I sigh, remembering. I had felt as if I were dancing on clouds. It had been the happiest night of my life.

"Why didn't you marry right away?" Amélie asks.

"Well, we needed time to plan the wedding, of course."

"Of course," she repeats in that dry way of hers.

"Plus Jack was still in school until May. He was at the teaching hospital around the clock—they worked the interns and residents to death. They slept on cots in closets and were constantly on call. And Jack's salary as an army major wasn't enough to really establish a household."

"I see," says Amélie, in that quiet, shrewish way that seems like an insult.

"And we already knew he was shipping out as soon as he graduated. Daddy thought it best I stay in college, and married women couldn't live in the dorms.

"And my mother . . . well, she had another reason she wanted me to wait. I was her only child, and she wanted only the best for me. 'What if he's terribly wounded?' she said. 'You might not want to be saddled for life to a man who is disfigured or loses a leg or is an invalid.'

"I was horrified. He was to tend the wounded, not get wounded himself! What was she thinking, to suggest such a thing could happen? I told her in no uncertain terms that I would always love Jack regardless of what condition he returned in.

"Of course, at that point, I never dreamed that he might return already married." I give Amélie a pointed look. "With a baby."

Amélie has the grace to look down.

"That's the part of the story I really want to know about," I press. "How did he come to marry you?"

"I am almost there. If you would like for me to continue . . ." Her eyebrows lift to an empirious high.

Oh, she is so aggravating! The words are bitter on my tongue. "Yes. Please."

"Very well." She rises from her chair in a fluid movement. "Would you like coffee or tea?"

"I—" I start to say I don't need a drink; I need her to get to the point. But my hospice counselor's words echo in my ear as I watch her walk to the kitchenette: *Patience and kindness, Miss Kat. Patience and kindness are the golden tickets.* "Tea, please."

She nods and settles the kettle on the stove. "I was about to tell you about the Normandy landing."

Finally, we are getting somewhere. "Jack shipped over to arrive just after D-day."

"Yes." She opens a cabinet and lifts out two china cups and saucers. She places them on a tray, along with cream and sugar, two spoons, and cloth napkins. She carries them over and sets them on the coffee table.

"He left just after his graduation," I say. "I was there, of course—at his graduation. My parents and I went to New Orleans and stayed at the Roosevelt Hotel. I was so terribly, terribly proud of him. He shipped out two days later with a Medical Corps unit. We learned later that it reached France right behind the Normandy landing."

"You did not make love with Jack before you sent him off to war?"

"Why—no!" The question stuns me. "No, of course not! I was not that kind of girl. Jack didn't ask . . . he didn't expect . . ." What did she think I was? In her world, I was probably a prude.

"Why, we hardly had any time alone together!" I sputter. "Besides, I was saving myself for marriage. That was the way it was done. That was what was expected."

"By Jack?" She looks at me intently. "You discussed this?"

"No. It needed no discussion. It was just how things were."

"Ah." She gives that small smile I find so annoying, then heads back to the kitchen, lifts the kettle from the stove, and pours boiling water into a little teapot with a single tea bag in it. I sigh; I should have known better than to let a Frenchwoman make me tea.

"You told him not to send you a breakup letter," Amélie says as she pours boiling water into a coffee carafe with a complicated press.

"It was a joke. I was teasing him, reversing the cliché." I sit and tap my toe, waiting for her to carry the carafe and teapot over to the table. She finally does. She leans forward and carefully pours me the weakest tea I have ever been served, outside of a Chinese restaurant. The cup, however, is thin as an eggshell, rimmed in gold with blue and purple flowers. It is absolutely stunning. So is the elaborate, heavy sterling teaspoon.

"You were about to tell me about the Normandy landing," I prompt.

"Yes," she says. "Yes, I am about to get to that part of the story."

God help me, I think, helping myself to a large spoonful of sugar. This story might take longer than the time I have left on earth.

28

AMÉLIE
1944

The Resistance became more organized and more effective as time went on. In large part it was because everyone listened to the BBC French broadcast from London. The Germans tried to scramble the signal, but they were never able to snuff out the broadcasts.

French citizens were not allowed to have radios, of course, but we all knew someone who had one, hidden in a washroom, a closet, or a pantry. The hotel had several radios for the Germans to use, and those radios always found their way to the French broadcast at night.

Over the airwaves, the British would send secret messages to the Resistance through the programming. *Jean has a very long mustache* might be a key for a southern pocket of the Resistance to block the train tracks in order to thwart a Nazi shipment of arms. The secret obscure messages became more frequent.

Acts of open sabotage against the Germans accelerated. The Boches retaliated by carting off large groups of French citizens, executing them and publicizing the punishment to halt further insurrection.

It did not stop us; it only made us more stealthy. We knew that the Allies were planning an invasion. The question was when, and where.

The Germans knew it was coming, too. They grew nervous and unsteady. Sometimes they ignored insults and bad behavior from the citizenry; at other times they responded with brutal force and twitchy trigger fingers.

I continued to serve as a courier. The need to get information to the Resistance had increased.

I met with Yvette less frequently. We were careful not to discuss specifics, but we shared general information. We usually talked as we walked along the Seine.

"The Germans are scared," she told me. "They believe the Allies' invasion will happen any day now."

"Mon Dieu, I hope it comes soon."

"I believe we will be singing by autumn."

I smiled. "So I have heard."

The code that the invasion was two weeks away would be the first line of the poem *"Chanson d'automne"*—"Song of Autumn."

"So tell me—how is your officer?"

"He is very sweet, actually."

"A sweet Nazi?"

"He is not at all like the last." She pulled out a cigarette and offered me one. I shook my head; I had only toyed with smoking, and now that everything was so scarce, I was glad I'd never taken to it. It was one less thing to yearn for. Bad enough to long for food.

Yvette lit a match and put it to her cigarette. "He is in love with me."

"How could he not be?" I teased.

"No, I mean it. He truly loves me." Her voice was very matter-of-fact, as if she were saying the sky was blue. "He loves me the way I loved Pierre."

The mention of my brother's name was a little dagger to my heart. "Do you still?"

"No." She lifted her shoulders and took another puff. "But perhaps I am still in love with the image I had of him as a little girl."

"You had a crush on him when we were younger?"

She nodded, then looked away, uncharacteristically shy for a girl who was usually so bold and confident. "Remember when we used to play house?"

My thoughts slipped back. We couldn't have been more than six or seven years old. Pierre always played the father, going off to work and teaching classes, and Yvette was the mother. Thomas and I were the children, relegated to taking orders, misbehaving, and being punished.

"I used to believe it could be that way. That we would be a couple like that we when grew up."

I had not realized she'd harbored any such dream. I had thought we'd told each other everything. Evidently not.

"When we started writing, after he joined the army and went away—well, I realized I'd been waiting my whole life for him to notice me. I think I was only interested in other boys as a way to try to attract his attention." She flicked away the ash of her cigarette. "But I was in love with a fantasy of Pierre instead of the real man. The real Pierre . . ." She broke off. "I shouldn't say bad things about your brother."

"He is no longer my brother," I said staunchly. "I have no brothers left."

We walked a while in silence.

"What about your Nazi?" I asked.

"Dierk is not really a Nazi."

Oh, no; she had gone over to the enemy!

My face must have looked as horror-stricken as I felt, because she grinned. "Do not look at me like that. It is not what you think."

"Then what is it?"

"I have learned that not all German soldiers are Nazis."

"You have been brainwashed."

"No. Dierk is German, yes. He is a soldier, yes. But he does not believe the Nazi doctrine and is not a member of the Nazi party. He is as horrified as we are at what is happening to the Jews and Gypsies and crippled."

"So why does he fight for them?"

"He fights for his fatherland, as his father and grandfather and great-grandfather and generations of family before him fought for their home. As our forebearers fought for France—for Napoleon, for example. If you recall your history lessons, he invaded other countries—countries who no doubt felt about the French as we feel about the Germans."

She drew another drag from her cigarette. "Dierk has a good and decent heart. Under any other circumstances, he would be an admirable man. His character—what he is like at the core—is steady and fair and intelligent, thoughtful and patient and, yes—I will say it—kind."

"Now I have heard everything," I said.

"German soldiers are just like French soldiers. They can be kind, they can be cruel. We all have both within us. It is a matter of what predominates. And in Dierk . . . he looks for the good in others. He wants to treat others well."

"You sound like a woman in love."

"No. I do not think I have it within me to love again. And I am well aware that he is the enemy. Even if he weren't, he is a married man—the father of three children, no less! Three children he adores—and he is cheating on his wife. And yet . . . he tries to give as much as he takes."

"From whom?"

"From everyone. But especially from me." She blew out a perfect circle of smoke.

"In the bedroom?" I questioned, frankly curious.

"Yes. Especially there."

We had never had the frank conversation about this that I longed for. "So what is it like?"

"It is good. Amazing, actually."

"Better than with Pierre?" What was I asking? I quickly added, "Not that I want details."

"Dierk is a generous lover. He understands a woman and he knows what he is doing. He seeks my pleasure before his own." Her hand arched gracefully as she tapped ash from her cigarette. "He is the type of man a woman could build a life with. He is not a perfect man, certainly, but he has many excellent qualities. I wonder if his wife knows how fortunate she is."

"It certainly sounds as if you love him."

"I enjoy his company. I like him. He gives me great pleasure. But all the same, I spy on him and his friends. I work to thwart his plans. I use him."

"He uses you, too."

"It truly does not feel that way. I have awakened to see him watching me when I sleep, his eyes full of tenderness."

"Does M. Henri know that you feel this way?" I said sharply.

"He knows that Dierk loves me."

"Does he know that you reciprocate?"

"I don't." She frowned at me. "Truly, I do not. I fear that the part of my heart that can love a man has been crushed forever. The only emotion I feel for him is this: I am not as full of hate as I should be." She tossed the cigarette to the pavement and ground it out with her foot. "That does not mean I will not kill him in his sleep if I am told to do so."

"Could you?"

"Yes. I would regret it, but yes." She sighed. "As I said, I am not as full of hate as I should be."

"There are no hard-and-fast rules," I said.

"But there should be, don't you think? There should be just a few. Simple ones, such as if you are French, you should hate all German occupiers. And I do hate them, collectively. It is on an individual basis that things become muddy."

I turned this over in my mind long after we went our separate ways. Was liking an individual German officer any worse than despising a member of your own family?

In the eyes of God, perhaps they are separate sides of the same coin.

29

AMÉLIE
June 5, 1944

"Did you hear it?" Tante Beatrice asked the moment she opened the door for me.

"Hear what?" I stepped inside, the onions and sulphur in the poultice wafting around me like the odor around soft cheese. The new bowl inside the basket did not contain the smell as well as the previous one—or perhaps the warmer weather was to blame.

"The BBC broadcast." The elderly woman's eyes gleamed with excitement. "'Wound my heart with a monotonous languor.'"

I was certain that Mme Zouet had lost her mind.

"Oh, mon Dieu!" gasped Mme Molin. "At last, at last! It's really about to happen!"

"What's about to happen?" I asked, feeling like a child whose parents were talking above my head.

"The Allies are coming! 'Wound my heart with a monotonous languor' is the second line of 'Chanson d'automne.'"

My heart raced. About ten days ago, the BBC had broadcast the first verse: "Long sobs of autumn violins." That was to put the Resistance on alert that the Allied invasion would happen within two weeks.

Mme Zouet had already taken my basket and was lifting my shirt to undo my waist packet. "You need to turn around and go right home."

"What? Why?"

"Because Pierre Manquin rode by wearing a green shirt, and I heard that the Curvaises had a green kerchief tied around the basket of acorns by their door."

"Plan vert!" cried Mme Molin.

Again, I felt like the left-out stepchild. "Which is?"

"It's a signal for the Résistance to sabotage the railroad system."

"Which railroad?"

"Only those who are to do it know. But you should get home as soon as possible, in case it is yours."

"Perhaps I should stay here," I said. The thought of tanks and guns and man-to-man combat—or of the Luftwaffe bombing the Allies, or the Allies bombing the Germans—seemed more terrifying in a city setting than in the country.

"No. We will need ears in Paris. You must leave now."

"Won't people think it is strange if I leave as soon as I arrive?"

"Simply say that I have a contagious rash and you were afraid you would catch it."

"That will work?"

"Like a charm," said Mme Molin. "If there's anything the Germans fear, it's illness."

Mme Molin drove me back to the station and I caught the first train back to Paris, hugging the knowledge to myself like a secret love. The Allies were coming! I wondered who else knew.

Right before the Toulouse stop, a small Frenchman from the side of the car ambled up and sat down beside me. "I love to sing in the autumn, don't you, Mademoiselle?"

I did not know if it was a trap. I kept my eyes straight ahead. For all I knew, he worked for the Germans. "I love music year-round," I said carefully.

"Yes, but especially in the autumn, *n'est-ce pas*?"

"I do not know what you mean."

"I see you on this train every few weeks."

"I go to visit my ailing aunt."

"Of course you do."

I did not like the slyness in his eye. "What about you? Why are you on the train so often?"

"I go to the country to trap."

With food so scarce, it was not an uncommon thing for Parisians to do. "What do you trap? Rabbits? Doves? Squirrel?"

He leaned forward as the train jerked to a halt. The motion of the train threw him into an intimate closeness. "Germans," he whispered, then rose and bounded off the train.

I watched him go. Such boldness was dangerous to us all, yet I could understand the emotion that prompted it. Over the next twenty-four hours, I was almost feverish with excitement, sneaking away to see if the radio was on. I could not believe so many people could keep such a wonderful and momentous secret. I wondered if perhaps Tante Beatrice and the stranger on the train were wrong.

The next morning, the Germans were somber and talking low. I passed by the radio room, and was delighted to see it strewn with coffee cups and beer steins. Straightening it up gave me an excuse to go in and listen.

Several German officers were huddled around the radio, their arms folded, their faces stern. The radio was set to the BBC, which was blaring in English. I, of course, pretended not to understand a word.

One of the junior officers was translating the English broadcast into German for his grave-faced superiors:

> *Supreme Allied Headquarters have issued an urgent warning to inhabitants of the enemy-occupied countries living near the coast. The warning said that a new phase in the Allied Air Offensive had begun. Shortly before this warning, the Germans reported that Havre, Calais, and Dunkirk were being heavily bombarded and that German naval units were engaged with Allied landing craft.*

I carried a tray of dirty glasses to the kitchen, trying hard not to smile. I went by the radio room again at mid-morning. *"D-day has come,"* the announcer said. I couldn't hear the next part because of the hubbub the Germans made following the translation. At length they quieted down, and I heard the following:

> *Under the command of General Eisenhower, Allied naval forces, supported by strong air forces, began landing Allied armies this morning on the northern coast of France.*

Again, an uproar obscured the broadcast. I picked up coffee cups that were closer to the radio.

> *The Allied Commander-in-chief General Eisenhower has issued an order of the day addressed to each individual of the Allied Expeditionary Force. He says, "Your task will not be an easy one. Your enemy is well trained, well equipped, and battle-hardened. He will fight savagely. But this is the year 1944. The tide has turned. The free men of the world are marching together to victory. I have full confidence in your courage, devotion to duty, and skill in battle. We will accept nothing less than full victory. Good luck, and let us all beseech the blessing of Almighty God upon this great and noble undertaking."*

I scurried from the room, my head down to hide my smile.

"What is going on?" Isolde asked me at lunch. "The Germans are all worried-looking and solemn."

My mouth itched to spill the news. It should not to come from me, however. I could not risk it.

"Maybe the Allies have landed," one of the assistant cooks said.

"Oh, do you think?" Isolde asked.

I hurried back to work, not trusting myself to keep my mouth buttoned.

Later that afternoon, I heard some high-ranking German officers talking in a meeting room as I swept the service hallway.

"Where was the führer during this landing?"

"Asleep at the Eagle's Nest in Berchtesgaden," said the second officer. "He left orders not to be disturbed, and no one dared wake him."

"I can understand. I would rather face hell itself than Herr Hitler's rage."

"His rage *is* hell itself."

"No. I fear hell is what is happening on the north coast—and what we are in for from here on out," said the third.

"What of Rommel? He's there on the coast. He could have directed the armored forces into action."

"He dared not," the first officer said. "The führer is the only one with that power, and he was asleep."

"We had units on hand that fought."

"Yes, but it was not enough. All of the tanks should have rolled into action immediately."

———

I sent word to Yvette to meet me. She, of course, had already heard the news. We hugged like giddy schoolgirls. "It has finally happened!" she said.

"It is just a matter of time now," I said.

"Chérie, we must think of what we will do when the war ends."

"What do you mean?"

"Well, do you want to work at the hotel for the rest of your life?"

"Of course not!"

"I have an aunt in America—my mother's youngest sister. I think we should go live with her."

"And leave France?" I could not imagine leaving my country, after working so hard to liberate her.

"Just for a while. Until things improve."

"They will improve once the Nazis leave."

"I will need a fresh start, Amélie." She looked at me with somber eyes. "I will need to put this behind me."

She was right, I realized solemnly. Yvette was likely to suffer reprisals for sharing a Nazi's bed, even though she had done so to help the

Resistance. She would benefit from a long voyage. No doubt I would, as well.

"When the Nazis no longer read our mail, I will write to her, and we will make our plans." Yvette bounced on the balls of her feet. "Oh, it's so wonderful that the war is finally, truly about to come to a close!"

"It is not over yet," I cautioned. "The Allies have only just now landed. *Il ne faut pas vendre la peau de l'ours avant de l'avoir tué.*"

30

KAT
2016

$\mathscr{I}$ cannot help but interrupt her. "What the hell does that mean?"

"Literally, 'Don't sell your pelts before the kill.'"

"I beg your pardon?"

"It's a very old saying from fur traders. It means don't count your chickens before they hatch."

Oh, for heaven's sake. I frown as hard as my Botox will allow. "Why didn't you just say that?"

"Because it is my story to tell." She leans forward and pours more coffee into her cup. "So. What were you doing on D-day?"

"Me? I was saying prayers for Jack. Whom, I would like to point out, you still haven't mentioned."

"He wasn't in France before D-day."

"I know. I don't understand why you didn't start this story with when you met him."

"You don't?" She cocks her head to one side like an inquisitive parrot and looks at me in a knowing way that just makes me want to strangle her.

All right—yes. I do know, actually. I have never really thought about the war from her perspective, and if she is telling the truth—and for all I know, she is completely whitewashing her role and dramatizing everything—her life has been significantly rougher than mine. All the same, if she believes that having a tough time during the war made it all right for her to seduce a man pledged to another, she has another think coming.

But patience is the key to getting the truth out of her. I draw a steadying breath and try to steer her back on track. "I gather you went to the north of France soon after D-day?" She must have, from the timing of the baby.

Her smile is like the Mona Lisa's, slight and enigmatic. "I will tell you in due time. Since you halted my story, however, I would like to hear, please, about your life after Jack left. Did you suspect that he was supporting the Allied landing?"

"Daddy did, when he heard the news."

June 6, 1944

My father shook me awake from a sound slumber—I had been at my friend Mary's house until late the night before, me and two other girls. We had played charades and drunk some wine—Mary was a Presbyterian, so it was all right by her religion, and I was at her house, so I decided when in Rome, do as the Romans.

We were celebrating the liberation of Rome, after all. The Allies had freed it that very day. It seems that everyone has forgotten about that, but the day before D-day was a huge victory for the Allies. We had gotten the Germans to evacuate Rome without destroying the city—really without much resistance at all. The pope had addressed the crowds and greeted the Allied commanders, and all of Rome was celebrating. We'd celebrated, too, by eating spaghetti and drinking wine.

Anyway, when Daddy woke me the morning of D-day, I was confused and a little fuzzy headed—as a Baptist, I wasn't used to drinking.

"Kat, wake up," Daddy said. "The radio just announced that the Allies have landed in France. I'll bet Jack is with them."

I sat up and rubbed my eyes. I didn't really understand the significance. "But Jack was sent to England."

"That's where the Allies came from," Daddy said. "They crossed the English Channel in the dark and landed on the north coast of France."

I got up, pulled on my bathrobe, and joined my parents in the living room, where the radio was on. New Orleans was seven or eight hours behind Europe time, so we were hearing reports of how many thousand troops had landed, and how many had been killed or wounded.

"They'll need the Medical Corps there right away," Daddy said. "Jack is probably in the thick of it."

That was the first time I feared for Jack's actual safety. "They'll wait until they stop shooting to send in the Medical Corps, won't they?" I asked.

"That's hard to say," Daddy said. "They'll set up a little behind the troops, but I bet he's on one of the ships, just itching to get on land and help."

"Didn't the announcer just say there were submarines bombing the Allied ships?"

My father had served in the First World War, mind you. He never talked about it, so I figured it hadn't been that big of a deal. I assumed that the Medical Corps were kept well out of harm's way.

But now Daddy looked worried. And the fact that my father was worried made me worried.

"It's war, Kat. We have to say our prayers and trust God to take care of things."

Father went to work, and Mother took me to visit my grandmother. She made sure to keep me busy throughout most of the day.

The mayor organized a service in the town square to pray for our servicemen that evening. The high school band played "America the Beautiful" and the national anthem, and a black woman sang "How Great Thou Art" in a way that gave everyone goose bumps. Three different ministers prayed, then everyone went home and listened to their radios. There were several boys from our town whom we suspected had landed on those beaches. One of them, Fred Corrigan, was married to a high school friend of mine—Peggy Hastings. They had dated all through high school and married as soon as he was drafted. They were the kind of couple who just seemed perfect for each other. The kind who seemed to tune out the whole world and only really need each other.

Peggy was crying during the service. "I had a dream last night that Fred came and kissed me good-bye," she whispered. "When I woke up and heard the news . . . oh, Kat, I'm so afraid it was real!"

"It was just a dream," I said, but it spooked me all the same.

"Did you dream about Jack?" she asked.

"No more than usual," I said. But I hadn't ever dreamed about him—not in the entire time I'd known him. I daydreamed, of course. I suddenly wondered if something was wrong with me—if I were somehow lacking.

If God allowed Jack's spirit to stop and say good-bye to just one person as it left the earth, would he come to visit me? He might go to see his mother—or my father. I hated to think it, but I wasn't sure if Jack and I were all that spiritually connected.

But then, I rationalized, Peggy and Fred were married. Once you were married and not just engaged, that's when the two-people-become-one thing would happen.

Like my parents. They were like that, weren't they?

Once again, I was suddenly unsure of something I had never doubted. Now that I thought about it, my father acted more like an indulgent parent toward my mother than a soul mate. He seemed to have more to say to Jack. They had in-depth discussions and laughed at the same things and, of course, had all the medical stuff in common.

I went home and wrote Jack a letter, telling him that I loved him and I was praying for his safety and that I'd had a dream about our wedding, and I just knew it was a sign from God that he would come home safe and sound. I thought that little white lie might reassure him.

When I knelt down by my bed that night, I asked God to watch over Jack and to bring him home soon. And I asked for a dream of Jack, and for Jack to have a dream of me.

I was disappointed the next morning when I could not recall a single dream. But when a dreaded telegram came for Peggy in July—it took weeks for word to reach us about the casualties—I was more than happy that the dream angel had skipped my bedpost.

31

AMÉLIE
June 6–August 1944

*A*ll through Paris that June, the French celebrated the Allied landing. As Brits and Americans fought their way through France over the next few weeks, Parisians who had suffered silently under German repression became emboldened. Street violence increased. Young people tossed Molotov cocktails into Nazi cars. Lone soldiers were shot or beaten on the street. A crowd would spontaneously erupt into rounds of "La Marseillaise."

The Germans were in no mood to humor us—but they seemed baffled as to how to respond. Reprisals were harsh but sporadic. They might do nothing, or they might open fire on a crowd. Life was chaotic, tense, and uncertain.

June stretched into July. On Bastille Day, everyone wore the blue, red, and white of the French flag. More than a thousand citizens gathered in the Place Maubert down the Boulevard Saint-Germain from the Sorbonne, singing and waving improvised French flags. The Nazis did nothing.

A week later we heard that a high-ranking Nazi had made an attempt on Hitler's life, convinced he was the reason the Germans were losing the war. There were whispers it was a conspiracy. As a result, many of the officers in charge of Paris were reshuffled.

German lorries increasingly rolled through the streets, carrying grim-looking German troops and officers to the front or back to Germany.

Incredibly, the roundup of Jews continued. At the hotel, I found orders for seizures of property, plans for raids of neighborhoods, and schedules for convoys to carry Jews from Drancy and Bobigny to Auschwitz, which I immediately reported.

As August arrived, all of Paris seemed stretched on tenterhooks, waiting for what would happen next. Parisians, already restive, grew increasingly violent.

I waited in vain for Yvette to meet me at our usual place, Terrasse du Bord de l'Eau, the last two Tuesdays in July and the first one in August. When she finally showed at our meeting place, she looked pale and sad. "Dierk is leaving," she told me.

"What will you do?"

"I don't know. He said he would get me a job at the hotel restaurant, but even if they hire me, they are sure to fire me as soon as the city is liberated." She drew a cigarette out of her bag. "They despise me for la collaboration horizontale. Are there any jobs at your hotel?"

"They're not hiring right now. When Paris is liberated, perhaps they will."

She gave a derisive snort and put the cigarette to her lips. "When Paris is liberated, I'm likely to be shot as a collaborateur."

My brow knitted in worry. Already, people were spitting at women known to have been mistresses of the Wehrmacht.

"It's not so much that they sleep with the Boches," I'd overheard the laundry supervisor say the previous week at lunch. "I don't really care about that. What I hate is that their tummies are full and fat and happy while my own children are starving." The other people at the table had nodded in agreement.

"Have you encountered much trouble?" I asked Yvette.

She lifted her shoulders. "Some."

I brushed a lock of her hair out of her eyes. "And that is why you are so sad?"

She shook her head. "That is only a small part of it."

My heart stood still for a minute. "Oh, Yvette—you're in love with your Boche after all!"

"No." She lifted her gaze, and I finally saw the depth of her worry. "But I am pregnant by him."

I reflexively clutched my own stomach. "Mon Dieu! Are you sure?"

She nodded. "I just missed my monthly, and last week I started throwing up. I can't even smoke anymore, although I still play with cigarettes." She pulled the unlit cigarette from between her lips and put it back in her purse, the end stained red with lipstick. "Dierk had a doctor check me, and he declared me officially *enceinte*."

"Oh, la! And what does Dierk say?"

"He said he makes pretty babies. He showed me photos of his children." Yvette gave a bittersweet smile. "He is right. They are beautiful."

She sat down heavily on a bench. "I thought about seeing one of the women who do the special operation, but I cannot do it."

"Oh, Yvette." The gravity of her situation pressed down on me. I sank beside her on the bench. "What will you do?"

"After the city is freed and the mail runs again, I will write my aunt. I will see if she can loan us money to go to America."

"That would be so wonderful for you!"

"And you. I will not go without you. Can I give her your address to write back? I have no idea where I will be living a few weeks from now."

"Certainly. But what will you do for food and money and living arrangements in the meantime?" Hildie was no longer an option; she had taken in a boarder to help make ends meet.

"My baby will eat; Dierk has given me a stockpile of powdered formula. And he said he will leave me some money, but he can't leave me much, because his wife needs it, too. He also said he will pay for me to stay at the hotel through the end of the month."

"At least you have that."

"Yes. I'm better off than other women who have just been dumped on the street." We both gazed at the Seine, which was strangely empty of boats. "He was in love with me, you know. He still is, a little."

"I am sure of it."

"But life goes on, does it not? His future is back in Germany, and I am not a part of it."

"Do you mind terribly?"

"I hate that my baby will be a *bâtard*, but personally, I don't mind so much." Her gaze remained fixed on the river. "I will manage. I managed during the worst of it. And because of Dierk, I provided the Resistance with a lot of important information about the movement of supplies to Paris."

In all our conversations, we had never talked about what, specifically, Dierk did. It fell under the rule of ignorance meant protection. "So he works with supplies."

She nodded. "He was one of the top officers in charge of logistics. The Resistance intercepted truckload after truckload of weapons, food, clothing, and artillery based on information I provided."

The importance of this was staggering. "You did a very good thing, Yvette."

"Not everyone will think that. They only know what they saw, which was a woman eating and laughing and sleeping with a German. They believe that is whole truth."

She sat very still for a moment. "Do you think my child will understand and forgive me?"

I put my arm around her. "I'm sure he or she will think you are the finest mother in the world."

Her eyes filled with tears. "Will you help me explain how things were, when it is time?"

"Oh, Yvette! I will help you and your child any way I can. You know I will. We will raise him or her together in America." We stood, and I gave her a hug. "You and I and your baby—we will be a family."

"We already are." She smiled at me. "We already are."

———

I mulled things over for a few days, then decided I should go see Pierre. The war was ending. Perhaps he would repent. If he did, perhaps Yvette would take him back; perhaps he would marry her and take care of the baby as if it were his own.

If that were the case, then perhaps, I, too, could forgive him. Perhaps, when all was said and done, he might even help me learn what happened to Joshua. Perhaps I would discover that he was alive after all.

Perhaps. I knew I was telling myself a fairy tale, one that began with *perhaps* instead of *once upon a time*, but hope was scant, and when hope is all you have, you cling to it like a child to a favorite blanket.

I went to the main police prefecture in the eleventh arrondissement. All of the officers were pulling off their caps and flooding out of the building.

"What is going on?" I asked one.

"We are on strike," he said.

More like trying to save your own skins, I thought darkly. The Nazis were fleeing the city like rats from a sinking ship, and the police were eager to get out of the uniforms that marked them as collaborateurs. I found one policeman still standing behind the front desk, although he was preoccupied gathering up his belongings. "Can you tell me where I can find my brother?" I asked. "His name is Pierre Michaud."

"Sorry, mademoiselle. I do not know."

"Can you look it up?"

"I'm afraid not."

All I knew to do was to go to Pierre's apartment. I had the address, but I had never been. It was in a building far nicer than I would have thought a policeman's salary could provide. I knocked, but got no answer. The concierge was out, so I knocked on the door of his neighbor. A stooped man with a nose like a turnip slowly opened it and peered through a crack.

"Excuse me. Do you happen to know the whereabouts of your next-door neighbor, Pierre Michaud?"

"The policeman?" His face screwed into a tight ball. "He moved back to his fancy family home a few weeks ago."

I felt my heart beat against my ribs. Was it true? Had Pierre been able to regain possession of our home? If anyone could, it would be he. He was the oldest son and therefore the legal heir. Perhaps, if he repented and we forgave him, he would let Yvette and me live there!

I thanked the man and breathlessly hurried to my old neighborhood. The train and Métro workers were on strike, so I walked the entire way, my feet throbbing at the heat of the pavement through the cardboard soles of my shoes. Now that it was summer, I could not bear to wear three pairs of socks to make Yvette's shoes stay on my feet, and had reverted to wearing my own.

When I reached my old home, the familiarity of it made me want to weep. The paint was peeling from the door and a black shutter hung from a hinge—but looking at it, I could still imagine my mother inside, wearing her favorite red apron, cooking dinner. As I climbed the steps and approached the door, I realized that the heavy brass knocker had been removed. I rapped on the wood with my knuckles.

A thin, middle-aged man answered, a pistol dangling from his right hand. "Yes?"

"Bonjour. I am looking for Pierre Michaud."

"You won't find him here."

"Do you know when he will be back?"

"Yes. Never."

"I—I don't understand. This is our home."

"Not anymore, it's not. The deed is in my name, notarized and recorded down at city hall."

"Oh. Oh, my." Tears unexpectedly filled my eyes. I hadn't cried in a long, long time, but having such high hopes, then having them dashed, all within the space of a couple of hours . . . well, it broke something inside me.

He scowled. "Who are you, anyway?"

"Pierre's sister. He—he sold it to you?"

His eyes hardened. "Same as. I won it as a gambling debt. Like I said, it's all registered at city hall."

My heart sank to my feet. "Do you have any idea where he is?"

"No."

"When did this happen?"

"A couple of weeks ago."

He started to close the door. I put my hand on the doorjamb to halt him. He stopped just shy of crushing my knuckles. "What about the furnishings?" I asked.

"Furnishings?" His voice held a mocking tone. "What furnishings?"

He opened the door wider. I saw the faded outline on the gold damask wallpaper where the picture of my grandmother had hung. The sideboard below it, where Maman had stored all her china and silver, was gone, as well. So was the piano across the entry hall—and all the furniture and paintings in the dining room. Only shadows remained. "The thieving Boches took everything."

"But . . ."

"I'm busy, mademoiselle." He started to close the door, then paused. "Look, if I were you, I wouldn't waste my time searching for that worthless brother of yours. I'm pretty sure he's no longer among the living."

"Wh-Why do you say that?"

"The SS came looking for him right after I moved in. Apparently he'd stolen something from one of their officials. They were plenty ticked off and out for blood."

"Did you tell them where to find him?"

"I told them where he liked to play cards." He looked at me, and his cold eyes warmed a couple of degrees. "I'll tell you, too, if you want to know, but I suggest you spare yourself the trouble."

I had to know. I owed it to my parents, to myself, and to Yvette, who had loved him. "Please," I whispered.

"The Silver Cat." He gave me the address. My heart was a hard knot somewhere near my collarbone as I made my way there.

It was a hole-in-the-wall in Montmartre, a dark cave that smelled like sour wine and acrid beer, with round tables surrounded by men playing cards. Every head lifted as I entered. I approached the barkeep, a tall man with pockmarked skin and a stained white apron, and stated my business as efficiently as I could.

"Pierre Michaud? Yeah, I knew him." The bartender ran a dirty rag across the counter. "He was dragged out of here by the SS. Heard them say he was going to wish he'd never been born."

"Do you know where they took him?"

"Does it matter? It's a safe bet he's never coming back."

I nodded my thanks, then left the bar, my eyes full, my head down. This time, I was unable to hold back my tears.

32

AMÉLIE
August 25, 1944

*T*he Allies are coming! The Allies are coming!" The cry echoed through the city as Yvette and I made our way through the thick throng to the Champs-Élysées.

It was a such a relief, so long overdue. The city had descended into anarchy over the previous two weeks. Paris had become a battlefield of haphazard gunfire as citizens took up the resistance cause and the Germans fired back to defend themselves, punish offenders, or simply buy time to escape. The violence was indiscriminate, with both sides firing at each other and into crowds. The carnage was terrifying and shocking.

To my mind, the insurrection of the people of Paris was completely uncalled for, because the Germans were already in retreat. But we had been under the thumb of the Boches for so long—had been so bullied and debased and disheartened—that many people felt the need to take action, even useless action.

They wanted to take back the city themselves. To that end, French citizens dug up street bricks, gathered sandbags, and built barricades. They fired on German soldiers with pistols and hunting rifles, they hurled homemade bombs, and they attacked any Boches foolish enough to go out alone or in pairs.

The violence was still occurring as the Allies marched into Paris and yet, Yvette and I and most of the city poured into the streets and headed to the Champs-Élysées.

"Look—here they come!" Yvette cried.

I tried to stand on tiptoe to see. I had gotten my shoes resoled, but due to the lack of leather, they were soled with wood. Consequently, I couldn't flex my feet, and had to settle for craning my neck to see through the crowd.

First came the French Second Armored Division. They were dressed in American uniforms, riding American Jeeps and tanks, so it was hard to tell that they were French—but when one young man bounded off a tank to hug a girl in a crowd, and another dashed from formation into a drugstore to telephone his mother, we realized they were our boys.

"Oh, isn't it marvelous! Just marvelous!" a woman standing next to me said.

"Papa!" a soldier yelled. He leapt off the back of the Jeep and ran into the crowd. An old man grabbed him by the cheeks and stared at him, then hugged him so hard and tight that the crowd eventually separated them, for fear one was smothering the other.

Yvette was crying. Everyone was crying. I put a hand to my face and realized my cheeks were wet, as well.

"At last. At last. At last!" Yvette kept repeating, grabbing my hand.

Behind the French troops came the Americans. They were for the most part taller and they all sported big, wide smiles.

"Why do the Americans smile so much?" said a lady behind me.

"Because they are happy to be in Paris," I said. "And seeing them here makes me smile, too!"

"Yes," the woman agreed. "Bien sûr, it is a joyous occasion!"

All in all, I have not ever seen—nor felt—such massive exultation, such collective joy, before or since. It was a force unto itself, a power that lightened and lifted us all. It was as if the law of gravity were momentarily suspended. Our hearts all soared like the highest, purest note of an aria, above and beyond us all.

"At last!" Yvette kept saying. "At last!"

Yes, at last—at long, long last.

And yet. And yet.

I am sure I was not alone in being struck, there amidst all the joy, by all that we had lost. Yes, we were liberated from our occupiers—but life would never be restored to "before." No one could ever give us back what the war had taken.

Paris was liberated, and my soul sang a hallelujah—but I couldn't help but wonder what meaning this really held, when everything and everyone that had made Paris my home was gone.

33

AMÉLIE
August 25–September 1944

*T*he euphoria of the Allies' arrival was quickly followed by some of the ugliest days of the war. *L'épuration sauvage*, the savage purge, began almost immediately. The French populace was eager for revenge, and they quickly turned on the collaborators—both those who had actively helped the Boche and those who had been guilty of la collaboration horizontale.

I walked with Yvette back to her hotel, noticing the venom with which she was treated. "*Putain*," a woman cursed as she walked by. *Whore.*

"Collaborateur," muttered another.

"Putain de merde."

By the next day, the crowd had been whipped into a frenzy to do something more than merely name call. I was in my room when a knock sounded. It was a doorman from the front of the hotel. He sheepishly looked down.

"Mademoiselle, the doorman at the Hotel Paris is my friend. He told me your sister has been taken by a mob to the Place de la République."

"Oh, mon Dieu! Why?"

His cheeks grew red. "They are punishing the collaborateurs."

I grabbed my purse and pulled out a coin to tip him.

"No, mademoiselle. I do not want your money. I just thought you would want to know."

"Merci. Merci beaucoup."

He nodded. "*De rien.* I am so sorry. I, too, have a sister, and . . ." He gave little shrug and turned to go.

"Wait."

He turned back around.

"What do you think . . . what are their . . ." I swallowed and asked the fear of my heart. "What do you think they intend to do to her?"

He lifted his shoulders again in an embarrassed shrug. "I do not know."

I changed out of my uniform and hurried to the square as fast as my feet would carry me, leaving word with a fellow maid to please tell the supervisor I had a family emergency. I knew she would not be pleased, but so many maids had simply disappeared or not shown up after yesterday's incredible celebration that I thought I would still have a job.

Through the city, shots still rang out. I do not know if it was fanatical German snipers, the Vichy equivalent of the SS, or a trigger-happy FiFi— a member of the Forces Françaises de l'Intérieur, as the Resistance was now called—but I kept going. I did not think that I was a target. I tried to maintain a profile like the "Brown Mice," as we called the German women who had been office workers under the Wehrmacht; I tried to be unobtrusive and bland and small, to blend in to the environment, to not stand out in any way or call attention to myself.

I heard the rumblings and jeers of the crowd from two blocks away. I turned onto the rue Beaurepaire, and gasped.

A makeshift platform had been set up. On it, three women, stripped to their undergarments, were seated in chairs, their hands tied behind them—as their heads were forcibly shaved.

Two of the *tondeurs*—shearers—were bearded men with cigarettes dangling from their mouths. The third was, shockingly, a woman—a woman with shoulder-length black hair that was curled and coiffed. She yanked her victim's head around by her remaining hair, more roughly than her male counterparts. The poor victim's scalp was nicked with cuts and gashes.

Tears poured down the flaming cheeks of the poor shorn women, who sat, miserably still, not daring to move for fear of their scalps being cut or of angering their captors to commit further violence against them.

They could do nothing but submit. Shame seemed to ooze from their very pores and hovered around them like a cloud of cigarette smoke.

As I watched, one of the tondeurs raised his hand, brandishing his razor in the air. "Voilà!" Two other Frenchmen immediately stepped forward and yanked the shorn victim, a rather flat-chested woman in her mid-thirties, to her feet. A woman from the crowd, a blonde wearing a red dress, ran up the steps, pulled a lipstick from her pocket, and drew a bright red swastika on the woman's forehead.

"There! Do you think a Boche would want to shove his filthy sausage in you now, eh?" the woman asked.

"Putain!" screamed someone in the crowd. "Ugly whore!"

"Just look at your mother, Ursule." The woman who'd painted the swastika—a woman who must have had some kind of axe to grind, I thought—grabbed the victim by the jaw and directed her head out to the crowd. "You are killing her. She is dying a thousand deaths from shame."

I could not see the poor mother in the crowd. The shorn woman on the platform sobbed, her bald head lowered so that I could not see her face.

Another woman wearing only a slip was roughly pulled onto the stage and pushed into the freshly vacated chair. Taunts, rude suggestions, and horrible curses erupted from the onlookers. Horrified, I covered my mouth with my hand and scoured the crowd for Yvette.

I was too short to see above the heads in front of me. Determined, I elbowed my way nearer the platform. At the very front, I saw a man and two women yanking the clothes off a familiar blonde.

"Stop!" I yelled, running toward her, pushing people out of the way.

Hands grasped at me, trying to hold me back. I wrested away and plunged through the crowd until I reached Yvette's side. I tried to pry the woman's hands off Yvette's rose dress—one of Yvette's favorites. It tore as she yanked it off Yvette's back, ripping the fabric.

Someone strong—a man—grabbed me from behind and held me in a choke hold.

"She was with the Resistance!" I gasped, trying to break free from his hold. "She worked for France!"

"She worked for the Germans—on her back," someone called.

The crowd laughed and catcalled.

"She lived at the Hotel Paris, feasting on German food while we starved," said another woman. "Look how plump her breasts are. Her belly was full, while I was too thin to make milk for my baby."

"You don't understand," I said. "She was a spy!"

"The Résistance did not need information on German dicks," said a man.

The crowd roared.

"And you . . ." The man holding me twisted me around to face him. He was older than I supposed, with weather-beaten skin and yellowed whites in his eyes. His breath was foul, scented with garlic, stale cigarettes, and rotten teeth. "I suppose you were a spy as well?"

"I—"

"She's one of them," said the woman who had torn off Yvette's dress. "I've seen her often at the hotel."

I felt the rip of fabric. The next thing I knew, my dress was gone. I stood there in my brassiere and panties. I had dressed quickly and had not put on a slip. I tried to cover myself, but my arms were quickly yanked behind my back. Terror and mortification waged a battle for the upper hand. I feared my pubic hair showed through the front of my panties.

"Please—leave her be!" Yvette pleaded. She was on the stage, being forced to sit in a chair. "She is a good girl. She had nothing to do with the Boches."

"Oh, you call them that, now, eh?" said the woman. "Before you simply called them *chéris*."

The crowd roared again.

"Do what you will with me, but leave her alone," Yvette begged.

She might as well have saved her breath. Rough hands guided me up bricks to the platform and shoved me into a chair. Sweat covered me like a film.

"Open your legs," yelled a man. "Show us what you showed the Krauts."

Oh, mon Dieu. I could not believe this was happening.

Yvette shot me an anguished look as she was forced into the chair beside me. "I'm so sorry," she whispered.

"Such beautiful hair," said the man with the razor, lifting Yvette's blond mane. "Such a shame!"

"*S'il vous plaît.*" Yvette turned and looked at him, her eyes imploring. "*Ayez pitié de nous.*" Have mercy on us.

"Why should he?" called out someone from the crowd.

"Slut. Whore. Collaborateur," hissed the woman who stood behind me, razor in hand. She roughly yanked my hair from my neck. "You are a disgrace to France."

The razor nicked my scalp. I jumped. "The more you move, the more you bleed," the woman said.

I wished that one of the men were shaving me. My *tondeuse* seemed filled with a vitriolic hatred.

"Sit still," Yvette murmured. "It will soon be over."

I folded my hands in my lap and bent my head. As my hair fell in my lap, I grabbed a fistful of it, and clutched it as if it were a magic talisman.

But it was not over after the shearing. The men piled *les femmes tondues*, about ten in all, into the back of an open-back lorry and trucked us slowly through Paris. Our tormenters insisted that we face outward, the women at the front of the truck bed seated, the rest of us standing, so we could all be seen by the crowds. We hung our heads and refused to meet the gaze of the onlookers—all of us except for one big-boned girl, who stared back with blazing hatred and hurled epithets right back at her mockers.

"Shut up," yelled the woman who had shaved me, who was in the back of the truck, holding a rifle. A man with a gun stood with her, as well.

"You are only mad because your husband slept with me," the large-boned woman said.

"You are a liar," the tondeuse said.

"You are angry because it is the truth."

The woman hit her with the butt of the rifle. She collapsed on the bed of the truck, knocking another *femme tondue* into me, causing both of us to fall.

Yvette helped us to our feet. The man guarding us rapped on the roof of cab, and the driver stopped. He came around to the back, and the two men pulled the unconscious, big-boned woman out of the truck and tossed her onto the pavement like a sack of potatoes. Her head hit with a nauseating thud.

"Is she dead?" asked a tondue, who had buried her face against my shoulder.

"If she was not before, she probably is now," Yvette said grimly.

It was hard, but I stood still. Years of watching the unthinkable had schooled me to follow the Resistance's advice: do not risk your life to save a comrade if he or she is already dead.

The truck resumed moving. The coiffed brunette prodded me to face the public, along with the trembling girl beside me. I could not believe the anger hurled at us. We were spat upon, hit with garbage, and doused with dishwater from balconies above. The hatred came from men, from women, and even from children—but the women were the worst.

Later that day, Yvette and I talked about it. "They are angry because they are jealous," she said.

"Non!"

"Yes. They were not attractive enough to be chosen by a German. They are furious we had an option that was closed to them."

I was not sure that I agreed with her, but I stayed silent. Perhaps it was Yvette's truth, something she needed to believe in order to deal with being bald. "Our hair will grow back and we will be pretty once again," she said. "They can have hair down to their waists, and it will not make them desirable."

When at last the horrible, nightmarish ride was over—I overheard a conversation among our captors about the scarcity of gasoline, their need for a bathroom, and a desire to eat—they stopped the lorry and just walked away, leaving us standing in the back.

"What do we do now?" I asked.

"We run," Yvette said.

We leapt down from the back of the truck and hurried through the streets. We must have made quite a sight. We were practically naked—me in my bra and panties, Yvette in her slip—and our heads were bald and bleeding. People pointed and laughed. American and British soldiers made rude propositions.

After hours of being jeered at from the back of the truck, you would think we would be inured to insults and threats, but that walk, with just the two of us, was worse. A path cleared and people lined up to gawk and stare and catcall and comment.

After what seemed like an eternity, we arrived back at Yvette's hotel.

The doorman stood unmoving in front of the entrance. "You cannot come in here."

"It is I, Jean-Paul," Yvette said. "I have a room!"

"I am sorry." His gaze was cold and distant. "You cannot be in the lobby in that state of . . . *deshabille*."

"Let's go around back," I urged. Every hotel, I had learned, had a staff entrance. We marched in, pretending not to see or hear the gasps, guffaws, snickers, and pointing fingers. I held my breath as we made our way to the service elevator.

The elevator operator, a small man with wire-rim glasses blinked at us. "You can't . . ."

"Fifth floor, please," Yvette said imperiously.

"But you're not . . . you shouldn't . . . you can't . . ."

"For God's sake, close the door and take us up," Yvette hissed, "or I will tell your management about the silver you helped the Nazis steal."

The slight man slid the metal wire gate shut, then the door to the elevator. We slowly ascended, the air so thick and hot with acrimony it stung the back of my throat to breathe.

"Thank you," Yvette said when we'd stopped in front of the numeral five and he'd slid the cage, and then the door, open. She stepped out as if she were a queen, her bald head held high.

I followed her down the hall, my hands folded in front of my crotch, and waited until she pulled a key out of her brassiere. She held the door and let me go in ahead of her, then she quickly entered and latched the chain.

"Oh, mon Dieu!" She froze in front of the bureau mirror. Her hands went to her head. "Mon Dieu! Look at me!"

Fresh tears formed in my eyes. "I know, Vettie. I know."

"And look at you!"

I didn't want to see, but she grabbed my hand and pulled me in front of the mirror with her. I stared at a girl I did not know—a girl with sad eyes and black stubble all over her scalp.

"I have a five-o'clock shadow on my head," I murmured.

"And I am bald as an egg." We regarded ourselves in the mirror. "We are ridiculous."

"Yes."

"All those times we fussed over our hair, thinking it didn't look good enough. Whoever would have thought we would be bald?"

"Not I."

"*Moi non plus.* But look at us. We are as bald as eagles."

She started to laugh. I worried for a moment that her sanity had left her.

"Oh, it is so funny!" she said, pointing at the mirror. "Just look at us!"

I looked, but I did not see anything remotely amusing.

She took both my hands. "Come on, chérie. We can laugh or we can cry; neither will make our hair grow faster. So let us laugh, because laughter feels so much better." She waved her arms like a bird. "Look at us—we are as bald as baby birds!"

She was acting so ridiculous that I grinned. I, too, flapped my arms. We swooped around the room, cawing, then ended up back in front of the mirror, laughing.

"Oh, just look at us!"

"All of Paris has been looking at us," I told her. "We have been paraded all over town, practically naked."

"Yes, but you know what, my little bald birdie? We are alive, and Paris is free."

"Yes," I said, thinking somberly of the belligerent tondue who had been hit with a rifle, then tossed into the street to die.

"Do you know what time it is?"

I had no watch. I shook my head.

"It is time to take a picture!"

"Oh, non! Non, non, non."

"Yes! Our hair will grow quickly. We will never be bald little chicka-dees again."

"You still have a camera?" I had returned mine to M. Henri when the Germans had left my hotel. There was still a war going on in the rest of France, and the Resistance—now called FiFi; I had trouble remembering that—would need the equipment elsewhere.

"I have one Dierk gave me—and it still has a roll of film in it." She reached under the bed and drew out a little camera, then pointed it at me. "Smile!"

"Oh, Yvette, no!"

"Smile! We will laugh at this one day."

"At least let me put on clothes."

"No."

I covered my crotch. She snapped a photo.

"Now your turn. Take one of me."

She thrust the camera toward me, then put her hands on her hips like Betty Grable and gave a big cheesecake smile. I snapped the button.

"Good! And now do you know what time it is?"

Her enthusiasm and energy was wearing me out.

"Non."

"It is time to try on *des chapeaux*!"

"Hats!" This, I realized, could be our saving grace.

"Yes. Gerhard and Dierk bought me several."

"But I cannot work in a hat," I said somberly, realizing the gravity of my situation. The hotel was not likely to take kindly to a maid being *une femme tondue*.

"No, but you can wear a kerchief under your maid's cap."

"I don't know why, but I saved some of my hair," I confessed.

"What? Where?"

"In my brassiere." I reached in and pulled out a wad of hair.

Yvette looked at the hair in my palm, her eyes thoughtful. With her hair gone, her eyes looked larger than ever. "We will cut it and glue it to ribbons. It will look like wisps around your temple and neck, and with a hat or kerchief, no one will know the difference."

"Oh, I think they will," I said dryly. "I live in a dormitory. I cannot wear the same kerchief night and day."

"As long as you can look respectable in public, Ammie, I am sure they will let you keep your job."

"I am not so sure."

"They will need you. But just in case: what do you know about the supervisor that could get her into trouble?"

"I know that she likes to tipple whiskey all day."

"That is good, but not enough. What else?"

"I believe that she and a night guard are having an affair in vacant rooms."

"Non! Really?"

I nodded. "I saw them come out of an unoccupied room a few weeks ago, and she gave me an overly elaborate explanation."

"Perfect! If she threatens to fire you, you get her alone and tell her that you would discourage her from that course of action, unless she wants her supervisor to learn about her tippling and twiddling."

"I couldn't!"

"You could, and you will." Her voice held a stern note of resolve. "You will do what you need to do. Isn't that how we have survived so far?"

She was right. I could—and I would—do whatever needed to be done.

KAT
2016

I frown at Amélie in the fading afternoon light. "So . . . your head was shaved when you met Jack?"

"It had grown back quite a bit by then."

"But how?" By my calculations, she must have conceived the baby by August or September. "When did you meet him?"

"It was in June 1945."

"No. That cannot be right." I have done the math, over and over. All the same, I recheck my calculations in my head, then lean forward. "So . . . you're admitting the baby wasn't his?"

"I admit nothing. To admit is to acknowledge some kind of wrongdoing, is it not?"

"But you lied about the baby!"

"To you? Non. I did not lie."

Anger flows through me like hot lava. "You most certainly did! You sashayed into Wedding Tree, claiming that you and Jack were married and had a baby."

"I said no such thing. I said nothing."

Oh, my stars—it had been *Jack*. Of course it was. He was the one who'd told me, who'd told my parents—who'd told everyone that the baby was his. "But why? Why would Jack lie?"

"You have interrupted before I could get to that part."

"But the baby . . . if it was not Jack's, whose was it?"

"Whose do you think?"

"Joshua's?"

"Alas, no." Amélie sinks back into the chair, as if her spine has shrunk. She suddenly seems small and weary and old. "I went to the Red Cross and asked, many times, if they had news of him. Years later, after I came to America, I learned that his name was among those of the many Jews exterminated at Auschwitz."

"I am sorry." And I am. If Joshua had lived, she would have left Jack alone. "But . . . if it wasn't Joshua, and it wasn't Jack, who was the baby's father? Were you carrying on with someone you haven't told me about?"

"No. I was carrying on, as you call it, with no one. But I've told you about the father." She straightens and gives me a little smile. She is enjoying this! I want to jump up and throttle her.

"One of the head shavers?"

"Oh, no, no, no." She shakes her head.

"Then who?"

She pauses a long moment, so long I fear I am going to have to endure a lengthy guessing game. "Dierk."

"Dierk?" I scrunch my forehead in a frown. "You had an affair with . . ." It dawns on me as I am saying it. "Wait. *You are not the mother?*"

"Not the birth mother, no. Elise was Yvette's child."

"Oh, my God in heaven!" My head reels. I have never been struck across the face, but I imagine this is how it must feel. I am stunned. It was right there in Amélie's story, but I'd believed something else to be true for so many decades that my mind refused to bend around this new information. "So Jack . . ." My thoughts swirl like water in a flushing toilet. "He knew all along that the baby was not his?"

"Of course."

"But he said it was his! Was that because he thought the baby was yours?"

"At first. But not when he told you." She glances at her watch, then slowly stands. "It is getting late. I think you should come back tomorrow."

She is going to end our conversation *now*—when we are finally getting to the part I care about? "No! I've waited my whole life for this information."

"That is not my problem." Amélie is now on her feet, looking down at me. "We will talk more tomorrow. I am very tired."

I can't believe she will just stop her story now. I am so angry and frustrated I want to stamp my foot. I stand and reach for my cane. "This is an outrage."

"I said I would talk to you on my terms. And my terms are that we are calling it a day."

Why does *she* get to make the rules? It is patently unfair. "I will be back in the morning."

"I am sure you will."

I reluctantly make my way to the door. "Don't you dare die in the night," I say, giving her my most authoritative glare.

Amélie gives me a weary smile. "I lived through the war, did I not?" She opens the door and holds it for me. "Good evening."

The door closes behind me the very moment I cross the threshold, so quickly it is almost rude. I hobble down the hallway, fumbling in my purse for my cell phone. I finally find it and punch in the number one, the number my great-granddaughter programmed that would signal her to come pick me up.

35

AMÉLIE
2016

I open the door at eight o'clock the next morning and there is Kat. I have not slept well. The old days have been piling on me like hay bales in a barn. "Back again, I see."

She gives me her wide-eyed beauty queen look. "You never doubted I would come, did you?"

I had not—not for a second. But for some reason, I don't want to give her the satisfaction of saying so. I lift my shoulders. "You could have changed your mind."

"Why? Because I don't want my ears worn out before you tell me what I want to know?"

Mon Dieu, but she is hard to be nice to! And here I have made up my mind to be kinder. I lay awake last night berating myself for not being more empathetic, more understanding.

"Actually, I thought that perhaps you wouldn't want to spend a second day in my company." It is hard to admit it—I have trouble with admissions, it seems—but I knew I was being difficult yesterday. I was not getting what I wanted from her, and that made me resentful. It also made me furious with myself; why am I seeking anything from this woman?

And what is it that I want from her? Understanding, I suppose. Understanding and forgiveness. Haven't I learned, in my ninety-three years on earth, to depend on no one's opinion but my own? Apparently not. Alas, we are all doomed to want the validation of others, up until we draw our very last breath.

"I came because I need to know what happened," she says stiffly.

"I know. And you deserve the truth."

She looks at me as if it is a trick. Being nice to her is a strategy that throws her for a loop, I see. Perhaps I should have tried it sooner.

"Come in, come in." I step back and hold the door wide. "Would you like a coffee? Or a tea?"

"Some water would be nice."

I go to the kitchen and pull a glass from the cabinet.

"Don't you have bottled water?" she asks.

Bottled water? When fresh clean water flows from a tap? How silly. Besides, she has cancer anyway. "No. Sorry."

All the same, I put ice in her glass—Americans always like their ice—and I use the filtered water from the refrigerator door, although the tap is faster. As I turn to head back to the living room, I see that she has settled in my chair.

I swallow back a burst of resentment. I offered her the chair to start with yesterday, had I not?

"I hope you don't mind," she says. "My back is a bit sore from the couch."

Of course I mind, when she puts it as a criticism of my sofa's comfort. Who on earth wouldn't? I blow out a little sigh. "Not at all," I lie, and move my coffee cup from the side table by the chair to the coffee table in front of the sofa.

"I could not sleep last night, thinking of how you deceived us about that baby."

Now that I look at her closely, I realize that she is fairly bristling with outrage. There is no use in pointing out that I had not deceived her; Jack had. "If you are angry now, you are only going to get angrier," I say. "Perhaps you should just go."

"No. Please." For a moment, she looks sincere—like a real person, with real emotions, not an image she is carefully curating for consumption. "I am just shocked that things are so different from how I always thought they were."

"I understand." I take a sip of my coffee. "Shall I continue?"

"Yes. Please do."

I settle on the sofa in the place I used to sit with Jack. I always sat on the right-hand side; Jack used to sit in the middle, beside me, with his arm slung across the back, his hand on my shoulder. Oh, how I miss the weight of his hand!

I close my eyes, letting the memories come. Time seems a thing that goes in circles instead of steadily moving forward. I let it pull me around and back, and then I start talking.

1945

The days after the liberation were, for me, worse than the war. As a shorn woman, I constantly kept my head covered and lived in fear of humiliation.

I believe that actual prostitutes had it better than I, because they had each other for support. The SS and Wermacht had commandeered twenty-two well-known brothels, such as Le Chabanais—it was a favorite of Goering during the war, and before that, King Edward VII had been a regular customer. The Germans would pay a sum equal to a senior officer's weekly pay for just one visit, plus they brought chocolates and champagne and cigarettes to their favorite girl, to maintain the illusion of decorum.

When I went back to the dormitory at my hotel the day of our shaving, I wore one of Yvette's dresses with a belt tightly cinched around my waist—she was taller and bigger in every way than me—and a little cloche on my head. I did not look too bad in street clothes. We had taken the hair I had saved, cut it into short strands, and glued it to two ribbons—one for me, one for Yvette. We had then carefully glued extra ribbons over them, and stitched them into place—then tied the ribbons around our head, letting little tendrils be exposed at our temples and the backs of our necks. It looked as if our hair was simply hidden under our hats.

We laughed at how Yvette looked as a brunette. It was a dramatic change for her.

The effect of the faux tendrils was not as convincing in the maid's cap I had to wear with my uniform. Also, since I had never before worn a kerchief over my dark curls, it was only natural that the other girls wanted to know why I was suddenly sporting one under my cap. I told the story Yvette and I had concocted; we had gone to a hair salon to celebrate the liberation with a new hairstyle, and we had tried one of the new permanent waves. The results, alas, had been disastrous, so awful that for the next few months, I would be wearing hats and kerchiefs.

I had to tell my story over and over. I could tell that people didn't believe me. For one thing, my hair had already been curly. Why would I want a permanent wave? I could tell that the hotel workers were all whispering about me behind my back.

Sure enough, as I had feared, my supervisor called me aside about a week later. One of my roommates, it seems, had peeked under my kerchief while I slept, and the report of my bald pate had made the rounds of the hotel staff and reached her ears. She insisted I remove my kerchief and let her see my head. I protested, but exposed my shorn scalp—by now covered with about a quarter-inch of dark stubble—all the same.

"I am sorry, Amélie, but I will have to let you go for moral turpitude."

"I have not been immoral!" Tears filled my eyes. Now that the war was over, it seemed I cried at the least little thing. It humiliated me that I was so unexpectedly at the mercy of my emotions. "I was in the wrong place at the wrong time, that's all, and I was mistaken for someone I am not."

She waved her hand. "It does not matter whether I believe you or not. We cannot have une femme tondue working at this hotel."

I took my lead from Yvette's handling of the employee elevator operator.

"Mme Hortense, if you find it necessary to fire me for moral reasons, I am afraid I will find it necessary to report to the hotel manager that I saw you and the night watchman leaving an unoccupied room together, looking quite disheveled, in the middle of your shift."

She gasped. "There—there is no way he would believe you."

"I would also find it necessary to report that your breath smells of whiskey first thing in the morning and all throughout the day, getting stronger as the afternoon progresses. All he would have to do is check for himself."

"I—I do not know what you are talking about."

"I think you do. And I also think that it would be in the best interests of both of us to each keep our own counsel. I will look for another position and leave this hotel as soon as I can. I expect an impeccable recommendation from you." I abruptly turned and went back to work.

Yvette's hotel evicted her the very next day.

"But my room is paid for through the end of the month!" she argued with the manager, a short, balding man who wore a gold chain prominently stretched across his vested suits.

"We do not rent to Germans or collaborateurs," was the reply.

"That's easy to say now, when you have Americans and British soldiers to fill the rooms. You had no trouble serving Germans and their women for the last four years."

He lifted his double chins. "You must move out by noon tomorrow."

"Then give me a refund."

"There is no record of any money ever being paid."

Yvette was certain that Dierk had not lied to her, but there was nothing to be done. She used the last of the money from Dierk to rent a little dump of an apartment and to buy us two black-market wigs, which, while not especially natural looking—the hair was very black and very straight, as if it had come from Asians—at least allowed us to be seen in public and find employment.

With the dark, straight, identical hair—it refused to hold a curl, although we tried and tried—we did look more like sisters. A Mutt and Jeff pair of sisters, perhaps, but sisters all the same.

I helped her lug all of her belongings—including the enormous boxes of baby formula—to the apartment. She had been clever in getting Gerhard and Dierk to buy things for her, so she had plenty of shoes and clothing, and even some jewelry that she could sell. I found a job at another hotel the following week, so I left the dormitory and moved in with her. Yvette got a job in a milliner's shop. She wrote her aunt again with our new address, asking for passage to America and promising prompt repayment.

She checked the mail every day. We knew that the mail was not reliable; Paris was still in shambles and France was still at war. But we did not lose hope. We talked often about what we would do in America.

Yvette planned to fashion herself as a young widow. No one need ever know that the father of her child had not been her husband—indeed, had not been French. In America, her child would have the best of opportunities.

Food was still rationed—everything was scarce in those days. The Red Cross provided some much-needed food for French civilians. The war raged on in eastern France as the Allies fought their way toward Germany. Yvette and I alternated our work schedules so that we could take turns standing in line for groceries. In the evenings we cooked in our single pot and hand-sewed baby clothes and maternity clothes. Yvette insisted on cutting down some of her dresses to fit me.

She repeatedly urged me to go out in the evenings. "You might meet a nice American," she told me.

Indeed, that seemed to be the hope of most single Frenchwomen in those days—to meet an American who would whisk her away to the land of plenty. Due to the wig and my slow-growing hair, I had no desire to meet a man. I was ashamed of the way I looked, afraid of having my wig discovered. What if a man put his fingers in my hair? I wanted to hide away and be invisible. I was quite content to stay home in the evenings with Yvette.

For her part, Yvette managed to hide her pregnancy for many months. Both of us were clever with a needle, and together we found ways to drape and layer her clothes to disguise her burgeoning belly.

All the same, near the end of her seventh month, her boss took her aside.

"Yvette, the time has come for you to stay in the back room. Your condition is inappropriate for a shopgirl."

Yvette did not even try to dissemble. "How long have you known?"

"About as long as I've known that you wear a wig," she said, not unkindly. "Surely your own hair is getting long enough now to reveal?"

I didn't think it was yet time to toss the wig—my hair still looked awfully short and boyish—but Yvette insisted we go to a salon near one of the expensive brothels. We were afraid to trust our obviously shorn hair to anyone who might want to take further vengeance against us, and we hoped that a hairstylist who catered to high-level prostitutes would not be shocked by a femme tondue patron.

We emerged with short, sassy hair such as that worn by movie star Jane Wyman. "The trick is to wear bright lipstick and fashionable clothes, and look as if we are the cutting edge of fashion," Yvette said. Indeed, if it weren't for her enormously pregnant belly, Yvette would have resembled Marilyn Monroe with her shorter hairdo.

"How does it feel to be blond again?" I asked her.

She tossed her head. "*Merveilleuse!*"

I, too, felt much lighter and freer. But I felt so much trepidation about going to work the first time without my wig that I continued to wear it for several weeks. I need not have worried; when I finally went to work sporting my real hair, my coworkers simply exclaimed over how much more attractive I looked.

Yvette grew larger and larger, and more and more uncomfortable. The only medical care we could afford was a midwife, a large woman with leathery skin who was not what I would call sympathetic.

"Who is the father?" she'd asked, when she'd come to see Yvette a month before she was due.

"A soldier."

She'd palpated Yvette's stomach so roughly Yvette had winced. "Was he a large man?"

"Yes."

"I figured as much," she muttered. "No doubt a Boche."

"I don't see why that matters," Yvette said.

"The Boches have huge babies. It is hard for Frenchwomen to bear them. Take off your underwear and lie down." Yvette meekly did as she said. The woman yanked up Yvette's skirt and roughly stuck three fingers inside her. I was appalled that she didn't bother to wash her hands first.

"Ow!" Yvette yelped.

"Oh, so you're a whiner, hmm?"

"No, I—I just . . . You didn't tell me what to expect."

"I bet you always knew what to expect from the Boches." She pulled out her fingers, her lips curled in a smirk.

I disliked the woman immensely. "There was no need to hurt her," I said.

"Hurt her? Ha! Wait until labor begins. This was nothing." She wiped her fingers on her skirt and turned to Yvette. "Your womb, it is still closed up tight. No baby for a while. Another month."

"A month! I cannot imagine getting a month larger!"

"As I said, the Boche babies are huge. Call me when your water breaks."

"I don't like her," I told Yvette when she left. "Let's find someone else."

"I had to pay half of her fee in advance," Yvette said. "I cannot afford to pay another one."

"But if she's not a good midwife . . ."

"She is," Yvette said. "She delivered Mme Steyvant's baby ten years ago, and all was well."

"She holds the baby's father against you."

"Yvette sighed. "Oui—but they all do. I approached two other midwives who simply refused to treat me."

"You did not tell me!"

"I did not want to worry you."

"How did they know the father was Boche?"

She lifted her shoulders. "Given the number of Germans who were in the city when the child was conceived, and the lack of Frenchmen, it is not a hard guess. Plus"—she ruefully looked down and smiled—"I am huge."

At least the news about the war was positive. The Allies were clearly winning.

And our downstairs neighbor, a widow named Nora Saurent who worked at a *boucherie*, befriended us, often bringing us meat scraps for soup. She was worried about Yvette having enough to eat, enough to nourish the baby.

On April 30, she knocked on our door. "Did you hear the news? Hitler is dead!"

We jumped around and cheered—or at least, I jumped; Yvette was enormous by then—then ran downstairs to listen to her radio and share a glass of wine.

The good news kept on coming. On May 7, we heard rumors Germany had surrendered—and on May 8, we learned it was true. Germany's unconditional surrender was ratified in Berlin on May 8.

The city went wild. Because of Yvette's condition, we stayed at home, again listening to the radio at Nora's apartment.

Yvette woke me around two in the morning that night. "Ammie, I think you need to go get the midwife."

"What's happened?" I sat up. "Did your water break?"

She nodded. "About two hours ago. I waited until the pains started coming, and now . . ." She doubled over, unable to speak, her hand on her belly.

"I will go get her right now. But first I'm going to get Nora to stay with you while I'm gone."

I threw on my clothes and knocked at Nora's apartment. She grabbed some clothing and hurried upstairs to stay with Yvette.

I ran to get the midwife, eight blocks away. It was nearly impossible to rouse her. I knocked and knocked, afraid she wasn't even home. She finally came to the door, her eyes half open, reeking of sour wine. At first she didn't want to come with me.

"There is no rush," she said. "First babies take forever."

"You need to come now," I said. "She is in much pain."

She blew out a dismissive hiss of air. "She thought it was painful when I examined her."

"Please. She paid you. You are needed now."

After much grumbling, she dressed, grabbed her bag, and came with me.

I could hear Yvette moaning as we approached the apartment. My heart raced with fear.

"You can wash your hands at the kitchen sink," I said as we entered, not wanting the midwife to repeat her unsanitary initial exam. I noticed that Nora already had a pan of water boiling on the stove.

I found Yvette writhing on the bed. I rushed to her side and took her hand. Fear tore through me. Too many women died in childbirth. If I lost Yvette, I would die, as well.

"The contractions are very close," Nora said.

"Let's have a look," said the midwife, drying her hands on a kitchen towel.

Her expression changed after she inspected Yvette. "She is having this baby now." She looked up at Yvette's face. "With the next pain, you need to push."

She opened her bag and pulled out some large forceps.

"I will go sanitize these for you," Nora said smoothly, taking them from her hand without giving her a choice otherwise. Nora also managed to boil the woman's scissors and sewing needle.

It seemed to take forever, but in reality, it was probably only thirty minutes later that Yvette's moan was joined by the high-pitched cry of a baby.

"She's not nearly as large as I expected," the midwife said, expertly wiping off the dark-haired baby with the warm water and clean washcloths that Nora had thought to provide.

"Did you say she?" Yvette asked.

"Yes. It's a girl."

"A girl!" she murmured. "Oh, a little girl!" She looked at me, her eyes shining. "I have a daughter!"

"She's beautiful," I said.

"Yes," Nora said. "Just like her mother."

"I will name her after mine." Yvette reached for the baby as the midwife finished wrapping her tightly in a blanket. She gazed into the red, still-squalling face. "Hello, Elise."

Tears poured down my cheeks. Yvette's mother should be here. How could a moment be so heartrendingly beautiful, and at the same time, so full of grief? Who knew such emotions could exist in equal portions at the same time?

"It is a wonderful omen," said Nora, "to be born just as the war ended."

"Yes. She is born in a free France," I said.

"But she will be raised as an American." Yvette looked at me. "Just as soon as we can, we will go."

———

Yvette did not rebound from childbirth the way we expected. She wanted to nurse the baby, despite all of Dierk's formula. The child constantly fussed and cried and spit up, but when we took her to a doctor, he said nursing was best, that formula would only make the baby worse. Yvette was exhausted, and continued to bleed well after the time she should have stopped. Both mother and child failed to thrive.

I tried to let Yvette rest by caring for the baby as much as possible, but there was only so much I could do. I would spend many an hour at night holding Elise and rocking her, trying to calm her crying.

As the weeks went by, Yvette took in some sewing, and the milliner who had employed her gave her some custom work to do at home. Yvette was determined to earn money for passage to America. Money was not the only obstacle we had to overcome; when I checked into the requirements, I learned that there were a very limited number of visas to America and thousands of Europeans wanting to immigrate there. We were hopeful that having Yvette's aunt sponsor us would help our cause.

We still heard no word from her aunt. Yvette wrote yet again.

At three months, the baby still cried and threw up all the time. Yvette was more fatigued than ever and seemed to have aged several years in a few months. We pooled our money and again took the child to a doctor. He said Elise was colicky and reassured us that she would outgrow it. He told Yvette to keep nursing her, to let her eat as much as she wanted. The baby was attached to poor Yvette's bosom almost continually.

Yvette lost weight, and the baby did not seem to be gaining.

And then, in October, when the child was five months old, Yvette took ill. It started with a headache, and then she developed a cough and a high fever. She could not eat, and she developed a horrible phlegmy hack that made nursing impossible.

Alarmed, Nora bought a baby bottle and we started Elise on the formula. I called the doctor, and he gave Yvette penicillin. Penicillin was very expensive in those days for non-military personnel—it took almost all our savings—but I insisted.

It didn't work. Three days later, her fever raged on. She was in and out of her head with delirium, and then, terrifyingly, she lay still and unresponsive, her breathing a shallow rattle. Nora fetched the doctor once again.

"It is the flu, which is viral," The doctor said. "There is nothing more medicine can do."

"What about a hospital?"

"I am sorry, but they are overcrowded and have no space to quarantine. They will not admit contagious patients."

"Will the baby get sick?" Nora asked worriedly.

"If she were going to, she probably would be ill already. It is likely her mother's milk gave her immunity." He packed up his bag. "If madame regains consciousness, give her liquids and aspirin." At the door he paused. "And call her priest."

My heart . . . it dropped into a bottomless pit. "It is as bad as that?"

The way he avoided looking me in the eye told me that it was. "She was weak from childbirth, and she is now very ill," he said in a low voice.

"But she might get better," I insisted. I could not accept what he was telling me.

"I have seen miracles before. And perhaps the priest can help pray for one."

A miracle? That is what it would take? I gazed at him, beside myself with grief. Yvette was the last of my family.

"I am sorry, mademoiselle." He closed the door behind him.

"I will go fetch Father Gaudet," Nora whispered.

I prepared a bottle for Elise and carried the child to Yvette's bedside. As I sat down, Yvette opened her eyes. "Ammie."

She was awake! Hope flooded my chest. "I am here."

"You will . . ." It took much effort for her to talk. Each breath was an ordeal. ". . . look after Elise for me."

"Of course. I will care for her until you are better."

"You will care for her . . . if I don't get better?"

"But you will! You must not talk like that."

"You will take Elise to America."

"We will all go together."

"I don't think I'm going to make it, Ammie."

My heart turned over. "Don't say that. Don't you even think that!" If she thought it, it could happen. I could not allow the possibility to exist. "Elise needs you to get well."

"We have always been . . ." Her chest rattled as she struggled to inhale. ". . . honest with each other. I don't have the strength to pretend. I need to know you will care for her—that you will get her to my family. Promise me."

"But . . ."

Her gaze cut through the protest on the tip of my tongue. "Promise me."

"Yes, yes, of course. Of course I promise. I will love her as if she were my own."

Her face relaxed. "Say a prayer for me."

"Yes." I bowed my head and said an Our Father. At the end of the prayer, she didn't open her eyes.

When Nora returned with Father Gaudet, they found me sitting on the bed beside Yvette, holding Elise and weeping. Somewhere between *Thine is the glory* and *forever*, Yvette had gone.

36

KAT
2016

*A*mélie sits quietly for a long, long moment, gazing at her hands.

I sit quietly, too, until I can stand the silence no longer. "I'm sorry about your friend."

"Thank you."

"After she died—that is when you went to the church and overheard Jack?"

She gives a single nod. "That happened a couple of weeks later. First I arranged for Yvette's burial. I had her interred in my family churchyard plot under the name Yvette Chaussant Michaud."

"Did the church know you lied about her name?"

She shoots me a withering glance. "The name was as true as anything ever was. She was my sister, in every sense of the word that matters. She was my family, and I was hers."

I don't think that Catholic officials, who seem very strict about rules, would accept this explanation. I decide not to point it out. Instead, I bring up what seems to be a bigger transgression of Catholic doctrine. "So she died without a final confession?"

"God and I knew all of her sins."

"But according to the Catholic faith . . ."

"I believe—and I think Yvette did, too, although we never talked about it—that if you have one person truly know you and love you and accept you anyway . . ." She looks thoughtfully at the wall. I follow her gaze to a carved wooden cross that I hadn't noticed before, placed among all her paintings and pictures. "Well, if you are fortunate enough to experience that, you have experienced God's grace. And you if know his grace, then you know his forgiveness."

"Hmmm." It has the ring of truth, but I don't like it. I don't like for anyone to break or bend the rules, especially when it comes to matters of religion. I resent hearing people say that God is larger than the confines of their denomination, because I feel as though they have a better deal than me. It's the spiritual equivalent of not wanting anyone to be smarter or more knowledgeable or prettier.

I realize this is probably one of those character defects my hospice counselor says I should address, but I don't care to examine it too closely. My counselor also says I should just let things go. This, I decide, will be one of those things. I turn my thoughts back to Jack and the story that Amélie is finally—finally!—about to tell.

"When you first started talking yesterday, you told me that you went to a church and heard Jack tell the priest the medic's confession. Is this what happened next?"

Amélie nods. "After Yvette's death, I was crushed—just devastated. Thank God for Nora. Elise and I moved in with her, and she helped me care for the baby. She urged me to turn to God. Her faith was very strong; mine—well, I wasn't sure I had any left.

"It was at her urging that I went to the church. I knelt low and prayed to God. I did not know if he was still there. I couldn't imagine why he would take Yvette now, when she had a child to raise, after helping her all the way through the war. I did not understand. I still do not.

"I prayed for guidance. I asked God to show me what to do, to help me find a way. And then I heard Jack telling the priest how the young medic had died in his arms and how he had confessed that he might have left a girl pregnant. And it seemed to me that it was a sign."

"A sign?"

She nods. "I had Jack's name—I'd read it on his bag. He'd told the priest the name of the hospital where he was working. He'd mentioned the name of the boy who'd saved his life—Doug Claiborne from White-fish, Montana. Thanks to my work for the Resistance, I was skilled at remembering names and details. I had entered the church hopeless and helpless, and now I had information and an idea."

My eyebrows rise nearly to my hairline. "So you decided God was telling you to seduce Jack?"

"No. That is not what happened." Her voice holds an impatient edge that does not bode well.

"But . . ."

She leans forward. "I know that you are going to want to interrupt me. My story will not fit your preconceived notion of what happened. You are likely to be displeased or even shocked. But if you want to hear the truth, I suggest you just sit and listen and let me speak."

"All right." I nod. "All right."

37

AMÉLIE
October 1945

I put the baby in a pink dress with white smocking, and tied a pink bow in her hair. I put her in a secondhand boiled wool coat. She looked adorable—and then, on the Métro, she had a horribly malodorous diaper explosion. I had a terrible time figuring out where I could change her—it was too cold to go to a park. I finally disembarked near a department store and changed her in the ladies' room. I debated what to do with the diaper; I couldn't really afford to just throw it away, but neither could I afford to meet the man whom I hoped would change my life smelling of poo. I decided to sacrifice the diaper, and tossed it in the trash.

I got back on the Métro and rode it all the way to Neuilly-sur-Seine. Elise was fussy, so I put the rubber nipple in her mouth and let her suckle herself to sleep. She was heavy in my arms.

I was wearing a rose-colored dress—one of Yvette's that I had cut down to fit me—and I had on my winter coat, as well. I wore a little rose hat at a saucy angle.

I entered the 365th army hospital—it had been the American Hospital of Paris before the U.S. Army took it over—and went to the information desk, which was manned by two women wearing army uniforms, complete with smart little pointed caps. "Excuse me," I said in French, thinking I should keep my ability to speak English under wraps. A farm girl from

Normandy was unlikely speak a foreign language. "I am looking for Dr. Jack O'Connor."

"Do you have an appointment?"

"No. I—I want to see him for a personal reason."

"Don't we all," sighed the second woman in the military uniform.

The one who was helping me shot her a sidelong smile. "May I tell him your name?"

"Yes, of course." I had thought long and hard about this. There was no reason, I'd decided, not to give him my real name. It would certainly simplify a passport or visa. "Amélie Michaud."

"And may I tell him the reason for your visit?"

"Yes. Please tell him that I am the fiancée of Doug Claiborne of White-fish, Montana."

She asked me to wait. The fact I had a baby made the other woman at the desk smile at me. I smiled back. At length, the first woman told me to go to a waiting room at the end of the hall on the second floor.

I went upstairs and took a seat. After a several minutes, a nurse came and escorted me into an office with a metal desk and two chairs opposite it. I sat down. My stomach was a hard knot of nerves.

After a few moments, the door opened. A young man with black hair and blue eyes walked in, wearing a heavily starched, immaculately white coat. "Mademoiselle Michaud?"

I rose to my feet, holding the sleeping Elise. "Yes."

"Bonjour. I am Jack O'Connor."

I was practically struck dumb. I had not seen him in the confessional; I had only heard his voice. I was unprepared for him to be so tall, or so good-looking. He was movie-star handsome—the kind of handsome that is universal, that anyone from any country would find handsome—and yet he was distinctly American. He had a wide American smile, and his eyes were kind. I could tell he had bad news to tell me and that it troubled him greatly to do so.

He held out his hand. I lifted one from around Elise and gave him a handshake—something Frenchwomen normally do not do. His hand completely engulfed mine in a firm hold, and he pumped my arm two times. So strange, these American customs!

He sat down beside me in the other chair in front of his desk. "I understand that you knew Doug Claiborne." Oh, there was something so sexy about a man speaking French with an American accent! He spoke it much better than most Americans I had met.

"Yes. We . . . he . . ." I looked down. I suddenly felt very shy in front of this man, and terrified about what I was about to do. "We were in love. Elise is his child."

"I see," he said. "She is very beautiful."

"Yes, she is, isn't she?" I had not yet grasped all that it meant to pretend that Elise was my child. As soon as the words left my mouth, it occurred to me that from a mother, they sounded, well, boastful. "I mean, thank you."

Flustered, I rushed ahead. "Doug mentioned you in a letter. He said he was serving with you and he spoke very highly of you. I figured that if anyone could tell me anything about Doug, it would be you. I do not know what happened to him, and I have tried to find out for a very long time. Many calls to many army personnel . . ."

He nodded somberly. "It's hard to get information through the army's bureaucracy in peacetime, much less in times of war. It's even harder if you don't speak English."

He was more sympathetic than I had dared hope. "Yes. The concierge at the hotel where I work—she speaks English and she knew someone with the Medical Corps. He looked up your posting, so here I am."

His eyes were somber. "I see."

I leaned forward. "M. O'Connor, I lost my family, my home—everything, really—in the war. Doug's baby—she is all I have. I am now living and working in Paris, but it is extremely hard, as an unmarried mother."

"I imagine it is."

"So, can you tell me . . . where is Doug? We were going to be married." I brushed my suddenly wet cheek.

The tears weren't an act; in talking to him, I felt my own loss and desperation. The loss of Yvette was a still-bleeding wound, and tears were always near my eyes. The circumstances I was relating were different, yes, but the story of a young woman alone with a baby, a woman who had lost all her family and the man she loved . . . it was my story, too.

Jack's eyes were full of bad news and empathy. His Adam's apple moved. "I am afraid I have something difficult to tell you."

I drew a deep breath.

"Doug is gone."

I closed my eyes and exhaled slowly. "Are you sure?"

He solemnly nodded. "I was with him when he died. He was very brave. He had gotten separated from his platoon . . ."

"Yes," I broke in. "We hid him at our farmhouse, my parents and I."

"For how long?" he asked.

I felt as though I were stepping in a minefield. Did he know the answer? I did not. If he did not, what would make the most sense? Too brief a time, I would look like a loose woman. Too much time, it might not seem believable. "Well, it was just a short while, but it felt like longer."

He nodded. "Under tense circumstances, people bond very quickly."

I nodded, grateful.

"When he showed up at the evacuation hospital, he said his life had been saved by a French family. He intended to rejoin his platoon, but they'd headed in another direction while he stayed behind to tend a dying soldier."

"Oui," I said, although this, of course, was new information to me. "He was so devoted to his fellow soldiers. So very kind."

"Yes. He was."

"So . . . how did he end up with you?"

He looked at me strangely. "Your friends with the Resistance brought him to the Sainte-Mère-Église evacuation hospital."

"Oh, right, right," I said. Oh, la—I couldn't afford to make a mistake. I needed to memorize the information in case I needed it in the future. Sainte-Mère-Église, Sainte-Mère-Église. I wiped my eyes. "I meant how did you first meet him?"

"Oh. At the mess tent, the morning after he'd arrived. He went right to work that day. Did your friends make it back okay?"

Oh, my—so many things I did not know! I hedged my bets. "Not all of them."

"Hell." Jack blew out a hard sigh. "He was worried about an ambush or a mine. He so appreciated being shown the way to the hospital."

"One of them never returned," I ventured.

"I am so sorry. Doug worked at the hospital while he waited for transport back to his platoon," Jack said. "Our commanding officer requested to keep him, because we were shorthanded and Doug was an excellent medic. It still wasn't settled if he was going to stay with us or go back to the front."

I dabbed my eyes. "How did he die?"

"Doug and I had gone to the edge of the hospital grounds to meet a truck carrying wounded from the front. We'd heard that some of them were barely hanging onto life. A German soldier—I think he was shell-shocked; he didn't walk steadily, and he seemed so surprised to see us—lurched out of the woods. He had a machine gun. He pointed it right at me."

He stared at the floor, then ran a hand across his jaw. "I think it was my white jacket. It had a medical insignia, and it must have looked like a target. He raised his gun and pointed right at it. And Doug . . ."

I couldn't help it; I burst into a little sob.

"He jumped right in front of me, pushing me to the ground. He pulled out a revolver—it wasn't military issue. He'd said he'd traded his for a smaller one from of one of his Resistance escorts."

"From one of my friends," I murmured. "That was so kind of Doug, to give him a better gun."

"They fired at exactly the same time. The German's gun shot off several rounds. The German fell as Doug collapsed on top of me."

I put my hand to my mouth, my horror real.

"I scrambled out from under him and immediately checked him over. He had a huge hole in his chest. It was a fatal wound; he could not be saved."

My tears fell on the baby's hat. My sorrow was genuine.

"He knew he was dying. He asked for a priest so he could give a final confession. He was worried about you. He said . . ."

"What did he say?"

"That he had done wrong by you. That he wanted to marry you."

"Oh, mon Dieu. Mon Dieu!"

"He cared very much for you."

"Oh, mon Dieu," I cried.

His eyes were full of sympathy. "I am so sorry I don't have better news to report."

"So . . . where is he?"

"His body was shipped home to his parents."

"To Whitefish, Montana?"

"Yes."

"So Doug saved your life," I murmured.

"Yes."

Tears ran down my face as I gazed at Elise. "So you are alive, and he is not."

His brow creased. He looked very troubled. "Yes."

"And his child has no father."

"Is there anything I can do to help you?"

I sat still for several heartbeats. "Can you help me get to America? My mother's sister and her family live in New York. That is the only family I have left."

"I will be glad to see what I can do."

"I am hoping that you will have some influence. I have checked on my own, and there are so many people wanting to go to America that I was told it might take years." My eyes welled up again. "Things are very harsh here in France, and I hear they may be difficult for many years to come. Doug wanted his child to be raised in America."

"I will see if I can help. How can I reach you?"

"I do not have a phone. However, I will write down my address." He handed me a piece of paper and a pen. I handed Elise to him to hold while I wrote. He held her as if she were spun glass and might break at the slightest bump.

"I work as a chambermaid at the Hotel du Chateau, so I can be reached there in an emergency, although they frown on employees getting phone calls. I will write down the name and address of the hotel, as well."

He nodded and gazed down at Elise. "What do you do with the baby all day?"

"I live with a widow and pay her rent, and she watches the baby for me. But we are three people in a one-bedroom flat, and it is very small. I dare not continue to impose indefinitely."

"I will check into things, and I will send word."

I rose. "Thank you."

"You are welcome." He stood as well, then reached in the back pocket of his pants. He pulled out his wallet. "I would like to give you some money."

"Oh, no. No!" I shook my head. "That would not be proper."

"I would like to help you. Please."

"You can best help me if you can find a way—any way at all—to get me and Elise to America."

He nodded, his eyes somber. "I will do what I can."

I thanked him and left the hospital, buoyed by the hope that this handsome young doctor could pull some strings. I believed that he had the power to do so. After all, German officers had exercised the power of life and death over us. Surely an American officer—especially one who was a doctor, who was highly educated—could do the same.

38

AMÉLIE
1945

I did not hear from Jack for a week. And then I got a package with wine, cheese, chocolate, and a dozen diapers. It contained a note: *I am still working on your request.*

More weeks went by. I received another packet, similar to the first, with the same message: *I am working on your request.*

November became December. On Christmas Eve, I heard a knock on the door. I opened it—and there stood Jack O'Connor.

My hand immediately went to my hair, which was in a kerchief. "Oh! Bonsoir," I said.

He held out two big boxes. "Bonsoir. And Merry Christmas."

"Oh, my! I—I didn't expect you!"

"I just wanted to drop off a Christmas gift for you and the baby."

"How—how thoughtful! Come in, come in!"

Nora came out of the kitchen, wiping her hand. She looked at me, and then at Jack, her eyes questioning. I had not told her about my visit to the hospital; she thought the gifts were from a gentleman I had met at work.

"Nora, this is Dr. Jack O'Connor—the man I told you about." I hoped she would pick up the clue to pretend she knew about him. "And this is my friend, Nora Saurent."

They exchanged greetings. Nora looked from Jack to me and back again. "It is a pleasure to meet you. You speak excellent French for an American!"

He gave a modest smile. "When I was young, I learned French from a Cajun nanny."

"Well, you learned very well!" Nora motioned to the small dining table. "We are readying *le réveillon*. We would be delighted if you would join us."

My heart pounded. If Jack stayed for Christmas Eve dinner, I would die of worry that Nora might inadvertently expose my lies.

"Oh, I'm sorry," Jack said. "I'm on my way to a dinner commitment. I just wanted to drop off the gifts on my way."

"That is very kind. We are honored to have you here. Let me get you a glass of wine. Sit, sit, both of you." Nora gestured to the sofa. Jack and I both sat on it, at opposites ends, as Nora bustled into the kitchen.

"Where is the baby?"

"She is asleep. Would you like to see her?"

"Yes."

I led him into the bedroom. The single bed, the cot where I slept, and the little crib were crowded into the tiny room. I felt embarrassed at how shabby the place looked.

Jack did not seem to notice. He went to the crib and bent down. Elise was sleeping like an angel. He stroked a finger across her forehead. "She is beautiful."

"Yes. I mean, thank you."

We went back into the living room and resettled on the sofa. Nora bustled in with two glasses. Jack stood. She handed a glass to Jack and the other to me.

"Won't you join us?" Jack asked.

"Oh, no, no. I best get back to the kitchen. You two visit." She disappeared around the corner.

I lifted my glass, feeling oddly embarrassed. "Well—*joyeux Nöel*."

He leaned forward and clinked his glass against mine in that American way. "Joyeux Nöel and *bonne année!*"

"Bonne année," I repeated, and took a sip.

I watched his lips as he fit them on the glass. He had wonderful lips. I watched the wine slide down his glass. It was hard to pull my eyes away. "Have you any news about a visa?"

"I'm afraid not. I've used every connection I can find. The immigration quotas are very tight, and they favor displaced persons."

"But I am a displaced person!"

"Yes, I would agree, but the government defines displaced persons as people who were forcibly removed or forced to flee their home countries. You're a Frenchwoman, still in France."

"Oh." My spirits sank.

"But." He set down his glass. "There might be something that will benefit you on the horizon. I understand that Congress is going to pass a War Brides Act in just a few days."

"A War Brides Act? What is that?"

"It is legislation that will clear the way for the wives and children and possibly the fiancées of American servicemen to come to the United States."

"Oh, that would be wonderful!"

"Yes. Since you have Doug's child, hopefully you will be included."

I practically vibrated with joy. This was exactly what Yvette would have wanted.

"I assume you have Doug listed as the father on the child's birth certificate?"

My spirits nosedived. "I—I do not have a birth certificate." My mouth was dry. My palms were suddenly damp. "Elise was delivered by midwife."

"I see." He took a sip of wine and looked thoughtful. "Well, I will find out what the requirements are. I should know in a few days."

"So there is hope."

"Yes." He took a sip of wine. "What about you? Do you have identification and a passport?"

"Yes." Yvette and I had applied for a passport at the local prefecture soon after Paris was liberated.

"That is good. If you didn't, I was going to offer to help you get them."

"That is kind."

"Yes, well . . . I wanted to let you know that I am shipping out in January."

Next month! I had only a few weeks before my only hope of help would be gone.

"I—I see." I forced a smile. "Do you have family in the United States?" I wondered if this was something I should know. I decided to clear the air on that. "Doug didn't write me about where you were from or your family—just that you were a wonderful doctor, very wise and capable, and how much he admired you."

His eyes took on a pained look. "I am so sorry Doug is gone."

"Yes." I looked down at my lap.

"To answer your question, yes, I have family—my mother, a sister, and a brother-in-law. They all live in a small town in Louisiana called Wedding Tree. *L'arbre du mariage.*"

"How lovely."

"I also have a fiancée."

"Oh. I see." For some reason, this depressed me immensely.

"Her father is a doctor. I plan to go into practice with him."

"In Wedding Tree?"

"Yes. He is the reason I became a doctor."

"He must be very special."

"He is. He cares a great deal about the people he treats. I hope to be as good a doctor as he someday."

"I am sure you already are."

"Oh, no. It will take a lifetime of practice." He took a sip of wine. "Will you open your gift?"

"But I have nothing to give you."

"Oh, I want nothing from you. But I wanted to give you something."

"I don't know that is it proper for me to . . ."

"Please," he interrupted. "I want to do it for Doug."

"Oh." My eyes inexplicably filled with tears. I was always on the verge of tears these days. "Oh, that is very kind of you."

"Here." He placed a large package on my lap.

I untied the big red bow and opened the box. Inside was a pair of black low-heeled shoes, made of the softest leather. "Oh, these are wonderful!"

"I guessed at your size. If they don't fit, I can exchange them."

I slid off my wooden-soled shoes and pulled the new ones on. They fit better than any shoes I had worn since I was sixteen—six long years ago.

"They are perfect!" I said.

"I noticed that your shoes looked uncomfortable the other day."

"Oh." My face heated. And here I'd thought I was dressed so well. I had painted the soles black, but the sound of wood on the hard floor had no doubt given me away. "Thank you. Thank you very much!"

"Will you open the gift for the baby?"

"Yes, of course." I opened the other box, and pulled out a pacifier, a blanket, and a little blue dress with buttons shaped like daisies. "Oh, it is so lovely!"

"You like it?"

"It's beautiful!"

Jack looked at his watch, then gazed up, his eyes regretful. "I must be going."

"Yes. I understand."

"I will let you know in a week or two if we can get you to America through the War Brides Act."

"Thank you. Thank you so much. Thanks for me, and on behalf of Elise." *And, especially, on behalf of Yvette*, I added silently.

"You are welcome." He looked at me, and his eyes were like the blue part of a flame. "Well, Merry Christmas."

I leaned in for la bise. His lips brushed one cheek, and then the other. A jolt of electricity shot through me. "Bonsoir," I murmured.

"À bientôt." *Until later*. Oh, how I hoped to see him again—and how I feared he would leave for America without helping me. He straightened and walked off into the night, his broad shoulders squared, taking with him all my hopes of fulfilling my promise to Yvette.

39

AMÉLIE
1946

Ten days later, I received a note from Jack that he would like to come by on Tuesday night.

I spent an inordinate amount of time trying to look my best. Monday evening I washed my hair and Nora helped me roll it. The next morning, she helped me arrange it in loose curls. It was finally getting long enough that I no longer looked like a poodle.

After his visit on Christmas Eve, I had told Nora all about Jack. Her breath had caught at the boldness of my lie. Her hands had folded across her heart. "Mon Dieu, mon Dieu," she had muttered, pausing to make the sign of the cross—but she understood that keeping my promise to Yvette was of tantamount importance. "Ma chérie, I pray that this is a case where *la fin justifie les moyens*"—the end justifies the means.

I put Elise in the dress Jack had given her for Christmas. She was still awake when a knock sounded on the door at seven.

Jack brought a bottle of wine, a bottle of olive oil—oh, how wonderful! Cooking oil was still very scarce—some formula, and some American chocolate. We exchanged la bise. He smelled good—like soap and shaving cream—and I felt a disconcerting little jump of my stomach.

Nora greeted him warmly and exclaimed over his gifts. She carried them to the kitchen, then returned to hand us each a glass of wine. She took the baby, freeing me to focus on Jack.

We settled on the sofa once again, each of us with a glass of wine.

"You have news?" I asked.

"Yes." He put down his glass, and I could immediately tell that the news was not good. "I am so sorry, but without a birth certificate, we cannot prove that the baby is Doug's. Without proof, she does not qualify under the War Brides Act to enter the U.S. And I am afraid that since you and Doug were not married, you are not qualified, either."

The words stung. I felt as if I were being judged by the entire U.S.A. and found lacking.

"But we were engaged!"

"I understand. But unfortunately, there are no provisions at this time for fiancées."

"But there may be in the future?"

"Yes, but . . ." He looked away. "My understanding is that they will only apply to servicemen who will marry the women within three months' time. There are no provisions for the fiancées or the . . ." He broke off and hesitated.

"What?"

"I know no gentle way to say this."

"So just say it."

I watched his Adam's apple bob. "There are no provisions for the illegitimate children of dead servicemen."

Elise was not mine—I knew that, logically; I knew it was all a lie. And yet I felt a powerful sense of shame at the word. Tears sprang to my eyes.

"I am so sorry," he said.

"I am, too." I swiped my face with hand. He pulled out a handkerchief and handed it to me. It smelled of starch and soap and man, and it was warm from his pocket. "When do you leave for America?"

"Next week."

"Next week," I repeated. "So soon!"

"I want to leave you some money."

"I do not want your money. I want your help getting Elise to America."

"I am sorry, but there is nothing I can do."

"Yes, there is."

His eyebrows quirked up. "There is?"

I nodded.

"Well, then, just name it."

I drew a deep breath and said the most daring words I have ever uttered, before or since, even bolder than my lie about being Doug's fiancée. "You can marry me."

KAT
2016

I feel as if an arrow has been shot through my chest. I sit perfectly still, letting my body adjust to the pain.

Oh, I had known it! I had known she tricked him—but I didn't know how sneakily!

"The whole marriage was your idea?"

"Yes."

"You lied to Jack about Doug, and then you flat-out asked him to marry you?"

"Yes."

"Ad he did so because he owed Doug his life."

"Yes."

"But the baby wasn't even Doug's."

"Yes."

"You ruined my whole life because you told a pack of lies!"

"Ruined your life?" Amélie's eyebrows rise. "You told me you had a wonderful life."

"Well, yes, but it wasn't the life I wanted back then. I was in love with Jack. I wanted to stay in Wedding Tree."

"And I wanted to stay in Paris."

"I do not believe you."

She shrugs. "Believe what you will. It is not my job to convince you. I am simply telling you what you want to know."

"Why would you not want to come to America?"

"Aside from the fact that I would be a foreigner in a strange country, where I would know no one? Would you want to do such a thing?"

"No, but I was not in your situation."

"No, you were not. So you are in no position to judge."

I feel that I am in the perfect position to judge. I am about to snap out a snippy reply, but she doesn't allow me the chance.

"Coming to America was Yvette's dream for Elise, not mine for myself, but I felt I had to honor her wishes for her child."

I can see how that might be so. But that is not what I am interested in learning. "It doesn't really make any difference to me. I want to hear about Jack."

"Of course you do."

"So tell me," I say. "What did Jack say when you proposed to him?"

AMÉLIE
1946

*J*ack looked at me as if I were crazy. "Marry you? I am engaged to another woman."

I leaned forward. "It wouldn't be a real marriage. We wouldn't . . ." I hesitated. The idea had occurred to me when he first mentioned the War Brides Act—how could it not?—but I had not thought it through. I was making it up as I talked. I was stopped by an indelicate word. Oh, what the hell—if he could say *illegitimate*, I could say this.

"We wouldn't consummate the marriage, of course. We would have a ceremony to get a marriage certificate, which would allow Elise and me to enter the country. Once there, you and I can get a quick annulment—you can get marriages annulled on the basis of it not being consummated, yes?—and then you can marry your fiancée as if nothing happened."

"Oh, I can't possibly do that."

"Why not?"

"It's deceitful. It wouldn't be right."

Years of pent-up frustration and anger swelled up in me. At that moment, I understood the expression *to see red*. Everything seemed hot and colored in a blood-hued haze.

"Wouldn't be *right*?" I exclaimed. "Tell me this: Is it *right* that Doug stepped forward, and took the machine gun fire intended for you? Is it *right* that you are alive and he is dead?"

He dropped his head.

"You would not be here if not for Doug. How is it *right* that you get to go home, to safety and family and plenty to eat and an opportunity to work, and Doug's child stays here with nothing?"

He continued staring at the floor.

"In war, the concept of 'right' stands on its head! It is not right to lie—and yet I lied over and over and over again to help the Résistance free my country. It is not right to go through people's private possessions, yet I went through Nazi coat pockets and briefcases and suitcases every chance I got. It is not right to murder, and yet in war, that is not only the job, but the duty and sacred trust of every soldier holding a gun and facing the enemy. Do not talk to me about what is right!"

"I understand," Jack said.

"All I ask is an opportunity for this baby to grow up in America—an opportunity she would have had if her father had not been killed. On your behalf, I might add! I am sure your fiancée would gladly postpone your wedding if she knew the circumstances."

"I think it would be a very difficult thing to explain."

"Difficult, but not impossible, no? Is she not sympathetic?"

He hesitated for a moment. "She sees things in very black-and-white terms."

"I would think she would be so grateful that you are alive that she would want you to help Doug's family in any way you can."

"She will not see it that way."

"She wouldn't want to help the child of the man who saved your life?"

"Her father would. Her father—he could talk to her."

"But you do not think your fiancée would have pity on a fatherless child?"

"She would not understand your position. She hasn't been in a war, so she can't understand what it feels like to think you will die. She doesn't know how quickly passions can rise, especially in extreme circumstances."

I had a flash of insight. "You and she have not made love."

"No. She does not believe it is right to have sex before marriage."

"So she will think I am a loose woman with a bastard baby—that Elise and I are not worthy of your help."

"I did not say that."

"You did not need to." I glared at him. "This fiancée of yours does not sound like a very nice person. And if you are like her, well, then perhaps you are not so nice, either."

"You judge her too harshly. She is young and inexperienced."

"And you? You would let her potential disapproval keep you from doing the right thing? You can go off and have a happy, carefree life in America, leaving Doug's child here?"

He blew out a hard sigh. He rose and strode across the room. He stared out the window. He walked back and sat down again.

"No. I could not live with myself if I go off and leave you two here. You are right. I owe it to Doug to help you get to America."

I paused, scarcely daring believe I had heard correctly. "Vraiment?"

"Yes. I will do it."

"When?"

"Tomorrow. The sooner we get the paperwork in order, the sooner I can see about getting you on a bride boat."

"A bride boat?"

"Yes. The Red Cross and the U.S. government will bring the wives of servicemen across on ships, at no charge to wives or the servicemen. They will start with a boat for officers' wives in a couple of weeks."

"Oh, this is wonderful news!"

Jack gave a tight smile. "I doubt that my fiancée will see it that way, but I must do what is in the best interests of the child. Do you know what is required for marriage?"

I nodded. A girl at the hotel had recently gotten married. "We must go to the town hall in my arrondissement. I will need identification papers and a witness, and so will you. I think you will need a passport and I will need proof of residency. I believe that is all."

"All right, then. I will bring a witness and come for you at ten o'clock in the morning."

AMÉLIE
January 1946

I had been worried that Jack might change his mind after sleeping on it, but he knocked on my door at 9:50 the next morning. With him was a man he introduced as Peter Barrett, who was also a U.S. Army doctor. Peter was an older man—maybe late thirties or early forties—and he wore a wedding ring. He looked at me with frank curiosity.

I had arranged to pay another neighbor, a woman with two children of her own, to watch Elise, and I had already taken her upstairs. I wore Yvette's yellow silk dress, which I had cut down to fit me, along with her matching hat, and the shoes that Jack had given me.

Nora handed Jack a small box as he entered the apartment. "This is a ring you can put on her finger," she said.

"Oh, Nora—not your wedding ring!" I protested.

"It is not mine. It was my mother's, and I have no need of it. You do."

"But . . ."

"But nothing. I want you to have it."

"You should wear it," Peter said. "A wedding ring is a very big thing to Americans."

It was to the French, as well. I gave Nora a hug and my heartfelt thanks.

Peter reached for the box. "In America, the best man keeps the ring until it is time for the groom to put it on the bride's finger."

The town hall was only about ten blocks from our apartment, so we walked. Nora insisted that we stop along the way so that Jack could buy me a bouquet and I could buy him a boutonniere.

"It will seem odd if you do not have it," she said. "You do not want to raise suspicions. And the official is likely to have a few. You two do not look like a couple in love."

Peter laughed heartily and winked at Nora. "They look more like a couple going to the guillotine."

"Or as if they had curdled milk for breakfast," Nora said.

Peter laughed again.

"They talk about us as if we are not here," I said to Jack.

He nodded, his face wooden.

"Are you all right?"

"Yes. Just very conflicted about what I am about to do."

"Me, too. But I am thinking of Elise."

"Yes. Elise, and Doug," Jack said.

The words pierced me like an dagger. I silently reminded myself of Nora's words: the ends justify the means.

At a corner flower stand, he bought me a little nosegay with a white rose in the center, and I bought him a single white rosebud. My hand shook as I fastened it on his jacket lapel.

Before I knew it, we were at 31 rue Peclet, standing in front of the town hall of the fifteenth arrondissement. We went inside and found the office where we filled out the application and showed our papers. Jack paid a fee, and then we were shown into a room where an *officier de l'état civil* would perform the ceremony.

It was a lovely room, with high ceilings and a small table up front. In the back were seats for the witnesses.

A tall, dignified gentleman who resembled General De Gaulle walked in, wearing a blue, red, and white sash. He examined the papers the outer office had given us, then instructed us to stand before him.

"I am old-fashioned, so I like my brides and grooms to exchange vows. Is this all right with you?"

I nodded. So did Jack.

"Do you have a ring?"

Peter produced it from his pocket and handed it to Jack.

"Please place this on her finger as you repeat after me. 'I, Jonathan Bradford O'Connor'—I had not known that Jack was a nickname, much less known his entire name!—'take you, Amélie Therese Michaud, to be my wedded wife. I promise to be faithful to you in happiness or in trials, in health or in sickness, and to love you all of my life.'"

Jack solemnly repeated the vow. He slid the ring onto my finger.

I repeated the same thing, holding his hand. His eyes were fixed steadily on mine. I knew it was not real, but Jack was so attractive and so kind, and it was easy to be swept into a fantasy. At the moment I said the age-old words, I meant them with all my heart.

The official then turned to Jack. "Jonathan Bradford O'Connor, do you want to take this woman as your lawfully wedded wife? If so, respond 'I want it.'"

"*Je te veut*," he said.

Nora twittered.

"The correct response is *Je le veut*," the official gently corrected.

"Pardon." Jack said. His cheeks colored, so I knew he realized what he'd just said: *I want you.*

"Mademoiselle, do you want to take this man as your lawfully wedded husband?"

"*Oui, je le veut.*" I grinned up at Jack's still embarrassed face. "*Et je te veux aussi.*"

Everyone laughed.

"I pronounce you husband and wife."

Nora and Peter applauded.

"You may kiss your bride," the official said.

Jack hesitated, then tentatively leaned down toward me. I tilted my head up. Our lips brushed, softly. It was a light kiss—a kiss that was little more than a peck, really—but I felt it all the way down to my toes. For reasons I cannot name, I pressed forward just as he was about to pull back. Our eyes locked, and something changed. He deepened the kiss and my eyes fluttered closed. This kiss was slower, more thorough, more intimate. Still brief, of course, but it was the kind of kiss a man gives when he desires a woman.

When he pulled away, he looked at me, his eyes dark and surprised, the expression so fleeting I wondered if I had only imagined it.

"Congratulations," said the official. He shook Jack's hand, then placed some documents on the table in front of us. "Now, if you and your wife will please sign the marriage certificate and two copies."

Jack signed, then I signed, then our witnesses signed.

"And now it is time for the photographs," the official said. He opened the door behind him and the woman from the front desk came in.

"Oh, we don't . . ." Jack began.

But Nora was already pulling Yvette's camera out of the case. "Wonderful. Let me take a photograph of the newlyweds with you, monsieur, and then perhaps your secretary will take a photo with all of us in it."

"Of course." The official stepped beside us, posed, and smiled.

"I don't think . . ." Jack began again.

"Elise will want the photos for when she is older," Nora told him.

And so a few photos were taken.

"Well. It's done," Jack said when we'd left the building and climbed down on the steps.

"Yes." I stood awkwardly on the sidewalk. I did not know what to say to this new husband of mine. "Thank you."

He shoved his hands in his pocket and gave a curt nod. His face looked strained. "It seemed the right thing to do under the circumstances."

Not exactly the words a bride dreams of hearing from her groom on her wedding day.

"You will have Elise's undying gratitude," I said. "And mine, too, of course."

"Let's go have some champagne!" Peter suggested.

"We have to get back to work," Jack said curtly.

"But it's nearly lunchtime," Peter protested. "Come on, man—you have to eat."

"I'll eat at the hospital. I need to get back." He gave me a slight bow. "I'll find out where I need to file this paperwork in order to get you on the first boat to the United States."

"Thank you," I said. "Will I—will I see you again before you ship out?"

"I don't know."

"All right. Well, then . . ."

He held out his palm, as if to shake my hand. I must have looked stricken, because he leaned in for la bise. "Sorry," he whispered. "I'm finding this whole thing very difficult."

Peter said his good-byes, as well. With an apologetic shrug, he turned toward Jack, and I watched them both walk away.

KAT
2016

"So marrying you—it bothered Jack's conscience?"

"Yes. He was very conflicted."

"Good." My spirits soar—until a detail of her story reins them in. "You said he kissed you like a man kisses a woman he desires."

"Yes."

"But you forced the kiss."

"I leaned in, that is all."

"Yes, well, Jack would have felt pressure to act appropriately. And he hadn't kissed a woman in over a year, so of course he was going to be receptive. He was only human, after all. Man is first and foremost an animal."

Amélie's expressive eyebrows rise. "Is that what you think?"

I smooth my hair. "Well, my father was a doctor, and he always said that man's basic instincts are the same as those of any mammal."

"Is that so?" She gives a small smile. "You never told me about when Jack first kissed you."

"Ah. It was after the high school homecoming dance. Jack bought me a corsage—six hothouse roses." *Unlike the single rose in your wedding nosegay*, I think with an edge of triumph. "It was my first formal dance. I wore a blue dress with a full tulle skirt and a sweetheart neckline, and Jack said I looked like a princess." I had felt like a princess that night. I had spent the whole day getting ready.

"On the way to the dance, Jack told me that he was going to graduate from high school that December—that he'd been accepted into the army's accelerated training program for college, and that he would have completed all the required high school courses at the end of the semester. It almost ruined things for me, knowing he would be leaving sooner than I had thought. I was irritated that he had chosen what should have been a perfect night to give me bad news.

"The dance was wonderful, though. I felt so beautiful in my dress, so proud to be on Jack's arm.

"When the dance ended, he walked me to my front door. I looked up at him expectantly. Sure enough, he leaned down and pulled me close, and then, well—it was wonderful. The fact we'd waited so long made the kiss all the sweeter. I could have kissed him all night long, but he ended it all too soon.

"I floated up to my bed and replayed it in my head, dreaming of the next time we would kiss, deliberately avoiding thinking about the fact he would be leaving in less than three months' time."

Amélie tilts her head. "Sounds like a scene from a teenaged movie."

I am afraid that there is some hidden snideness in her remark, but I can't find it. "Yes, it was." I need to get her talking again. "I am sorry I interrupted. Did you see Jack again before he left?"

"No. The next time we met was in New York."

"Tell me about it."

"In due course. First I must tell you about the trip over."

I do not care about that, but Amélie is determined to tell this in her own way. I squash my impatience and settle back for another long story.

Book
Two

AMÉLIE
1946

*N*ora had tears in her eyes as she stood with me at the train station two weeks later. "Are you sure about this?"

"Yes. Absolutely."

"I'm worried that you never heard from Yvette's aunt and uncle."

I was, too, but I wouldn't admit it. The mail was still unpredictable. "I will send you back your ring. I will send it through more reliable means than the mail, however."

"I want you to keep it. Sell it, if you need to. It is yours. I give it to you with no strings attached."

My eyes filled with tears. I grasped her hands. "Will you be all right?"

"Yes. I am thinking that I might apply for a job at the milliner's shop where Yvette worked."

"Oh, you would be very good at that!"

"I think I would enjoy it."

"You have been like a mother to me—and to Yvette, and Elise. I don't know what any of us would have done without you."

"It was my pleasure."

"You must to come visit me, once I get settled."

"Yes. Or perhaps you will bring Elise back for a visit."

"Oh, I most definitely want to do that."

We hugged. We were both crying. Elise started to cry, too, and that was the thing that pulled us through—tending to her.

A lady with a Red Cross armband raised her hand.

"That is our escort," I told Nora. "She's signaling that it's time to go."

Nora smiled bravely. "Off with you, then. You and Elise will have a wonderful new life. God bless and bon voyage!"

"Merci. Au revoir!" With a final hug, I took Elise from her arms, gathered up my purse and diaper bag, and boarded the train.

I was traveling with a group of other officers' wives to Le Havre, where we would board the ship. The Red Cross had organized the entire trip. The representative helped me with my luggage and showed me to the assigned railcar.

I sank into a seat beside a young woman with blond hair. "Oh, what a beautiful baby," she said, holding out her finger to Elise.

"Thank you." I had gotten better at claiming credit for Elise's beauty, because that was what people seemed to want from me.

"How long has it been since you've seen your husband?" she asked.

"Two weeks."

"Oh, you're so lucky! I haven't seen mine in seven months."

"Seven months!"

"Yes. And he hasn't seen me like this." She cast a rueful look at her pregnant belly. "Was that your mother?"

It took me a moment to realize she meant Nora. "No. She was a neighbor. My mother died during the war."

"I'm so sorry to hear it."

"Yes."

You must live in Paris, since a neighbor came to see you off."

"Yes. And you?"

"Near Marseilles. My name is Heloise Bradley."

I introduced myself, as well.

"I came to Paris yesterday," Heloise said. "The Red Cross put me up in a hotel." She smiled. "I'd never been to Paris before. I wish I'd had more time here to see the sights. I was glad the Eiffel Tower was not bombed."

"We were mostly spared the bombs," I said.

"Did you meet your husband in Paris?" she asked. "How long have you been married?"

I couldn't very well say just a few weeks—not with Elise. I decided to tell the Doug story, substituting Jack for Doug. "We met in Normandy, where I was staying with my aunt and uncle at their farm."

"Oh, our ship sails from Normandy!" the girl said. "You'll have to tell me all about the area. Will you see your aunt and uncle?"

Oh, la! Right off the bat, I was about to be caught in a lie. "Non. They did not make it through the war."

"I'm so sorry. Were they far from Le Havre?"

"Yes. They were out in the country." I turned to the window and dabbed my eyes, hoping to discourage further conversation.

Heloise held her tongue for not quite a minute. "How did you meet your husband?"

I would need to remember whatever I told her, because I would probably have to repeat the story to many other brides on the ship. I decided to give few details and to stick close to Doug's story. "Jack became separated from his unit. My family hid him for ten days. We fell in love and became engaged, and later married in Paris."

"Oh, how marvelous! A Paris wedding! Was it a big celebration?"

"No, very small. And you?"

"Oh, I met my Ronnie in November of '44, when the Americans landed in Marseilles. My friends and I were greeting the soldiers—giving them flowers, just letting them know how very happy we were to see them. I also handed out little thank-you notes with my name and address with my flowers. He was one of five soldiers who wrote me, and we started a correspondence. He got leave seven months ago, right after the war ended, and he came to meet my family—and, well, sparks just flew. He asked my father asked if he could marry me—it was funny, because his French is terrible, and my father didn't understand English; he thought Ronnie wanted to work for him!

"Anyway, we were married at the local courthouse. My mother cried that we didn't get married in a church, but she understood. I wore her wedding dress. We honeymooned at a hotel in Nice—oh, it was so lovely! But it was only three days. That was all the leave extension we could get, and then he went back to the U.S. He's at Fort Benning. That's in Georgia. I can't wait to see him again!"

"How wonderful," I said. "So you will live in Georgia?"

"Yes, until he musters out of the army. Do you know where you are going to live?"

"Yes. In New York City."

"Oh, so you'll be home as soon as we disembark."

"Yes." Dear God, I hoped so. I would not admit, even to myself, how concerned I was about not hearing from Yvette's aunt. I feared we would not be welcome—or that they would welcome Elise, but not me.

I shoved the worries into a closet in my mind and locked the door. I would find a way to stay near to Elise, or I would die trying. In the meantime, I would deal with what must be done today to move forward.

It took more than three hours by train to get to Le Havre. Once there, the trip was not over. We were herded onto buses for transport to the Philip Morris camp near Gainneville, France. Built after the Normandy invasion as a staging areas for troops arriving in Europe, Philip Morris was one of several "Cigarette Camps" named after brands of American cigarettes. Now, it was used to process troops—and their brides—on the way back to the U.S. We were to be there a week, during which we would be given physicals and vaccinations, exchange our francs for U.S. dollars, and receive instructions about life in America.

It was an austere, treeless camp of Quonset huts and long, low buildings with pitched roofs. After standing in line and filling out even more paperwork for what seemed like forever, we were assigned to barracks. We slept in a Quonset hut lined with bunk beds, with a big coal stove in the middle. The women close to it were uncomfortably hot and the ones at the ends were freezing. Heloise and I managed to find bunks about halfway down—as close to ideal as possible. Our belongings were stashed at the end of our bunks.

The bathrooms were in a separate building. It was cold and damp and windy to get to it, and I pitied the pregnant women—who, if they were anything like Yvette, would need to make multiple nighttime trips.

We were told our bunkhouse was scheduled for the first seating for dinner, so we cleaned up and went to the dining hall.

There we found a pleasant surprise—delicious food. Lots and lots of it, too—more food than I had seen in ages. We were served meatloaf and mashed potatoes and gravy, along with green beans and bread and pudding. Our plates were served by stout Germans—apparently prisoners of war.

"Look how fat they are," said a woman with curly red hair. "They've been eating American food while we've been barely surviving on rations. Hardly seems fair."

It was hard not to feel bitter, especially after having seen the French prisoners of war returning from the German prison camps. I had seen some in Paris, getting off a train; they'd looked like walking skeletons, their arms the size of twigs, their cheeks so sunken their faces looked like skulls.

The Quonset hut mess hall was filled to capacity, and there were two other seatings. Six hundred brides, we learned, from all over France as well as Italy, Germany, Belgium, and who knows where else, were to sail on January 18.

"I've heard they're using luxury liners to transport some brides," my new friend, who never seemed to shut up for a second, nattered on the next morning at breakfast. "But apparently we're not going to get one of those. We're sailing on a Liberty ship."

"What is that?" I asked.

"A cargo ship. One built on an assembly line in the U.S., churned out in a matter of weeks during the war."

"Well, as long as it stays afloat and crosses the Atlantic, it'll be good enough for me," I said.

A week later, I was ready to eat those words. Eight women, plus Elise and two other babies, were crammed into a tiny cabin aboard the SS *Zebulon*

B. Vance. The room was built for no more than four, and most probably two. Heloise had arranged things so that she was rooming with me—I don't know why she gravitated to me, but she had, and as annoying as her constant chatter could be, it was good to have a familiar face.

There were four two-decker bunk beds in each cabin, so those of us with babies had to share our narrow mattress with our child. I was accustomed to sleeping with Elise, and she was now eight months old—but one of the women with a young infant was terrified of rolling over onto her child or having the baby fall out the bed. I took an upper berth—Elise would sleep against the wall, so I could make sure she did not fall—so that Heloise could have a lower bunk. The other two women with babies also took lower bunks: Lucia, an Italian from Naples who hardly spoke any French and only a little English, and Stephanie, a rail-thin brunette from Normandy, who seemed very shy and seldom said anything. A woman from Cannes, an extremely well dressed and pretty woman who radiated an aura of entitlement, claimed the last lower bunk without even questioning if one of the other women needed it.

The bathroom situation was nightmarish at the beginning, and that was when things were still clean. Instead of a bathroom for each room, which we heard the ocean liners provided, we made do with rows of toilets lined up in the hull of the ship—side by side, back-to-back, with no privacy whatsoever. The showers also had no privacy.

I double-diapered Elise at night, and yet we both still sometimes woke up soaked.

Food on the ship, like at the camp, was excellent and plentiful, but seasickness was so rampant that hardly anyone could eat it. We were all ill in varying degrees. As a cargo ship, the *Vance* did not have the ballast that passenger vessels had; consequently we were tossed and sloshed by every wave.

I was nauseous, but not as bad as poor Heloise. At first, she couldn't keep anything down. We went to see the Red Cross, and they told us we had to take care of each other in our room, that the infirmary was full.

I talked to a bride in another cabin who had worked as a nurse's aide during the war. "Tell her to go back to the infirmary again. She needs to insist on getting an IV. It's very easy for pregnant women and babies to get dehydrated, which makes the vomiting worse. An IV is the only thing that will help."

I escorted her back to the infirmary and insisted that she be treated. A nurse, somewhat reluctantly, gave her an IV, and Heloise perked up immediately.

The trip, which took only six to eight days on an ocean liner, was supposed to take twelve on a cargo ship like the *Zebulon B. Vance*. It ended up taking sixteen due to bad weather. The toilets stopped working about halfway across. The smell was beyond atrocious. By the end of the trip, we were wading through excrement to go to the bathroom.

Worst off were the small babies. Soon after we boarded, the Red Cross asked all the mothers to surrender their formula, so that they could handle mixing and heating the bottles.

"Don't do it," I whispered to the two young mothers in my cabin. "You don't know how well they will sterilize things." Stephanie heeded my warning, but Lucia either didn't understand me or was afraid to not follow orders.

As it turned out, I was right. Stephanie used her tea water to mix her baby's formula, as I did for Elise, since the tea water was boiled. Many of the other babies grew very ill.

Toward the end of the trip, Lucia's baby reached the point where she was practically unconscious. Her crying produced no tears. Lucia took her to the infirmary, and was sent away.

I insisted on accompanying them back there again while Stephanie watched Elise.

"I'm sorry, but there's nothing we can do," said the nurse in the small reception room.

"Yes, there is. This child is dehydrated and needs an IV immediately." I headed for the door behind her.

"You can't go in there," the nurse said, but I had already guided Lucia and her frail infant into the treatment room. It was crammed with women laying on cots or in chairs, many holding babies. "Where is the doctor?"

"He is busy."

I saw a door marked "Doctor's Office." Below it was a sign: "Do Not Enter." I pushed it open anyway.

"Stop! You can't . . ."

But it was too late. I saw the doctor, his eyes closed, leaning back in his desk chair behind a desk littered with paperwork—but what drew my eye were three large ice coolers lined up against the wall, with six little lumps covered with pillowcases. One of them was not entirely covered; I stared at the little baby toes sticking out beneath it.

"Mon Dieu!" My hands flew over my mouth in horror.

Lucia, behind me, let out a sound that was half whimper, half cry.

The doctor, a man with a gray fringe of hair around his balding head, jerked awake. He rose from his chair, along with the heavy scent of whiskey. "You are not supposed to be in here."

"Those babies are dead!" I gasped.

"You are not to be in here," he repeated.

"We are here to keep another baby from dying. This child is dehydrated."

He looked at Lucia, rather than the child in her arms. "It looks like it's too late," he said. "I have very few IVs left, and I have to save them."

"For whom?"

"The—the crew. I can't run out of supplies."

It was because Lucia was Italian. I instinctively knew it. I drew up to my tallest height. "If you don't give this child an IV, I'm going to the dining room and announcing that there are six dead babies in here, that the ship's doctor is drunk, and that you are withholding treatment that could save another baby. You will have six hundred women beating down your door to kill you."

"It is not my fault!"

"If you don't want me to make an announcement, you will put an IV in this child immediately."

I do not know where my authoritative tone came from, but it worked. The doctor fumed and harrumphed, but he told the nurse, in English, to get an IV and a baby cot for the hallway.

"And a chair," I added, also in English. "The mother will stay here with her child tonight."

Two Red Cross nurses came forward. "You must not say anything about what you saw," said one who wore a Supervisor pin on her shirt.

"I will say whatever I want."

"It will cause mass panic. We will dock tomorrow. The mothers will be better off learning the fate of their children when they are with their husbands."

"They don't know?" My heart sank for the poor, unfortunate mothers of those poor, unfortunate babies. "What are you telling them in the meantime?"

"That the doctor is treating their children. That he's doing all he can and that they can't see them because they must be quarantined."

"Do you have a plan for telling them?"

"Yes. We will call their husbands aboard so they will have support, then the chaplain will break the news."

I weighed the consequences. There was no good way to handle this terrible problem; at least the plan seemed humane. "Very well. I will say nothing until I am off the ship. But Lucia will stay here with her baby tonight, and she will get the best treatment available. Furthermore, any other baby that comes in will automatically get an IV, as long as there is one single IV left. You will hold nothing back for the crew. Do we have a deal?"

"Yes," the head nurse agreed.

Just to be sure, I sat with Lucia until midnight, then crawled into my bunk and fell heavily asleep beside my own sweet Elise.

AMÉLIE
1946

*W*e're here! We're here!" Heloise rushed into the cabin the next morning. She had been on deck since before daybreak, watching as we neared New York. "Come, Amélie—you have to come see the Statue of Liberty!"

"I'll watch Elise," Stephanie promised, looking at my sleeping child.

I tied a scarf over my head and grabbed my coat. I followed Heloise out the door and down the narrow hall, then clanged up the narrow metal stairway to the deck.

I had already been to the infirmary that morning. Lucia's baby had made it through the night and was showing signs of great improvement. I'd brought a bottle of formula—Stephanie's formula, made with water from my tea—and the child had eagerly gulped it all. The head nurse said that if she kept it down, the IV would be removed and she would be cleared to leave.

My heart ached for the women who were about to discover that the babies they'd given life to no longer lived.

The wind cut me, stealing my breath as I pushed through the heavy metal door and stepped onto the deck. Heloise and I were the only women outside. The rest were staying warm and, more importantly, protecting their hairstyles—most of us had rolled our hair the night before and were doing everything possible to look our best for our husbands. It was very difficult, with the bathroom situation as disgusting as is it was. With my short hair and natural curls, I was less worried than many of the others.

We sailed right past the Statue of Liberty. Oh, she was a beautiful sight, so large and stately and tall! I thought we were going to stop there—I had read that Ellis Island was the entry point for all immigrants—but we kept going and sailed straight into New York Harbor. As the wives of servicemen, we had special visas.

People were already milling around on the dock, waiting for the ship. Lots of men, a few middle-aged couples and some families—in-laws, no doubt, anxious to meet their new daughters-in-law. My heart turned over. Oh, how lucky these girls were, to have loving husbands eagerly waiting to welcome them to America!

"Do you see your husband?" Heloise asked me.

"No." I didn't expect to—not until the afternoon, at any rate. The instructions had said that we would disembark some time after noon. "Do you see yours?"

"No. But I don't want to look yet. I want to get myself glammed up before he sees me."

"And if you don't see him, he won't see you?"

She laughed. "Something like that."

We hurried below deck and packed up the last of our things. We went to breakfast, but not many of us could eat. Seasickness still dogged many of us, and excitement had dampened the appetites of others.

The previous evening, we had been given instructions for disembarking.

"You are to gather in the dining hall," a Red Cross official had told us. "We will use a loudspeaker to announce your names as your husbands arrive. No one will be allowed off the ship unless your husband or a family member is here."

"Pardon." A bride I did not know raised a tentative hand. "What if a husband is delayed and he cannot send someone else? What happens to the bride?"

"I am sorry, but in that event, the woman must stay on the ship and return to France."

Every woman moaned.

"I am afraid that will happen to me," Stephanie murmured.

Surprised, I turned to her. Her eyes were wet with tears.

"The last time my husband wrote, he said perhaps we had made a mistake. I wrote to him, begging him to give us a chance. I told him things would be better in America, that I would be a good wife—but I fear he will not come."

"Oh, you cannot seriously think this!" Heloise said.

"I do. I do, and . . . I'm afraid."

"Why didn't you say anything?"

"I—I was ashamed. And I didn't know what else to do."

"Do you know anyone in America?" I asked.

"I have a cousin in Florida."

"Well, then—we must get you to her."

"But first I have to get off the ship." Tears rolled down her cheeks.

I handed her a handkerchief and helped her pack up her things. We pulled our suitcases and our belongings into the dining room, where we waited as name after name was called. The names were in random order—apparently they were called according to the order that the husbands signed in onshore.

"Mrs. Bradley." The name resounded over the ship's loudspeaker. "Mrs. Ronald Bradley."

"That's me! That's my Ronnie!" Heloise said excitedly.

I gave her a hug. "I'm going to go up and watch you join him."

"Oh, me, too!" said Stephanie. All of the brides from our room, except for the stuck-up one who had not become any friendlier, did the same.

We went to the railing and watched. Heloise made her way down the gangplank. About halfway down, she apparently caught sight of her husband, for she waved, smiled madly, and began to trot, her hugely pregnant belly going before her.

"She better be careful or she's going to trip!" Stephanie said.

A man in a black suit and tie picked her up off her feet and swung her around, despite her size. He handed her flowers and kissed her, then picked her up again.

"She's a lucky devil," sighed Stephanie. "No question her husband wants her here."

"Yes."

"What about you, Amélie? Do you see your husband?"

I looked out over the sea of people, my heart tight and anxious. I didn't want to say it, but I, too, had questions about whether or not Jack would come. His life would be far easier if he just did not show up.

But I was fairly sure, even though I had only seen him a few times, that Dr. Jack O'Connor was a man of his word. After all, he'd gone to a church to convey the confession of a dying man, hadn't he? And he'd provided Christmas gifts and other items for Elise. And he'd gone through with the marriage, hadn't he?

Yes, he would be here. I was certain of it.

But poor Stephanie! We went back inside and sat side by side, each of us trying to quiet our fussing babies, but the children seemed to pick up on our nervousness—especially her poor baby. He wailed and wailed inconsolably. Our wait was punctuated by going outside to see off the remainder of our roommates, then sitting again, on pins and needles, listening to the names being called.

We were down to about fifty brides remaining in the waiting room when, finally, around four-thirty in the afternoon, it came. "Mrs. O'Connor. Mrs. Jonathan O'Connor."

"That's you!"

It took me a moment to recognize my name. I rose, picking up Elise. I hugged Lucia and Stephanie good-bye.

"I hope I'm not going back to France," she said.

"I'll speak to Jack and see if we can do something to help," I said.

I hurried down the gangplank, trying to see over the head of the sailor ahead of me, who was carrying someone's bags. As I neared the end of the slanted board, I saw him—tall and handsome, his dark hair freshly cut and shining in the sun.

I lifted my hand. He did the same. I rushed toward him, then stopped abruptly, suddenly unsure of how to greet him. We awkwardly exchanged la bise. He smelled like aftershave and starch, and the scent of him made my heart flutter. I reminded myself that he did not know I spoke English.

"Bonjour," I said, feeling like a tongue-tied idiot.

"Bonjour. *Bienvenue aux États-Unis.*"

"Merci." I was aware of how weirdly stilted and formal we were with each other, especially when surrounded by the effusive greetings of the other couples.

Jack gave Elise a wide smile. "Hello, little one," he said in French.

She regarded him somberly, then broke into a wide smile. He smiled back.

"She remembers you," I said.

"Do you think?"

"Yes."

"Did you have a good trip?"

"Oh, Jack—it was . . ." My eyes suddenly filled with tears.

His forehead creased in concern. "Is something the matter?"

I didn't want my first words to be a complaint against his country's treatment of us. I shook my head. "It was very tiring."

"I'm sure! I hear you ran into some bad weather. Is this the only bag you have?" He lifted my battered brown suitcase.

I nodded.

"Well, then, let's go."

"Wait." I put one hand on his arm, then quickly withdrew it. Touching him made me feel very self-conscious and nervous. "I'm worried that one of my roommates won't have anyone to meet her."

"What?"

"She said . . . her husband seems to have had a change of heart. The last note she got from him, he said he thought their marriage was a mistake."

"And she came anyway?"

"Yes. She has a baby, and she didn't know what else to do. But the Red Cross told us that if a husband or the husband's family doesn't show up to meet one of us, well, then that bride won't be allowed to get off the boat. So, Jack—do you have a friend here? Someone who could pretend to be her husband?"

His eyes widened. "You want me to ask a friend to lie?"

"Jack, you have no idea of the conditions."

"I know it's bad in France, but . . ."

"I don't mean in France. I mean on that ship." The words came tumbling out. "Jack, the toilets didn't work after the first week. There was human waste all over the floor. There was no ballast on the boat and everyone was seasick. There weren't enough buckets for the vomit. And the babies who drank formula—oh, Jack, I saw six of them dead."

"What?"

"In the infirmary. I took a friend whose child was nearly dead from dehydration. The doctor was drunk, and I saw six dead babies on ice, lying in coolers under pillowcases . . ."

He looked at me as if I were mad. "That ship is operated by the U.S. military. Do you realize how ludicrous this sounds?"

"Yes, yes, I know, but it is the truth. I fear my roommate's baby would not survive the trip back. Do you have a friend who can say he is her husband?"

"No!" His eyes flashed with indignation. "And if I did, I would never ask anyone to commit that kind of deception."

"Well, then, perhaps you can say you are her husband's cousin. She has a cousin Florida. If we can just get her off that boat . . ."

"Attention, please," came a woman's voice through the loudspeaker. "We have a few women who as yet have not had family claim them. Is anyone here for Mrs. Nat Spencer, Mrs. Cyril Freud, Mrs. Arthur Smith, Mrs. Jules Tervot, or Mrs. Sherman Rolls?"

"That's her! Mrs. Sherman Rolls. Stephanie Rolls. You must help her."

"I will not lie. And frankly, Amélie, I'm appalled that you'd ask that of me."

I realized I had made a grave error in judgment, but I didn't know what to do. "Well, we can't just leave her and her baby on the ship."

"This is a matter for the officials to handle."

"She needs our help. Please, Jack."

He blew out an exasperated sigh, then turned and stared at the ship. "Take Elise into the terminal and get her warm," he said. "I'll see what I can do."

I headed into the terminal. From the window, I watched him talk to the Red Cross worker on the gangplank. She would not let him aboard, but she signaled a crewmember, said something to him, and the crewmember went inside the ship. I waited an hour, alternately sitting on my suitcase and walking Elise. I watched Jack talk to a ship's officer. I left my perch at the window once to go change Elise's diaper, and when I came back, I saw Jack talking to yet another Red Cross worker.

At length Jack returned, threading his way through the thinning crowd in the terminal.

"Well?"

"Your friend's husband came and collected her."

"Oh, how wonderful!"

"Apparently he'd had a case of cold feet, but he got over it. They were billing and cooing like a pair of turtle doves."

"I'm so relieved!"

"I suspect she might be in for a tough time, though. He had a black eye, and he reeked of whiskey."

"Well, at least he came for her, and she's off that ship. That's the important thing."

His blue eyes regarded me somberly. "I have to say, Amélie, I'm shocked that you asked me to lie like that."

"Jack, if you had seen the conditions on the boat, you would have done anything to get her off it."

"I asked the Red Cross representative about sanitation on the boat, and she said everything was shipshape."

"Of course she did! They won't want it known how badly they bungled things."

"I asked to speak to a ship's officer, and the bursar came down and talked to me. He said things got a bit bumpy during the storm and there was a lot of seasickness. He also said that several of the foreign women didn't have the best hygiene, and that their children fell ill because of it."

"It was not the hygiene of the women! He is lying to you!"

"He knew nothing of any dead babies."

"I saw them, Jack!"

Jack blew out a hard sigh. "Well, if what you say is true, it will come out soon enough." There was an iciness to his voice that had not been there before, and it filled me with grim foreboding.

He didn't believe me. The irony of it all—that he had believed my lies, but not my truth—left a bitter taste in my mouth. "I suppose it will."

He picked up my bag. "Well, let's get going."

Elise cried at the shock of the cold wind and the loud noises of traffic as we left the terminal. I held her close as Jack hailed a cab.

"What is the address of your aunt's home?"

"It's 1926 Fairster Street. I believe it's in an area called the Bronx."

Jack gave the address to the cabdriver in English, and the taxi pulled away from the curb.

New York had much more traffic than Paris, and the city seemed to go on forever. The skyscrapers were so tall that they made the streets seem like canyons. I gazed out the window in awe, then turned my attention to Jack.

"How was your flight over?" I asked. I knew from our conversations in Paris that it would be his first time on an airplane.

"It was very pleasant, thank you. Very exciting. It's a wonderful way to travel."

"And did you muster out?"

"Yes—finally. I was discharged last week."

"Have you talked to your fiancée?"

"Just briefly. I will call her again tonight, then head to Louisiana as soon as I get you and Elise settled." He twisted toward me and cleared his throat. "I have done some checking. We must be established residents in a state in order to get an annulment."

"Oh?"

"I'm a resident in Louisiana. It will take six months there."

"Oh, la!"

"It will take less time in Reno or Las Vegas, Nevada. Only six weeks."

"I see. Is that near to New York?"

"No. It's not near Louisiana, either."

My chest tightened. "I am sorry if this is a problem."

He lifted his shoulders. "Six weeks is not long in the course of a lifetime. All in all, it is a small price for bringing Doug's child to America."

"I hope your fiancée sees things that way."

"I do, as well."

"So you haven't told her about . . ." I started to say *our marriage*, then thought better of using those words. ". . . about the way you're helping us?"

"No. It is the sort of thing I need to tell her in person."

"So what do you write to her about?"

He lifted his shoulders. "Ordinary things."

"Such as?"

"The weather. Medical cases."

"And what does she write to you?"

"News about what she's doing, about the town . . . but mainly questions about the wedding. She is dying to set a date. Apparently her mother has reserved three different dates at the church and the country club."

"Oh, la."

"I have tried to explain, in vague terms, that I want do additional medical training in Reno before we marry. I can do that while I wait for the annulment. She suggested we get married first, so she can come with me to Nevada. I must see her to explain."

"I understand. "

"Here we are," the cab driver said.

The cab had stopped beside an empty lot filled with rubble.

"Where?" Jack asked.

"Right there." The cabdriver pointed to what looked like the remains of a demolished building. "That's the address you gave me—1926 Fairster."

My stomach lurched. "This can't be right."

"Please wait for us," Jack said to the driver.

I got out of the cab, holding Elise. My knees felt like pudding.

"This is the only address you have?" Jack asked.

"Yes." I handed him a piece of paper with the names and address of Yvette's aunt and her husband. "This is it."

Jack took my elbow and led me across the street, into a small grocery store. "Is that 1926 Fairster Street across the street?" he asked the man behind the counter, who wore a butcher-style apron.

"Yep," the man replied.

"Can you tell us what happened?"

"The building burned down about six, seven months ago."

"Do you know where the residents went?"

"Oh, pretty much all over."

He glanced at the paper. "We're looking for Angelique and John Brown."

"Oh, yes. We knew them." A short woman wearing a white apron over a bright floral dress walked up from the back of the store. "She was French, right?"

"Yes."

"They moved out west."

"The west side of the city?" Jack asked.

"No. To California or Washington or Oregon or somewhere."

"Do you know what city?"

"City?" the man laughed. "Hell, we don't know what state."

"Do you know anyone who could tell us?"

The woman frowned thoughtfully, then shook her head. "All of their close friends were in the building, and they've all moved way."

"Do you know if the Browns belonged to a local church? Did the children go to school?"

"They had a boy and a girl, both grown and married. They didn't live here," the woman said. "I believe the Browns were Catholic, though."

Jack turned to me and translated.

"We can ask at the local church," I ventured in French.

"Do you know which church they went to?" Jack asked the couple.

"There's a Catholic church down the street," the woman volunteered.

"Thank you. We'll try there."

We got back in the cab. Jack looked as if he were working hard to control a rising tide of anger. His voice was controlled, but his eyes flashed as he turned to me. "When did you last hear from your aunt and uncle?"

"It was . . . during the war."

"How long ago?"

My insides felt as if they were shrinking. "A year . . . or two."

His gaze was incredulous. "They didn't know you were coming?"

"Oh, yes! I wrote to them!"

"And they wrote back?"

I felt seasick all over again. "The mail—it wasn't reliable. Especially the incoming mail. We were told that mail posted out, however."

He stared straight ahead, as if he couldn't bear to look at me. "You told me they were expecting you." His voice was flat and cold.

"Yes. Because I wrote them."

"But you didn't hear back," he repeated.

"N-no. I couldn't imagine . . . I had no way of knowing . . . I never dreamed they would move."

"You didn't send them a telegram when you learned your departure date?"

"I—I did not think of it."

He gazed at me, his expression one of disbelief and icy fury.

"It—It just didn't occur to me," I said.

"I see."

"No, I think you do not. From the angry look on your face, it appears the only thing you see is that I am an idiot or that I am somehow trying to trick you."

His eyes snapped. "I just can't believe you would cross an ocean—and marry a stranger!—on the off chance that your aunt and uncle had received your letter."

"You are right. It was very stupid of me." It was not an act for tears to course down my face.

"I'm trying to understand, to give you every benefit of the doubt, but it doesn't make any sense. Why wouldn't you send a telegram?"

All of my Resistance training came back to me, especially the words of Mme Dupard: *Stick as close to the truth as possible. Tell the truth whenever you can.*

"A telegraph was like a . . . a big steak, or an airplane ride. So beyond my reach or everyday thinking that it wasn't in my frame of reference. During the war, telegrams only came for Germans. The French people— at least the ones I knew—never received them. Not when someone died, or was arriving . . . Never." I met his eyes, though mine were blurred with tears. "The last I heard, my aunt loved her home and neighborhood. I never dreamed she would move. It never occurred to me that a tragedy such as a fire could happen here. Those were horrors that belonged to war. In my mind, America was paradise—a place where everything was always good." Elise was asleep, and slipping down in my arms. I struggled to readjust her.

Jack inhaled a long slow breath. He seemed to be pulling something into himself, some something stronger than air. He took Elise from me and gently cradled her. She opened her eyes and looked at him. I thought she would cry, but she just closed her eyelids again.

"You have been through an ordeal that is hard for an outsider to understand," he said at length, as the taxi stopped before a small church. "Come on. Let's see if the priest can tell us anything about your family."

The church was deserted. At length a woman dressed all in black came in to light a candle.

"Do you know where we can find the priest?" Jack asked her.

"The rectory is around the back."

Jack translated into French. I realized that I probably should have told him I spoke English when I first got off the ship, but I had thought I would only be with him for an hour or two, and an explanation would have involved more lies. Now, when he was already viewing me as either an idiot or a con artist, it seemed too awkward to tell him. For the time being, at least, I would let sleeping cats lie.

We knocked on the door, interrupting the priest's supper.

Jack explained our situation.

"Ah—the Browns. Such a tragedy, that apartment fire! So many parishioners lost everything, but everyone escaped with their lives, praise God."

"Do you know where they went?"

"I know Mr. Brown had a married sister in California—or was it Texas? It was out west, I'm sure of that. Maybe Oregon or Arizona."

"Do you know his sister's married name?"

"I'm sorry—no. I never met her. I only saw Mr. Brown on a couple of occasions. He seldom came to church. He was a Protestant, I believe. The missus, though—she was fairly devout."

"Were the children christened here? Maybe the aunt was a god-mother."

"Sorry, no. They were older when they moved to the neighborhood." The priest gave an apologetic smile. "I'm sorry I can't be of any real help."

Jack turned to me once we were outside. "Do you happen to know what your uncle's occupation was? Perhaps we can track them down that way."

"He—he was a construction worker," I invented.

"Did he have a specialty? Iron work, perhaps?"

I shook my head. "He—he changed jobs quite often. It was a worry to my aunt."

Jack marched to the taxi and yanked open the door for me, his face hard.

I couldn't help it. I cried. I tried not to, but tears rolled down my cheeks. He handed me a handkerchief. I wiped my face. Elise awoke and howled. I took her back from Jack and cradled her in my arms.

"What does she need?" Jack asked.

"She's hungry."

"What does she eat at this age?"

"Formula and soft foods."

"Let's go get dinner, then, and try to figure this out."

———

We went to Schrafft's. It was large and modern and unlike any restaurant I'd seen in Paris. It had glass blocks on the outside, and mahogany on the interior. "This looks terribly expensive."

"Oh, no, don't worry. The prices are very reasonable."

"I—I still don't think I can afford this," I said.

"I wouldn't dream of letting you pay."

"Are you sure?"

"Absolutely."

A waitress with a thick accent—I think it was Irish, but my English wasn't precise enough for me to tell—approached our table. I wasn't sure what to order, so Jack did it for me. He ordered a steak—maybe because I'd mentioned steak as one of the things that was beyond the scope of my world in France, like a telegram—with a baked potato, green beans, a salad, and warm rolls with butter.

"Oh, my—oh, this is enough for four people!" I said when a white-aproned waitress set a heaping plate in front of me.

"That's just for you and Elise."

"Well, we must save the rest."

"We have no place to keep it."

All the same, I put a roll in my purse.

Jack ate a steak as well, and then he looked at me. "I've made a decision."

"Yes?"

"I have a hotel room for the night. We'll get another room for you and Elise, then in the morning, we'll catch a train for Whitefish. Since we can't find your family, we'll take you to Doug's."

My stomach suddenly felt as if I had just eaten a box of rocks. "But . . . I don't know them. And they're not expecting me! I bet they don't even know that Doug and I . . ."

He leaned forward. "I'm sure they'll be thrilled. But just to avoid anything like what we just encountered, I'm going to give them a telephone call."

"Oh, la!"

"Don't worry, I'll do all the talking, since you don't speak English."

Thank God I hadn't told him I spoke English! "I'll tell them that I'm coming to see them, and that I'm bringing them a surprise from Doug."

I numbly nodded.

"Once they see you and Elise, why, there's no way they'll want to do anything but welcome you with open arms, don't you think?"

All I could do was once more, dumbly, nod my head. "I hope so," I murmured.

"I'm sure they'll want their grandchild close," Jack said. "Doug was an only child, so Elise will be their only close family."

He helped me gather up my belongings. Yvette's camera fell from my shoulder tote.

He picked it up and looked at it. "Looks like you have one photo left."

"Let me take a photo of you, then. But you'll have to hold the baby so I have my hands free." I handed the baby to him.

"Would you like for me to take a picture of all of you together?" asked a gentleman at the next table.

"Why, that would be very nice," Jack said.

We stood together and smiled as he raised the camera.

"Why don't you put your arm around your wife," he said to Jack.

"Oh, she's . . ." Jack abruptly broke off. I could tell he'd been about to say that I was not his wife, and then he must have realized I was. His ears reddened. "Yes," he conceded. "Good idea."

His arm came around my shoulders, and I leaned in toward him.

We were in the middle of a brightly lit restaurant. It was a pose, that is all. There was nothing genuine about it—much less anything romantic or sentimental or sexual. And yet, my heart started to pound. I inhaled the scent of him—the warm, man-scented wool of his jacket, the clean starchiness of his shirt, that undernote of soap and shaving cream and testosterone—and I felt slightly woozy. My skin felt strangely vibrant and alive where we touched, as if those were the only places on my body where blood flowed freely. The warmth of his arm, the feel of his fingers, gave me goose bumps. Being close to him made me want to inch even nearer.

I told myself it was the suggestibility of it all. The man taking our photo had referred to me as Jack's wife. The man thought he was taking a family photo—and yes, we were married in name. Still, it was both a relief and a letdown when the photo was over and we pulled away from each other.

It was a few moments, that was all, less than a minute in total. And yet being that close to Jack for even that short a time—well, it changed something. I found myself increasingly, uncomfortably aware that he was a very attractive, appealing man.

46

KAT
2016

$\mathscr{S}$he has finally admitted it. "You were attracted to him!"

"I didn't want to be," Amélie says. "I didn't want to think of him that way at all. I knew he was taken."

"But you were attracted. And you were willing to go to Montana and tell these poor people who had lost a son that you were the mother of their granddaughter? You were willing to pass Elise off as their blood kin?"

"I wouldn't say I was willing, no."

"But you were going to, all the same."

"That was Jack's plan, yes. At that moment, I didn't know what to do but go along with it."

"Good heavens! The deceit!"

"Well, I was in a difficult position. I had the baby. And my biggest fear was that Jack was going to march me back to the Red Cross and put Elise and I on that death boat."

Oh, but that they had! I am fairly quivering with indignation. "In the meantime, I was sitting in Wedding Tree, expecting Jack to come home and marry me, and I didn't have a clue what was going on!"

"I know he called you that night."

Oh, I remember that call! I'd been waiting and waiting for it. He'd called when he'd first landed in the U.S., but it had been a very unsatisfying conversation. He had been at a USO club and it was noisy, with a lot of confusion in the background and a five-minute time limit. Mother and I had wanted to go meet him, but he'd flown to San Antonio, where he'd been put to work at a burn unit at the base hospital. He said he was living on base and he was very busy and wouldn't be able to spend time with us.

When he called from New York, I was surprised to learn he'd left San Antonio—and I didn't learn until later that he'd already mustered out of the service. I was shocked when he told me he was heading out west.

"Military orders?"

"Um, not exactly," he'd said. "I'm going to see the family of the man who saved my life."

"Oh, Jack, no! Just write to them. That should be good enough."

"I have something I need to take them."

"Good heavens. Why don't you just send it?"

"This is something that needs to be delivered in person. I'll tell you all about it when I get to Wedding Tree."

"Well, I don't understand," I'd told him. "Not at all. And Mother is wanting to know which date is the best for the wedding."

"As I told you, it's going to take a few weeks to finish up my obligations. Then I'll come home and see you, but I need to do six weeks' training in Reno before we marry."

"How many weeks, in total? Do you know how long I've waited? All our friends are already married!"

"It's not a contest, honey."

"I know, I know. It's just, I'm so eager . . ."

"I know, darling. I understand. Truly. Say, can I speak to your father?"

"Yes, of course."

It was a relief to turn the phone over to Daddy. Mother had immediately demanded, "Did he give you a date?" I'd shaken my head. She'd bitten her lip, all agitated.

I halfway listened to Daddy. "The womenfolk here are in a tizzy about the wedding plans, wanting a firm date."

He was silent for a long time. Apparently Jack was talking at length.

"I see. Well, do what you have to do. I respect your opinion. Maybe we should tell them to just set a summer date."

"Summer? No!" I practically stomped my foot.

When Daddy hung up, I was immediately all over him.

"What did he tell you?"

"Same thing he told you, I'm sure. He had some business in New York, and now he's headed out to see the family of the man who saved his life. Then he's coming here, but he'll have to go back for a six-week training stint in Nevada before you marry."

"Well, I think the trip to Montana is ridiculous."

"I think it's very admirable," Daddy said.

"I think he's being inconsiderate."

"Depends on whom you want him to be considerate of."

"Of me, of course! I'm his fiancée, and I haven't seen him in nearly a year!"

"Listen Kat—he's been through a lot. He's seen people shot. He's pulled bullets and shrapnel out of young men who will never be the same. You have no idea how difficult war is, how it changes a man. You can't expect the same carefree person who left here to just sashay through the door. He has a lot to sort out. He has to learn how to live with the fact that he's alive and a lot of good men aren't."

"I just feel something is wrong, Daddy. I feel like he doesn't love me like he did."

"Well, I don't imagine he feels about anything the way he did before he left. War will do that to a man. But it doesn't mean he won't bounce back."

But I knew something wasn't right. I lay in bed that night, staring up at the ceiling, and I thought I should get on a train and go meet him—maybe catch up with him in Whitefish. If his love for me was growing cold, maybe I could reignite it.

"He seemed so different, and I thought it was up to me to help him, to pull him back to the way he'd been before," I find myself telling Amélie. "I felt it, and I didn't act on it. There was something I should have done that I didn't do. Do you have any idea what that feels like?"

"I do," she replies. "I felt like I let down Yvette and Joshua and my parents, although in reality, there was nothing I could have done to save them. But because I'd felt that way, I was determined that I was not—absolutely was *not*—going to let down Elise. She had her whole life ahead of her. Thank heavens Jack also wanted to make sure Elise found a home in America."

"That was because he thought she was Doug's child."

"Yes."

"But she wasn't." My chest is hot with indignation. "So how could you let him take you to Whitefish to meet Doug's family?"

"The question I asked myself at the time was, *How can I stop him?* If I told him the truth and he learned the extent of all my lies—if I did that, then and there, he would put me back on that ship, and Elise might die. I only saw two courses of action: forward with Jack, or back on the boat. I couldn't get back on the boat. I saw no other option."

"There's always another option," I hiss.

"Oh, yes?" Her gaze is sharp as a hatpin. "What would you have done?"

"Well, I wouldn't have gotten myself in your situation in the first place," I huff.

"And I would not have been in yours," she says. "Because if I had been you, I would have married Jack before he left home."

I feel as if all the air has been sucked from the room. It takes me a moment to regain my breath. How dare she? It is a blow straight to the heart, a direct hit to my most vulnerable spot. It is, quite possibly, the one regret of my life—or would be, if I allowed myself to believe in regrets.

Amélie leans forward. "Are you all right?"

I have to unclench my teeth to answer. I will not—*not*—let her know that her remark had cut me to the quick.

"Yes," I say at length. "Please go on with your story."

AMÉLIE
1946

*O*nce I started adjusting to the idea of going to Montana, I began
thinking, would it be so bad, really, if Elise grew up believing that these strangers were her grandparents? It was a place to go,
and these people were likely to love her. But could I tell such a lie to
such vulnerable people? Could I live such a lie for my entire life? I
doubted it.

When in doubt, buy some time. It was a lesson I had learned in the
Resistance. I didn't have to decide about Doug's parents right now; right
now, I simply had to get away from that dreadful ship until it had set sail.

Not knowing what else to do, I went along with Jack's suggestions.
We took the cab back to the hotel where he was staying. Along the way,
he held Elise and jollied her out of a bad mood. He charmed her completely; he had been able to do that, even in Paris. Jack had a way with
her; he talked softly, he smiled, he held her gaze. He treated her the way
I began to wish he'd treat me.

When we got to the hotel—it was a nice place, not overly fancy, but
with doormen and bellmen—there was not another room to be had.

"Well, then, we'll just have to share," Jack said to the clerk.

The man peered over his glasses, his mouth pursed, as if Jack were
suggesting something immoral. "Are you two married?"

Jack's ears turned pink. "As a matter of fact, we are."

"I will need to see some identification."

Jack asked me, in French, to hand the clerk my passport, which had been changed to my married name.

The clerk's face was red as he handed it back. "I'm sorry. It's just that this hotel has certain standards, and since you first asked for separate rooms, I thought . . ."

"My wife has just arrived from France, and . . . and . . . it's been a long separation," Jack awkwardly explained. "I thought that perhaps she and the baby would be more comfortable in their own room this evening."

"I see." The clerk was clearly as discomfited as Jack. I was amused that an American hotel would try to police the morality of its guests. "Well, I can send up a crib for the baby."

"That would be very helpful. Thank you."

Jack put his hand on the small of my back and steered me toward the elevator. We went up to the twelfth floor—far higher than I was accustomed to.

"You take the bed," he said. "I'll sleep on the sofa."

The room had—merci Dieu!—its own bath. After the ship, it seemed like an unimaginable luxury. I bathed Elise, then put her in the crib. When she fell asleep, I went in the bathroom and drew a bath for myself. I sighed with pleasure as I sank into the warm water.

Through the door, I heard Jack on the phone. I heard him murmur in a low tone. I thought I caught the word *darling*. A stab of envy shot through me. The woman whom he was to marry was a lucky girl. She would have stability and a home. Her children would have a caring, loving father and never have to worry about their next meal.

And she would have Jack in her bed. This last thought made my stomach flutter.

He tapped lightly on the door. "I'm going to run down and get some extra blankets," he called. "I'll be back in a few minutes."

I murmured my assent. I came out, wrapped in my old robe, and was glad for the chance to brush my hair and climb into bed without him in the room.

He let himself in with the key a few minutes after I had settled myself under the covers. The bed was soft and lush and large, with clean-smelling sheets. It felt like heaven. I realized I had not been in a bed that comfortable since before the war.

Jack made up a bed on the sofa across the room, then went into the bathroom and showered. I was exhausted and by all rights should have fallen asleep right away, but I was keenly aware that he was naked on the other side of the door. He came out, bringing soap-scented steam into the room, and settled on the sofa.

"*Bonne nuit,*" I whispered.

"Bonne nuit," he replied.

I could hear his bedclothes rustling, then hear him breathing—not the regular, slow breathing of someone asleep, but the breathing of someone lying awake in the dark, just like I was.

I thought about saying something, but I couldn't figure out what to say, so I just lay there. I listened to the city—a city very different from Paris—a city with different sirens, louder traffic, and people speaking English. I listened to Elise's slow, somnolent puffs of air. I listened to Jack's steady breathing in the dark. I listened to the overly loud pounding of my heart.

Sometime in the early morning hours, I must have fallen asleep, because when I was awakened by water running in the bathroom, sunlight was streaming in the window.

AMÉLIE
1946

*J*ack came out of the bathroom freshly shaved and smelling like toothpaste, wearing a sleeveless undershirt. His chest was broad and his arms were muscled. Our eyes met, and he froze.

"Bonjour," he said.

"Bonjour." I saw his gaze lower to my chest. I realized my nightgown was washed thin, nearly transparent. I rapidly reached for my robe.

Almost simultaneously, he grabbed a shirt from his suitcase and pulled it on, then turned his attention to Elise, who was sitting up in her crib, cooing. "Good morning, sunshine!" he said.

I struggled into my robe and tightly belted it. "I'm sure she's a bit cloudy in her diaper."

He smiled. "I'll take care of it."

I was surprised, but I welcomed the opportunity to visit the bathroom myself. When I came out, his shirt was buttoned and tucked in, and he was leaning over Elise, who was now lying on a towel-covered part of the sofa.

His face was a study of concentration as he tried to insert a diaper pin. "I'm afraid of poking her or making the diaper too tight, but instead, I end up making it too loose."

"I'll get it." I reached over. My arm brushed his. His skin was warm where it touched mine. We both pulled back abruptly.

"This isn't something they taught in medical school," he said.

"Maybe they should."

He grinned. "Probably so. That diaper pin is as sharp as a scalpel."

"It doesn't require the same degree of expertise."

"Elise would probably disagree." We smiled at each other for a moment. "Why don't I go find us some breakfast? That way you'll have a chance to get dressed in private. "

"That would be very nice."

He brought back tea, coffee, milk, juice, fruit, and an assortment of pastries. I mixed Elise's formula with the water from the teapot. We sat at the table, with Elise on my lap, sipping from her bottle and eating bites of muffin and fruit from my plate.

"When did you wean her?" he asked.

"Wean?" I wasn't sure what he meant, since she was still drinking from a bottle.

"Stop breastfeeding her."

"Oh! I, uh, never did that."

"Really?" The surprise in his voice put me on high alert.

"I heard that formula was better."

"Some doctors—and I'm one of them—think that nature is always best." He looked at me intently. "How did you afford it? Wasn't it hard to come by?"

"Well, um, one of my friends . . . she became pregnant, too. Her baby's father acquired a shipment of formula and stockpiled it for her."

"He stole it?"

"I don't think it is stealing if it belonged to the Nazis." I had to think fast. "Anyway, she miscarried—and . . . and I got it."

"I'm surprised the father didn't want it back to sell it."

"He was gone by then."

"He was caught?"

"We think so." Oh, why couldn't my mind work more quickly? "In the war, people sometimes just disappeared. He worked for the Resistance."

"I see. This friend . . . where did you know her from?"

"We met at the hotel where I worked."

"This was before Elise was born?"

I was getting in over my head. I didn't know when he thought I'd started working at a hotel. "Um . . . yes."

"So you were in Paris before Elise was born? I thought she was born in Normandy."

Oh, la; I was getting in deeper and deeper. *Stick to the truth.* "She, um . . . no. Elise was born in Paris. I went there after my parents' home was bombed."

His brow creased. "But you said the she was delivered by a midwife. That's why she didn't have a birth certificate."

"She was delivered by a midwife in Paris. I was very poor. Life was very grim. I didn't have money for a hospital."

"I see."

What he saw, I feared, was that I was lying. I gathered Elise onto my lap and made a show of looking at the clock on the bureau.

"Oh, my—look at the time! The morning is slipping away. Shouldn't we be heading to the train station?"

"Yes, we should."

We moved on to packing up our things and talking about other topics, but I could see that the doubts he'd had about me since my arrival had rekindled in his mind.

49

AMÉLIE
1946

*M*y worries increased as we left the hotel. Jack had asked the concierge for directions to the train station, then headed the other way.

"Where are we going?" I clutched Elise as Jack guided us down the crowded sidewalk.

"We need to pick up something."

"What?"

He grinned down at me. "Your photos."

"My . . . photos?" I froze, and was almost knocked down by a man walking close behind me. "From the camera? Oh, I can't possibly afford . . ."

"Oh, it's my treat. I saw an all-night photo shop around the block, so I took the film last night while you were in the bathtub. They said the pictures would be ready this morning."

"That is very considerate of you," I managed. It was, of course. Very considerate and kind and . . . nosy. Or was it just my paranoia? Oh, la— what was on that roll of film? Yvette had owned the camera.

I hurried beside him as he turned into the store.

Jack greeted the man behind the counter. "I'm here to pick up some photos. The name is Jack O'Connor."

"Oh, yes." He smiled at me. "Your hair looks much better now than it did in the pictures."

I must have looked shocked. I remembered, gratefully, that I was not supposed to understand English.

"Don't you want to look at them?" Jack asked. "I'll hold the baby."

"Not now," I said. "Later, when I'm sitting down."

"We'll have plenty of time on the train." He handed me the packet, and I tucked it into my purse. We went back outside, into the noisy, chilly air, and crossed the street, where he hailed a cab.

"Penn Station, please," Jack told the driver.

The ticket clerk looked down at a printed schedule. "It's a twenty-two-hour trip to Chicago, and then you'll have to change trains. From there you'll take a train to Williston, North Dakota, and change trains again. That's about a fifty-six-hour trip. Then it's just a twelve-hour trip on to Whitefish."

"All right," Jack said. "How many days are we talking?"

"With wait time between trains, four."

Jack blew out a sigh. "Okay. We need two tickets for the whole way, with separate sleeping berths for the overnight portions, please."

The man peered over his wire-rim glasses, his expression curious. "It's just you and the missus, right?"

"Well, yes—and the baby."

"One double berth should work. The baby can sleep in one of your suitcases. That's what most folks do. There's just enough space on the floor."

"We'd like separate berths, please."

"Separate?" He glanced at me and back at Jack, then quickly looked down. "I'll, um, see what I can do. We're awfully full up, what with the war over and everyone being transferred around and trying to get home and such." He went to a Teletype machine, keyed something in, then pulled out a small piece of paper. He carried it back to the window. "I'm sorry, but you'll have to double up for at least part of the trip, if you want to leave today. If you insist on separate berths the whole way, you'll have to wait . . ." He punched more keys. "Whew—looks like three weeks. We've got a bunch of military movements coming up."

"Three weeks!" Jack exclaimed.

The man's eyebrows rose. "You two are married, right? So there's really no reason that you can't share."

"Well, yes. It's just . . . well, we . . . I—I—I snore."

Jack was a hysterically horrible liar! I don't know if it was my fatigue, Jack's obvious discomfort, the clerk's confused expression, or a combination, but I couldn't help it; I burst out laughing.

Jack stared at me, his expression so odd I thought he was signaling me to corroborate his story.

"He snores like a freight train," I said. "It usually doesn't bother me, but, well, I'm pregnant, so I don't sleep very soundly. But we'll be fine with a double berth."

The clerk smiled, his eyes friendly. "Congratulations on the new little one! My wife is expecting, too."

He turned back to his machine, but Jack continued to stare at me. It was then—only then—that I realized he was looking at me strangely because I'd understood, then spoken, English.

My heart sank. Mon Dieu! I'd made it through the war pretending that I couldn't understand a word of either German or English, keeping my secret for years. One day in Jack's company, and I'd already given myself away.

I turned aside, pretending that Elise needed rocking, and stared at the passengers streaming off a train while Jack paid for the tickets. I was sick with anxiety.

He carried both of our suitcases, but still managed to take me firmly by the elbow. He steered me toward a bench. "I didn't know that you spoke English."

"I—I don't," I responded in French. "N-not much."

"You seemed pretty fluent a moment ago."

"I—" I bounced Elise as I tried and failed to think of an excuse. I was too nervous to sit down.

A nerve flicked in Jack's jaw. He was angry. Very angry.

"Where does a Normandy farm girl learn to speak perfect English?" he asked in English.

It was futile to continue the ruse. I responded in his language. "My English isn't perfect."

"You seem to understand me quite clearly. Don't pretend you don't."

I lifted my shoulders.

"When did you learn?"

"As a girl." *Stick to the truth. Act as if you are forthcoming.* "It so happens I speak German, as well."

"Good God." He stared at me. "How?"

Tweak the truth. That way the story rings true. "My friend's father was a linguistics professor."

"A linguistics professor—in a rural farming community?"

Have a logical explanation. Keep it simple. "He was paralyzed. A—a motor accident. He and his wife and daughter moved there to live on his father's farm. He taught my friend and me and my brothers English and German. He tutored us after school and in the summers."

"And your parents went along with this?"

"My parents were simple, but they understood the value of a good education. They wanted a better life for me and my brothers."

"Why did you hide this from me?"

"I . . . didn't. You spoke French so well that it just never came up."

His lips were tight, and his eyes flashed. I wasn't afraid of him, exactly, but I was glad we were in a public setting so he couldn't give his temper full rein. "You never once tried to talk to me in my own language, and you let me translate everything everyone has said since you got here. Why? Why on earth—*why*?"

Elise pulled at my hair. I adjusted the collar on her dress. "It just seemed awkward."

"Awkward?" He scowled at me. "As if translating everything wasn't awkward for me! What kind of answer is that?"

"I wanted to tell you, but I couldn't find the right moment, and then it had gone on so long that it seemed as though I'd lost the opportunity. I just didn't know how."

"How about saying, 'By the way, I speak English beautifully?'"

"I didn't want you to think I had a problem with your French. I—I didn't want to be rude."

"Rude?" A vein stood out in his temple, beside his eyebrow. "You thought making me translate everything was being *polite*?"

When he put it like that, I felt like an idiot. "I didn't say anything at first, because I was in the habit of hiding the fact I could understand what was going on around me. And then, when I realized I should tell you, well, it had gone on so long that I was embarrassed."

"Whoa. Hold it right there." He put up his hand.

Elise chose that moment to start crying. She no doubt could feel the tension between us. "Excuse me," I said. "I need to find a place to change her diaper."

―――――――

When I returned, Jack seemed to have calmed down quite a bit. He waited for me to sit on the bench and settle Elise on my lap, then he sat down beside me. "What did you mean, you became used to hiding the fact you could understand what was being said around you?"

"Well, you know I worked for the Resistance during the occupation. I continued to do so after I moved to Paris. I got a job as a maid at a hotel and used my language skills to spy on German officers."

"You worked while you were pregnant?"

It made me very nervous, talking about myself. I was afraid I would say something that would contradict what I'd already told him. "Yes. I didn't show very much, and I am clever with a needle. I was able to hide my pregnancy until the very end. I worked until a month before Elise was born."

He sat still for a moment. He no longer seemed angry. "You said something to me in France about going through Nazis' coat pockets and suitcases. This is what you did at the hotel?"

I nodded. "I went through their belongings and I listened to their conversations. None of them imagined a maid could understand their language."

A train roared into the station on the far track, heading the opposite way. It slowed and squealed to a halt. That's what I needed to do with this conversation, I thought—get it on another track, going in a different direction.

"I had to work because I was destitute and homeless. But I don't suppose you'd know anything about that. You said you learned French from a nanny, so I assume your family is very wealthy. I suppose you look down on me because I'm poor."

"Oh, no! No, I don't blame anyone for being poor. And you're wrong; my family wasn't wealthy. We fell on extremely hard times after my father died."

The rumble of another approaching train made it impossible to talk. Elise fussed as the train grew closer and louder and the air grew heavy with the scent of diesel. The brakes squealed, and the engine slowed as it passed by us. At length it stopped, the passenger cars in front of us.

"This is our train to Chicago," Jack said.

———

We ended up in a private alcove with seats facing each other that would fold down into a bed, with a bunk bed on top. Heavy green curtains, which would give privacy at night, were tied back at the sides on brass hooks.

Boarding the train and getting settled provided a much-needed distraction. Elise was in a playful mood, which helped dispel the tension between us. I didn't give Jack a chance to start questioning me again; as soon as the train began moving, I posed questions of my own. "You said your family fell on hard times when your father died. Does that mean you once were wealthy?"

"No. Well, my mother . . . she came from a family of means in Charleston, and she was accustomed to the finer things. She was a debutante, and my father was a strawberry farmer in Louisiana."

"How did they end up together?"

"They met during the Great War and fell madly in love. Her parents objected to him, but she ran away and married him anyway."

"Goodness!"

"She should have listened to her parents. Their differences . . . well, you can hardly imagine a more unlikely pair. Lots of turmoil, lots of arguments, lots of shouting matches." He shook his head. "One thing about growing up in a household like that—it teaches you what you don't want your life to be like."

"I would imagine so."

"That's one reason I'm marrying my fiancée. I want a home life that will be calm and peaceful."

It struck me as an odd thing to say. "And how do you know your fiancée will be provide such a thing?"

"Well, she's just like her mother, and I'm very much like her father. He's very rational and logically minded, and she's home-oriented and sociable. I feel like I've seen a prototype of what our lives will be like."

"So that's the reason you're engaged?"

"I think it's a very good reason."

"What about love?"

"Well, that, too, of course."

"You didn't mention it."

"I didn't think I had to. I'm marrying her, aren't I?"

"I see." I was not sure that I did. "What is her name?"

"Kat."

"Like the animal?"

"It's short for Katherine. But she has big green eyes like a cat."

"She sounds beautiful."

"Oh, she is."

"Do you have a picture?"

"Yes."

He pulled a professional photo out of his wallet. I felt a stab of jealousy; the woman looked like an actress or a model. "She's gorgeous."

He smiled. "Yes."

"What has Kat been doing while you've been away?"

"Going to college."

I felt another stab of envy. "What is she studying?"

"Home economics. She wants to be the best wife and mother possible."

"I see." I didn't understand how college could help with that, but then, there was a lot I didn't know.

"So . . . how did you two meet?"

"Through church. I suppose I'd known her all my life, but we connected because her father was a doctor and I wished to talk to him about the profession."

"Did you date all through school?"

"No. She is two years behind me in school, so I didn't start dating her until a few months before I graduated high school."

"Was she your first girlfriend?"

He shook his head. "There was another girl, Beth Ann, when I was younger. She moved away."

"Did you love her?"

"Well, I thought I did, but when you are so young . . . well, it's easy for emotions to overtake you."

"And did your emotions overtake you?"

He cut a look at me. "You mean the way yours did with Doug?"

I felt a blush along the roots of my hair. "I suppose that's what I'm asking."

"I don't think that's an appropriate question, do you?"

"I think you just answered it."

He looked away, but a nerve twitched in his jaw. He was pretty good at keeping a poker face, but he had little tells.

"So you are concerned about what Kat will say about our . . . arrangement?"

"Yes. She won't like it."

"How do you intend to tell her?"

"Well, first, I thought I would tell her father. He'll understand that this was the right thing to do. His opinion is very important."

"To her, or to you?"

He looked surprised at the question. "To both of us, I suppose. Then I'll take Kat aside and I'll assure her, first, that there is nothing romantic between you and me."

The words stung a little bit.

"And then I'll tell her about Doug," Jack continued.

"You haven't told her?"

He shifted on the seat. "She knows a medic died saving my life, but I haven't told her how it affected me."

"It can be hard to put emotions on paper." I put my hand on his arm, a spontaneous gesture of sympathy. The moment I did, I was keenly aware of the muscles of his arm, of the heat radiating through his jacket. I pulled my hand away. "It will be much easier to talk when you are face-to-face."

"I hope so." He looked away. "Sometimes I find it hard to talk to people."

"You seem to have no problem with me."

"That's true." He smiled. "Maybe it's because we both experienced the war."

"Yes." My thoughts flickered back and forth between his comment "there is nothing romantic between you and me" and the way his arm had felt under my palm. I forced myself to carry on the conversation. "Do you think Kat's feelings will be hurt?"

He tilted his head, considering the question. "No, not really. As long as word of our marriage doesn't get out in Wedding Tree, I think she'll mainly just be inconvenienced."

"Inconvenienced?"

"Yes. That I'll have to spend six weeks in Reno in order to get our annulment, and that we'll have to postpone the wedding."

"I'm so sorry I put you in a bind." I was genuinely chagrined. "If you want, you can head back to Louisiana from Chicago, and I'll go on to Montana by myself. I don't know why I didn't think of it earlier." In fact, traveling alone would give me the option of going somewhere other than Montana.

"No. It would be too difficult for you to manage with the baby—and Kat and I can't marry until the annulment is finalized, anyway. Besides, I told Doug's parents I was coming, and I always try to keep my word."

"That's very admirable."

"Yes, well, I believe in being trustworthy. Too many people aren't."

I suppressed a shiver. Dear God, I hope he never learned the truth about me! "I sense some interesting stories behind that statement."

"I don't know how interesting they are, but yes, I've had some experiences."

"Tell me about one."

He gazed out the window at the passing cityscape. "When I was a boy, my friend Tim lived at the horse ranch next to our farm. Tim had asthma. It wasn't a well-understood condition at the time; people called it 'weak lungs.' His father had taken him to see the local doctor—that would be Kat's father, Dr. Thompson—several times. The best that he could offer was a shot of epinephrine for an acute attack. They didn't have inhalers then—at least, not in rural Louisiana.

"Dr. Thompson thought that Tim had allergies, probably to hay, dust, and horses, and suggested that he stay away from them. Well, this didn't sit well with his father, who expected Tim to help out and eventually take over the business, so Tim continued doing all the things that could make his condition worse."

"Oh, la," I murmured.

"At the height of the Depression, a shyster came by Tim's home claiming he had a cure. He had a special tonic and a harness-like device. He said that if asthma sufferers wore it at night, it would pull back the shoulders and open up the lungs. Tim's parents couldn't afford it—like everyone, they were barely scraping by—but they bought the contraption and a year's supply of the medicine anyway.

"Tim told me that the harness hurt so bad that sometimes he'd just lie in bed and cry like a baby. When he'd take the medicine, his heart raced and his face sweated and he lost his appetite. But he was determined to stick with it, both because he wanted to be cured and because his parents had invested so much in it.

"Over a few months' time, Tim lost a lot of weight and looked awful. And then, on the way home from school one day—we used to walk together to and from school, which was a couple of miles from our farm—he had a horrible asthma attack." Jack closed his eyes for a moment.

"I tried to help him, but he couldn't breathe. Finally someone came along in a car and picked us up and took us to town to Dr. Thompson's office. By the time we got there, Tim was dead.

"Dr. Thompson was mad as hell when I told him about the device and the medicine. He said it sounded as if the medicine had cocaine or amphetamine in it, which would only exacerbate the condition, and that the salesman's lies had killed Tim just as sure as if he'd shot him. He said Tim's parents were fools for falling for a snake-oil pitch. He calmed down by the time the parents got there—he didn't want to make them feel any worse than they did—but he did tell them that the treatment had been worthless.

"Tim's mother died of a stroke within the year. Everyone said it was the stress and grief, and I don't doubt it. Tim's father took to the bottle, and he ended up losing the farm. The other kids went off to live with relatives in other towns." Jack stared out the window. "And meanwhile, that self-serving, lying quack was still out there, deceiving other people desperate for a miracle."

"How terrible!"

"Yeah, it was."

"Was that what made you want to become a doctor?"

"That was part of it. I'd already been thinking in that direction, and having Tim die like that—well, it made me want to learn how to help people, instead of just being a bystander."

I thought of how I'd felt when the Nazis had firebombed the farmhouse and I'd sat in the cart, not knowing what to do. My heart went out to him.

"Tim was the first person to die in my arms," Jack said. "Two years later, my father was the second."

"Oh, Jack!" I breathed.

He stared out the window, but I don't think he was seeing the outskirts of the city. "We were fishing on a lake—I was rowing the boat, and he was casting a line. All of a sudden, his fishing pole clattered to the bottom of the boat, and he grabbed his chest and keeled over. I scrambled over to him—I nearly tipped over the boat, trying to get to him—and he was unconscious. I yelled to some other men fishing from the shore, then rowed over to them as fast as I could. They helped me take Dad home and put him to bed. Dr. Thompson came, and, well, Dad never woke up."

"I'm so sorry! How old were you?"

"Fourteen. I felt terribly guilty, thinking I should have been able to save him. I asked Dr. Thompson what I should have done differently. He said there was nothing. He said it was a heart attack, and that I had done all anyone could."

"Oh, Jack."

"Dr. Thompson said I'd probably make a good doctor myself someday, but I felt discouraged. A few weeks after the funeral, I went by his office and had a conversation with him. I asked, 'How can you stand having patients die of things that you can't help?' And I'll never forget what he told me."

I leaned toward him as the train swayed. "What did he say?"

"He said, 'A doctor isn't God. I don't care how well trained you are, you can't always keep someone from dying. But very few people make it from birth to death without having a sore throat or breaking a leg or having some other health problem. So whenever a patient dies, I try to remember that during his or her life, I or another doctor probably helped them. We can't fix everything, but we help where we can.'"

"He sounds like a very wise man."

"Oh, he is. I admire him more than anyone in the world. I really look forward to going into practice with him."

I studied him from the corner of my eye while pretending to smooth Elise's hair. "It's convenient that you fell in love with his daughter."

"What do you mean?"

"Just . . . you're fortunate he'll get to be your father-in-law." And he had spoken more passionately about Dr. Thompson than I'd ever heard him speak about the fiancée. But perhaps this was just his way. "Is his daughter interested in medicine also?"

"Oh, no. The sight of blood makes Kat queasy. But she's like her mother, so she'll make a very good doctor's wife."

At the time, I thought *il l'assomme avec des fleurs*—he's knocking her with flowers. I've since learned the English phrase: damning her with faint praise.

50

AMÉLIE
1946

We went to the dining car for lunch, and when we came back to our alcove, Elise fell asleep in Jack's arms. I leaned back my head and closed my eyes for a moment, my purse in my lap. The motion of the train and the rhythm of the track lulled me to sleep. A clatter suddenly jolted me awake. I opened my eyes to discover that my purse had fallen open on the floor. To my horror, photos were spilled all over our feet.

"I'll get them," Jack said. He passed Elise to me before I could form a protest, then dropped to his knees and began picking up pictures. "I was wondering when you were going to look at these." He picked up a picture of us at the restaurant, and then of us at our wedding. He suddenly froze, staring down at a photo in his hand.

I leaned forward to see the picture, and felt my blood turned to ice. It was a photo of Yvette and me—together, smiling, our arms out like birds, our heads shorn. The shadow of swastikas were faintly visible on our scalps.

He held the photo in front of me, his face red, his mouth a hard line. "What is this?"

"Oh, that—that's nothing." I tried to take the photo from him. My first instinct was to make it disappear, to downplay it, to act as if it were not important.

He twisted away and continued holding it. "This is not nothing." He picked the other pictures off the floor, then riffled through them.

My stomach turned. I thought I would be sick.

"You were a femme tondue."

"It's—it's not what you think. I wasn't . . . I never . . ."

He held up another photo—and then another. Oh, mon Dieu—they showed Dierk, shirtless in bed, leering at the camera. Dierk in his uniform at a restaurant table. Dierk by the Seine.

"Don't lie to me. I know all about it, how the French turned on the women who had slept with the enemy. I was there. I saw it in rural France."

"It is not what it seems. It is not! I never slept or made love or even kissed a Boche. I was simply trying to help my friend—to keep her from being stripped and shaved and I didn't know what else. In the chaos of the moment, the mob grabbed me, as well."

The next photo—oh, how horrible!—was of Dierk and me at a table at a sidewalk café, the one day I had joined Yvette and him for Sunday lunch. Dierk's hand rested on the back of my chair.

Jack's eyes narrowed as he waved the photo in my face. "You expect me to believe you?"

A sense of despair engulfed me. "That was not my camera. My friend—she took the photos."

"The very best conclusion I can draw is that you were bosom buddies with a woman who slept with German soldiers."

"It wasn't like that. Well, it became that way, at the end . . . but she only did it to gather information for the Resistance."

"An undercover agent, I suppose."

I wasn't familiar with the term, but I recognized the sarcasm in his voice. "It so happens she provided some very important information."

"Why should I believe you?"

"Why should you not?"

He flipped to another picture and held it out. I wanted to slide under the seat. There I was, my arms out like a swan's wings, my head bald as an egg and marked with a swastika, gallivanting around a luxurious room.

"This is not the grim time in Paris you described." His voice was low and controlled. It was scarier than if he had shouted. "Look here. That is your dress in the armoire. That is your hat on the rack. You obviously lived there."

"I did not. This was Yvette's room. It was the day before she was kicked out, the day after the Germans all fled and the Americans arrived. The clothes were all Yvette's. All of my clothes were once Yvette's."

"And where is this Yvette?"

"She is dead."

He must have seen something in my face, because I could tell he believed that.

"She died of the flu. What you said about someone dying in your arms . . . I know about that. I was at her bedside. At our apartment."

"Where?"

"Upstairs from Nora. When Yvette became ill, the hospital wouldn't take her, because she was contagious. I—wear her clothes. I had none of my own that weren't maid's uniforms, except for the dress I was wearing when I came to Paris."

He flipped through the photos.

The last one, thank God, showed Dierk and Yvette, holding hands. I felt a jolt of relief.

"See? The camera—it was Yvette's. Dierk gave it to her. That is why she isn't in most of the photos. It's because she was the one taking the pictures. And she is wearing the yellow dress I wore to marry you."

He looked up, his gaze still harsh. "Why did you not tell me the camera was not yours?"

"When would I have done that? It isn't the sort of thing I would just announce—not any more than I would have announced that the clothes were not mine."

He sat there for a moment. I could tell he was struggling to sort the facts. "I would like an explanation."

"Of what?"

"Of everything. Who was this Yvette? Did she work with you? Was she the friend who left you the baby formula?"

Fear—cold, gripping, paralyzing—flashed through me. If I said yes, he might put it all together. "Yvette was my dearest friend. She was like a sister to me. We grew up together."

"In the country?"

"Yes. And she came to Paris with me."

"Was it her father who taught you English and German?"

"Yes."

Why didn't you tell me of this?"

"Again, when would I have told you?"

"Nora knew her?"

"Yes."

"And yet neither of you mentioned her."

"I don't know when it would have come up. You and I did not spend much time together before we married."

He knew I had a point, but he scowled all the same. He went back to the first photo, the one of Yvette and me with our hair freshly shorn. "Why the hell were you frolicking around in this picture, as if it's all just some kind of a lark?"

Oh, mon Dieu. How to explain? "That day—it had been the most awful, humiliating experience of our lives. We were stripped to our undergarments and put in an open truck with other women—some of them prostitutes—and driven through the streets of Paris. People spat on us and threw garbage at us and ridiculed us. It was horrible. The hotel wouldn't even let us into the lobby—we had to go through the servants' entrance. And once we were in Yvette's room, we saw ourselves in a mirror for the first time.

"That might have been the worst part of all—seeing ourselves with no hair. I wanted to die. And then Yvette said that we could cry or we could laugh; neither would make our hair grow back faster, but laughing would make us feel better about it. And she started teasing me about looking like a little bald bird, and she started clowning around, and after all of the shame and humiliation and crying . . . well, she made me laugh. And she got out her camera, and . . ." I gestured at the photos. ". . . voilà."

He was silent for a long moment.

"Yvette had a powerful, uplifting spirit," I said. "She found a way to make that horrible situation bearable. That day, after laughing together, we were able to figure out a way to hide our baldness, and we were able to survive."

He lifted his gaze from the photo, looked at me, then blew out a sigh. "She sounds like a remarkable woman."

"She was. She truly was." I wiped at the tears that were sliding down my face.

Elise started to fuss. I pulled her diaper bag from under the seat and rose, holding her. "I need to change her diaper."

When I returned from the ladies' room, Jack apologized.

"I'm sorry I was angry. I know the war wasn't easy, and when I learned you were a femme tondue, well, it was a shock. You were pregnant with Elise, and thinking that you . . . while you were carrying Doug's baby . . . Well, I'm sure you only did what you had to do."

"I did not do *that*. I was shaved because I was in the wrong place at the wrong time, trying to protect Yvette."

"It doesn't matter."

"It does matter!" Although when I searched for a reason, there was none I could voice. I couldn't say, *You are a good man, and the opinion of a good man matters a great deal to me, because I have done many things that are neither black nor white. I want the validation that I am on the lighter shade of gray.* But that was the truth of it.

We sat in silence for a long moment. "Did you ever consider it? Going with a German?"

"No."

"Why not?"

"Yvette—well, she'd had her heart broken and she was sure she'd never love again. She did not value lovemaking, but she knew it could be a crucial tool for gathering information. I could not see it that way for myself."

"So your head was shaved because you were trying to help Yvette," he said at length.

"That's right."

We sat in silence for several moments, the tracks rumbling loudly beneath us. He seemed to be deep in thought.

"Okay," he said at length.

"Okay, what?"

"Okay. I believe you."

The comment left me angry. Why, I do not know, since I desperately wanted his good opinion. Maybe that—the wanting—was the reason for my anger. "And I'm supposed to feel good about that?"

He leaned forward, clearly exasperated. "What do you want from me?"

Understanding. Validation. To feel that you think I'm a good person. Because if I can convince you, perhaps I can believe it a bit myself.

"I honestly don't know." I stared at Elise, asleep in my arms. "To not feel judged, I suppose. To not feel as if you're doing me some kind of favor." I was immediately stricken. "Although you are, of course. Marrying me—it was a tremendous favor." I leaned back my head and closed my eyes for a moment. "I owe you a great deal. Thank you. I have no right to complain about anything you say or do."

"Of course you do. It's natural that you wouldn't want to be thought of as a woman of . . . of . . ."

"Ill repute?"

He gave a sheepish grin. "That sounds really stuffy, doesn't it?"

I smiled back. "I've always wondered why one never hears of men of ill repute, even though they are equally to blame. Maybe more so, since they're the ones who create the demand for services."

"You're right. It's unjust. But that is how it is." He looked at me. "You don't talk like a country girl. Your school provided you with a surprisingly good education."

"Yes, it did." I looked away. Oh, how I hated all the lies that stood between us! It was time to turn the conversation in his direction.

"What about you? You were raised in the country, as well. What did you say your father grew?"

"He started out with strawberries, then added a small dairy."

"What was he like?"

"Oh, my father . . ." His face tightened. "Lots of charm, lots of big plans. He was always off chasing a new scheme." He gazed out the window. "I guess you would describe him as a man of excessive passions."

"Ah. You are very different."

"Yes."

"And that is not by accident, I take it?"

He smiled at me. "You are a student of human nature."

"I am just naturally curious."

"About everything and everyone?"

"About you." The minute I said it, I realized it sounded too personal. "Anytime someone speaks of excessive passions, well, it sounds as if there is a story there, and I am a big fan of stories."

"Well, then, you would have loved my father, because he could always spin a good one."

"Yes?"

"After he married, my father started looking for a get-rich-quick scheme. That's when he started brewing and shipping bootleg whiskey."

"What is bootleg?"

"There was a thing in the United States called Prohibition. It was illegal to have or serve alcohol."

I had heard of this. The American prohibition had hurt France's wine industry, because we lost a major export market. As a Frenchwoman, however, I could not understand it. "That is very strange. Why would the government do such a thing?"

He laughed. "Your reaction is the one that logical people should have had. The government thought it would cure many social problems, but outlawing alcohol didn't stop people from drinking. It just made them buy alcohol through illegal means."

"You mean the black market." Here, now, was a concept I fully understood.

"Yes. My father made a good amount of money at it. He needed it, because my mother had expensive tastes. She insisted on a large house, a piano, maids, and a nanny. But when Prohibition was repealed, his business crashed. And then the Depression was upon us, and money was tight."

"Oh, la."

"And my father . . . well, he had made very little provision for making an honest living. And then he died."

"That must have been very difficult for your family."

He nodded. "Extremely difficult. I worked and went to school and worried about money. I took over the books for my father's business. My mother claimed she had no head for business; I think she was afraid of what she would find. And I wouldn't have wanted her to have seen what was in those books."

"Why? What did you find?"

"Father had spent money he didn't have. We had very little. He'd mortgaged the farm. And there were other things . . ."

"What things?"

"Other women."

"No!"

"Yes. After he died, I discovered we had virtually nothing left. And Father had not invested in fertilizer or new plows or any of the things we needed to run the farm efficiently."

"What did you do?"

"I worked the farm and made the mortgage payments, and in the summer I worked as a laborer on other farms in exchange for being able to use their equipment. And then my mother remarried and moved to town. She wed the local banker, a man who was quite a bit older than she was. That's why I was able to leave for college. I had a scholarship, so I didn't need money for myself, but I couldn't have left my sister, so . . ."

"Doctor!" called an urgent voice.

I turned and craned my head. The conductor was coming down the railcar aisle. "Is there a doctor on board?"

Jack rose and stepped out into the aisle. "I'm a doctor. What's the problem?"

"A boy in car four is having a fit."

Jack grabbed his bag from under his seat. "I'll follow you." He rested his hand on my shoulder for a moment. "Excuse me."

"Of course," I said.

He returned about an hour later. Elise was awake and playing with a rag doll.

"Is everything okay?"

"Yes." He sat down heavily. "It was a young man having an epileptic seizure."

"Is he all right?"

"He is now, but the people seated around him were really unnerved." He shook his head. "One woman insisted he was demon-possessed."

"Oh, la!"

"The conductor wanted to put him off the train."

"Why? Is it likely to happen again?"

"Not anytime soon. He took some medicine that will prevent it. I spent more time calming down the conductor and his seatmates than I did actually treating him. Fortunately, his destination is the next stop."

"What causes epilepsy?"

"There are lots of theories, but sometimes we see it begin after brain trauma. We'll have a lot more of that with the war veterans returning. But in about half the cases, it appears to be hereditary. There's a lot of good research going on right now, and in the next few years, we should have better answers and better treatments." He looked at me. "I'm surprised you know what it is."

"I've read about it."

"For a farm girl, you're awfully well read."

"Well, I'm interested in a lot of topics. But speaking of well read—as a small-town doctor, you will have to know about all sorts of different diseases and disorders."

He nodded. "And one of the most important things to know is when I don't know enough and when to refer a patient to a specialist."

The train started to slow. "Cleveland," called the conductor. "Next station stop, Cleveland."

Jack rose again. "I'm going to go help my patient and his mother get off the train."

"That's very kind of you."

"Well, he may be feeling a little weak. We'll get some supper after this stop, okay?"

"Yes."

I watched him go, thinking he was one of the kindest, most considerate men I'd ever known. His fiancée was one lucky girl, indeed.

I also uncharitably wondered if she deserved him. Did she have any idea just how special he was?

51

KAT
2016

I know I said I would keep quiet, but I just can't do it anymore.

"Of course I knew he was special," I huff.

"Yes," Amélie replies. "I see that now."

"You were falling in love with him."

She nods. "I didn't realize it at the time, but I was. I didn't want to be, but I couldn't help it."

"Jack always had that effect on women. He was so good-looking."

"Yes, but his appeal was far more than his appearance. What was truly devastating was his kind heart."

"Kind!" I glower at her. "You think it was kind of him to practically jilt me at the altar?"

"He felt terrible about that," Amélie says. "If you knew him at all, you must realize how difficult that was for him."

It couldn't have been more difficult than it was for me. I sniff. "So did you seduce him that night?"

"Non." Amélie crosses her legs. "We slept in the bunk beds. He was a perfect gentleman. He took the top bunk. He gave me privacy to undress and ready myself for bed. Nothing happened. Nothing at all. It was on the second train that everything changed."

Now we are getting somewhere. I lean forward.

"Are you sure you want to hear this?" Amélie asks. "Perhaps it will be too painful."

"No, no, no! Don't you dare stop now!"

She dips her head in a graceful nod. "All right, I will continue. But you must be quiet and let me talk."

"I will."

"I realize this will not be easy for you to hear."

"Please. I want to know."

"Do you want to hear the things he said about you?"

"Oh, yes. I especially want to know that." *Unless you are making it up to hurt me.*

"It might make you angry."

"I have been angry for years."

She lifts her brows and gives a little smile, as if I have said something amusing.

"I will become angry only if I think you are lying to me or not telling me everything," I say.

"I have no reason to lie or withhold information—if you are sure you can bear to hear it."

"You cannot tell me anything that will make me hurt worse than I have already," I say.

"All right, then. Here goes."

52

AMÉLIE
1946

*O*e changed trains in Chicago the next morning. We handed our tickets to the conductor and he led us to a Pullman car, where the porter greeted us with a big smile and carried my bag through the doorway to a room immediately to the right. Jack carried Elise.

I paused at the door. "This can't be right."

The porter looked at the ticket. "Oh, yes, ma'am. This is your room. Says right here."

"But . . . it looks like there's just one bed."

"That's right. A double."

Or maybe a triple. The bed took up the entirety of the room. There was barely space to get in it or around it. There was certainly no space to put a cot, or even for a person to stretch out and sleep on the floor.

The porter showed off the room as if it were his pride and joy. "An' over here, you have a toilet an' a wash sink behind that li'l wall. An' that li'l space right here in front of it will work great as a spot for the baby to sleep in a suitcase."

Jack cleared his throat. "This room—it isn't what I paid for. It's much too fine."

"Sometimes the agent will upgrade a lucky client. The 'spensive rooms don' always sell out."

An upgrade. This was what I had gotten for saying I was pregnant. I looked at Jack and knew he was thinking the same thing.

Jack cleared his throat. "Well, um, is there any way we can change to just two bunks in a sleeping car?"

"You don' like this room?" His eyes grew wide and round.

"Well, it's very nice," Jack said, "but it doesn't seem right."

"It don' cost you no more."

"Still, could we just have two bunks?"

His forehead wrinkled like a prune. "Why you wanna change?"

"Well, we uh . . ." Jack paused, cleared his throat, ran his hand across his jaw, then jammed both hands in his pockets. "Can you do it or not?"

"No, suh, I can't. All the sleepin' accomm'dations are all full. An' I don' have no authority to go changin' accomm'dations. You'd have to get off and talk to the ticket agent, but I can tell you, you'll just end up havin' to wait a day or two for the next train."

Jack looked so distraught that I almost laughed. "It's all right, dear," I said. "I'm so tired, I'm sure I can sleep through all your tossing and turning and snoring. Even your teeth grinding and sleep kicking probably won't bother me."

The porter's large teeth gleamed. "Well, goody, then! Y'all let me know if I can get you anything." He pulled the door closed behind him.

Jack carefully laid the sleeping Elise on the bed, then looked at me, his right eyebrow cocked high. "Sleep kicking?"

I lifted my shoulders. "I thought you'd prefer that to me saying that you wet the bed."

"You wouldn't have dared!"

"Oh, no?" I grinned. "I really can't resist a good dare, so if you're challenging me, I'll just call back the porter, and . . ." I turned as if I were going to the door.

He took a step toward me. "You wouldn't."

"Oh, but I would. And I think I should. I think the porter would love a good bed-wetting tale to share with his coworkers." I stepped closer to the door and put my hand on the doorknob. "He looked like he'd enjoy a laugh, didn't he?"

Jack picked me up and hauled me away from the door. Laughing, I kicked my feet in the air. He finally set me down.

"You're just pure trouble, aren't you?"

"Yes, pretty much." Laughter bubbled out of me. "Oh, you should have seen your face! You looked so shocked and outraged!"

His lips curved in a rueful smile. "It took me a moment to realize you were kidding. I'm not used to being teased."

"You need more of it."

"Maybe I do."

He still had his hands on my arms, and we were standing very close together, just smiling at each other, and suddenly the air changed. It crackled, like radio signals. His eyes darkened, becoming all pupil. I found it hard to breathe.

His gaze slid to my lips, and his fingers tightened on my arm. We moved closer. I wasn't sure who moved first. It seemed as if the very ground were moving.

And then I realized it was. The train was pulling away from the station.

Jack abruptly dropped his hands and stepped back, as if awakening from a trance. "Well. We seem to be under way."

"Yes."

But something else was under way, as well—something as powerful as a locomotive, and possibly just as hard to stop.

———

Jack moved toward the door. "I'll go find the porter and tell him that I'm a doctor. With a train this size, they're likely to need one at some point."

He headed out of the cabin, closing the door behind him.

When he came back, we both tried to act as before, but we were too polite, too stiff, too oddly formal. We read, we talked, we played with Elise. We tried to ignore the enormous bed in the center of the room—the bed we would be sharing.

After about an hour, Jack finally addressed the elephant in the room.

"I would offer to sleep on the floor, but there's no room to stretch out."

"Don't be ridiculous. It's a huge bed. We'll just each keep to our side."

Jack sighed. "Kat won't like this."

"Then don't tell her. There's no need for her to know everything."

"If she asks, I'll be obligated to tell her."

"If she loves you, I'm sure she trusts you. You're worrying about it too much."

He was quiet for a moment. "I know what I'll do; I'll ask for extra pillows. We'll put them down the center of the bed."

"Why don't you just ask for that prickly fence the cowboys use in the movies?"

"Barbed wire?"

"Yes. That's it."

"Very funny."

"I'd hoped you'd think so." I stopped smiling when I saw that he was still frowning. "You're really worried about it, aren't you?"

"It seems improper."

"It's not much more improper than sharing a room, which we've already done for two nights." He was still frowning. "If Kat is as wonderful a girl as you deserve, she will be understanding. You are doing a very kind thing for me and the baby."

"And Doug. And Doug's parents."

I had completely forgotten about them. Guilt burned in my chest. "Bien sûr. Yes, for them, too."

We got off the train and grabbed a sandwich at Glenview, then climbed back on.

"Y'all know there's a sittin' room you're free to use, don' you?" the porter said.

"Really?" Jack said.

He nodded. "This Pullman was 'specially outfitted for groups travelin' together. People often rent out the whole car, but no one did this time. So there's a room with a sofa and chairs in the center. You can sit out there instead of stayin' in that li'l room all the time."

"Why, thank you," I said.

It was our saving grace. We met up with our fellow passengers—all of whom seemed be very well-heeled. One older couple, Rose and Wilbur

Atkins, took to Elise immediately. Rose was a petite woman with immaculately styled silver hair and a British accent. Wilbur was a bulky man with a wide, friendly face.

"Oh, what a beautiful baby!" Rose said. "She looks like a perfect blend of her mommy and daddy."

Jack opened his mouth to speak. I could tell he was about to correct her assumption, but what would that do but muddy the waters? I jumped in. "Doesn't she? And Jack is wonderful with her. She absolutely adores him."

"A real daddy's girl," Rose said. Elise cooed, then reached for Jack's ear. Jack was standing her on his lap, his hands on her waist, and Elise was doing knee bends.

"She looks like she's full of mischief," Wilbur said.

"She gets that from her mother," Jack said, giving me a sidelong look.

"Well, with that face, she could get away with anything."

"Again, just like her mother," Jack said.

I gave him a slight kick, but the flirtatiousness of the remark thrilled me.

We learned that the couple was from Chicago, going to California to celebrate their thirtieth wedding anniversary.

"Rose wants to see where the movie stars live," Wilbur said.

"Oh, how exciting!" I exclaimed.

Rose and I talked about movies and movie stars, while Jack and Wilbur discussed business. When he learned Jack's background, Wilbur was extremely impressed.

"This young man is a doctor," he told his wife. "He just got out of the army after serving overseas."

"Oh, how marvelous! Is that how you two met?"

"Yes," I said. "He was working in a hospital in Paris."

"Oh, my! We had a wartime courtship, as well," Rose said. "The first war, of course. I lived in England, and he was based there. We'd known each other only three days before he asked me to marry him."

"Goodness!" I said.

"When it's right, you just know it," Wilbur said. "I figured, why waste time?"

"How did you know it was right?" I asked. "Did you have a lot in common?"

"Oh, no. We were polar opposites," Rose said. "We still are. He loves watching sports, I can't stand them. I love opera, he hates it. I think the house is always too cold, he thinks it's too warm. He's very conservative about politics, and I'm a progressive."

"But you seem very happy all the same," I said.

"Oh, we are. We've learned to appreciate our differences, rather than fight about them."

Wilbur, it turned out, was a stockbroker who had managed to liquidate most of his holdings before the big crash.

"How did you know to do that?" Jack asked.

Wilbur lifted his shoulders. "I followed a hunch."

The concept fascinated me. "Like a premonition?"

"Well, it wasn't a dream or vision or anything like that. It was more just a feeling, a sense that things were about to change. Investors were getting a little too reckless, and the economy had stopped growing. I'm sure a lot of people noticed the same things. The only difference is, I acted on it."

Jack leaned forward. "Can you say why?"

Wilbur lifted his bulky shoulders. "Danged if I know! The good Lord was watching out for me, maybe. I always try to start my day talking to him. Anyway, I decided to liquidate just about everything and invest in real estate. As they say, no one can make more land. Before I could buy very much, though, the market crashed."

"Good thing you followed your instincts."

Wilbur nodded. "I've never regretted a decision I made with my gut. It was like that when I met Rose."

"Where did you meet?" I asked.

"At a dance for servicemen put on by a women's auxiliary in London. I just knew, early on, that she was the one." He smiled over at her, and took her hand.

"He told me he felt as though we'd already met," Rose said. "And the funny thing is, I did, too."

"Like déjà vu?" I asked.

"No, more just a sense that she was familiar." He gave her an adoring look. "She was exactly what I'd been longing for all my life, and I recognized her when I met her."

"That's so beautiful!" I said.

Rose nodded, her eyes a little misty.

Wilbur patted her hand, then glanced at us. "You two probably felt the same way."

"I definitely felt like I'd been looking for Jack." I shot him a mischievous glance.

It was his turn to kick me under the table.

"I think intuition plays a bigger role in life than most people realize." Wilbur turned to Jack. "Do you ever get hunches in your line of work?"

To my surprise, Jack—logical, rational Jack!—nodded. "Actually, I have. I've had hunches to run a certain test or look for symptoms that didn't seem obvious. But I'm sure you're right. No doubt I was subconsciously picking up on little signals and signs."

Elise chose that moment to set up a squall. "I think that's a sign she's tired," I said with a smile. "It's time for her nap."

"Why don't you two join us for dinner?" Wilbur asked. "As our guests, of course."

"Oh, we don't want to impose," Jack said.

"It wouldn't be an imposition. It would be our pleasure."

"I think it sounds marvelous," I piped up. Being around another couple helped defuse the tension between us.

"All right," Jack conceded. "But we will pay our own way."

"No, no, no. Listen, son." The older man leaned forward and clapped Jack on the back. "I have the highest respect for doctors and servicemen, and I would be absolutely honored to have you as our guests at every meal for the rest of your time on this train."

"Why, how wonderful!" I said. "That sounds delightful, doesn't it, Jack?"

"And furthermore, my maid Sue can watch little Elise so you two don't have to have her in your lap nonstop," Rose said.

"Why thank you," I said, touched at the generosity.

"In fact, anytime you'd like a break, Sue would be happy to watch her. She watched our two boys when they were young, and she's as reliable as the day is long. She can't wait to take care of the grandkids in California."

———

Dinner with the Atkinses was filled with much joviality and laughter.

"When is your actual anniversary?" I asked Rose.

"Next week," said Wilbur. "We'll celebrate in Los Angeles with our sons and their families."

"Thirty years—that is so wonderful!" I said. "What is the secret to a long and happy marriage?"

"Putting little notes under each other's pillows." Wilbur gave Rose a wink.

Rose blushed, and hit him on the arm. "Give them advice they can use," she scolded.

"Well, I think our notes help keep things lively," Wilbur said. "It's important to have a secret way to communicate with each other."

"Here's a piece of advice that's actually helpful," Rose said. I think she was trying to cover her embarrassment. "You need to care more about getting along than about being right."

"Oh, that's very good advice," I said.

"And you need to have a sense of humor," Rose continued. "Life together should be adventurous and fun."

"I think the war was adventure enough to last a lifetime," Jack said.

"I imagine it was. So now it's time for the fun part," Rose said.

"Yes," Wilbur added. "And with such a beautiful, personable bride, I'd say you're all set in that department."

I didn't know what "all set" meant, but from the context, I knew it was a compliment—and from Jack's embarrassed expression, I could tell he was incapable of forming a response.

I leaned over and kissed Jack's cheek. "With such a handsome, charming husband, I'm all set in that department, too," I said.

"Why all the questions about a happy marriage?" Jack grumbled when we'd collected Elise from the maid's room and gone back to our own.

I settled the sleeping baby in my half-emptied suitcase. "Well, you'll be getting married soon—for real, I mean—and I thought you could use the advice."

"I don't need any advice, thank you." He sounded very grumpy.

"Oh? So you expect that you and Kit will be as happy as Rose and Wilbur in thirty years?"

"Her name is Kat. And I don't think most people are ever that happy," Jack said, pulling off his tie. "They're an anomaly."

It was a new word for me, but I could guess its meaning. "Does Kit have a sense of humor?"

"It's Kat. And yes, of course she does."

"So you two tease each other and make each other laugh?"

"We're not really like that."

"So what do you laugh at?"

He concentrated on unknotting his tie. "We both like funny movies."

I rolled my eyes. "Oh, my, what a special bond!"

He shot me a dark look. "It works for us." He busied himself in neatly rolling up his tie like a cinnamon bun. "I'm not much of one for teasing."

"Ah."

"I'm not looking to marry a comedienne. I just want a calm, peaceful, orderly existence. Someone who will run the house and let me focus on medicine."

"Sounds like you need a maid and cook instead of a wife."

A knock sounded at the door. Jack opened it.

"'cuse me, sir." The porter peered around Jack and lifted his cap. "Ma'am. I was jes' wondering if there was anythin' I could get you 'fore y'all retire for the night."

"Yes," Jack said. "Could you bring us some extra pillows?"

"Certainly, sir."

"And do you have a rubber sheet?" I added.

Jack turned to me, his face murderous.

"A . . . rubber sheet?" The porter's eyebrows rose.

"Yes. For . . . how do you say . . . the bed-wetting?"

Jack's face flamed.

"Oh! Well, um . . ." The porter seemed taken aback.

I waited for several dangerous moments, letting the discomfort thicken in the air, and then I gave my sweetest smile. "It's for the baby."

"Oh! Why, of course. Yes, ma'am. I can bring you an old vinyl tablecloth liner, and some extra sheets. Will that work?"

"That would be perfect. Thank you."

"I'll be right back." He closed the door.

Jack's glare would have melted a glacier.

I smiled at him. "What's the matter?"

"Don't play all innocent with me."

"You seem upset." I nonchalantly turned away. "I can't imagine why."

"Oh, can't you?"

"No." I busied myself unfolding my nightgown.

"Bed-wetting," he muttered.

I couldn't help it—I giggled. My hand over my mouth, I turned to look at him.

His scowl softened. A grin tugged at the corners of his lips.

"I thought you were going to explode when I asked for a rubber sheet."

"I thought you were ready for a rubber room."

"What is a rubber room?"

"It's where they put crazy people."

"Oh, really? People who do things like this?" I threw a pillow at him.

"Yes. People who need to be put in straitjackets."

"What is a straitjacket?"

"It's something that restrains people from doing harmful things."

"How does it restrain them?"

"I think I need to show you."

"You will have to catch me first."

"Is that a dare?"

"Absolutely."

He climbed over the bed to the other side and threw me onto the mattress.

I squealed and scrambled on top of him. "I don't feel restrained. But perhaps you do."

He flipped me onto my back. "How about now?"

"A little."

I looked up at him, smiling. His eyes were dark, and his breath smelled like chocolate. My heart pounded. Our smiling stopped, but our eyes never broke contact. Our breathing seemed to fall into sync. The moment, so lighthearted one second ago, turned tense. "But another part of me feels very unrestrained," I whispered.

"Amélie." He breathed my name onto my lips as he lowered his mouth to mine.

And then . . . oh mon Dieu! I was swept away, sucked into a whirlpool, lost in a storm of Jack—his mouth, his taste, his hands in my hair—I could not tell where I stopped and he began. I did not want to know. He kissed me as if my lips contained his oxygen, and I was sure his contained mine.

And then . . . the porter rapped on the door.

We jumped apart, as if we'd been hosed by firemen.

"This can't happen." Jack rolled off me and sat on the edge of the bed.

I sat up beside him, chagrined at his chagrin. "No. No, you are right."

"It's because of this situation. It's unnatural, having everyone think we're married."

"But we are married."

"You know what I mean."

I did. He looked at my mouth. I looked at his. Time hung like a still pendant, and the pull toward each other seemed stronger than gravity.

The knock sounded again.

Jack stood and straightened his shirt. "I'd better get that, or else he'll think we're . . ."

I grinned. "Doing what we were doing."

His forehead creased, and his mouth was stern. "We cannot—we must not—do that again."

But from that moment on, it was all I could think about.

53

AMÉLIE
1946

*N*othing further happened that night. Shortly after the porter dropped off the pillows, extra sheets, and vinyl tablecloth, Jack put his tie and coat back on, took his doctor's bag, and headed out the door.

"Where are you going?" I asked.

"I think I should sleep in the sitting room tonight."

"There is no need. We have the pillows to keep us apart."

"I fear it might take more than pillows."

So he left.

The next morning, Mrs. Atkins took me aside on the way to breakfast. Her brow furrowed in a worried frown. "I understand that you and Jack had a lovers' tiff last night."

"What?"

"I heard that he slept in the lounge. Everyone in the car knows it. So I figured that you two must have had an argument."

"Oh, it wasn't that. He wasn't sleepy, and he didn't want to disturb me, so . . ."

She waved her hand impatiently. "There's no need to pretend with me, dear. I know how it can be. But honey, it's important that you patch things up right away. You shouldn't go to bed angry. And you certainly shouldn't sleep apart!"

"Jack is very stubborn."

"Well, I'm sure he is. But you can't let him walk out and sleep elsewhere. You have to nip this in the bud."

"Nip in the bud? I do not understand."

"It means you mustn't let disagreements go too far. That's the key to a long and successful marriage."

She looped arms with me as we walked toward the dining car. "I can tell that you love each other very much."

My head turned toward her in surprise. "You can?"

"Oh, yes. I see the way you look at each other."

My pulse thrummed in my throat. I feared I was not good at hiding my attraction to Jack, but I didn't know if it was reciprocated. "Does Jack—look at me that way?"

"Oh, my dear, it is plain that he adores you! Even Wilbur mentioned how smitten Jack seems with you."

My heart soared at her words.

"And any fool can see that you feel the same about him."

I numbly nodded. I hadn't meant to, but I was falling in love with him. How could I not? He was exactly the kind of man I had dreamed of. He was smart, strong, protective, caring, kind, and handsome. He could even be funny when he let himself.

"You know, there's a great deal of power in the physical side of marriage," Rose told me. "It smooths over many hurt feelings and harsh words. It's the best way to show that you forgive and are forgiven, that you accept and are accepted, just as you really are."

Oh, how I longed to be accepted and forgiven! The closer the train chugged to Whitefish, the heavier guilt weighed on me. How could I perpetrate such a tremendous charade on Doug's innocent parents? How could I spend my life pretending that I had loved someone I had never known?

How could I stay behind and watch Jack leave? The very thought plunged me into despair.

"That is wise advice, I am sure," I said. "But Jack is determined to keep his distance from me. I suspect he will once again spend the night in the lounge."

"Well, I can make sure that doesn't happen," she said. "I'll get the porter to tell him it is against the rules—that each guest must retire to his own quarters after midnight."

My heart quickened. "Thank you. That will help."

"And why don't you let Sue keep the baby tonight? After dinner, Sue can say that Elise was fussy and had trouble falling asleep, that it would be a shame to awaken her to carry her to another room. I know Sue would love it."

"Oh, I wouldn't want to inconvenience her."

"Nonsense. She asked me if she might keep Elise all night. She adores babies."

"Well, then . . . all right."

"And one other thing. A little alcohol helps to boost along amorous impulses."

"Yes, but Jack usually doesn't drink."

"He will if Wilbur toasts to things he cannot refuse to raise a glass to. This is our last night together, so there will be many things to toast. I will see to it." She smiled at me. "All you need to do is look beautiful and act sweet. When you retire to your cabin after dinner, I daresay all differences and disagreements between you will melt away."

"Thank you, Rose. You are such a wonderful friend."

"So are you, dear. So are you."

54

KAT
2016

I knew it! I knew that she'd deliberately set a trap for Jack. "And so you seduced him?"

Amélie lifts her shoulders. "Call it what you will. Perhaps yes, or perhaps it was mutual. Do you want to hear it, or not?"

"Oh, yes, I want to hear. I want to hear every single detail."

"Very well. But if you interrupt during this next part, I will stop talking."

"I will be quiet," I say, and hold my tongue between my teeth.

AMÉLIE
1946

*J*ack was civil but distant all day. Rose told Jack that she wanted to help me dress for dinner—"I always wanted a daughter, and all I had were rowdy boys!"—so I went to her cabin in the late afternoon.

Rose pulled a dress out of a box filled with delicate tissue paper. It was apricot shantung silk, fitted, very beautiful, and, I'm sure, very expensive.

"Oh, how gorgeous!" I sighed.

"I bought it in New York when I was shopping for my daughters-in-law," she said. "I'm bringing them both several dresses. I couldn't decide which one to give this dress to—it isn't really right for either one of them—but it was so exquisite, I couldn't pass it up. The moment I saw you, I said to myself, 'Amélie would look heavenly in that the dress!' So I really, really want you to have it."

"Are you sure? It's divine!"

"I'm certain. I don't know why I didn't think of it earlier. And let's have Sue help style your hair."

When Jack saw me that evening, he froze in his tracks. I saw his Adam's apple bob as he swallowed. "You, um . . . you look very nice."

"Doesn't she?" Rose said. "Dressing her up was more fun than I ever had playing dolls as a girl."

"Looks like we've got a couple of living dolls, doesn't it, son?" Wilbur winked and smacked Jack on the shoulder. "They smell nice, too."

Rose had loaned me her perfume, as well.

Dinner was a high-spirited event. As promised, Wilbur offered toast after toast, keeping my glass and Jack's glass always topped off. He insisted on ordering after-dinner brandies. At length, Wilbur covered a yawn and said he was ready to turn in. When Jack and I went to Sue's room to pick up Elise, she suggested that Elise stay the night with her— that she was teething and fussy, and it would be a shame to awaken her to move her. I agreed.

And so Jack and I returned to our room alone. The train was curving its way through the mountains, and I had to hold on to the seats to steady myself as I walked through the car.

"It was a wonderful evening, wasn't it?" I said as Jack unlocked our little room.

We stepped in and he closed the door. The porter had left a nightlight on. The bed was turned down with extra pillows on the mattress.

"All of Wilbur's toasts to wives and marriage and happiness made me very uncomfortable," Jack said, pulling off his jacket and hanging it on the wall-mounted coatrack.

"They think we had a taff because you slept in the lounge last night."

"A what?"

"A taff. That's what Rose said."

He laughed and loosened his tie. "It's 'tiff.' So Rose talked to you about this, hmm? Now all the toasts make sense." He pulled off his tie. "They are trying to get us to kiss and make up. Is that why she wanted to dress you up?"

"Yes," I admitted.

"Well, it was all wasted effort."

I couldn't help it. My eyes welled with tears.

"Oh, hell—I didn't mean that the way it sounded. You look beautiful. But then, you always do. You don't need to get gussied up to look breathtaking."

My tears fell harder.

He stepped closer and wiped my tears. The train jerked.

"Hey—did I hurt your feelings?"

"No. It's just . . . I hate that the trip is ending."

"It will all work out in Whitefish. Doug's parents sounded swell on the phone."

The train shifted, throwing us together. His hands gripped my arms. His eyes burned into mine in the dim light. The train lurched and the lights flickered. "That isn't why I'm sad," I whispered.

The train bumped us closer. The lights blinked again. My heart felt as if it were in my throat. "Is it a sin to desire someone you shouldn't, even if you are legally married to the one you desire?"

"You shouldn't ask such things."

"I have to. If my thoughts will send me to hell, well, I would like to taste heaven first. And your kiss last night—it was like being there."

"Amélie . . ."

"And we are married. How could it be so wrong?"

The train rounded a bend, and the lights went out. Our arms gripped each other's, and we inched closer, and then, somehow, our lips met in the dark. It was a match striking flint over the driest kindling. Instant sparks, instant heat, instantly leaping to uproarious flames.

After a long, drugged kiss, he pulled away enough to whisper in my ear. "If we continue, I'm afraid I won't be able to stop. My self-control is all worn down, I've had too much to drink, and I'm barred from staying in the lounge tonight. We're playing with fire."

"I am burning for you already, and I am not playing," I whispered.

"Amélie . . ." His lips reclaimed my mouth. His fingers found the zipper on my dress. I unbuttoned his shirt, eager to feel his skin against mine.

His chest was hard and muscular, covered with soft springy hair. I had never felt a man's naked chest before, and I thrilled at the difference between his body and mine. The dim light flickered back on. He edged my open dress off my shoulders. The silk pooled at my feet, along with my slip. I stepped out of the garments as we edged our way to the bed, still kissing. It was only a matter of inches to the mattress in that cramped room. Together we fell on it. He reached around and unhooked my bra, then slid it off.

"Beautiful," he murmured, gazing at my breasts. "So beautiful."

His hand cupped me, and his mouth followed. A bolt of pleasure shot straight south as he kissed and fondled each breast.

I moaned, and his hand moved to my thigh. He unfastened my garters, then pulled off my stockings, rolling them down gently. He kissed his way back up my leg, his five-o'clock shadow a thrilling scruff against my skin. When he reached my inner thighs and pulled off my panties, I thought I would die of pleasure.

And then he was over me, his lips on mine. I unfastened his belt buckle. He pulled away for a moment to shuck off his pants, as well as his underwear.

I had never seen a naked man, much less one who was aroused. I was fascinated and slightly terrified as I watched him cross the room and pull a packet of something from his doctor's bag. However would he fit inside me?

The mattress dipped as he rejoined me on it, and his lips reclaimed mine. His kisses moved to my neck, my ears, then down to my breasts, spending equal time on each. And then he kissed his way down my belly, down to the part of me that was throbbing for him.

He kissed me there, his fingers working some kind of magic. I was at first embarrassed, but I was soon too enthralled by the sensations to remain self-conscious. I gave myself over to the delicious feelings, to the growing sense of tension and desire. He coaxed something from my body that I did not know it could do, something wild and full and beyond my control. It gave me an exquisite sense of release and joy. I lay there, panting and weak and sated.

He kissed his way back up my body to my mouth. I reached for his shaft. It was hard as steel, but so warm, with such warm, soft skin. It jerked as my hand enfolded it.

"Amélie—" His voice was a raw croak. "I can't wait."

"I don't want you to," I whispered.

He turned away for a moment. I heard a rip of foil, and then he was back over me, covering me, sliding into me.

The sensation—the opening, the filling, the gentle expansion—made me tremble with pleasure. I unfolded to him, giving him slow access to the softest, most vulnerable, most loving parts of me. I was riding on a cloud of delectable pleasure—until, suddenly, I was pierced by a sharp stab of pain.

Oh, mon Dieu! I felt as if I were being ripped in two. I tried not to cry out, but Jack sensed something was wrong.

He froze inside me. I feared he would pull out, that I wouldn't be able to give him the pleasure he had given me—and I deeply, achingly wanted to give him that pleasure. Biting my inner lip, I gripped him tighter and remembered what Yvette had told me: *Men love it if you move beneath them.* I pushed my hips forward. Jack responded with an answering thrust, so I did it again and again, and his body seemed to completely take over. At length he tensed and gave a low moan.

He lay atop me, spent, for a long moment. In that moment, I felt a sense of completeness, of contentment, of all-encompassing love—a wholeness of body and soul that I had never known, not even before the war.

And then he rolled off me. His eyes glowed with a soft light I had never seen there before. "Jesus, Amélie," he said. "It's almost as if you were a virgin."

My guard was down, and he must have read the truth on my face. He abruptly sat up and stared at the sheet between us. I followed his gaze to a spot of blood.

He jumped from the bed as if it were full of snakes. "Good God. You *were* a virgin!"

I was too stunned to think quickly enough come up with a cover story. I hadn't thought of this.

I could see his scientific mind rolling through the ramifications. "Damn it all to damnation." He pulled off the condom, then stared at it as he strode to the trash by the sink. "Oh, no. Oh, *hell*! Freaking bloody *hell*!" He hit the sink with his palm, so hard it made the wall jerk. "Bloody, bastard-soaked, rotting hellfire *hell!*"

"What is wrong?" I asked.

"You're a friggin' virgin, and I think the condom busted!"

"It . . . busted?"

"Broke. Ripped. Tore." The train rocked around a bend, and the lights went out. "I *hope* it broke when I started to pull it off, but it sure as hell seemed like it was already busted." The lights blinked off again while he did something at the sink. When they blinked back on, he was beside me with a damp washcloth. He handed it to me. His eyes were hot coals in a face drained of color.

"Good God, Amélie." I could see the wheels turning in his brain. He stared at me as if I had suddenly sprouted horns, or another head. "If you're a virgin, you're not Elise's mother."

A lump the size of the Eiffel Tower formed in my throat.

"Which means you couldn't have had Doug's baby." His voice was rising in volume, but getting lower and more guttural with every word. "You were never with Doug!"

"No," I whisper.

"Holy *fuck*!"

It struck me that I had never before heard him use this word. But before tonight, I had never even heard him say *damn*.

He loomed in front of me, his face a terrifying thundercloud. "So tell me this, Amélie—and you better goddamned tell me the truth."

I leaned back against the wall, clutching the covers.

"Who the hell are you, and who the hell's baby do you have?"

56

AMÉLIE
1946

I had no other option, so I told him the truth.

We stayed awake most of the night. I explained that I was the daughter of a linguistics professor, that I had grown up in Paris with my brothers, and that I had known Yvette all my life. I told him all about the beginning of the war and meeting Joshua, then fleeing Paris. I told him about losing my parents and my home. I described life in occupied Paris, the fear, the hunger, the desperation. I told him about working for la Résistance, about Pierre. I told him about becoming une femme tondue, about Yvette's pregnancy and death.

He seemed to be sympathetic. He seemed to be softening. "And how does Doug fit into all this?"

So I told him how I had overheard him giving Doug's confession by proxy.

This infuriated him all over again—more than any of my other deceptions, more even than learning that Elise was not my biological child. He let out a string of epithets I didn't understand, but realized were viler than any he had probably ever uttered in his life. "Why?" Jack asked, his hands on his head. "Why did you set me up like that?"

"Because I was desperate, and you seemed like a gift from God."

"You could have just asked me! I would have tried to help."

"You would not have married me."

"No. I would not. And I don't know that I can ever forgive you for taking that choice from me."

"You always had a choice."

"You played on my sense of guilt, damn it! And now I've betrayed Kat and her family and myself—all for your personal gain."

"No. I did it for Elise."

"Oh, really?"

"Yes. It wasn't for me. I decided to do this before I set eyes on you. You could have been an old ugly toad of a man, for all I knew."

"You not only tricked me into marrying you—you tricked me into taking your virginity!"

"I didn't trick you into that," I protested. "And what does my virginity have to do with anything?"

"It shouldn't have a damn thing." He rose from the bed and stood in the narrow space between the bed and wall. Lifting the shade, he stared out the window at the passing night, then turned to me. "Tell me this: What were you planning to do in Montana? How long did you think you could pass off Elise as Doug's child?"

Shame scoured me like a metal-bristled brush. All I could do was bow my head. "I . . . I do not know."

"You were going to dupe Doug's parents into taking in you and the child?"

"It was not my choice. It was yours."

"Because I believed you, damn it! But you—you were going to let it happen?"

"I—I do not know. It has been heavy on my heart. I have not known what to do since we started this journey. I believe I would have told you on the next train."

"You *believe* you would have? What kind of woman are you?"

"A desperate one," I replied. "I do not believe I am a bad one."

He made a scoffing sound from the back of his throat. "Even you don't know for sure."

I lifted my head. "I know this. I never meant any harm. I only want what is best for Elise."

"If you think I'm going to reorder my life to accommodate some scheme of yours, you're dead wrong."

"What?"

"Last night doesn't change the fact you're a liar and a schemer."

"Last night was because I grew to care for you, to want you. You know that I wanted you. You are a man. You are a doctor. You know the signs of desire, signs a woman cannot fake."

He stared out the window.

"I have no designs, no schemes on you, aside from getting Elise to America. Last night—well, that, I admit, was selfish; I made love with you because I wanted you so badly. It is the only thing I have sought purely for myself, aside from survival, since I was sixteen years old." I lifted my chin. "And I do not regret it."

"Well, I do."

"I am sorry. I felt it was so good, so right, so exactly as it ought to have felt."

"How could it be good or right, when it was built on a stack of lies? I betrayed my fiancée for a woman who lied to me and used me for her own purposes."

"You make me sound awful. I never meant harm. I only lied because I wanted the best for my child."

"The child is not even yours. Good grief, you don't even have a legal claim to her!"

"I have the claim of love. I have the claim of being with her all of her life, and of being the only mother she knows."

"By all rights, I should report you to the authorities."

My heart stopped, then pounded so hard he must have been able to hear it. "What . . . what would happen then?"

"Elise would probably be sent to social services and you would be deported."

"Oh, no!" The terror of losing Elise was far, far worse than any fear I had felt in the war. My blood felt as though it had turned to ice. "That cannot be what is best for the child. Please. Let us get an annulment as planned."

"And how will you live? How will you support her, without friends or family to watch her while you work? Where will you live?"

"I—I'll figure it out. I have a much better chance here than in France. Here there is food. There are jobs. There is opportunity."

"I honestly don't know what to do with you. I don't know what to think."

We went round and round all night, talking and arguing. Sometime toward morning, we fell into an exhausted sleep. We skipped breakfast and readied ourselves to change trains.

I went to get Elise from Sue and ran into Rose.

"Did it work?" she asked eagerly.

"Yes, and no," I answered, my heart heavy. "We made love, but then we had another argument, and it was worse than before. And it is all my fault."

"No argument is ever the fault of just one party."

"This one was," I said sadly. "I was untruthful to him about some very important things from my past."

She patted my back. "My dear, love can conquer anything. Keep him close, be patient, and remember the power of the physical side of your relationship."

There was no point in telling her that her advice was useless. Advice about love only worked if both parties felt it. I mustered a small smile. "Thank you for all you have done."

Rose handed me a card with her address. "If you ever are in Chicago, or if you ever need anything, you can reach me at this address or this phone number."

I tucked it in my purse. During the war, I had learned the importance of having supportive people in my life and not being too proud to take their help when I needed it. It was almost as important as being there to support others in their time of need. "Thank you, Rose, for the dress and the advice and the encouragement."

"God bless, my dear." She kissed my cheek. "And welcome to America!"

If only, I thought, I could be sure I would get to stay.

57

We changed trains in Williston, North Dakota. Jack carried my bag. He helped me with Elise. But he did not speak to me.

We sat across from each other for hours. He read a book. I tried to distract a very fussy baby—I don't know if Elise was really teething or just picking up on my tension—and I stared out the window. The scenery was magnificent—snowcapped mountains, rivers full of ice floes, and meadows ridged with snowdrifts—but none of it registered. I was too terrified of what would happen to me.

At last, Jack broke his silence. "The Claibornes are meeting us at Whitefish. Since you can't be trusted to open your mouth without lying, you are to say nothing beyond 'Hello' and 'Nice to meet you.' In fact, why don't you pretend as if you don't speak English? You've proven you can do that convincingly enough."

His words stung. "And what will you tell them?"

"That I was with their son when he died. As for you—I will not support any of your lies. You never met him. You will not say you did." He gazed out the window, his mouth as hard and craggy as the mountains. "We'll stay the night, and we'll leave tomorrow."

"Afterward—what will happen to Elise and me?"

"I don't know yet." He didn't deign to look at me. "And if I did, I'd make you wait to find out."

"You are trying to punish me."

"No. I am keeping you from finding a way to work against me behind my back. You are not to be trusted."

Tears sprang to my eyes. "You are wrong. I am completely trustworthy, if I am on your side of things."

He gave a disbelieving snort.

"Look at how faithfully I served France. Look at how good a friend I have been to Yvette, and how good a mother to Elise. The problem is, when I first met you, I did not know that you were . . ." I hesitated. What could I say? *That you were so fine, so upright, and respectable? Too decent to lie to?* "So . . . honorable."

"Would that have changed your plans?"

I blew out a sigh. "Probably not. I had made a vow to Yvette, and you seemed the only option I had of keeping it. And I never meant to be such a problem to you. I thought you would help me get to New York, and then we would go our separate ways. I had no idea things would get so . . . involved."

"Were the Browns really your family?"

I had no reason to withhold the truth about anything anymore. "They were Yvette's family—Elise's family. I know they would have given us a place to live while I got a job and got on my feet."

"We'll never know that now, will we?"

And then, about a half hour later, he asked another question. "Why did you lie about the dead babies on the ship?"

Tears sprang to my eyes. "I didn't! That was the truth."

"A very convenient truth, considering it kept me from putting you back on the ship to France when we couldn't find your family."

"That is not how it was."

He shook his head. "When I count up the lies you've told me, it boggles the mind. I don't even know which one is the worst."

"I am sorry. At the time I told each one, I felt it was necessary."

"How about the lie of omission?"

"I don't know what you mean."

"Why the hell didn't you tell me you were a virgin?"

I didn't understand why he was scowling so darkly at me. "What does that have to do with anything?"

"Nothing! It should have nothing to do with a blasted damned thing." Although, I could tell, in his mind it did.

AMÉLIE
1946

*W*e arrived at Whitefish a few minutes after ten in the evening. The Claibornes were waiting for us at the station—a large Tudor-looking building, far more grand than I would have expected out in the wilds of the country.

The Claibornes were both blue-eyed and large-boned and tall. To my mind, they looked like Germans, or possibly Swedes. The woman's graying hair was pulled back into a severe bun. She had a thin mouth but kind eyes. She wore what looked like an Indian blanket draped around a shearling-lined overcoat. Her face wore the familiar signs of recent grief—circles around the eyes, furrows in her forehead, the gaunt, angular look of someone who had suddenly lost weight. The man was tall and broad-shouldered, with thinning, white-streaked hair and a white beard. He wore a heavy suede coat, also lined in shearling. He had the ruddy skin of a man who spent much time outdoors.

"My family surprised me in New York, so I brought them with me," Jack said. "I hope we're not inconveniencing you."

"No, not at all. The more the merrier! I'm Daniel Claiborne, and this is Gustava."

"Please, call us Dan and Gustie," she said, holding out her hand to me.

I still found it odd, this American custom of shaking hands. I awkwardly did so.

"*Enchanté*," I said. "I am Amélie. And this is Elise."

"Oh, my—what a beautiful child!"

"Thank you," I murmured.

Jack gave me a meaningful look. "I'm afraid Amélie doesn't speak much English."

"I'm sure we'll get along just fine." She looked at me hopefully. "Did you know Doug, too?"

"No." Jack responded at the same time I did.

An awkward pause followed our odd unison reply. "Well, I can't wait to hear everything you can tell us about our boy." Gustie looked at Jack, her plain face bright with anticipation.

"Now, Gustie," Dan admonished. "It's late, and our visitors have had a long trip. Let's get them home and let them get some sleep, and then we can all talk tomorrow."

"Yes. Yes, that's a very good idea."

They took our bags, placed them in the Claibornes' ramshackle Ford, and drove several miles outside of town. Their home was a small, two-story clapboard farmhouse.

"I've put you in the guest room," Gustie said.

"Thank you," I said.

"The bathroom is down the hall," Dan said. "If you like, I can get Doug's old crib out of the attic for the baby. Gustie insisted on saving it for our grandchildren. Now, I guess, we'll never . . ." His voice petered off.

Gustie's fist went to her mouth.

My heart went out to her. "I am so sorry for your loss."

"Thank you." Dan looked at me, his eyes kind. "Say, I think your English is pretty good."

I could feel the heat of a warning in Jack's gaze and decided to ignore it. "Thank you. Jack has taught me much," I replied. "Please don't bother about the baby bed. She has been sleeping in my suitcase. I take out a few clothes, put a sheet across the others, and she has been perfectly comfortable."

Gustie bustled around, getting an extra sheet and blanket for the baby's bedding, asking if we wanted anything to eat or drink. Mercifully, Jack said we were tired.

Gustie held the baby while I fixed the suitcase bed. When I turned, I caught Gustie gazing at Elise with the rapt tenderness of someone falling in love. This, I thought, is what she lost in the war—her very own beloved child, the heart of her very heart. I had wondered if a mother ever really moved beyond that all-encompassing early love—that stay-up-all-night, feed-you-with-my-own-body, she-bear-ferocious love. Apparently not.

The thought of Jack separating me from Elise made my stomach knot.

Gustie softly placed Elise in her little bed as if she were made of the most delicate porcelain. "Oh, she's the sweetest thing."

"Thank you," I murmured.

Later, when Jack and I were alone, I remarked how very nice the Claibornes were. "And they really seem to like babies," I added.

He glowered at me. "If you're suggesting that we revert to your original scheme . . ."

"No! No, of course not. And you're forgetting that it was never my idea." What did he think I was?

And yet, how far from the truth was he? Because in the back of my mind, I was calculating how I might be able to stay with them instead of being shipped back to France. I was also thinking that I had Rose Atkins's card from the train. I was evaluating my options. The problem was that I had no money.

I knew that Jack had a big wad of money in his bag. I had seen it in the corner. If I took out enough to buy train tickets, I would be able to keep Elise in America.

I waited until he went down the hall to the bathroom, and I opened his bag. I stared at the money. There was a lot—maybe three thousand dollars in cash. He probably wouldn't even miss a couple of hundred-dollar bills.

I had learned many hard lessons during the war. The most lasting one was this: It was up to me, and me alone, to protect my loved ones. I could rely on no one else.

And yet . . . I was not a thief. If I had to become one to protect Elise, I would not steal from a man who had done nothing but help me. I closed the bag and put it back exactly where Jack had left it.

The bed was large and the room was cold. There were no extra blankets. All the same, Jack lay down on the floor.

"Don't be ridiculous. There is plenty of room in the bed for both of us."

"I will not share your bed."

"Very well. Then I will sleep on the floor and you can have the bed."

"No."

"Then we will both sleep on the floor." I hauled off the bedding, gave half to him, and covered myself with the other half.

"What are you doing?"

"I am not going to lie in comfort while you're on the floor. So if this is what you're going to do, then it's what I'll do, as well."

"Suit yourself," he said.

So I did. I lay on the floor on the right side, and he lay on the left. A big feather mattress lay between us, with no one—ridiculously—upon it.

I awakened early in the morning to sounds in the kitchen. Jack was gone. I gathered up the sheets and blankets and made the bed, trying to remember exactly how Gustie had the bedding arranged, then went to the bathroom, washed up, and brushed my teeth. I even managed to get dressed and fix my hair before I awakened and dressed Elise.

I took her downstairs to find Jack sitting with Gustie and Dan before a fire in the kitchen.

"Come in, come in," Gustie urged. "What can I fix for you and the little one?"

She warmed some water for Elise's formula and poured a cup of coffee for me while getting us each a bowl of oatmeal. "Your wonderful husband was just telling us about his service during the war," she said. "You must be so proud of him."

"Yes," I said.

"Where did you two meet?"

I looked at Jack, remembering I wasn't supposed to know much English. I decided to let him fend for himself.

"In Paris," he said. "She visited the hospital where I worked."

"Judging from the size of your baby, that must have been when you just arrived in France," Dan said. "You couldn't have wasted much time."

"It was a—how do you say—tornado romance," I supplied.

"She means whirlwind romance."

They both laughed.

"Doug didn't mention that you were married." Gustie frowned at Jack as she put some toast on my plate. "In fact, I thought he wrote something about you planning to practice medicine with your fiancée's father in Louisiana."

I saw Jack's ears flame. "War has a way of changing a person's plans."

"Are you going back to Louisiana?" Dan asked.

"Yes. But first I have to spend six weeks in Reno to get some extra training. In fact, we're catching a train there this afternoon."

I looked at Jack, startled. This was the first I'd heard of this.

"So soon?" Gustie asked. "But you just got here."

"We really can't stay. But I did want to come meet you and tell you what a fine man you'd raised."

Gustie's eyes grew wet. Even Dan's looked suspiciously moist. "Well, we appreciate that."

"You said on the phone that you had something from Doug for us?" Gustie said. "A surprise of some kind."

"Yes." He reached into his pocket and pulled out a stack of bills wrapped with a rubber band. "He wanted me to give you this." He handed the bills to Dan.

The large man thumbed through the thick wad of bills. "But how . . . how on earth did he get this much money?"

"Doug became quite a poker player. He routinely cleaned the table. And he kept his winnings—said he was saving up to help you get some new equipment, I believe. And, well, he asked me to see that you got this."

Dan's heavily wrinkled eyes widened. "There's twelve hundred dollars here!"

"Like I said—he was quite a poker player."

"And he wanted us to have it?" Dan's voice quavered.

Jack nodded. "I wanted to give it to you in person." His voice, too, shook with emotion. "Your son saved my life. I owe him—and you—a debt I can never repay."

"Thank you." Gustie dabbed at her eyes with the hem of her apron. "That means a lot."

Dan sniffed and cleared his throat, then rubbed his eyes with his thumbs.

"He was an excellent medic. He did a lot of good and helped a lot of people," Jack added.

Dan nodded. Gustie wiped her eyes again.

"Well." Jack's chair squeaked on the linoleum as he pushed it back. "If it's not too much trouble, can you take us back to the train station? There's a train that leaves at three thirty that we need to be on."

"Sure, no problem." Dan looked at the clock and put down his coffee cup. "I need to go feed the cattle first. Would you like to come?"

"I'd love to," Jack said. He shot me another warning look. "*Ne fait pas quelque chose stupide en mon absence.*"

"D'accord," I said sweetly. "I adore you, too."

"Your English is really quite good," Gustie said.

Thank heavens, I thought, *I can't say the same about your French.*

AMÉLIE
1946

I didn't get a chance to ask Jack about our future plans until we were on the train and pulling away from the station, because he deftly avoided being alone with me at the farmhouse. I waved to the Claibornes as the train began to move, then turned to Jack, who was seated across from me. We were in a Pullman car, but it was once again a double bunk, as on the first leg of our trip. We sat opposite each other in an alcove formed by the folding bottom mattress.

"Are we really going to stay in Reno for six weeks?" I asked.

"That's the required residency time to get an annulment. I have a doctor friend there, and I'm hoping he can pull some strings so we don't have to wait that long."

Merci Dieu—apparently he wasn't going to send me back to France or put Elise into foster care! "So you don't have to be there a full six weeks to complete the training course?"

"It's not a course, exactly. My friend specializes in wound care. I can learn a lot from working with him."

"You made it sound like a formal program."

"Did I?"

"Yes, and you know it." It felt like a small victory, catching Jack misrepresenting the truth.

"Well, then, your bad habits must be rubbing off on me. The sooner I'm rid of your influence, the better off I'll be."

His words hit me like a blow. "Am I really so awful?"

He hesitated so long I didn't think he was going to answer. At length he blew out a long sigh. "No. I don't think you're awful. I just can't trust you."

"Is there anything I can do to restore your faith in me?"

"At this point? No." He rose from his seat. "If you'll excuse me, I'm going to take a walk."

We hardly spoke to each other the rest of the day. At dinnertime, Elise was fussy. She refused to eat, and her cheeks looked flushed.

"I think she feels a little warm," I said to Jack. "Do you think she has a fever?"

He took her temperature under her arm. It was 99.9.

"It's a little high, but babies tend to have higher temperatures than adults. She looks like she has a little cold."

I didn't think she looked well. She cried, her eyes were red and her nose was running. She didn't even want to drink her formula or juice.

Jack took the upper berth. Elise and I bunked down in the bottom one. I was so exhausted that I fell right asleep, but Elise woke me up crying in the middle of the night.

"Jack," I called.

He climbed down immediately. "Yes?"

"Elise is burning up."

He took her temperature. It was 104 Fahrenheit. "Let's see if we can get her to drink some fluids. And I'll get a damp washcloth to put on her head."

He headed for the lavatory at the end of the railcar. I rocked the crying baby, smoothing back her hair, trying to tamp down a rising sense of alarm. She had never been seriously ill before. She'd had the sniffles, and she'd had a short-lived little stomach bug, but she'd never had a fever like this. I felt helpless. I was relieved when Jack returned.

He put the washcloth on her head. "I'll give her a little aspirin," he said, rummaging in his doctor's bag.

He sat beside me on the berth, and helped me coax some apple juice down her. I rocked her, singing her a French lullaby.

"That's very pretty."

"It's a song my mother used to sing to me." I looked at him. "Do you think she'll be okay?"

"Oh, yes. I'm sure she will."

"What do you think it is?"

"It's too soon to tell—probably some kind of virus. It could be the flu—or possibly the measles or chicken pox. We'll have to wait and see if she develops any other symptoms."

"Oh, I hope it's not the flu!" I bit my lip, trying to hold back my tears.

Jack's gaze was gentler than it had been in a while. "Most people recover from it just fine. You said your friend was in a weakened state."

I nodded. If anything happened to Elise . . . The very thought made my chest feel as if it were strapped with steel bands.

"She'll be fine," Jack said. "Why don't you go to the upper bunk and try to get some sleep?"

"I don't want to leave her."

"You won't be of any use to her if you get sick, too. It will be a long night. We'll take turns. I'll watch her for a while, then I'll wake you and we'll switch places."

If it had been anyone else, I couldn't have left her, but Jack was a doctor. I nodded. "Okay."

I crawled into the upper bunk. The pillow smelled deliciously of Jack. I clutched it and fell into a deep slumber. When I awoke, dawn glinted through the edges of the window shade.

I scrambled down the ladder as quietly as I could. Jack and Elise were both asleep on their backs on the lower bunk. The sight of them made my heart rise and swell like leavened bread. What a picture they made! Elise, small and helpless and perfectly formed, cradled in Jack's arm—her long lashes dusting her chubby, fever-pinkened cheeks, her cherub mouth puffing out tender breaths.

His hand looked so large and masculine against the pale pink of her romper. His hair was black against the pillow, a perfect contrast. I gazed at him, enraptured by the opportunity to let my eyes drink their fill of his straight nose, his high cheekbones, his cleft chin, his sensuous mouth. It occurred to me that Jack either didn't know or didn't care that he was incredibly handsome. His indifference to his own physical attractiveness was part of his appeal. Most good-looking men capitalized on the effect they had on women, but not Jack.

This, I thought, was a truly good man—perhaps the best man I'd ever known.

The weight of all I'd done to him settled heavily on my chest. I had lied and deceived and tricked him. Worse, I had compromised and possibly even corrupted him. I had brought him nothing but grief.

The question Jack had asked me earlier echoed in my brain: what kind of person was I? I had not meant to harm him. I had not meant to harm anyone, ever—except the Germans, and that was while we were at war.

Elise whimpered, then opened her eyes. She saw me and stretched out her arms. I was leaning over to pick her up when Jack's eyes fluttered open.

"Bonjour," I said.

His expression, so relaxed in sleep, grew wary. It was like a fresh dagger to the heart. Mon Dieu—does he distrust me so much? But then, how could he not? If the circumstances were reversed, I would no doubt feel the same way.

Elise grew progressively more ill as the day wore on. She developed a cough. Jack peered into her throat with a light and said her throat was red. By the end of the day when he checked her again, Jack said she had tonsillitis and possibly strep.

By evening, she was limp and listless. We tried to cool her brow and the back of her neck with wet washcloths, and Jack kept her on a constant round of aspirin. It was hard to get her to drink anything, so Jack bought her Coca-Cola, which she loved.

When we got off the train in Reno, we checked into a small hotel a block from the station. For economy's sake, we shared a room with two beds. The hotel provided a crib for Elise. As Elise and I settled in, Jack wrote a prescription for penicillin, cough medicine, and a painkiller on his army hospital stationery, then left to find a pharmacy. He returned with two bottles of medicine and a syringe.

It was the first time Elise had had a shot. I loosened her diaper so Jack could have access to her little bottom, then held her. I cried when she let out a howl of pain. "How can you bear to do that?" I asked Jack.

"I think of the outcome." He wiped the injection site with another swab of alcohol, then attached a small bandage. "It is a necessary evil in order for her to get well, far better than the alternative."

"A necessary evil." I had never heard the term before. "Like the lies I told you to get her to America. They, too, were a necessary evil."

His look was withering. "It's hardly the same thing."

"Isn't it?" A sense of outrage swelled in my chest as I rocked Elise, trying to console her. I had done wrong, yes, but was it really so heinous?

"No," he said, sounding infuriatingly certain, as if he were the voice of God.

"Oh, you are right; there is one major difference." Over Elise's head, I shot Jack a look that I hoped was as scalding as the indignation boiling in my chest. "Elise will forgive you."

Thanks to the codeine in the cough syrup, Elise had a more restful night. I did not. I heard trains rattle by, and a neon sign across the street leaked flashing light around the edges of the curtains. I finally nodded off, and awoke around two in the morning to see Jack beside Elise's crib, propping her up to give her her aspirin dissolved in Coca-Cola. He gave her several more sips, then tenderly laid her down and covered her with the blanket. He stood beside her, his hand on her tummy, for long minutes until her breathing resumed its slumbering rhythm. His gentleness with her made me weep. He was such a wonderful, kind, caring man—to everyone but me.

I awoke a couple of hours later and checked Elise for myself. As I withdrew my hand from her forehead—she felt cool, thank God—I felt

Jack's eyes on me. When I say I felt them, I mean his gaze touched me like a hand, making me turn around.

Sure enough, he had raised up from his pillow to watch me. His eyes were different. I realized I was standing there in just my nightgown—a worn pink flannel that had been washed so many times it was nearly translucent. The neon sign outside flashed bright, and his face was clearly lit for a moment. The expression in his eyes—I recognized it. There was no mistaking it; it was desire. I could not breathe, I could not think. I stood there, staring back. He did not look away for the longest time. We stayed like that, gazing at each other in the night, for what seemed like forever.

And then he rolled over onto his side, away from me, his head back down on his pillow.

I stood there a second longer, then crawled back into my bed, my back to him. I lay there, awake, wondering what would have happened if I'd walked over to his bed. I alternated between hating that I had not done so, and then hating that I had even considered it.

The next morning, Jack went out and brought us breakfast. Elise had a croupy cough. Jack said it was good she was coughing, because her lungs sounded a little wet, which worried me.

Jack went down to the lobby—back then, not all hotels had phones in every room—and called his doctor friend, who contacted a judge he knew at civil court. Arrangements were made for us both to appear in his chambers at two o'clock.

Judge Sanders was a tall, middle-aged man in a gray suit, wearing something I found quite bizarre around his neck—a thin, silver-tipped rope run through a piece of jewelry with a large aqua stone. I later learned this was called a bolo tie and that the stone was turquoise. It was not unusual attire for a man in Reno at that time. The judge also wore a large silver watch and several rings. I was not accustomed to seeing so much jewelry on a man.

He shook Jack's hand, then nodded at me, as my hands were busy holding Elise. He regarded the baby somewhat curiously as we sat down in the two chairs in front of his large, ornate desk. Elise cried fussily and reached out for Jack. Jack took her from me, and she calmed in his big arms.

The judge cleared his throat. "I understand from Dr. Forrester that you two would like an expedited annulment."

"That's right," Jack said.

The judge raised his eyebrows. "Looking at the little one here, it seems a divorce is more in order."

"No, it needs to be an annulment. The child—she's, um, not mine." Jack's ears were turning red, the only sign that he ever gave that he was embarrassed or flustered. "Amélie already had her when we met."

"I see." The judge rested his elbows on the table and tapped his fingers together. "On what grounds do you seek this annulment?"

Jack patted Elise's back. "It is, um, not a marriage in the true sense of the word."

The judge leaned forward. "I am afraid I need to put this in very blunt terms. The law requires that I ask you this, and you have to be willing to put it in writing, under oath: has the marriage been consummated?"

Jack and I looked at each other for a heartbeat.

"No," I lied very quickly.

Jack closed his eyes, drew in a deep breath, and exhaled it in a sigh. "Well, yes—but only once. It hasn't—and it won't—happen again."

"Hmmm." Judge Sanders tapped his fingers together and looked from one of us to the other, his gaze settling on me. "Is there any chance of a child resulting from this union?"

I didn't understand the question. "Pardon?"

"Could you be pregnant?"

"Oh, no," I said quickly, knowing it was the answer he wanted.

Jack turned to me. "You're absolutely sure?"

Whose side was he on? "How would I be sure?"

He looked at me incredulously. The judge suppressed a chortle.

"Excuse us for a moment," Jack said.

"Certainly." The judge grinned.

Holding Elise in one arm, Jack used the other to pull me out into the hallway. "When were your last menses?"

"My what?" I was unfamiliar with the word.

"Monthly bleeding. Surely you know that's related to conception."

I was indignant. "Well, of course! I did not know the word, that is all." *Menses* wasn't something listed in vocabulary books or taught by my father. "It is too soon to have missed a monthly."

He said the English word for *merde*. Elise stirred in her sleep. "When did you last bleed?"

"I was on the ship."

There was that word again. So uncharacteristic for Jack. "When, exactly, did the bleeding start? How many weeks ago?"

"About two and a half, I think."

His jaw went tight. "So when we made love, it was two weeks later?" I nodded.

He said a worse word—the one that means copulation, the word he had uttered when he'd learned Elise was not Doug's baby. He paced three steps, turned around, and paced three more. He raked his hand through his hair. "That is the most fertile time. And the condom—I don't know for certain, but I fear . . . I mean, there is at least a fifty-fifty chance—no, probably more likely sixty-forty, or seventy-thirty. Hell, maybe even eighty-twenty—that it broke while we . . . when we . . . ." He ran his hand down his face and he drew a deep breath. Elise squirmed, picking up on his tension.

He resettled her in his right arm, then opened the door to the judge's chamber with his left. He nodded his head, indicating I was to walk in before him. I did so, then sat back down.

He sat as well, settling Elise, who was now awake and whimpering, in his lap. "We won't know for sure for two or three more weeks."

Judge Sanders sat still for a long moment, then tapped his fingers on his desk. "Here is what I am prepared to do. As a friend of Dr. Forrester's, I'm willing to fudge on the dates you've been in Reno. I'm even willing to overlook your, uh, single marital act in order to grant you an annulment." He splayed his hands to the table and leaned forward. "But I must know for certain that no children will result from this union before I dissolve it. Come back when you can tell me that."

Jack nodded. "I understand. Thank you for your generosity."

The judge rose. So did Jack. I took back the fussing baby so the two men could shake hands.

"We'll see you in two or three weeks," Jack said.

The judge nodded. "Take care of that little one."

"Will do." Jack headed for the door.

"I realize it's none of my business," the judge called, making Jack stop and turn around. "But in my opinion, you two should consider staying together. You make a really nice little family."

Hearing the hope I hadn't dared admit to myself voiced aloud made tears form in my eyes. I had learned during the war not to think about things that I could not have. Thinking about them set up longing, and longing led to yearning, and yearning would lead me right back into tempting Jack to do what he was determined we must not do.

We were silent on the way out of the courthouse and on the taxi ride back to the hotel. Once in the room, Jack took Elise's temperature under her arm—her cheeks were bright red again and her eyes were glassy. "Her fever's up again," he said. He gave her some aspirin and fetched a cool washcloth, his hands so gentle as he placed it on her forehead that my throat grew tight with emotion. Then he turned to me and crushed any seeds of hope.

"I need to call Kat and my mother. I haven't spoken to them since we left New York, and I know they're worried."

"Of course."

"Are you okay with the baby by yourself for a little while?"

"Yes."

He went down to use the pay phone in the lobby again, while I held Elise against my chest and tried not to want what I could not have.

60

KAT
2016

I remember that phone call. I remember every word of it."

"I would be interested in hearing about it." Amélie has moved to the kitchen and is pouring us coffee. I take the cup she offers me, then settle back on the sofa and into the past.

1946

I had been waiting for a call from Jack for well over a week. And what a week it had been! Mama had had the maid stay at the house to answer the phone when we were gone, because we'd spent more time at the hospital than at the house.

I answered the phone in the kitchen, grabbing it up after the first ring. "Hello?"

"Hi, Kat—it's Jack."

He didn't need to say his name; I knew his voice well enough. In retrospect, it was odd that he did. It spoke of a space between us that hadn't existed before.

"Where have you been? Where are you? We've all been frantic."

"I told you I had to go to Montana. Now I'm in Reno."

"Heavens to Betsy! Are you on your way back here?"

"Well, that's what I called about."

I could tell there was a stall coming, and I didn't even want to hear it. "Jack, something terrible has happened. Daddy's had a stroke. He's in the hospital."

There was a heartbeat of silence. "How bad?"

"Well, we think his left side is paralyzed, and he can't talk, and he's asleep all the time. Mama is beside herself."

"Holy Jesus, Kat—I'm so sorry."

I had never heard him use the Lord's name like that.

"He's at the parish hospital? Who's his doctor?" Jack demanded.

I answered his questions, then said, "There's more news. Have you talked to your sister?"

"No. Why?"

"Well, your mother's in the hospital, too. She went in with pneumonia—it started out as flu; half the town has the flu, and there's no doctor here, and everyone is in a state, and . . ."

"Tell me about my mother," Jack cut in.

"Well, like I said, she's in the hospital with pneumonia. That's about all I know."

Jack was silent for so long I thought we might have lost our connection. And then he asked, "Who's her doctor?"

"I—I'm not sure."

"Is she in the parish hospital, too?" His voice held a sharp note.

"Yes."

"Did they do an X-ray?"

"I don't know."

"You don't *know*?"

I'd never heard him sound that impatient with me. It occurred to me for the first time that I should have been shown more concern for his mother's condition. "I—I—I've been so distraught with Daddy. Jack, you need to get back here as soon as possible."

He blew out a hard sigh. "Yeah. Sounds like it. Look, I'm going to hang up now and call the hospital and my sister."

"Okay. Call me back with your travel arrangements."

"Will do."

"Jack—I love you."

"Yeah. Look, I've got to go."

I hung up the phone. Mother was looking at me funny, so I tried to act like everything was fine, but it wasn't. Something had changed. Jack was different. He'd never not responded to an *I love you* without at least saying, *Me, too.* But I had just told him some bad news, I reasoned; he probably needed some time to let it sink in. At least, that's what I tried to tell myself.

"What did Jack say?" Mother asked.

"He was upset."

"I imagine so. Is he coming home? Where is he?"

"In Reno."

"Reno, Nevada? What in mercy's sake is he doing there?"

"I didn't get a chance to find out."

"That's one of those gambling towns. I hope he didn't pick up a vice overseas."

"Mother, don't be ridiculous. He probably was just passing through on his way home."

Mother rolled her eyes. "I see why you got that C in geography."

I went into Daddy's library and pulled down an atlas. Sure enough, Reno was even further west than Montana. I stared at it and frowned. I remembered he'd said something about going there to do some training, but he hadn't planned on doing that until after he came home. I should have asked him what was going on, but I didn't get the feeling the question would be welcomed—and he didn't really give me a chance. He'd been different—distant, detached. Like a stranger, almost.

Well, it didn't matter why he was in Reno, I decided. He was coming home.

I didn't go back to the hospital with Mother that evening. I stayed by the phone, waiting for another call about when he'd be arriving. Why, oh why hadn't I asked where he was staying so that I could call him? I had so many unanswered questions.

That night, I slept downstairs on the sofa so I could hear the phone in the kitchen. It never rang. But the next morning, I got a telegram:

On the way. Meet me at the station in Baton Rouge on Thursday at 6:30 p.m.—Jack.

"Baton Rouge is an hour and a half away," Mother grumbled. "If he can take the train to Baton Rouge, seems like he could take it to Hammond."

"I reckon he just can't wait to see me," I said.

"Well, he needs to get home as soon as possible, that's for sure," Mother said.

61

AMÉLIE
1946

*J*ack was gone a long time, far longer than it takes to make a phone call. When he came back to the hotel room, almost two hours had passed.

His expression was wooden when he walked through the door. He did not say hello—in France, we always say hello and good-bye—and he moved more like a machine than a man.

"What is wrong?" I asked.

"You mean aside from the fact my mother is in the hospital with pneumonia and Dr. Thompson has had a stroke that has left him in a coma?"

"Oh, Jack! Your mother is ill?"

"Yes." He sank onto the edge of the bed. "She caught the flu, and it went into pneumonia."

"The flu!" Despite what Jack said, the flu, in my mind, was worse than cancer. "Oh, Jack, I am so sorry! And—you said Dr. Thompson had a stroke?"

"Yes." He put down a brown paper bag on the bedside table. I saw that it held a bottle of whiskey. He rose and strode over to the baby bed. He gazed down at Elise, who, thankfully, was sleeping.

"How bad?"

"Very bad. I talked to his physician. He may live, but he will never be able to practice medicine again."

"Oh, Jack!"

"And his patients . . . the flu is rampant, and there is no doctor within thirty miles."

My heart turned over in my chest. I knew immediately what I must say. "You must go to Wedding Tree immediately. Elise and I will stay here until the annulment goes through."

"How will you care for Elise by yourself?"

"I will manage. I managed after the war."

"You had Nora. You can't even carry Elise and a suitcase at the same time."

"I—I could get a stroller. And if you will loan me just a little money, I will find a place to live—perhaps at a boardinghouse. I will get a job. We will be all right, Jack."

"How will you work and care for her?"

"I will find someone to watch her. That has always been the plan."

"What about when she is sick, as she is now?"

How did he expect me to respond to questions that had no answer? "I will manage."

"And if you're pregnant?"

"That is very unlikely, yes?"

"That is hard to say. Given the timing and the broken condom, it may be just as likely as unlikely."

"Well, we will deal with that if the need arises."

"No. We must deal with it now."

I didn't know what he was saying. Was he suggesting I get some kind of procedure—the procedure I knew some women underwent to terminate an unwanted pregnancy? Because if he was suggesting that, there was no way—no way under heaven!—I was going to agree. "We can just wait. Two or three weeks isn't that long."

"Damn it, Amélie—in two or three weeks, Dr. Thompson might be dead."

"I told you to go home. You must be with him and your mother and the flu patients as soon as possible."

"I can't just leave you here—not with Elise so sick. It's possible you'll get sick, as well. How will you care for her if you're ill?"

"I will be fine. You are borrowing trouble."

"Here's the bottom line, Amélie. I have to go home, and I can't leave you here. You have to go with me."

"But . . ."

"Listen to me!"

I had never heard him sound so commanding, so authoritative. I sank onto the bed.

"I'm in a real pickle here. I've been walking and thinking, thinking and walking, wrestling with my conscience. If you are pregnant, I intend to stay married to you so that we can raise our child together. I would, of course, want to raise Elise as my own, as well."

Oh, my traitorous heart—how it leapt in my chest!

"If you are not pregnant, well, there is another matter that I have been loath to address, but address it I must, if I am to live with myself in peace and consider myself an honorable man." He took in a long breath and slowly blew it out. "I took your virginity. The way I was raised, if a man compromises the virtue of a woman, he marries her. And the fact of the matter is, I compromised your virtue—even though I had no idea I was doing so at the time, no idea at all, which strikes me as incredibly unfair. But—I did it. It is done."

"Jack, you don't need . . ."

"Don't tell me what I need and don't need! You're not my conscience!" His brow was furrowed, his voice angry. He strode back and forth, pacing the room.

"If I must stay married to you—and it is now clear to me that, either way, I must—it will be far easier for everyone in Wedding Tree to accept you and Elise if they believe that she is my daughter. There would be no questions of Elise's fatherhood or legitimacy, no questions of your moral fiber, if they think we married for love and she is my biological child. This is not a story that can wait two or three weeks' time; it is a story we must present from the very beginning."

"But what—what will you tell Kat?"

"The same story we tell everyone else."

My mind whirred. If he was expecting everyone to believe Elise was his child, then a year and a half had gone by. "What about all that time? All the letters you wrote to Kat?"

He blew out a harsh breath. "That's the worst part. That's what I can't explain. It makes me sick to think how deceptive that will look—responding to her questions about wedding flowers and so on." He looked up, his eyes hard. "It sickens me, it really does."

I swallowed, miserable. It was all my fault, and he blamed me. "I understand."

"Oh, do you?" The sarcasm in his voice stung. "You understand being sick about deception?"

"Yes," I whispered. "Oh, yes, I do."

My response seemed to take the heat out of his anger. He sat down beside me on the bed, his shoulders slumped. "I've been trying to figure out a way to let Kat down gently, and I can't find one. I'll just tell her that I met you and we married, and I will apologize. It's better for her to think me a cad and a coward. That way she'll get over me more quickly."

"Oh, Jack . . ." I put my hand on his arm.

He shrugged me off and rose. "Don't try to comfort me. I'm so angry that you duped me that I don't know if I can ever get over it. You've been a bad influence on me from the beginning. I stretched one rule, and then another, until I was in a hole so deep that I couldn't climb out. Just looking back and seeing how far I've fallen leaves me reeling." He blew out a hard sigh. "I am not the man I was before I met you."

"Perhaps you are better."

His eyes flashed. "How on earth can you say that?"

"Well, you are following your heart instead of your head. Your heart is a truer compass of what is truly right."

He looked at me as if I were deranged. "I sometimes wonder if you are completely depraved."

"You are upset—and it is no wonder. You don't have to make permanent decisions now."

"Yes, I do. I already have. We are to stay married."

"And if I refuse?"

"Are you refusing?"

What, really, were my options? I had no idea how I would care for Elise alone. And even with his anger—I couldn't deny that I was secretly, inwardly thrilled. "No," I whispered. "I will do whatever you think is best."

"It's settled, then." He shot me a heated glare. "But don't think for one minute that this will be a real marriage. A real marriage is based on truth and trust, and I don't trust you any further than I could throw a locomotive."

AMÉLIE
1946

*B*y the time we arrived in Baton Rouge, we were both as frayed as worn washcloths. It took us nearly three days to get there. We slept in a regular public Pullman car with bunk beds. Jack was pale and had dark circles under his eyes. Elise was still ill, but better, better enough to squirm and whine and generally be difficult. I was so tired that I felt as though I were sleepwalking when I was awake, and when I was asleep, I still felt half awake.

Jack's demeanor toward me was cold verging on icy. He was distant but polite except when dealing with Elise. When it came to her, he was caring and tender and warm. He barely talked to me, except when conversation was essential. At dinner, he might say, "pass the salt, please," but my attempts at conversation—including benign comments about the scenery—went largely unanswered. He had little appetite. I was worried that perhaps he was coming down with Elise's illness.

As Baton Rouge neared, I sensed a growing nervousness about him. "What do you want Elise and me to do when we disembark?" I asked. "Should we pretend we don't know you?"

His look cut me to the quick. "Is your first reaction always one of deception?"

My face heated. "You know that is not true."

"Do I?"

I bristled. "Yes, but it makes you feel better to think the worst of me. I was simply thinking of Kat's feelings. It might be a worse shock for her to see us together before you have a chance to explain things to her."

"She won't think we're together. She'll think you're simply a fellow traveler I'm helping off the train."

"And once we're off the train? Should Elise and I just stand beside you?"

I think he finally saw my point. "No. Just . . . just step aside or have a seat on a bench or something and let me talk to her."

The porter called out the approaching stop. We gathered our suitcases and belongings. My heart roared in my ears like the train wheels on the tracks.

The brakes screeched as the train ground to a halt. I peered out the window, looking for a young woman. I didn't see her until I actually stepped off the train, Jack right behind me.

When I did, my stomach felt as if I'd swallowed a cannon ball. She was a beautiful blonde with perfectly coiffed shoulder-length hair, wearing an immaculate white wool coat. I couldn't imagine the luxury of a white coat! She looked like a movie star or beauty queen as she raced toward Jack.

So this was Kat. Oh, mon Dieu, what an exquisite creature! I caught a smile as wide and bright as sunshine and a whiff of soft perfume. Jack set down the suitcases—mine and his—as she hurled herself at him. He caught her, and she clung to him so tightly—or perhaps the clinging was mutual, it was hard for me to tell—that her feet left the ground. He set her down quickly, then averted his face as she aimed her lips at his.

"Oh, Jack, don't be so shy!" she said, laughing.

I was suddenly, acutely aware of my rumpled clothes, my unstyled hair, the general griminess of having spent three days on a train. Next to Kat, I felt like a hobo.

Elise squirmed and whimpered. I needed her bag, which Jack had carried off the train. As surreptitiously as possible, I edged close and picked it up. Kat's gaze flew to me, her eyes widened with alarm.

"Thank you," I murmured in Jack's general direction, and walked away, as if he were a polite stranger who had aided me because I was traveling with an infant.

I sat on a bench on the far side of the depot, my heart pounding, my breath hard to catch. I tried not to watch them, but my eyes were drawn to them like a sore tooth draws the tongue.

63

KAT
2016

I set down my teacup and lean forward on the sofa. After all these years, you'd think my insides wouldn't boil like reheated coffee whenever I think of that day, but there it is again—that hot, acidic churning.

"When you took the bag from Jack," I say, "I thought you were a Gypsy. I'd never seen one, but I'd heard of them—dark-haired, foreign-looking thieves who frequented crowds and used babies and strange clothing as distractions."

Amélie gives me an indulgent smile—the kind you might give a small child or a mentally impaired person who has committed a faux pas, but can't be held accountable. "I realized you thought I was stealing."

"I did. But then you said 'Thank you' and Jack kind of nodded, so I figured he'd helped you off the train and the bag was yours."

"Yes."

"After you walked away, it was as if no one else was in the train station except for me and Jack. I had waited so long for him to come home, and finally, there he was."

I close my eyes and remember.

1946

He stepped back and I just gazed at him, my heart unfurling and billowing like the sail of a boat. He was still so handsome—so incredibly handsome!—but he was different than I remembered. His body was harder and leaner, his face more somber. His cheeks had hollows I didn't recall, and lines radiated out from around his eyes. I thought, *He looks like a man who has been through a war*, and of course that was exactly right.

I tried to kiss him again—or, more accurately, get him to kiss me—but he averted his face. That was the moment I knew for certain that something was horribly, terribly wrong. He wasn't avoiding kissing me just because we were in public. There was another reason—something serious, something sinister. The sense of dread I'd had from the phone call coiled like a snake in my stomach. "What is it, Jack?"

"We need to talk."

Oh, my Lord. Are there any four more terrifying words in the English language?

I grabbed his arm. "Is it Daddy? Is he gone?"

Even as I said it, I realized the question made no sense. Jack had been on a train; how could he have received word before me? And yet it was the only thing I could think of that could have caused that expression on his face. Then I remembered his own mother was ill. That was of far less priority to me than the health of my father—and in my mind, I'd assumed it would be less important in Jack's mind, too—but maybe I had misjudged. "Is it your mother?" Again, as I spoke, I realized it made no more sense than the question about Daddy.

"You would have more current information about both of them than I. How were they when you left this morning?"

"Fine. I mean, unchanged, as far as I know. So what's wrong? Why do you look so grim?"

"Come and sit down, Kat."

The fact he said my name . . . So funny that it only now occurred to me that Jack seldom used my name when talking to me. My insides turned to ice. "I don't want to sit down." All the same, I was clinging to his arm and my knees were shaking. I let him lead me to an empty bench and I perched on the edge of it. He sank down heavily beside me.

"You're scaring me, Jack. What's this about?"

"It's about us."

My stomach just plummeted. My mouth went dry.

"I have to tell you something very difficult."

"No." I shook my head. I was vaguely, ridiculously aware that it made my curls bounce on my shoulders in a way I had practiced in front of the mirror. I wasn't doing it now to be fetching; I simply wanted him to stop talking.

"I've been hiding something." The words were heavy, as if they were made of lead. "I should have told you this when it first happened, but I didn't know how. I didn't want to just write or call—I wanted to tell you in person—but, well, I shouldn't have waited."

He'd been unfaithful—that's what this was about. I knew it, knew it in my soul. Inexplicably, a wave of relief rolled over me. I could deal with this. If I didn't have details, if it happened overseas and in the past, I could pretend it never happened at all. I put my hand on his arm. "It's okay, Jack. Whatever you did during the war—you don't need to confess. I don't want to know. I forgive you, whatever it is. Let's just put it behind us and move on as if it never happened. Please don't tell me."

"I have to."

"No, Jack. I'm fine with whatever you did."

"I married someone else."

The words did not make sense. They were foreign, alien, unlike anything I expected to hear. He might as well have been speaking Swahili. "What?"

"I'm married. And . . . and I have a child."

I have never been so shocked, so stunned, so utterly unsure I could trust my own hearing in all my life. "Is this a joke? Because it's not funny."

"It's not a joke, Kat."

I swatted at his arm, trying but failing to be playful. "Stop this nonsense, and stop it right now." I sounded like my mother. It was what she used to say when I persisted in mischief as a child.

"I'm telling you the truth."

I suddenly felt as if I might lose my lunch. And yet, I still didn't entirely believe him. "If you're married and have a child, where are they? Back in France?" My mouth was a Teletype machine, spewing words as soon as they hit my mind. "That's very far away. And when you were there—it was like another lifetime. No one here need know. You can just leave them behind and we'll go on with the wedding as planned, and later you can hire an attorney or someone in France, and if we need to, we'll remarry privately somewhere to make it all perfectly legal, and . . ."

"They're not in France," Jack cut in. "They're here."

"Here?" I pointed down to the floor. "*Here* here? Here in the station?"

He nodded. I stood and whirled around, looking, I suppose, for someone who resembled me. I rotated in a complete 360-degree circle. After a process of elimination, my gaze landed on the little Gypsy with the sick-looking baby.

I stared—bug-eyed, no doubt, like a cartoon character. Her gaze met mine, then she quickly looked down at the baby. "Her?" I pointed, although Mother had taught me that pointing is rude. "You jilted me for *her*?"

"I didn't mean to hurt you, Kat." Jack was on his feet beside me. "It just happened."

"It just *happened*?" Rainstorms happen. Car accidents, coffee spills, broken fingernails happen. Sexual attraction, even affairs can happen. But marriage? It requires a proposal, a decision, some kind of wedding.

I stared at the Gypsy. She looked so rumpled, so drab, so incredibly plain. She rose from the bench and carried the baby some distance away. She was tiny. Maybe not even five feet tall.

"Why, Jack?"

"I'm sorry, Kat." His face was the very picture of misery. "I hate that I've hurt you."

The full implications of this situation started to sink in. Hurt? I would be more than hurt; I would be humiliated. I would have to call off the elaborate wedding I'd been crowing about for a year and a half—and everyone in town would know why. "Oh, my God. How will I hold my head up? What will I tell people? I'll be a laughingstock. People will feel *sorry* for me!" I, who had always been admired and envied, would be *pitied*! It was an unbearable thought. "I can't believe this."

"I know it must be a shock."

Shock didn't begin to describe it. Another reaction was edging in as the dominant emotion—something darker and heavier and more dangerous. Anger. Outrage. Fury. "Why? Why the hell did you marry her? Why couldn't you just fuck her like every other man probably has?"

I'd never heard his voice so steely. "That's enough, Kat."

I realized I was practically yelling, that I was creating a spectacle. People were staring. I didn't care.

"It's not enough. You jilted me for a French whore and expect me to just be quiet about it?"

He grabbed my arm. "I will not stand for you talking about her that way."

"You can't stop me. How do you know the child is even yours?"

"It's mine."

"How do you know?"

He stepped close. His voice was low, as ominous as thunder. "Amélie was untouched when I married her."

Amélie. Hearing her name was a knife to my gut. "Untouched, my ass!"

He grabbed my wrist and pulled me close, his mouth next to my ear. "I am a doctor. I know these things. And if you spread lies about her virtue, well, I can do the same about yours."

I gasped. Was he threatening me? Yes, he was! He was threatening to say he didn't marry me because I was impure.

"You wouldn't!"

"I wouldn't want to."

"It would be a lie!"

"So would anything you have to say about Amélie."

I felt as if I'd been slapped. "My God, Jack, you've changed. You're not the man I thought I was going to marry."

"That's true," he said. "You should be glad you dodged that bullet."

I started to cry. He took my arm and urged me to sit back down. "Look, Kat—it was never my intention to hurt you or your family. I have behaved in a manner unbecoming a gentleman, and you have my deepest apologies. I bear all blame and responsibility."

"You damn sure do!"

"I wronged you. You have every right to be angry. But be angry at me, not at Amélie. Do not take it out on her or my child."

"Your child!" A sob left my throat. "Do you have any idea how it pains me to hear you say that?"

"I wish to God I'd handled this differently." He pulled a handkerchief from his pocket and pressed it into my palm. "I asked you to meet me here so I could tell you before we arrive in Wedding Tree. I wanted to give you advance warning."

"Wow, isn't that just swell of you!"

"I hope to spare you all the embarrassment I can. I'm the one who bears all the blame. I know that, and I accept it."

A train rolled in just then on the opposite track, loud and clanging, the brakes hissing. "That is our train to Wedding Tree. Amélie and I must get on it."

"You and your little family are just going to roll into Wedding Tree and act as if I don't exist?"

"I will never forget that you exist, Kat. I will never get over the shame and regret of treating you this way. Believe me, this is not easy for me, either."

I stared at him. "I hate you."

"I understand."

"I loathe you, I detest you. I wish I'd never set eyes on you."

"I understand." He gathered the bags and started across the station toward her.

I didn't mean to, but I found myself running after him. I put my hand on his arm. "Just tell me this—did you ever love me?"

His blue eyes were dark as troubled water. "No matter what I say, the opposite answer is likely to make this easier for you. And so, Kat, I will simply say good-bye."

And with that, he headed toward the little Gypsy and the baby. She rose and walked with him to a train car. The porter took his luggage, then Jack took her elbow and helped her up the steps onto the train.

64

AMÉLIE
1946

I f the train ride from Reno to Baton Rouge was awkward, the one from Baton Rouge to Hammond was excruciating. We rode in silence for about half an hour, Jack's jaw looking as if it were set in cement.

The saving grace was Elise, who fussed and cried and demanded constant attention. Jack gave her medicine and then she reached for him, giving her gummy smile. That's the wonderful thing about babies; they bring you out of yourself and into the present moment. When a baby smiles at you, you just have to smile back, and that changes your mood. Jack took Elise onto his lap and the tension between us melted a little.

"I know that telling Kat was very difficult for you," I ventured. "I'm sorry it didn't go more smoothly."

"She was shocked," Jack said. "It was a hard and unexpected blow."

"She seemed more concerned about what people would think than about losing you," I remarked.

"She was shocked," Jack repeated. "Shock makes people react in odd ways."

"In my experience, it usually shows a person's true character."

"You can't judge her on how she responded."

Yes, I can, I thought. "Based on the language she used, I'd say you're the one who dodged a bullet."

"I'm sorry you heard that."

"The entire train station heard it."

"She was not herself. I'd just turned her world upside down. And she was already reeling from the blow about her father." He gazed out the window and sighed. "I feel like the worst kind of cad."

"Well, I know the truth, and I think you are very noble."

"Noble?" His voice and his glance were bitter. "I broke her heart."

"I don't think it's her heart you broke."

"What the hell do you know about it?"

He was right; I knew nothing. I wanted to dislike her because she was so beautiful. My heart was seething with something very much like jealousy. No; it *was* jealousy.

I hated to think that Jack loved another and was stuck, instead, with me.

On the trip to Hammond, Jack and I discussed what we would tell people when they, inevitably, asked about the circumstances of our meeting. Jack's family knew that he originally had been with an evacuation hospital in La Cambe. Since I had, truthfully, worked as a courier for the Résistance, we agreed that the story would be this: We had met when I arrived at the hospital to deliver a message to Jack's camp commander. I asked the first American officer I saw—Jack, of course—to take me to him. Because of troop movements, I was unable to leave the hospital for several weeks. That is when we fell in love and married.

Jack's sister, Caroline, and her husband, Bruce, met us at the Hammond train station. Caroline bore a striking resemblance to Jack—she, too, was tall, black-haired, and blue-eyed. My first impression was of a lovely woman in a navy coat and red hat, calling Jack's name and running toward him. Jack set down the bags, caught her in a bear hug, and swung her around.

"Jack! Oh, it's so good to see you! Let me look at you." She stepped back. "You look older."

"I am older. And, if I may point it out, so are you."

She gave him a playful hit on the arm.

"You know I told you on the phone I was bringing a surprise?" Jack said.

"I hope it's champagne," she said.

"It's better." He turned and motioned me to come forward. "Caroline, this is my wife, Amélie, and our daughter, Elise."

"Oh, the army has turned you into jokester, has it?" She turned to me and smiled. "Let me guess; he met you on the train and convinced you to play this role. He's very persuasive, our Jack." She shook her finger at Jack. "Take my advice and don't try this on Kat; she won't find it one bit funny. She . . ."

Caroline froze in mid-sentence. Her mouth not only stopped, but slightly opened. She looked from Jack to me then back again, apparently reading the truth in our expressions. She put her palm over her mouth. "Oh. My. Word!"

I shifted Elise to one arm, stepped forward and held out my hand. "It's very nice to meet you, Caroline."

She limply shook my hand, all the while looking at Jack. "You're serious?"

He nodded grimly.

"Does Kat know?"

"She drove to Baton Rouge and I told her."

"Just now? She just now found out?"'

"Yes."

Caroline was clearly flummoxed. "But this baby . . . how long have you . . ."

It was clear I needed to step in and fix the situation. I'd been turning it over in my mind ever since Baton Rouge, when it had become clear that jilting Kat would cast Jack in a very bad light. "We married in July in La Cambe," I said. "And I'm afraid the secrecy is all my fault."

"Amélie." Jack's voice was a warning.

I tried to imitate my mother's flinty-eyed determination. "No. You tried to protect me when you spoke to Kat, but it's not right. You should not shoulder blame that's not yours."

"Stop it," he said.

I ignored him. "We met shortly after he arrived in France. I was working for the French Resistance, and I delivered a note from Paris to the commander at Jack's evacuation hospital. We married two weeks later. It was very sudden, very impetuous. The war . . . well, when you think you're likely to die at any moment, time speeds up and things happen very quickly. Jack wrote a letter to Kat and gave it to me to mail. I am sorry to say that I did not mail it."

"Amélie." Jack's expression was so dark I had to look away. "Don't do this."

"It's okay, Jack. It's better to tell all." I turned back to Caroline. "At first I forgot. The day I returned to Paris, I learned my mother had fallen and broken her hip in my absence. Then she developed complications and it looked like she would never walk again. I am an only child; I couldn't just desert her and move to America.

"So I wrote Jack that I must stay in France to care for my mother. I loved him, but I didn't want to ruin his life, so I told him that the best thing would be for us to divorce and for him to go ahead and marry Kat. I told him I had not mailed his letter to her breaking off the romance.

"And then, when the army mistakenly sent a letter from Kat to my address—which was also listed as Jack's address—well, I wrote her back."

"She didn't recognize it wasn't Jack's handwriting?"

"I am an expert calligrapher. Part of what I did for the Resistance was forge false identity papers for Jews and travel papers for resistance workers."

"Stop it, Amélie." Jack's face was hard and cold. "Caroline, she's just trying to put me in a better light."

"No. I can prove it," I insisted. "I will show you my calligraphy skills. Jack is trying to protect me, so I won't be hated in Wedding Tree. But I think it is better for everyone to know that it was my fault and not Jack's, and that he tried to act honorably."

"She's right, Jack," Caroline said. "If you're to be trusted as a doctor here, you can't be seen as someone who would so callously jilt his fiancée. For goodness' sake, let her talk."

"I discovered I was pregnant, and then my mother died," I said. "After that, there was no reason I had to stay in Paris. I still loved Jack, and I wanted my baby to grow up with her father. So Jack and I made up, and I came on a bride boat to America."

"Oh, my goodness!" Caroline turned to her brother. "But, Jack—why didn't you mention your marriage in any of your letters to the family?"

I had thought this out ahead of time. "He couldn't," I said, "because Kat did not yet know. She needed to be told first."

"Oh, of course." Caroline seemed stunned.

"Here is the part of which I'm most ashamed," I continued. "I only admitted to Jack that I had been writing to Kat, pretending the letters were from him, right before he left for the United States. He was very, very angry."

Jack glowered at me, unwittingly reinforcing my story.

I hurried on. "I persuaded him that since things had gone on so long, it was better to tell Kat in person rather than to tell her over the phone. He planned to come to Wedding Tree a couple of days before I did—he thought it would be easier if I weren't yet in the picture—and talk to her father. He was going to try to gently break the news to her while she was surrounded by her family. But when he called her to arrange that, he learned her father had suffered a stroke and your mother has pneumonia, and our baby was sick, too sick for me to manage alone, so . . . here we are, all together."

"Oh, my! Oh, heavens! Oh, you poor dears! Oh, what a mess!"'

"We were, each of us, only trying to do what seemed right at the time, but I have put poor Jack in a terrible situation, and I'm afraid he is horribly angry with me."

I smiled at Jack. His face was, indeed, thunderous.

"I warn you, Caroline—he will say I am lying," I continued. "He will do anything to try to protect me. He told me he is worried that I will be hated and ostrich-ized."

Caroline's husband howled with laughter. "I think you mean ostracized."

"Yes. He is willing to take the blame fully on his shoulders. He is such a hero that way. But I need for you to spread the word that it was I, not Jack, who kept the secret from Kat for so long."

"Yes. Yes, of course! I will go talk to Kat."

The conversation, thankfully, moved on to the topic of Jack and Caroline's mother as we piled into Bruce's Ford and arranged our luggage in the trunk. Jack and I climbed into the backseat.

"And how is Dr. Thompson?" Jack asked.

"He's awakened from his coma, but he's paralyzed on the left side, and he can barely talk."

Jack's face grew somber.

"Kat's mother is in denial that he was ever unconscious," Caroline said. "She insists he was only resting."

A gloom of silence hung in the car. At length I said, "Bruce, I understand you served in the Pacific."

He nodded. "I left a kidney in Guam."

"He's lucky to be alive," Caroline said.

I had hoped to steer the conversation onto more cheerful topics, so I said, "Jack tells me you are an attorney in Wedding Tree."

"Yes, that's right. Mainly wills and probate—not very interesting, I'm afraid."

"Oh, some of the things people put in their wills are quite interesting," Caroline said. "And he does a little criminal defense, as well. Bruce, tell them about the boy who tried to drive the bread truck over a car!"

Bruce launched into a comical story. Jack smiled and laughed at the appropriate part, but he did not say a word to me the entire trip.

Bruce drove us to his and Caroline's house—a charming two-story Acadian-style home with three bedrooms and two—two!—full bathrooms upstairs, and a powder room below. I could scarcely imagine the luxury.

I settled into one of the bedrooms with Elise. Bruce drove Caroline and Jack to the hospital to see their mother and Dr. Thompson.

While they were gone, I rummaged through Jack's bag for an example of his handwriting. I found some notes about a new method for removing a gallbladder.

I tore a page out of a notebook I had brought from France, crumpled it just a bit, then smoothed it and, copying Jack's handwriting, carefully penned a letter to Kat. I dated it July 9, 1944. I folded and refolded it several times, making it the size to fit into a small envelope.

Reaching under the bed, I found some dust against the baseboard. I had learned as a hotel maid that no matter how good the housecleaning, there is almost always dust on under-bed baseboards. I rubbed a tiny bit onto the edges and folds of the paper, where dirt settles on a document. I handled it a little more to make it look aged and worn, then I tucked it into the bottom of my suitcase.

I gave Elise a bath, then foraged in the kitchen. I pulled on a red-checked apron I found hanging in the pantry, then located some leftover chicken in the fridge, as well as a half-opened bottle of wine. I added some potatoes, carrots, celery, and spices, and set it on to simmer.

"Something smells wonderful!" Caroline said when she and Bruce came through the door around six o'clock.

"It is coq au vin."

"But how did you find anything to cook? There was barely any food in the house!"

"Barely any food?" After what I had gone through in France, I was truly shocked. "You had a feast in your refrigerator!"

"It was just leftovers," Caroline said.

"Well, it was more than enough for a meal."

Caroline lifted the lid off the pot and inhaled appreciatively. "You're a miracle worker! No wonder Jack married you."

Jack had no idea whether I even knew how to boil water, I reflected. "Where is Jack?"

"He's gone to see some patients. There's a flu epidemic, and word spread that Jack has returned."

I stirred the stew. "How did things go at the hospital?"

Bruce and Caroline looked at each other for a moment. Oh, la; I could read in their expressions that it had been a difficult visit.

"How is your mother?"

"She was very glad to see Jack," Caroline said. "She's feeling much better."

"Better enough to be a pain in the neck," Bruce grumbled.

"She asked for her makeup and perfume and hair rollers and a lace bed jacket," Caroline said.

"And her cigarettes," Bruce added. "She's on oxygen, and she wanted her cigarettes!"

Jack had not said much about his mother's personality, aside from telling me she never got over being a debutante. He'd also said that she'd been widowed by the banker two years ago, and was now in the market for a new husband. "How did she react to the news of Jack's marriage to me?"

Again, Caroline and Bruce exchanged a glance. My palms grew damp.

"She wasn't happy," Caroline admitted. "She and Kat are thick as thieves."

"She had been looking forward to playing a leading role at a big wedding," Bruce said dryly.

"She will come around," Caroline said. "Don't worry about it. Jack takes everything Mother says with a grain of salt."

"Should be with a shot of vodka," Bruce grumbled.

"How about Dr. Thompson?"

Caroline pulled a serving bowl down from the cabinet. Bruce bent to play with Elise, who was on a blanket, banging a wooden spoon.

"It was a difficult visit," Caroline said. "He is very weak."

My heart squeezed. "Did Jack tell him about . . . our marriage?"

Caroline nodded, her eyes somber.

"What did Jack say?" I was anxious to hear how he talked about us.

"That he knew he'd broken Kat's heart, and that he felt horrible. The doctor made some moaning sounds and closed his eyes."

"What did Jack do?"

Caroline hesitated.

"Tell me," I urged. "I need to know. Please be very blunt."

"He cried."

Tears sprang to my eyes. My hand flew to my chest, where my heart felt like melting wax.

"Jack said that you all will leave Wedding Tree once Mother gets better."

Jack leave Wedding Tree? All he could talk about in Paris was coming back to his hometown. He'd made Wedding Tree sound like Eden! In fact, he'd talked about the town and the doctor and the practice they would have together far more than he'd talked about his fiancée. I couldn't imagine him even considering the idea of moving.

"What did Dr. Thompson say?"

"His voice is like a grunt, but he talked very slowly and was quite clear. He said, 'You can't leave now. The town needs a doctor.'"

"How did Jack respond?"

"Well, Mrs. Thompson showed up just then. Kat had come home, and of course, she'd told her all about . . . about . . ." Caroline hesitated, obviously searching for a kind way to put it.

"About me."

She nodded.

"And . . . she was angry?"

"Oh . . . furious! She gave Jack a real tongue-lashing. Used some very un-Christian words and actually threw him out of the room. She was especially angry that he'd led Kat on for months in his letters."

"Oh, dear!"

Caroline pulled some napkins out of the drawer. "So I hope you don't mind, but I dropped by Kat's house on the way home. I thought it might help her to know what you'd told me—that Jack had written to her before the marriage, and that you hadn't mailed the letter because you thought you might not be able to leave France. I told her that you then received her letters, so you'd forged Jack's replies, because you didn't want to ruin Jack's chances with her when it looked like you couldn't leave France."

"And?"

"Well, she was surrounded by her minions."

"I don't understand."

"Kat was Miss Popularity in high school. She still is. She had six friends with her, trying to console her, all outraged at Jack on her behalf. The worst one is Minxy."

"Minxy?"

"That's her nickname. Her father gave her a coat with a mink collar when she was in junior high and the name stuck." Caroline placed the napkins around the kitchen table. "Anyway, I pulled Kat aside and told her what you'd told me. She immediately trotted back to her friends and repeated everything I'd said."

"Did it help?"

"Well, I think it took the edge off their anger at Jack. But several were skeptical. Minxy didn't think anyone could forge handwriting convincingly enough."

"I'll show you. Get a piece of paper and write something, and I will write in your handwriting."

She grabbed an envelope and pen from the counter and wrote her name and address.

I took the envelope, studied it for a moment, then carefully wrote her name and address beneath it, matching her handwriting nearly exactly.

Caroline picked it up. "This is amazing! If I hadn't seen you write it, I would think I wrote this myself!"

I lifted my shoulders. "It's a skill that came in handy during the war. And here is Jack's handwriting." Jack's script was fresh enough in my mind that I didn't need an example in front of me. *I wrote Jack's letters,* I scrawled.

"That's incredible!" Caroline picked up the envelope. "Can I take this to Kat and show her?"

"Of course. And I have something else she should have." I straightened and rubbed my hands on the apron. "I have the letter that Jack wrote to her—the one I did not mail."

Her eyes rounded. "You brought it with you?"

"Yes. It is in my suitcase. It was never mine to keep, and now, of course, I know I should have mailed it. Would you take it to her?"

"Oh, of course! Oh, that will be so helpful!" Caroline clapped her hands together. "I'll take it to her right after dinner—along with this example of how well you can imitate handwriting."

65

KAT
2016

My fingers grip the arms of Amélie's chair so tightly it is a wonder my fingernails don't cut the fabric. She forged the letter from Jack? And she'd done it after arriving in Wedding Tree? She is more duplicitous and conniving than I had even imagined! "I can't believe you just lied and lied, then forged a letter!"

She lifts her shoulders in that graceful French way of hers, an expression that seemed to say *So what?* or *No big deal.* "I wanted to help preserve Jack's reputation as much as I could. I thought the note would be a convincing touch."

Oh, it had been. It had been convincing, indeed! At the time, it had certainly convinced me.

Caroline had brought it to me the evening Jack returned to Wedding Tree, as Mother and I were cleaning up from a dinner we'd barely touched.

"Amélie and I talked at great length tonight," Caroline had said. "She showed me how she can replicate handwriting—it's truly amazing! She could write exactly like me."

"Well, isn't that a worthwhile talent," I'd sniffed. "Almost as wonderful as pickpocketing."

"She knows calligraphy. It's no wonder she could write letters that you believed came from Jack." Caroline had reached in her purse and pulled out a folded piece of paper. "She gave me the letter that Jack wrote you a year and a half ago—the one she didn't mail. She said you should have it."

I'd snatched it out of her hand, and run into the living room. I'd sunk onto the chair by the window, unfolded it, and read it like a starved wolf devouring a squirrel.

Over the next weeks and months, I reread it so often I committed it to memory:

Dear Kat,

It breaks my heart to write this, but I must tell you that our engagement is off. I will put this in very straightforward terms: I am about to marry a Frenchwoman.

I know this must be a shock. It is shocking to me, as well. I find it hard to explain and I am sure you will find it hard to understand, but life is very different here, and I am very different. I go to another evacuation hospital closer to the front in two days' time; a similar hospital was just bombed, and I fear I will not make it home in one piece. Everything here is urgent and intense and uncertain. The uncertainty demands rapid action. Amélie and I fell into a madness of love and will marry at one o'clock today.

I regret making promises to you that I can't keep, but it would be unfair to you for me to even try.

I want you to be free to find a new love of your own. From this vintage point, our plans for the future seem like a childish fairy tale we told ourselves. Life must be seized as it happens.

I know that such a beautiful woman as you will be quickly snapped. I envy the man that you someday will marry, and I will always cherish your memory.

Love always, Jack

Right now, I am so angry at Amélie that I want to slap her. I hold my right hand with my left one to stop myself, because I know my impulse control is no longer very good.

That letter has been a huge consolation to me over the years, and now she is taking that away from me.

When I first read it all those years ago, I thought it was an admission that Jack had fallen into some kind of madness and acted rashly. I figured that he'd probably been seduced, had carnal relations and fallen under a spell of lust. I wondered if he had been drunk or somehow drugged or even shell-shocked. I wondered if he'd had a terrible fear of being wounded and wanted to spare me from caring for him as a cripple.

I drew special comfort from the fact he said I was beautiful and that he would envy the man I eventually married. That meant he wasn't over me, didn't it? That he'd never be over me. And the sign-off, *Love always*—a man wouldn't write that to someone he wouldn't always long for. That helped me make it through the hard days ahead of me.

And now . . . Amélie is snatching that sole consolation away from me by telling me Jack never wrote such things, that she wrote them herself after arriving in Wedding Tree.

But, then . . . of course. It should have become obvious to me when she told me they hadn't even met until shortly before Jack's return to the States. All the implications of that one fact, all the ways it changes what I know—or thought I knew—of the past, has not soaked in yet.

And oh, there are so many implications! My brain is not as agile as it once was—or perhaps it is just overwhelmed by receiving so much information so fast.

"You look upset," she says to me.

"I am." My voice holds an unflattering virulence. I try to modulate it. "Of course I am!"

"I thought that letter was a kindness to you."

"Oh, really?"

"Yes. I deliberately wrote things I thought would soothe your rumpled feathers."

"The phrase is 'smooth your ruffled feathers,'" I correct in a curt tone. Some odd wordings in the letter are suddenly thrust into a new light. *Vintage point*—surely Jack would have known that the correct word was "vantage." *Fallen into the madness of love*—Amélie probably meant "fell madly in love." *You will soon be snapped*—I'm sure she meant "snapped up." I'd thought Jack had just been in a hurry or an emotional state and simply left out a word.

"Ah. Well, you understand the meaning," Amélie says. "I confess, however, that your feelings were not the primary reason I wrote it. I did it for Jack. If he was to live and work in Wedding Tree, it was important that he be seen as an honorable man."

"Honorable," I scoff.

"Yes, honorable. Jack was not a perfect man, but he was a man of honor. He tried to do the right thing. When he made a mistake, he tried to correct it, even when that meant putting his own wishes aside for someone else's best interests."

"And whose best interests did he serve by bringing you here?" My tone is sharp. "Yours?"

"Oh, no. He did it for Elise. He did not want to be married to me back then—not at all. He only stayed married to me because he feared I might be pregnant, and if I had been, he wanted to be able to claim Elise as his own, as well." Amélie tilts her head at a speculative angle. "You know, if you had slept with him before he left for the war, I'm sure none of this would have happened."

The utter gall of the woman! "Of course not," I say indignantly.

"But you wanted to wait for a big wedding." Amélie shakes her head. "I have never understood women who put the ceremony of getting married ahead of the actuality of being married."

I will not let her hurt me with this line of reasoning. I refuse to deal in regrets. I lift my chin. "A wedding is a common girlhood dream."

"Yes, I suppose. Did you have your dream wedding when you married your husband?"

"Oh, yes. We had a big extravaganza in Dallas. I had nine brides-maids and a reception at the Dallas Country Club and a European honeymoon."

"Well, then. Sounds like you had everything you ever could have wanted!"

"Yes. Everything and more." And yet, I have always felt a vague dissatisfaction. Lately I've been wondering if I wanted the wrong things, if I somehow sailed right past what was truly important. I have wondered if my dissatisfaction has to do with Jack.

Well, that is why I am here now—to find out.

"Go back to your story," I urge her. "Tell me about your married life in Wedding Tree."

"You know the beginning of it."

"Yes, but not from your perspective. I want to know what happened between you and Jack."

66

AMÉLIE
1946

*E*lise and I went to bed early that first night. Jack didn't come home until after eleven. Bruce and Caroline were already in bed. I pretended to be asleep when he crept into the room, thinking that he might climb into bed with me if he thought I wouldn't know it. My heart pounded hard. Instead, to my disappointment, he pulled out a blanket from the closet and slept on the floor.

He left the house before the sunrise, leaving a note that he was going to the hospital to be there when the doctors for his mother and Dr. Thompson made rounds.

I decided to lay low for the day. "Elise is still getting well," I said to Caroline that morning. "I want to keep her away from sick people until she's a little stronger, and I desperately need to do some laundry."

Caroline had nodded. "Best to give things a little time to simmer down, anyway. I'll show you how to use the washing machine."

Jack came home in the middle of the morning, when Elise was down for her increasingly short morning nap. The moment I saw his face, my spirits sank. His eyes blazed with anger, and his lips were pressed so hard together that his mouth nearly disappeared. He advanced toward me until I was backed against the stove. "You forged a letter from me?"

"I thought it would help your cause."

"My *cause*? My *cause* is to live an honest life! Yet every time I turn around, there's a new lie I have to deal with."

"I did it to shift the blame where it belongs—from you to me."

He glowered at me. "Amélie, you forged a letter!"

"It was the type of letter you surely would have written if the circumstances were as we say, yes? In the real world, you would have written Kat before you married another."

"Damn it, Amélie, *this* is the real world. That letter is a falsehood!"

"It is proof you are a caring man. I did it as a kindness. I don't see how that is so wrong."

He threw out his hands. "It's wrong because it's a lie! You don't seem to grasp that simple, basic fact."

"I do—of course I do! But in times of war, everything is turned upside down."

"We are no longer at war!"

"Oh, no?" I glared back at him. "You and I seem to be very much at war right now."

"This. Must. Stop!" He pounded the counter with the flat of his palm, accentuating every word. "No more lies!"

"Jack, we are living a lie."

He raked a hand through his hair. "I get that. But no more new lies, Amélie! No more embellishments, no more exaggerations. Do you understand me?"

"I have never exaggerated anything."

His mouth curled. "Dead babies on the ship? Come on."

"It was the truth!"

He turned on his heel, walked away, and then paced back. "Look, I understand how hard—impossible, even—it can be to back down from a lie once you've told it and defended it. I'm not pressuring you to admit it. Just . . . no more." He made a slashing gesture with his hand.

Despair filled my soul. "Jack, that was the truth!"

"I lose a little more respect for you every time you say that, so let's just not discuss it."

Tears filled my eyes. It was so unfair—and yet, how could I blame him?

He leaned forward, his eyes hot as blue flames. "I refuse to live my life walking on eggshells, always afraid to find out what you've said or are about to say. If I learn of any more new lies, I'll get custody of Elise and send you packing back to France. If you're pregnant, I'll get custody of that child, as well. Are we clear?"

"Y-yes," I stammered.

He stared at me, as if he were trying to see behind my eyes, into my mind, into my soul.

"I wish to God I could believe you," he said.

He turned on his heel and left the house without another word.

67

AMÉLIE
1946

*T*he evening after our argument, Jack came home with a stroller, a high chair, a baby bed, baby sheets, a baby swing, and about a dozen toys. Caroline and I were in the kitchen fixing dinner and saw him struggling to get the stroller out of the trunk. In those days, strollers didn't fold.

Bruce went out to the car to help him carry everything inside.

"Oh, Jack, how wonderful!" I said when I saw all the baby paraphernalia. Jack pulled Elise into his arms and gave her a big kiss, then guardedly gave me la bise—only, I am sure, because Caroline and Bruce were watching.

"A patient gave me all this." Jack shot Bruce an apologetic look as he set the high chair in the breakfast room. "I promise we're not permanently moving in with you."

"You're welcome to stay as long as you like," Bruce said.

"I've checked into rental property, and there's nothing available right now," Jack said.

"Why don't you just buy a house?" Caroline asked.

"I'm, uh, waiting to see what happens with Dr. Thompson."

My chest tightened. Did this mean Jack was still considering leaving Wedding Tree? Or was he holding off because he might divorce me?

I was tense during dinner. Caroline and Bruce carried most of the conversation. Jack was polite but quiet; he had nothing to say to me directly. I was uneasy about where we stood with each other.

I was thrilled when he followed me into the bedroom as Caroline and Bruce retired for the night. Perhaps we were going to talk. Perhaps we were even going to kiss and make up.

I turned toward him, my heart pounding as he closed the door.

"Tomorrow you can take Elise downtown in the stroller and buy both of you some new clothes." He handed me five twenty-dollar bills. "And there's a grocery store on Oak Street, just off the town square." He peeled off two more twenties.

I looked at the money. It was a fortune in those days—especially to me. It was far more than I could imagine spending on clothes or food. I smiled. "Thank you, Jack."

"You're welcome."

I stepped toward him, wanting to give him a kiss, thinking this heralded a new beginning.

He stepped back, his expression cold and remote. "I'm going back downstairs to read for a while." He opened the door and left, closing it quietly behind him.

———

The next morning, Jack once again was gone before anyone awakened. Apparently he had admitted a couple of patients to the hospital, and he also wanted to confer with his mother's doctor and the physician treating Dr. Thompson.

The weather was lovely. In Fahrenheit, it was about 65 degrees. After breakfast, I bundled Elise into her coat, put her in the new stroller, and headed downtown. This was my first chance to really see Wedding Tree.

The town was centered on a redbrick courthouse in a parklike town square. The square had a fountain and benches, and was filled with enormous live oaks and magnolia trees that stayed green in the winter. Stores lined the streets facing the square on all four sides. I was totally charmed by this lovely American village.

I glimpsed a shop with children's clothing in the window and went inside.

"Hello," said a middle-aged woman with her hair in a fishnet snood, standing behind the counter. I thought she wore too much rouge and the green of her dress was all wrong for her complexion, but she was attractive all the same. "May I help you with something?"

"I am looking for clothes for my baby," I said.

Apparently my accent immediately called attention to me, because two women in the back of the store turned from a rack of clothes. They looked at each other, then marched up to me, like soldiers advancing on an enemy. "You must be the war bride," said the one in front, a curvaceous woman dressed all in pink with short platinum blond hair, heavy red lipstick, and large button earrings.

I tensed. I wasn't sure what I disliked more—the term, or the way she said it. "I am married to Jack O'Connor, yes," I said.

"Well, I have to say, what you did was just awful."

I froze, unsure if she was unbelievably rude or if there were a slang meaning for "awful" that I didn't understand. "Pardon?"

"You stole Kat's fiancé, then didn't have the decency to even mail the letter Jack wrote telling her about it." The other woman leaned in. "And I heard you wrote phony letters to Kat to string her along."

I didn't know what "stringing along" was, but I knew it sounded malicious. "That is not true."

"Jack's own sister said you did."

"I wrote the letters, but not for any stringing. I did it because I thought I might have to stay in France with my ailing mother and I thought Jack might return to Kat. I didn't want to ruin their lives."

The blonde sneered. "You'd already done that when you stole Jack from her."

"That is impossible."

"What?"

"A man can't be stolen, like a—a watch, or a pocketbook, or a potato."

"A potato? Who would steal a potato?" The two women looked at each other and laughed.

"Someone who is starving," I said in a low, somber voice. "Someone trying to feed a family during a war."

The blonde quit laughing, but she didn't apologize. "Well, our men aren't potatoes, and we don't take kindly to you Frenchies stealing them. So don't expect to find yourself welcomed in Wedding Tree." She turned to her friend. "Come on, Maura. It smells in here."

"Yeah. It smells like frog." They both giggled as they minced out the door.

I stood there, feeling small and devastated.

"Were you looking for something specific?" the clerk asked.

"No. No, thank you."

I, too, headed out the door, blinking back tears. I turned the wrong way, but finally found the grocery store. It seemed that everyone there stared at me. Several women at the meat counter stood together, whispering and pointing. I bought a piece of beef, some fruits and vegetables.

"Did you find everything you were looking for?" The cashier, a fortyish brunette with a friendly face, smiled at me as she punched in the numbers on the large black cash register.

"Yes, thank you."

"Why, you don't sound like you're from around here, honey. Where are you from?"

"France."

"France! Heavens to Betsy! What brings you all the way to Louisiana?"

"This is my husband's home."

"Oh, yeah? Who're you married to?"

"Jack O'Connor."

Her brow crinkled. "I thought he was marrying the doctor's daughter."

Oh, here we went again! "That plan changed."

"Why, just last week, she was in here, talking about her wedding."

I fumbled with my wallet, my head down.

"Isn't her father in the hospital? I heard—"

"I'm very sorry," I broke in. "I'm in a hurry, so if I can just pay for my purchases . . ."

"Oh, yeah, honey. Sure thing."

I hurried out of the store and down the sidewalk. As I pushed the carriage, struggling to balance my groceries atop the umbrella cover, I noticed that cars slowed down and people gawked at me.

I felt a hot flush of shame rush over me. It was not unlike being une femme tondue all over again.

———

That evening, I told Caroline what had happened.

"Oh, the platinum blonde—that had to be Minxy. She's horrid! She used to make fun of me because I lived on a farm. One time in high school she asked me, in front of a group of her snotty friends, if the polka dots on my dress were milk from one of our cows. Once she wouldn't stand next to me in the lunch line because she said I smelled like manure."

"How cruel!"

Caroline nodded. "It wasn't true, of course. Mother was such a priss about raising me to be a lady, she wouldn't let me within a mile of the dairy. Anyway, Minxy is a jealous, petty busybody. Ignore her."

"It wasn't just Minxy. In the store and all the way home—people were staring and whispering and pointing at me."

"Well, you are quite the town topic. It'll die down eventually. Just smile, go about your business, and ignore it."

But to do that, I feared I was going to have to ignore the whole town.

———

One person I couldn't ignore was Jack's mother—who, unfortunately, warmed to me no faster than Minxy. The next day, Caroline agreed to watch Elise in the hospital lobby—they didn't allow children on the rooms with patients in those days—while Jack took me to the newly added second floor to meet her.

"Now don't let Mother upset you," Caroline warned. "She's very outspoken, and . . . well, she's a big fan of Kat's."

Hiding my trepidation, I plastered a smile on my face as Jack opened the door to her room.

"Mother, this is my wife, Amélie."

She was a beautiful woman, with dark hair and blue eyes like Jack's. She reminded me of an older Vivien Leigh. She arched her delicate eyebrows as she looked me over. "So you're the girl who turned my son's world upside down."

"He did the same for me." I said, with my most charming smile. "That's what love does."

Jack crossed the room, picked up his mother's medical chart, and began perusing it.

"Yes, but I'm afraid you've made his life here very difficult." Her gaze raked me from head to toe. I was sure she was trying to figure out what Jack saw in me. "So tell me, Amélie, was your marriage to Jack a shotgun wedding?"

I had never heard the term. "A what?"

"Did he marry you because you were pregnant?"

"No!"

Jack looked up from her chart. "I already told you that, Mother."

"Yes, but I wanted to ask her for myself. Kat says the baby is huge."

Oh, mon Dieu! She was going to be what I believe Americans call a tough biscuit. I decided to distract her. "I am anxious for you to meet your granddaughter. She is such a delight. She's here at the hospital, but regulations prevent children from visiting on this wing."

"That's just as well. I'm far too young to be a grandmother. In fact, I'm worried it'll make me less desirable to eligible men."

Beside me, Jack stiffened. "Mother, I hardly think a man your age would hold a grandchild against you."

"Who said I'm looking for a man my age? I've been told I look a decade younger than my years."

One thing I knew how to do well was to flatter. "You are very beautiful," I said. "You certainly do not look old enough to be Jack's mother."

The remark earned me a small lift of the corner of her mouth, but it didn't seem to improve her opinion of me. "Jack, I've been thinking. When I get out of here, I'm moving to New Orleans."

Jack put down the chart. "That's a big decision, and you are still ill enough to be on oxygen. There will be plenty of time to discuss this when you get home and feel better."

"I've been considering it for some time. I'm bored here, and the city has a lot more to offer." She fluffed her hair. "With this scandal of yours, Jack, I think you should consider moving, too."

"Getting married is hardly a scandal."

"Jilting the most eligible girl in the parish and coming home with a war bride and a baby big enough to be your sibling—that is indeed a scandal, Jack. A big one, in a town this small." She turned and gave me an insincere little smile. "Sorry, dear, but that's just how things are."

A nerve ticked in Jack's jaw. "They'll get over it when the next bit of gossip comes along."

"Will they? I fear it will hamper your practice. And anyway, I don't see why you don't want to go for a specialty that can make you some real money."

"Because I've always wanted to be a general practitioner. I want to treat entire families, to know my patients outside of sickness, to be a part of their community."

"Well, you can do that perfectly well in New Orleans."

"The type of practice I want is only available in a small town."

"If you're expecting to socially interact with your patients, I think you're going to be disappointed. I hear you're already being shunned."

His features settled into the unreadable set I knew too well. He stiffly kissed her forehead. "Get some rest, Mother."

I walked beside him in silence as we left the room. "Is she right, Jack? Am I ruining your practice?"

He shook his head. "Sick people need a doctor, and right now there are a lot of sick people. My mother has always been overly concerned with the opinions of others."

"You, too, must be concerned about the opinion of those you care about."

"I hate that I've hurt Kat and Dr. Thompson."

"Caroline told me you're considering leaving Wedding Tree."

He blew out a sigh and nodded. "I am trying to find a doctor to take over Dr. Thompson's practice, but it's not easy. I've promised to stay here in the meantime."

"Oh, Jack! I am so sorry I put you is this position."

He stared at the elevator door as it closed. "I put myself in it. I accept responsibility for my own actions." His eyes briefly met mine. His gaze was cool, but I sensed a undertone of still-hot anger. "What I have trouble accepting is that I made my decision based on false information."

"I am so very, very sor—"

He held up his hand. "Save your apologies. I am sick of them, and they don't fix anything."

"But . . ."

The door slid open, and we were no longer alone. My heart was heavy. I didn't know if Jack would ever be able to forgive me. And if he could not, how would I ever be able to forgive myself?

68

AMÉLIE
1946

The next day was Saturday, and the weather was again gorgeous. Winter in southern Louisiana was much like spring in Paris, I was learning—varying from chilly to warm, then back again. This day was another gift of sunshine.

At breakfast, Caroline suggested that we take a picnic to see the town's namesake. Jack tried to beg off, but Bruce insisted. "You need to spend time with your wife, Jack. It won't hurt you to take off half a day to show her around her new hometown."

As Caroline and I washed the dishes, she confided that Bruce had found Jack asleep on the sofa on Thursday when he'd gone down to the kitchen in the middle of the night.

"Bruce is worried about your marriage," Caroline said.

My face heated. "We're fine."

"A lot of couples come to Bruce wanting to divorce," Caroline said, drying a plate. "He always tries to talk them out of it. He says there's one thing those couples all have in common by the time they seek an attorney." She placed the plate atop a stack of clean ones, carefully keeping her eyes on it. "They're always sleeping apart."

My face flamed. I felt very exposed and vulnerable.

"I can tell Jack is angry," Caroline told me.

"Yes." I scrubbed a plate more vigorously than necessary. "He's furious at me for writing to Kat."

"He can be very stubborn."

I nodded.

Caroline picked up another plate and rubbed the dish towel over it. "Sometimes the best way to get over a rough patch in a marriage is to just move forward and create positive new memories." She smiled at me. "That's why Bruce and I planned an outing for the four of us today."

After we finished cleaning the kitchen, Caroline fussed over what I should wear—"Wearing something special makes the day feel special," she said—and insisted on helping me style my hair. She was up to something, I could tell that, but I thought it was just a clumsy attempt to make me more attractive to my own husband, which, quite frankly, embarrassed me to death.

I ended up wearing a dress of Yvette's that I had cut down to fit me—it was light pink with a full skirt. We drove out of town and into the woods, Jack behind the wheel. He was dressed in a suit and tie, because he was going to see patients later.

"This forest reminds me of France," I said.

He parked near a wide spot in the road. We climbed out of the car and walked down a well-worn path through tall oaks and pines. "There it is," Caroline said. "The Wedding Tree."

I stared where she pointed. It was actually two enormous live oaks, connected by a single, continuous branch that formed an arch.

"Oh, my!" I breathed.

"It's called inosculation," Jack said. "The branches rub against each other and wear off the bark, and the two trees graft together."

"It's like that Cole Porter song, 'I've Got You Under My Skin,'" Bruce said, hugging Caroline.

"The part that grows together is the cambium," Jack said.

Caroline rolled her eyes. "Trust Jack to know all the scientific terms."

"They're usually called husband and wife trees, or marriage trees, but the local settlers got it slightly wrong," Bruce added.

I gazed up at the thick branch. "You can't tell where one tree ends and the other begins."

"Like a really long, strong marriage. Isn't it beautiful?" Caroline said.

"They've been completely grafted together for at least a couple of centuries. They share water and nutrients through that branch, too."

My throat grew strangely tight. "That's lovely."

"Isn't it?" Caroline agreed. "There's a legend that if you kiss under the tree, you'll always be together."

Bruce grabbed Caroline, bent her over backward, and gave her a thorough smooch.

"Now it's your turn," Caroline said to Jack.

He raised his hands and stepped away from me. "I don't believe in superstitions."

"Oh, right," Caroline said. "I remember Kat complaining that you wouldn't kiss her here."

Jack's eyebrows quirked up. "She told you that?"

"Yes." She imitated Kat's breathy voice. "Jack said it's a bunch of nonsense and he refuses to participate in a pagan ritual."

"I'm sure I didn't call it a pagan ritual. I probably said I don't believe in perpetuating superstitions."

"It's not a superstition, it's a tradition," Caroline said. "And speaking of tradition, I asked Adelaide McCauley to come take a picture of you and Amélie kissing beneath it."

Jack's eyebrows rose. "What?"

"Well, you know she's a very gifted wedding photographer. You shouldn't miss out on having an Adelaide McCauley photo just because you're already married. You'll treasure it when you're old and gray, and so will your children."

Jack frowned. "I don't think . . ."

"Oh, look!" interrupted Caroline. "Here comes Addie now!"

I turned in the direction Caroline was facing and saw a slender brunette coming down the path, clutching a professional-looking camera. I thought she resembled Katharine Hepburn. Caroline waved and walked toward her.

"Were you in on this?" Jack asked Bruce.

Bruce sheepishly raised his shoulders. "You know your sister. When she gets an idea in her head, there's no stopping her."

The woman wore a blue shirtwaist and wide smile. "So you're Jack's new bride. I'm Addie. Welcome to Wedding Tree!" Instead of shaking my hand, she gave me a hug and patted Elise's arm. "Oh, what a beautiful child!"

Elise smiled and cooed at her.

"Welcome home, Jack." Adelaide gave him a peck on the cheek.

"Thanks. How's Charlie?" Jack asked. "I heard he lost part of a foot in the war."

"He's doing much better, thanks." She greeted Bruce, then lifted the camera hanging around her neck. "The light is just perfect, so we'd better get busy and take advantage of it."

"I'll hold Elise," Caroline said.

I passed the baby to her.

"Jack and Amélie, stand right here and face each other," Addie directed. "That's right. Now, Jack, put one hand on your wife's waist, and the other hand around her back. Amélie, put one hand on Jack's chest and the other around his neck."

We awkwardly posed as she directed. She stepped back and focused her camera for what seemed like forever. The nearness of Jack—the smell of his shaving cream and the starch in his shirt and the scent of his skin—made me feel a little light-headed.

"Okay—now kiss!"

Jack leaned in and lightly touched my lips in what must have been the world's shortest peck. Bruce laughed.

"You'd think you two were total strangers," Bruce said. "How'd you make a baby, kissing like that?"

Jack's ears turned red.

"You need to hold the kiss longer," Adelaide said gently. "Let's do it again."

This time our lips met and held. I melted a little against him, and he seemed to thaw a bit, too.

"This is awkward," I whispered to him.

"No kidding," he replied.

"Again!"

We kissed again.

Adelaide repositioned us several times. With every kiss, things grew both more comfortable between us—and more tense. I was enjoying it, I feared, way too much.

"Okay. I've got it!" Adelaide said at last.

"Thank you so much," Caroline said.

Elise started to fuss and reached for us.

"Oh, wait—let's take a few with the baby! Both of you kiss her, one on each cheek."

We did as Adelaide directed. She snapped away, then lowered her camera.

"Wonderful! I can't wait to get these developed."

"I can't wait, either!" Caroline said.

"Amélie, I want to throw a little dinner party to welcome you to town," Addie said. "How about next Saturday? Bruce and Caroline, I want you to come, of course—and Kurt and Alice Sullivan, and the Marches."

"That sounds wonderful!" Caroline said.

I looked at Jack. He nodded. "Sure. I'd love to see Charlie."

"What can we bring?" Caroline asked.

"Just yourselves. I'll send out an invitation with the particulars. Oh, this will be so much fun!" With a wave, Addie headed up the path to her car.

We ate our picnic lunch, then drove back to the house. Jack left to check on some patients, and Caroline and Bruce went to a movie, with plans to go out to dinner. They invited me to go with them, but I thought they might want some time alone as a couple.

Oh, what I would give for Jack and me to truly be a couple! The kisses had ignited a longing deep in my soul.

I had heard the saying "the way to a man's heart is through his stomach." I was sure it was not a French saying—Frenchwomen know otherwise—but still, I figured it couldn't hurt to cook a nice dinner for Jack. I decided to brave the grocery store again.

I bought a small chicken. I'd just placed it in the oven to roast and had put Elise down for an afternoon nap when Jack came home.

I had hoped that the kisses had warmed him up, as they had me, but his expression was distant, his manner aloof. "Where are Caroline and Bruce?"

"They've gone out to a movie and dinner."

He scowled. "No doubt another of their little romantic plots to leave us alone together." He turned toward the door.

"Where are you going?" I asked.

"Out."

I hurried across the room toward him. "But I'm cooking dinner for you."

"Don't bother." He reached for the doorknob. "I'll grab something at the diner."

"Jack," I said.

He reluctantly turned toward me.

I pulled off my apron and placed it on the side table. "I want to make things better between us, but I don't know how."

"I don't think it's possible."

"Maybe if you don't . . ." I stared at his brown loafers. It took me a moment to gather my courage. "You don't have to sleep on the floor anymore." I looked up at him. "We are married, after all."

"I don't feel married."

"I don't, either. But I want to have that with you. To build that with you."

His eyes were remote, his features hard as granite. "Because of you, I've hurt a lot of people I genuinely care about. If I had my way, I wouldn't be sharing a house, much less a bedroom, with you. The truth is . . ." He heaved a hard, frustrated sigh. "Damn it, Amélie! I'm so furious at you that it's hard for me to be around you."

"We need to fix that." I stepped closer to him. "To fix your anger."

"How the hell do you propose to do that?"

I don't know where the courage came from. My heart was fluttering in my chest like a caged bird trying to escape. I moved toward Jack, put my hands around his neck and drew him down. "Like this," I whispered.

I pressed my mouth to his lips, and angled my groin to fit against his.

He did not move. For a long, heart-stopping moment, I thought he was going to push me away—which, I must tell you, would have killed me.

He remained as still as a rock for so long that I began to tremble. But then, his lips moved on mine, hot and hungry, his tongue demanding entrance. His hands tangled in my hair, then moved down to my breasts, my waist, my bottom. He cupped my buttocks, lifted me and carried me to the kitchen counter, where he set me down.

He wasn't gentle, but it wasn't gentleness I wanted. I wanted raw, primal passion. I wanted to be possessed, to be claimed, to be marked as his.

He unbuttoned my dress, pushed aside my bra, and took my breast in his mouth. His movements were rough and urgent and thrilling. A rush of pleasure shot straight to my groin. He claimed me with his hands and his mouth—my breast, then under my dress, sliding up my thighs— all the way up, stroking me through my underwear until I thought I would die, and then he lifted me again, set me back on the floor, and pulled off my panties.

"Turn around." It was an order, low and raspy, and I quickly complied.

He leaned me over the counter. I heard the clink of his belt unbuckling, the soft whish of his pant zipper, and then he bunched up the fabric of my dress. One hand circled around and stroked me in front on my most sensitive spot, and then . . . Oh, mon Dieu, he filled me. This time there was no pain—only pleasure. Oh, what pleasure! He stroked in and out, continuing to use his hand, as well. Tension built and coiled inside me until it reached an aching, back-arching need, which spiraled to a breath-holding crescendo. I shattered, like glass broken by a soprano's purest note. Jack's completion followed right behind.

He leaned against me, his lips on the back of my neck, breathing hard. I felt a sense of joy and fulfillment and yes . . . love.

And then the kitchen door burst open.

"Oh—excuse me!" I heard Bruce's voice say. I looked up to see the door rapidly slamming shut.

"Merde," Jack said.

"Mon Dieu!" I whispered.

Jack backed away and straightened his clothes. "Go upstairs and get decent."

I scurried upstairs, but paused around the corner to listen as Jack opened the door.

"Hey, really sorry to disturb you, buddy," Bruce said.

"I was, uh, just . . ."

"Hey, no need to explain." I heard Bruce chuckle. "I'm just glad to see you two are getting along better."

I couldn't hear Jack's response. I don't know if he made one.

"Caroline needed a sweater. Good thing she waited in the car, right?" I heard the closet door open. "Say—we saw Betty Costley at the movie, and she asked if you could stop by to see her mother tomorrow. Her arthritis is worse and she's got some kind of new pain that keeps her from sleeping and she's miserable."

"Okay," I heard Jack say. "Do the Costleys still live over on Pine Street?"

"Yeah." The closet door banged shut. "Well, again, sorry to interrupt." I heard what sounded like a backslap and a chortle. "Gotta say, you're a lucky man, bud. Most women won't do anything unless it's dark and the lights are all out!"

I headed to the bathroom so Jack wouldn't catch me eavesdropping. When I came out, Elise was awake from her afternoon nap, and Jack was gone.

69

KAT
2016

*H*earing Amélie talk about lovemaking with Jack makes my stomach hurt, even though I'd told her I wanted the details. I hadn't counted on being able to fit her stories into the context of my memories.

"I think I saw Jack at the hospital that night," I say. "You'd been in town for about two weeks?"

"Yes," Amélie says.

I sink back in the chair, and my mind sinks back, as well.

1946

It was a wonder I hadn't run into Jack more often, because it seemed like I was at the hospital all the time that winter. I wasn't, of course—not nearly as much as Mother. Not nearly as much as I should have been, actually, because the truth of the matter is, I hate sick people and I can't stand hospitals.

Oh, I don't really hate sick people; I just hate being around them. My great-grandmother was very old when I was a child, and I remember how she scared me. Her eyes were milky and they would get crusty in the corners, and she would spill food when she ate. My mother always fluttered around and fussed over her, but Gran-Gran was grouchy, and it made Mother anxious to be around her, and well, I guess sick people have always had that effect on me. They make me feel anxious and uneasy and a little sick myself.

So. I hadn't run into Jack that week, but I had reports of "Jack sightings" from all of my friends—they kept me abreast, it seemed, of his every move.

Unfortunately, I also knew every move of that French whore and her bastard. I knew it wasn't Christian to call them that, but I couldn't seem to help it. That was how I thought of them. I couldn't believe that Jack—the wonderful Jack whom I'd known and loved with all my girlish heart—had so blatantly, so thoroughly, so publicly thrown me over! I was heartbroken. I was stunned. I was humiliated.

That Frenchwoman had gotten her claws into him and tricked him somehow. My hopes, my dreams, my plans to be the wife of the hometown doctor—why, that trollop had stolen my entire future right out from under me!

I hated to hear about her, and yet I became obsessed with learning all I could. From my friends, who were also friends with Jack's sister, I knew that Amélie had worked for the Resistance during the war. I knew, of course, that she had forged documents and supposedly smuggled papers and had worked as a maid at a hotel, spying in Nazis' rooms.

"Oh, I just bet she worked at a hotel!" I'd told Minxy. "On her back, no doubt."

According to Caroline (who apparently just thought Amélie was wonderful; that chafed, because she'd never thought *I* was wonderful), Amélie had had a close call when a house was bombed, and she'd lost both parents and two brothers in the war. Even her ocean crossing was dramatic.

I found it all hard to believe. She was really quite ordinary—she looked like a little brown mouse if you saw her sitting still across a room. But then, she never seemed to sit completely still, and when she moved, she was as graceful as Ginger Rogers. She had something invisible—an energy or vitality or something. I figured she must be like Wallis Simpson, who looked rather plain in photographs but was so captivating that the future king of England had given up his throne to marry her.

Anyway, I heard that she and Jack had been on a picnic to the

Wedding Tree that day. Thank God they hadn't gone out and about as a couple in town—that would have rubbed salt in the wound. Mother had told Daddy to warn Jack not to humiliate me any more than he had, and he'd promised to talk to him about it. I don't know if he ever did.

I knew Daddy was just sick about the way things had turned out with Jack. I also knew that he wanted to go to Dallas for therapy—there was a special doctor there who worked with stroke patients and was getting remarkable results. Jack, of course, had found the doctor. How convenient for him and his war bride!

"Oh, Mother—how can you fall for that?" I'd asked when she told me this. "Jack just wants to run us out of town!"

"I spoke with the doctors at the hospital, and it's true. There's a live-in rehabilitation facility where they're doing therapy for stroke patients, and they're having very exciting results. Daddy will stay there for several months, and they say they can help him regain function of at least his hands and maybe even his legs."

"What will we do while he's there?"

"We'll go with him, of course. There's lodging for families next door."

"Will we ever come back?"

"Of course. We'd still have the house here." Mother had reached out and smoothed my hair, as she used to when I was a child. I hated it when she did that, because I always fixed my hair just so. "It will be good for you, too, dear, to get away for a little while. Daddy says Jack plans to move; he's trying to find another doctor to practice in Wedding Tree. If he can, life will be so much easier for you."

I didn't want to go to Dallas. I told Mother it was because I didn't want to leave my friends, but the truth was, I hated to leave Jack.

It was illogical, and I knew it, but the heart is not a logical organ.

Mother tried to talk sense into me. "You can't possibly want him back, Kat. Even if he divorced her, he'd always be tied to her through that baby. And you'd be marrying a divorced man! Worse than that, you'd be marrying a man who had thrown you over for someone else. You can't want that. Why, the rest of your life, you'd be looking over your shoulder to see if he was about to do it again!"

On one level, she was right. My pride revolted at the thought of being second best. On another level . . . oh, if he had asked, I would have taken him back in a flash. I would have left Wedding Tree with him and started over somewhere else, and . . .

These were the thoughts stirring in my mind as I walked toward my father's room in that dinky parish hospital, back when hospitals smelled like antiseptic and alcohol and sickness.

Jack was coming out the door just as I neared it, and we almost crashed into each other. "Kat," he said, putting his hands on my arms to steady me.

I wanted to give him the cold shoulder—to walk right by without acknowledging him—but I couldn't. I wanted—I needed—something more.

So I stood tall and faced him down. His ears were red, and his eyes held a depth of misery that almost moved me. Maybe it did move me, a little, but my own misery was so all-consuming that any pain he felt was only a fraction of what he deserved.

"I want to know why." My voice was shrill, and I didn't like the way it sounded.

"I can't explain it."

"Try. I think you owe me that."

"It was one of those things. There's really no excuse to give."

"You won't even make an effort?"

"I . . . fell for her."

"You love her?"

"Do you really want to hear me say it?"

No. What I want to hear you say is that you love me. I wanted to crumple to the floor. Instead I asked, "Are you sure that baby is yours?"

"Her name is Elise. And yes, she's my child."

I didn't want to look weak, and yet, I couldn't help it. Tears sprang to my eyes. "What of me? You have left me in a terrible position. What am I to do, Jack?"

"You'll find someone else, a fine man who is worthy of you, a man who will love you as you deserve to be loved."

"Doesn't that bother you at all—the thought of me with another man?"

"I try not to think about it."

All I can think about is you with her. The thought fairly screamed in my head. My blood started to heat and boil. "I just don't understand what you see in her! She's so foreign, so small, so . . . so . . . strange!"

"I won't listen to this."

"And all that espionage rubbish—I don't believe any of it is true."

"It doesn't matter what you believe."

"She trapped you, didn't she?"

He got that flat, tight-lipped look I knew all too well. When Jack got his mule face on, there was no changing his mind. "All I can say is I'm sorry for how I treated you."

"This town isn't big enough for both of us." I realized that was a line from a movie, that it sounded ridiculous, but it was true. I lifted my chin. "I understand you'll be leaving?"

"Yes. As soon as I can find a doctor to take over your father's practice, I'll get out of your way."

"You do that, Jack. You and your foreign wife and your little feral child—you get out of my way, and you stay out of my way."

I flounced down the hall, right past my father's room, like a car going too fast to brake. I couldn't have stood to see my father right then. I was angry at him for having a stroke—although I knew, logically, that it wasn't his fault and certainly wasn't his choice. I was angry all the same—angry at him for keeping Jack in Wedding Tree, angry that he wanted to have anything to do with Jack. At that moment, my feelings for Jack turned a corner. They were still there, still just as intense, but what had been love and longing transformed into fury and hellfire.

Over the next few months, that anger would be my saving grace, because it held me together until I could meet another man.

70

AMÉLIE
1946

*J*ack and I turned a corner, too, after our angry lovemaking. I waited up for him that night and turned on the light when he entered the bedroom. I had taken the advice from Rose and Wilbur on the train, and had tucked a little note under Jack's pillow: *J'ai aimé faire l'amour avec toi.* I loved making love with you.

He wore the look of a man returning from combat.

"What is wrong?" I asked, scooting up on the pillows. "What has happened? Is it Dr. Thompson?"

"No. Although I did have a run-in with Kat earlier this evening." He loosened his tie.

My stomach made a sick little dip. "She must have really upset you."

He shook his head. "I'm upset because a patient died."

"Oh, Jack! From the flu?"

"No. He was eighty-nine and had multiple health problems. He had been bedbound for a while."

"I am so sorry."

"I believe he's now in heaven and free of pain. But still—it was heartbreaking for his wife and children." He took off his jacket and hung it in the closet.

"Heartbreaking for you, as well."

"It's never easy to lose a patient." He pulled off his tie. "Although I have to say, it's easier to say good-bye to someone who has lived a long and useful life than it was to lose soldiers younger than me."

"I am sure. It must have been extremely difficult."

"It weighs on me still."

"I know you did your best to save them."

He blew out a long sigh. "When I couldn't, I didn't have time to mourn them—I had to turn to the next patient, and the next, and the one after that. There was always a line of injured. I still have nightmares about needing to hurry, about someone dying because I took too much time caring for the one before." He sank onto the bed beside me. "The only thing that would be worse than losing a patient because I didn't treat him fast enough would be losing one because I didn't treat him carefully enough. I wonder, sometimes, if any soldiers died because of me."

I put my hand on his back. "Dr. Thompson told you physicians aren't God. Well, none of us are, Jack. We are all only human, and sometimes humans grope in the dark." It occurred to me that Joshua had said something very similar to me, long ago, and it had given me strength. "When we can't see any light, we must move forward in the direction that seems the least black. We must trust we are being guided to do the next right thing."

"I prayed that I was."

"Then you must have faith that it was so."

He looked at me, really looked at me, in a way he had not since we had arrived in Wedding Tree. It was a look that reached beyond our eyes. I felt a connection to him that went all the way through the skin, into our innermost being. The air between us sweetened and softened. "Thank you, Amélie," he whispered. I thought, for a moment, that he might embrace me.

Instead, he rose. He opened the closet door and pulled out the blanket to spread it on the floor.

"Don't, Jack," I said softly. "There is plenty of room in the bed."

I saw him swallow. "Amélie—I am sorry for what happened earlier."

"Why?"

"Because lovemaking shouldn't be like that. It should be tender."

"I think it can be all kinds of ways. Didn't it feel good?"

"Oh, my God." His gaze warmed my skin. "I have thought of little else."

"So . . ." I flipped back the covers and patted the bed.

He shook his head. "I have hurt so many people. It seems wrong for me to enjoy the pleasures of married life."

"I see." Was he in love with Kat after all? Hadn't he said he'd had a run-in with her earlier? I felt as if a boulder had been rolled on top of my chest. "Well, Jack, do you want to divorce?"

"No."

I swallowed hard, my mouth dry. "If we divorced, you could marry Kat."

"No. She would never marry me now. I knew that when I brought you here. That bridge is crossed and burned. And even it if weren't, I don't believe that I could . . . that I would want . . ."

He broke off talking.

"What?"

He sank onto the edge of the bed, leaning his forearms on his thighs. He shook his head. "So many things are not as I thought they would be. I wanted to be an honest man, an upright man, to do what was right."

"You are, and you have."

"I have hurt many people I love."

"You did it out of the generosity of your spirit. You are the one who has been hurt most of all, and it is my fault." I put my hand on his back again. "I want to make it right for you. You are a wonderful man, and I want to give you what you want. Please, Jack. Just tell me what that is."

He twisted around to look at me. His eyes burned into mine, clear and bright. "You. Amélie, I want you."

I reached out for him, and just like that, he was in my arms—kissing me and loving me, his hands and mouth burning trails all over my body. I did the same to him, exploring his body with my fingertips and lips. He covered me with his body, his weight a welcome warmth.

When we joined together, we knew just what to do—how to move, how to read each other's sighs and moans, what to do next. He rolled me over so that I was on top, and the transition was seamless. He used his hand again to caress that small sweet spot as he filled me, and pleasure spun tighter, spiraling me higher and higher until I started to cry out. He gave a soft moan and finished with me. I lay on his chest, still joined to him, and felt a sense of joy and belonging that I had never known.

When we pulled apart, there was blood on the sheets.

"Are you okay?" he asked.

"Yes. I think I . . ." I felt acutely embarrassed. "I have gotten my menses."

"Oh." His face looked drawn.

Disappointment keened through me, along with surprise at the reaction. Had I wanted to be pregnant? Yes; now that I thought about it, of course. It would have tied me to Jack. I loved him. Oh, my God—I loved him!

I tried for a far lighter tone than I felt. "So . . . I guess I'm not pregnant."

He gave a wry smile. "I gathered it didn't mean you're a virgin again."

I didn't know how to respond to that. His face had a funny, tight look. Was he disappointed, or relieved? Was he angry all over again, thinking about the lies I had told? Was he upset that he had brought me to Wedding Tree for no purpose?

Because . . . oh, God. If I wasn't pregnant, I could have stayed in Reno and gotten an annulment. Jack could have quietly explained things to Kat, and no one else in town, aside from probably her parents, would need know he had ever married me.

But that is not the way things unfolded. I wondered if he regretted it.

But of course he regretted it, I thought. He must. He was only human!

I pulled on my bathrobe, and grabbed a Kotex from my baggage— thank God I still had a few left!—and the Kotex belt with the girdle straps that would hold it between my legs. I picked up my pajamas and padded quietly down the hall to the bathroom. I washed up, and brought a washcloth back to the bedroom to try to get the stains out of the sheets. Jack headed down the hall as I returned.

He crawled into bed with me instead of sleeping on the floor, but he stayed firmly on his side of the bed, not forming the spoons in a drawer as I had hoped. Disappointment lay on me like bedclothes. On his side, I imagined, regret lay just as heavy on him. We did not move, and we did not talk, but we both stayed awake for a long, long time.

I did not know that he'd found my note. But in the morning, I smiled when I found one under my pillow: *Moi aussi.* Me, too.

AMÉLIE
1946

"C̲ome in, come in!" Adelaide McCauley stood at the door of her home, a lovely two-story Victorian on Oak Street. I stepped inside and she gave me a hug. Jack followed close behind me, with Caroline and Bruce on our heels.

Inside, the house smelled of baking bread, sautéed garlic, and mouthwatering spices.

"Amélie, Jack, I'd like you to meet Kurt Sullivan. He's the president of the local chamber of commerce. This is his wife, Alice. She's a master gardener and the mother of three adorable boys. Kurt, Alice, let me introduce you to Jack and Amélie O'Connor. Jack is a doctor, and his wife just moved here from France."

We shook hands, then she brought us into the living room and introduced us to a local builder, Henry March, and his wife, Frieda, as well as a hardware sales representative, George Ruston and his wife, Poppy.

Next Addie drew me over to a tall, thin man standing by the fireplace. "This is my husband, Charlie. Charlie and his father run the local lumberyard."

Jack greeted Charlie with a handshake. "Hey there! How's your foot doing?"

"Much better, much better." Charlie looked at me, his gaze frankly curious. "So this is your new bride! How are you liking America?"

"For the most part, it is wonderful. It is a beautiful country. The people are friendly, and the stores have so much food!"

"You had a tough time under the Nazis," Kurt said.

"Oh, yes. Yes, it was very difficult."

"Amélie lost her home and all of her family in the war," Caroline said. "And she worked for the French Resistance as a spy and a courier and a document forger."

"Oh, my word!" Adelaide exclaimed. "You're a heroine!"

"No. I only did what I could to help my people. The heroes were men like Charlie and Jack and Bruce who left their own homes and fought for freedom. I can never thank them enough."

The conversation, thank God, drifted to other topics. Jack talked about an overnight trip he was making to New Orleans on Monday for a symposium on communicable diseases, Charlie explained how the lumberyard was now carrying premade lattice panels, and the builder talked about the trend toward one-story houses, called ranch-style. Caroline told an amusing story about how enamored I was with American washing machines.

At length, Adelaide called us to the dinner table. Throughout the meal—which centered on a delicious Cajun dish, called shrimp étouffée—the guests repeatedly tried to steer the conversation back to me and the war. I kept trying to deflect the topic, but it grew very tiresome.

"I understand that you're taking over Dr. Thompson's practice," Kurt Sullivan said to Jack.

"Temporarily, yes."

"Temporarily? Why not permanently? Wedding Tree desperately needs a doctor. Why, the city council was just talking about it."

"I'm helping Dr. Thompson look for another doctor to move here. I'll stay here in the meantime."

My hands knotted in my lap. I hated that Jack was going to leave Wedding Tree because of me, but I understood that he didn't want to make life more difficult for Kat.

"Where are you moving?" Mrs. Sullivan asked.

"I'm not exactly sure yet."

"Well, then, why would you move?"

"Yeah," chimed in Mr. March. "I'd love to build you a beautiful home. I've got some tracts on the east side where we're putting up brick ranches. Thanks to the GI bill, you can get a VA loan and a very reasonable mortgage."

I felt Jack's body grow stiff beside me. I had gotten rather good at reading his body language. In the last week, we had grown much closer. "Yes, well, I'm afraid the situation is rather complicated."

"What do you mean?" Mr. Ruston asked. "How complicated can . . . Ow!" He looked at his wife.

"So sorry, dear." She gave him a placid smile. "I accidentally stepped on your foot."

Across the table, Frieda tittered.

Adelaide rose. "Who would like seconds?"

"Oh, not me." Mr. Sullivan patted his belly. "I'm stuffed!"

The others groaned their agreement.

"I'll help you clear the plates," I said to Adelaide, picking up mine and that of Mr. Sullivan, who was seated beside me.

Adelaide followed me to the kitchen. "I'm so sorry if things grew awkward."

"It's not your fault. I'm getting used to it."

I went back and retrieved more plates. "Where do you want me to put the scraps?" I asked when I returned to the kitchen.

Caroline just emptied uneaten food in the trash, which I found an abomination. Adelaide smiled. "Scrape them onto this plate, and we'll put them in the garden for the birds and squirrels." Adelaide turned on the percolator, then popped her head into the dining room. "We're going to move into the living room for coffee and dessert," she said.

"In the meantime, I'll take anyone who's interested on a tour of the garden and show you some of those lattice panels," Charlie said.

I excused myself and went to the powder room, where I took several long, deep breaths and regained my composure.

As I walked back toward the kitchen, I saw Adelaide's husband through the window, showing Caroline, Bruce, and Jack the garden. I was about to go join Adelaide in the kitchen when I heard Jack's name mentioned in the living room. I stepped forward and listened from the hallway.

"Jack was engaged to the doctor's daughter, Kat—she's a real looker, that one—and then he came home married to the Frenchie," one of the men was relating. I wasn't sure, but I thought the voice belonged to George Ruston.

"Oh, boy. That's awkward," said one of the other men.

"Wait, it gets worse. Kat hadn't received his letter breaking off the engagement—Amélie deliberately didn't mail it—so here poor Kat is, planning a wedding, only to learn that her fiancé is already hitched. To make matters worse, Amélie had forged Jack's handwriting and continued to send love letters to Kat."

"Why on earth would she do that?"

"The way I understand it, she wasn't sure she wanted to come to America—something was wrong with her mother—and she thought she was helping Jack by keeping his options open with Kat."

"How very odd!"

"Everything about her is odd. I'm not sure she's the type of gal a fellow like Jack would normally have married."

"Such a shame. He had such a bright future and everyone just loves him."

"Not so much anymore."

"Why on earth *did* he marry her?" one of the women asked. "She's lovely and very charming, but Kat . . . well, Kat looks like Miss America."

"There's a baby," the man said.

Another woman gasped. "Well, if that isn't the oldest trick in the book!"

"Kat is just crushed. I heard the doctor and his family are leaving town for a few months," said the first woman. "The official story is that Dr. Thompson is going for physical rehabilitation, but it'll give everyone some breathing room until Jack can find another doctor to take over the practice."

"I hate that he has to leave Wedding Tree," said one of the men. "He didn't look very happy about it, did he?"

"No, sirree. I passed a chain gang on the road today—and those men wore looks of total resignation. Jack had that same look when he talked about leaving Wedding Tree."

"You're right about people snubbing Jack," the woman said. "I heard Ben Campbell really gave him an earful yesterday—told him outright that his behavior was ungentlemanly. Jack put him in his place—told him he shouldn't speak about things he knew nothing about. But that sort of thing is happening quite regularly to him, I'm afraid."

"Yes," said the man I thought was Mr. Ruston. "He greeted a couple of old friends at the drugstore yesterday, and their wives just dragged them away—wouldn't even let their husbands talk to him. It's a darn shame, seeing a fine young man all caught up in a woman's web like that."

"Well, now, it's not entirely her fault," said one of the women. "It takes two to make a baby."

"Yes, but you know what they say about those Frenchwomen—they really know how to get their hooks in a man. And you can bet it was deliberate. From what I hear, every one of them wants to snag an American husband. And as poor a shape as everything is in over there, you can't really blame them. Still, it's not right."

"I'm sure she didn't hold a gun to his head," the woman said.

"She might have held something else, though."

Everyone laughed.

My knees nearly buckled. Oh, mon Dieu—how had I not realized what I was doing to Jack? I was driving him away from his home and friends, making him lose face in front of people he respected, thwarting all of his plans for the future.

What kind of horrible situation had I put this man in? He was a good man, a noble man, a kind man who had only tried to help me—and how was I repaying him? I was ruining his entire life. A man like Jack deserved a well-respected, upstanding wife—not a lying, conniving one who had tricked him into marriage. I wasn't good enough for Jack.

He was a man of his word, so he would stand by me, even if I made him completely miserable. He'd made that decision when he'd brought me here. What had he said? *That bridge is crossed and burned.*

Not exactly the words of a man in love. Well, he might have burned the bridge to Kat—although I wasn't entirely sure about that; I suspected she would still take him back—but even with Kat out of the picture, I was still faced with the hard, cold truth: Jack was saddled with a woman he didn't love, and I was bringing him nothing but heartache.

Jack deserved to be married to someone he adored, the way I adored him. It wasn't fair to keep him bound to me through a sense of duty. He deserved a happy marriage.

The little group was coming in from the garden. I pasted a smile on my face and went into the kitchen, where Addie was slicing cake.

"Are you all right?" Jack asked as he walked through the kitchen door. "You don't look well."

His attentiveness touched me. "I have a bit of a headache."

"Let me get you some aspirin." He left to fetch his bag, which he'd left in the car.

I knew what I had to do. The realization, as swift and hard as a Nazi's fist, left me reeling. I loved Jack; therefore, I had to leave him. I was making him miserable and standing in the way of all he wanted and deserved. I would have to be the one to leave, because he was too honorable to leave me.

And I would have to do it in a way that would free him from his sense of obligation and justify him in the eyes of the community.

He returned with aspirin. I took two with a glass of water. How I wished they could treat the pain in my heart.

"Would you like to go home?" he asked me.

"As soon as we possibly can."

He smiled in a way that was touchingly conspiratorial. It felt, for that brief moment, as if we were a team, a real couple, as if it were he and I against the world. "A doctor always has an out," he whispered. He turned to Adelaide. "May I use your phone? I need to check in with my service."

"Certainly. It's right over here." She led him to the hallway.

As he left the room, Jack gave me a little wink. My heart turned over, and I blinked back sudden tears.

AMÉLIE
1946

I waited until after lunch on Monday, when Jack departed for his symposium in New Orleans. Caroline drove him to the train station in Hammond. I declined to go along, saying Elise needed her nap. As soon as the car puttered out of sight, I quickly packed a bag.

I had been by the bus station on Sunday—while Jack was visiting patients and Caroline and Bruce were at church, I took Elise on a walk—and learned that a bus to Baton Rouge left at two p.m. From there, I could catch connections to Reno.

I changed into my blue polka-dot dress and pulled on my overcoat, because the weather had turned cold. I put Elise in her coat and situated her in her stroller, then placed a note I'd carefully written in English on the kitchen table:

Dear Jack,

I am going to Reno to get an annulment. Our marriage can be dissolved this way because it was based on fraud.

I know that you have grown to love Elise, but Jack, I need to confess that she is not your child. I hate to tell you this, but it is for the best that you know the truth. I cannot live a lie any longer. You are not the father. I lied to you in order to bring Elise to America. I hope you can forgive me.

I see now that you and I are simply too different to spend a lifetime together.

I hope that your friends and family will not hold my sins against you. I am so sorry that I have sullied your name and reputation.

Elise and I are going back to France, where we belong. I will have the annulment papers sent to you at this address.

Thank you for everything.

> *Regretfully,*
> *Amélie*

I wrote him another letter in French and stuck it underneath his pillow. That one said:

Dear Jack,

Please use the other letter to explain things to your friends and family. I am so sorry for placing you in a difficult position. Now, hopefully, you can stay in Wedding Tree. Please place all blame on me. Feel free to show them the other letter and to talk badly about me; it will help your cause.

Please know that I respect and admire you more than any man I have ever known. It was an honor to be your wife. I envy Kat or whatever woman eventually becomes the object of your love and adoration.

> *Je t'aime toujours,*
> *Amélie*

Before I placed the letter, I lifted his pillow to my nose and inhaled his scent one last time. I wished his scent to become part of me. I wanted to memorize it so I could conjure it up when I needed reassurance that life was worth living. If such a man could exist in this world, then perhaps the world was not so awful a place.

The wind whipped hard as I left the house. Elise protested and I adjusted a blanket tightly around her. She was already cranky about missing her nap; the chilly weather didn't help.

My spirits were too low for tears as I wheeled the baby carriage to the bus station, pushing it with one hand and carrying my suitcase with the other. I had known grief and despondency before, but this was different. This time, there was no war that I could hope would end and no new beginning I could look forward to. Any future without Jack could not be as bright as the few bright spots I'd shared with him. This time, I was leaving my fondest hopes behind me.

The thought of starting over filled me with nothing but dread. I had no intention of going back to France; I fully intended to keep my word to Yvette and raise Elise in America, and I was certain Jack would know that. I'd only put that in the letter in order to satisfy Kat or whoever he showed the letter to that I was well and truly gone.

I had no idea how I would make it on my own in this new country. In the back of my mind, I thought I might get a job as a seamstress or maid in Reno, although how I would work and care for a baby, I had no clue. Perhaps God would help me, if I had not strayed too far from what he could forgive. If he did not want to help me, perhaps he would help Elise.

The six blocks to the bus station felt like six kilometers that day. It had rained the night before, and large puddles impeded my progress.

I finally arrived at the station, which was also a small grocery store, and bought a ticket to Reno with just a few minutes to spare. I took Elise from the stroller and settled on a bus bench outside, the baby on my lap. A woman in a nubby black coat sat down beside us. The yellow-and-black-striped scarf she wore over her gray hair made me think of a bee.

"Are you waiting for someone?" she asked.

"No," I said, hoping to discourage conversation. It was a futile attempt.

"Then you must be going somewhere."

I nodded.

"I'm here to meet my son. He was just discharged from the navy."

"How wonderful," I said.

"How old is your baby?" she asked.

"Nine months."

"Oh, she's beautiful!"

She smiled at Elise, then started playing peekaboo, which made Elise laugh and coo. It softened my resolve not to engage with her. "You're very good with children," I said.

"Oh, I ought to be. Raised six of my own, and now I have ten grand-children, with another on the way. The oldest is fifteen; I can't believe I'm old enough to have a grandchild that age! That one belongs to my eldest son, Steven Earl. He's married to a girl from . . ."

I tuned out her words, my thoughts on Jack. What would our child have looked like? My chest ached with longing. If I had been pregnant, it would have changed everything.

I gazed at the filling station across the street. It was a small ramshackle clapboard building, only a little bigger than a shed, with two pumps out front and an attached garage on the side. An empty black Chevrolet sedan sat at the first pump. Through the open door, I saw a little boy, maybe four years old, with dark hair and chubby cheeks. He was bouncing up and down on his heels, obviously wanting his mother's attention, as she paid the attendant.

Jack and I might have had a little boy like that one, I mused.

". . . and my second-oldest grandchild is thirteen," the woman ram-bled on. "That one's a girl. She just loves horses, and . . ."

Inside the gas station, the attendant handed the woman some change. She leaned down and gave the little boy a coin. It must have been a penny, because he went to the gumball machine and tried to put it in. The coin slipped through his chubby fingers. He dropped to his knees and crawled after it.

A large blue Buick pulled up to the second pump. The service atten-dant tipped his hat to the woman with the boy, then loped outside, a cigarette dangling from his lips.

The driver of the Buick rolled down the window. Oh, my heavens—it was Minxy! I slunk down on the bench and pulled up the collar of my coat, my heart pounding, not wanting to be seen.

I immediately realized that the concern was absurd—Minxy would be nothing but delighted to see that I was leaving town. Given the way she'd snubbed me at the children's shop, I had no reason to fear she'd cross the street to start a conversation.

No. It wasn't fear that had me slinking down, hoping to become invisible, I realized; it was shame. I was ashamed of what I'd done to Jack's reputation—ashamed to be seen in Wedding Tree, and ashamed to be seen leaving it. Oh, dear God. I was a vessel full of shame!

Beside me, the woman—I mentally dubbed her the bee woman— droned on. ". . . her mother worked in Covington at the coffee grinding company during the war, and . . ."

Across the street, I realized I needn't have worried about Minxy; she didn't glance my way at all. She spoke to the attendant and climbed out of her car. She was wearing a burgundy dress with a fitted skirt and high heels. She must have been somewhere fancy for lunch. I watched her swing her hips as she walked into the station, stepping around the little boy, who was still crawling on the floor, searching for the penny. Minxy plucked a key attached to a large wooden *L* key fob off a peg on the wall, and turned to the left, toward what must be the ladies' room.

The attendant watched her, too, his cigarette dangling from his lips as he unscrewed the gas cap on her Buick and fitted the nozzle into the tank. Minxy had disappeared, but he kept his eyes on the open door and watched for her reappearance.

Something about the scene struck me as wrong. My stomach clenched with primal foreboding. My gaze latched on the glow at the end of his cigarette. As I watched, some ashes dropped.

There was a loud whooshing sound, and then an explosion and a blinding flash.

Oh, mon Dieu! It was the French farmhouse all over again! But this time, I knew what to do. I jumped to my feet.

"What's happening?" the woman asked.

I thrust Elise into her arms. "Take the baby and go inside."

I dashed across the street. The gas pump was an inferno, and fire was snaking across the pavement, toward the building. But my attention was riveted on the attendant. The right shirtsleeve and pant leg of his gabardine uniform were ablaze. He ran in circles, flapping his flaming arm, screaming.

I tackled him and knocked him to the ground, only a few yards from the fire. I rolled him over, smothering the flames. We rolled right into a big mud puddle. I heard the hissing of his burning clothes—and maybe his burning skin—being extinguished.

I jumped to my feet and yanked him up by the back of his jacket. Where I found the strength, I do not know. "Across the street," I ordered. "Go!"

He was in a daze. He stared at me. "Go!" I roughly shoved him. "Cross the street. Now!"

He staggered off in that direction.

The fire was leaping high. Minxy's car was ablaze, as well as an oil drum beside the pump. The wind carried the flames to both the Chevrolet and to the wooden shingle roof of the station.

I dashed inside and found the woman trying to pull her child out from under a tabletop display of motor oil. Her skirt was too tight to allow her to kneel down. "My car," she said, her voice shrill with panic. "I've got to get my car out of here!"

"No. There's no time." I crawled under the table and grabbed her child.

"Hey!" She tried to pull her child from my arms, but I straightened and headed for the door. She trotted alongside me as I hurried outside, away from her car, to the grass at the side of the building.

Another explosion rent the air. I pushed the woman to the ground and fell on top of her, the little boy between us. Glass and metal rained down around us. After a moment, I got up, and pulled both of them to their feet. "Run across the street. Now!"

The woman lifted her wailing child into her shaking arms and staggered away from the fire, toward the bus station.

I turned around and surveyed the situation. The woman's car had just exploded. The gas station itself was now ablaze and Minxy was still inside.

I pulled off my overcoat, dunked it in a puddle, and headed back into the building. One of the explosions had blown out the glass, and flames were leaping inside around the display of motor oil cans.

The coat over my head, I ran to the back, and to the left. I could hardly see through the smoke. I pounded on the restroom door.

"Wait your turn!" Minxy yelled.

"Fire!" I bellowed. I tried the door. It was, of course, locked.

A can of motor oil exploded. Flames crawled across the floor.

I ran to the cash register, praying that they kept extra keys to the restrooms. Thank God—there was a key with an *L* key fob in the drawer under the register. I ran back and unlocked the door just as Minxy was flushing the toilet.

"How dare you!" she said, eyes flashing.

"The building is on fire." I took a gulp of air; the metal door to the bathroom had kept out most of the smoke. "We must leave now."

Her eyes grew large as she smelled the smoke and saw flames outside the door. "Oh, my God. Oh, God!"

"Come on. We have to go."

"I can't go out there! There's a fire."

"You can't stay in here. There are no windows, no exit."

I pulled at her. She wouldn't budge. She was as frozen as a glacier.

I threw my coat over her head. Like a parrot in a covered cage, the darkness seemed to calm her. "Just walk with me," I told her. "Hold on, and walk with me."

It was almost too smoky to see. Holding my breath, I guided her through the garage and onto the grass, then took my coat off her head. She blinked and stared at the building. As we watched, the roof collapsed.

"Where is my car?"

"It exploded."

"That's impossible," she said. "It's brand new."

The disconnect between what one wants and what one gets can

sometimes make the brain misfire. "Come on." I herded her across the street. As we neared the bus station, another explosion rattled my teeth.

———

The ticket agent was standing outside. He stepped toward me, his mouth hanging loose from the jaw. "I never saw nothin' like that in all my live-long life, and I was in the first war."

"I was in the second," I said.

He held the door open for me, then reached out his hand. "Here, ma'am—let me take your coat."

I realized the overcoat I was clutching was charred, mud-soaked, and sopping wet. I handed it to him, then went indoors and took Elise from the arms of the bee woman.

She was, thankfully, speechless. The ticket agent handed me my purse and diaper bag, which I guess he had collected from the bench outdoors. He set my suitcase beside me.

Just then, a bus pulled into the station. The door wheezed open, and a man around thirty years of age bounded down the stairs. "What the hell's going on across the street?"

The woman who'd held Elise ran toward him, sobbing. He caught her in bear hug. "Hi, Mom. What's with the fire?"

Sirens sounded in the distance. The bus driver rose from behind the wheel and hefted himself down the stairs. He opened the storage bay on the side of the bus and quickly extracted a bag. The young man— apparently the bee woman's son—picked it up.

"Any passengers for Baton Rouge need to board right now," the driver yelled. "Can't have the bus this close to a fire."

"This little lady is getting on," said the ticket agent. He put my suitcase in the bus's storage compartment.

"I need to take the baby carriage, too," I said.

"It's too big," the driver said. "It's against regulations."

"She gets to take whatever she wants," the ticket agent told him. "She just single-handedly saved four lives."

I climbed up the steps onto the bus. It was half full of people, most of whom were gaping out the windows at the blazing gas station on their right. Several, I noticed, turned and also gawked at me.

The sirens were getting closer.

I sat with Elise in an empty row on the left side about three seats down. Elise reached for my face and touched it. When she pulled away her hand, her palm was black.

Oh, dear. I looked at my lap. My dress was splattered with mud, pocked with burn holes and singed at the hem. My hands were filthy. So, I noticed, were my arms—and apparently my face. I must look like I'd been rolling around in a bin of coal.

Well, I might be filthy on the outside, but I hadn't added to the sins of my soul. For once, the right course of action had been clear, and no lies had been required to justify it.

I rested my head on the back of the seat, thinking it was a good thing they had headrest covers to protect the fabric. In France, they were called antimacassars, to protect furniture from the macassar oil men used on their hair at the turn of the century.

If only, I thought, cradling Elise, there were antimacassars to protect those I loved from the consequences of my misdeeds.

73

KAT
1946

*M*other and I saw the smoke as we were driving back from the hospital around four in the afternoon. It was billowing toward the sky, a huge malevolent cloud, boiling and churning and spreading.

"Merciful heavens—what's on fire?"

"I don't know," Mother said. "I hope it's not our house."

But the fire was too dark, too heavy to be a house. As we neared Wedding Tree, we began to guess that it was the filling station.

I wanted to drive down and see what was going on, but Mother wanted to get home and check the house.

"Why? It's fine. It's on the opposite side of town."

"Yes, but I need to check. Whenever something bad happens, I have to make sure our life is unaffected."

Interesting words, those. I didn't really ponder the significance until later. I walked in the house with Mother, crinkling my nose at the way the foul, oily smoke hung in the air. I fully intended to turn around and drive to the station to see what was going on, but the phone was ringing. I answered it.

"You'll never guess what happened!" It was Minxy, and her voice was breathless.

"Is the gas station on fire?"

"Yes. Yes! And I was in the ladies' room when it happened!"

"No! You were there? Are you all right?"

"I lost my brand-new car. It exploded!"

"No!"

"Yes. And my new shoes—the red high-heeled ones—they're ruined. And my burgundy dress—it has burn holes all over the skirt. But I walked through an inferno—an absolute inferno!—and I'm okay. And you'll never guess who saved me."

"Who?"

"The war bride."

I sat down on the floor, my back against the wall. "No."

"Yes! She saved Ernie, and Mrs. Anderson and little Lukie, and then came back for me."

"What was she doing at a filling station? I didn't even know she could drive."

"She was waiting for a bus across the street."

"A bus?" None of this was making sense. "To where? Where was she going?"

"She got on a bus to Baton Rouge."

"Why?"

"I don't know. But she was sitting there with Mrs. Palinsky, and there was a big boom, and Ernie's clothes caught on fire. Quick as lightning, she handed her baby to Mrs. Palinsky and dashed over to help. She tackled Ernie and rolled him in a mud puddle. And then she ran into the building and got Mrs. Anderson and little Lukie. And Mrs. Anderson wanted to go to her car and drive away, but Amélie grabbed the child, and Mrs. Anderson had no choice but to follow, and then Amélie pushed them down and covered them with her body when their car exploded!"

I switched the phone to my other ear, unable to process what I was hearing. "Wait. Amélie did all this?"

"Yes! And then she came back in for me! I was in the bathroom. I'd heard some explosions, but I thought Ernie just had a radio program on too loud, and then I was mad when I heard someone pounding on the door, because I thought someone was being rude and trying to hurry me."

I switched the phone back to my right ear.

"So she went and got the extra key and came in anyway and got me out. She threw her coat over my head—it was sopping wet and muddy and smelled all charred and awful, but thank goodness she did, because Daddy says that probably kept my hair from catching on fire. And she led me out through the garage and across the street, right before another car blew up. I don't really remember how we got out—it was all dark and smoky, and Daddy says I must have been in shock. And then . . . well, she just took her baby and her purse and her suitcase and the baby carriage, and got on the bus!"

My heart quickened. "She left town?" I rose to my feet. "Why?"

"Nobody knows. I've been trying to reach Caroline, but I don't get any answer."

74

AMÉLIE
1946

I had to change buses in Baton Rouge, so when they took my suitcase and the baby carriage out of the bus's storage bay, I put Elise in the carriage and rolled her to the restroom so I could clean up and change clothes. My face and hands were filthy, and I had burns on my hands, arms, feet, and legs. The bottom of my hair was singed on one side. I used manicure scissors and cut it into a layer, then cut a layer in the other side to match. I thought it came out surprisingly well. I was grateful, right then, to have curly hair, because curls can hide a multitude of irregularities. Could a person have a curly soul? I certainly was in need of one.

I washed my hair in the bathroom sink, using bar soap and cupping my hands to pour water over my head. I received strange looks from women coming in and out of the restroom, but I didn't care. I didn't mind disdain directed at me as long as it didn't reflect badly on someone I loved.

It was dark when we boarded the bus for El Paso, where I was to change buses again. We rode and rode and rode. It took all night and all the next day, with stops at what seemed like a thousand little towns along the way. Elise was so cranky I feared she was getting sick again. She wanted to crawl, and there was no safe place for a baby to crawl on a bus. I stood her in the seat beside me, sang softly to her, played patty-cake, and read to her from the three picture books I had packed in her diaper bag. I fed her little bits of sandwiches and snacks I bought at the little towns along the way. A woman with a thick Texas twang sat beside us for a couple of hours, and she helped occupy Elise. Elise finally drifted off into a sound sleep as evening fell for the second night. I closed my eyes and tried to sleep, as well.

Sleep wouldn't come, even though I was so very, very tired. I couldn't get comfortable. My back hurt, my arms hurt, my legs hurt. I had pulled muscles in places I didn't even know I had muscles.

But worst of all, my heart hurt. I was heartsick over what I had done to Jack—heartsick I had hurt him, heartsick I had soiled his reputation, heartsick that, like a dab of arsenic in a well, I had poisoned his life.

He would have been better off if he'd never met me. There was no question in my mind of that.

And yet—God help me!—I could not entirely regret our time together, because with him, I had discovered depths of the heart I never knew existed. He had shown me that despite all I had lived through, all I had lost, and all the sins I had committed, there was still compassion and kindness and selflessness in the world. He had helped me regain my faith in God.

The glow of streetlamps filtered through my closed eyelids. I blinked and sat up; we were driving through a city. The bus lurched to a halt at several stoplights, made a couple of turns, then pulled into a brightly lit bus station.

The bus shuddered to a stop. The driver killed the engine, and opened the door.

"El Paso," he announced.

He climbed out and opened the storage bay on the side of the bus. Out the window, I watched two men in Greyhound uniforms hoist out suitcases and set them on the pavement. I gathered up the baby's bag and my purse, and gently lifted Elise. She was sleeping soundly now, so soundly she felt as limp as soft rags in my arms.

Not wanting to awaken her, I waited until everyone else had disembarked, then carefully made my way up the aisle and down the steps.

My eyes were on the baby carriage. I gently set Elise inside it, being careful not to wake her. Without lifting my head, I bent to pick up my suitcase. As I reached out, a masculine hand beat me to the handle.

Something about that hand registered with my heart. I lifted my gaze to the arm, then the chest, then the face connected to it.

My pulse stopped, my breath hitched, and I thought I was hallucinating. Perhaps I had inhaled a damaging amount of smoke, after all. "Jack?" My voice did not sound like my own.

"Amélie." He grinned at me.

"What are you doing here?"

"I came for you."

Oh, dear. Had I messed up again? Because of me, he was missing his symposium in New Orleans. He had left his patients in Wedding Tree. He'd left his sister and mother and Dr. Thompson. My brow knitted in a frown. "Have I created another problem for you?"

"I'll say you have."

My heart sank further. "Jack, I'm so . . ."

"If you're going to say you're sorry again, I'm going to turn you over my knee and spank you."

"What?"

"It's an expression."

"Oh." I looked at him, feeling uncertain and a little dizzy. He was smiling. It sounded a little . . . naughty. "What does it mean?"

"It means . . ." He shook his head. "I'll tell you later. We have more important things to discuss." He peered in the carriage. "Elise is all right?"

"Yes. She's fine. She's been terribly fussy and she just fell asleep."

"Well, let's go inside and try not to wake her."

He put his hand on the small of my back. It was a small touch, but I felt it in my bones. I shivered.

"You don't have your coat."

"No."

"I heard what happened to it." He held open the door to the terminal, and I pushed the carriage inside. He led me to a quiet corner, away from the ticket desk and waiting passengers.

"Why don't you have a seat?"

"If you don't mind, I'd rather stand." As the Resistance had taught me, if you're in a threatening situation, it's always better to be on your feet. "How did you get here before me?"

"I flew."

I was so stunned to see him that for a moment I pictured him flapping his arms like a bird. "You took a plane?"

He nodded. "Caroline called me in New Orleans. I was at the front desk of the hotel, just checking in. She told me what happened at the filling station."

"She knows about that?"

"Are you kidding? The whole state knows about it. Heck, probably the whole country."

"Really?"

"Amélie, when she first told me about the fire, and that you were there, I thought you'd been . . . I thought you were . . ." He looked down and cleared his throat. "I thought she was calling to tell me I'd lost you. She was telling me of all your heroics, but all I could do was think, 'Thank God she's safe, Elise is safe, they're safe.' And then she read me your note."

"The one I left on the kitchen table."

He nodded. "I immediately told her you were lying, that Elise is definitely my child—that you were trying to give me an excuse, an out from the marriage, and that she was not to repeat a word of what you'd written to anyone." He frowned at me ferociously. "You are not to ever tell another soul that Elise is not my child. Is that clear?"

I bobbed my head.

"Swear it."

"I—I swear."

"Good. Anyway, next I asked Caroline to go look under the pillow on our bed." His mouth curved in that slight, sidewise grin. "She read me that letter, too."

I frowned. "But it was in French."

"She speaks French as well as I do. We had the same nanny."

"Oh—bien sûr!" I hadn't thought of that. I'd only thought I wanted the first letter to be for public consumption, and the letter under the pillow for Jack's eyes only. I tried to remember what I'd written in it.

"You signed it *Je t'aime toujours*."

"Yes, well . . . it's an expression. Like you saying you wanted to take me for a spank on your knee."

He grinned. "Is it true?"

"Is what true?"

"What you wrote . . . is it true?"

He was an impossible man. What did he want to do? Humiliate me? Make me say what I had no right to feel? Or try to make me lie again? I wouldn't lie to him anymore, damn it! "Well, of course I love you. Why else would I be leaving you?"

He laughed. Threw back his head and laughed! "That's just about the most ridiculous thing I've ever heard."

I bristled. I was tired, burned, sore, and heartsick. And now I had to be insulted? "It's ridiculous for me to want you to have a happy life, a good life, the life you deserve with your friends and family in your hometown? It's ridiculous to not want people to think less of you because of me?"

"It's ridiculous to care what other people think."

"Jack, I heard people talking at the dinner party. They think I trapped you. They feel sorry for you. They think you deserve better. And you do."

"I get to decide who is best for me."

"No. I gave you no choice. I lied to you and bent the truth to my own purposes."

"You were not alone in bending the truth, Amélie." He moved closer to me. His eyes were somber. "I bent it to fit my boyish ideal of how life is supposed to be. I proposed to Kat because she was so very beautiful and we'd been dating a long time, and it seemed like the next logical step, especially since I planned to go into practice with her father."

His hands settled on my arms. "I told myself that since we didn't argue, we'd have a good life together. I didn't stop to think that maybe we didn't argue because we didn't have much to say to each other—that maybe the lack of conflict was really a lack of connection. Not fighting is not a good enough reason to get married."

"You didn't love her?"

"I thought I did. But then you showed me what love really is. I didn't understand love until you and Elise came into my life."

He took my hands. "Amélie, I have been stubborn and unforgiving. I looked only at the lies, and not at the truth behind them. I focused on how you wronged me, and refused to see the kind intentions and brave heart and love for Elise that spurred your actions. I am so sorry."

My heart pounded hard against my ribs. I tried not to let the wings of hope unfurling inside me take flight.

"Amélie, it doesn't matter where we live. Wedding Tree isn't home. You are. Elise is. And what you did in that fire . . . Jesus, Amélie! You risked your life for strangers and a woman who treated you badly!"

"I only did what needed to be done."

"Not everyone would see it that way. Very few people would put everything on the line just because it was the right thing to do. But Amélie—that's all you've ever done. For your country. For Yvette. For Elise." He stepped closer. "And for me. And if you think I'm going to let you get away, well, you don't know me very well."

"What are you saying, Jack?"

"I'm saying I love you. I want to live with you and have babies with you and grow old with you. Will you stay married to me and be my wife, for real and for true?"

I looked at him. He was suddenly blurry because my eyes had filled with tears.

"Only if you will be my forever husband."

"I already am." He drew me into an embrace and kissed me. When we pulled away, he looked at me with the kind of love my heart had never thought it would find. "Let's get out of here and go home."

KAT
2016

I sit there, letting her story settle in my mind. The things she's told me mingle with my own memories. They all float around in my brain like flakes in a snow globe.

The day after the fire, the newspaper came out with the headline, "War Bride Braves Inferno, Saves Four Lives."

Overnight, Amélie went from persona non grata to the toast of the town. Everyone raved about her strength of character, her selflessness, her generosity of spirit. Caroline's stories about her work for the Resistance were repeated, growing more stupendous and outrageous with every telling. Even Daddy sang her praises.

"A woman who does a thing like that—well, sometimes God puts a certain person in a certain place at certain time to do a certain thing. Ernie and Minxy and the Andersons would all agree that Amélie was meant to be in Wedding Tree."

Oh, just peachy, I'd thought—my own father believed God had conspired for Jack to jilt me for a Frenchie! Caroline had circulated the word that Amélie had gone to visit a sick relative. The whole town was planning a hero's welcome for her when she returned. I couldn't get out of Wedding Tree fast enough.

My thoughts circle back around to Amélie's words.

"So Jack really said all that at the bus station?"

"Yes." Her expression is somber, her eyes kind. "I didn't tell you that to hurt you."

I wave my hand. "Oh, I'm not interested in that he-loved-you-more-than-me stuff. Of course he thought he loved you more; he'd had sex with you. Men think with their little heads. They always think sex is love."

Amélie's eyebrows fly upward, as if this surprises her. How could it? She is a woman, after all. Plus she is French.

I lean forward. "What I want to know is, did he really say the other part?"

"What other part?"

Her refusal to see the obvious irritates me. "Did Jack really say I was very beautiful?"

"Oh! Yes. Yes, of course, Kat." She cocks her head in that graceful, birdlike way. "He said you were beautiful many times. And you were. You were gorgeous. You still are."

I sit back and clutch this information to my chest like a beloved doll. "That's all I ever had, you know." I know I was never particularly smart or funny or brave. "I only had my beauty."

"That's all any of us have."

"No." I refuse to let her take away my specialness by pretending it isn't so special. "Not everyone has real beauty."

Her eyes catch the light in way that reminds me of an owl at night. "Yes, they do. Some have more than others, of course—and some people have more on the inside than the out."

I think about it for a moment. "Well, I suppose that's true. You're one of those, aren't you?"

She laughs, as if I'd said something extremely amusing. "That's not for me to say. What's the English expression? 'Beauty is in the eye of the beholder.'"

"Jack was one of those people who had lots of both."

"Yes. Yes, he was." She tilts her head. "And your husband?"

"Oh, he was good-looking—very handsome. And he had the beauty of being rich."

Amélie laughs again. She makes me feel as if I am a most amusing person.

"He adored me," I say.

"Then you are a most fortunate woman. I hope the adoration was mutual."

I nod, but I'm not quite sure. So many memories are swirling around, I still feel like a shaken snow globe.

"I've always wondered about something." Amélie leans forward. "You and your family never returned to Wedding Tree—not even to move. As I recall, a moving service came and packed up everything and shipped it all to Dallas. Was that because of Jack and me?"

"No. No, not at all!" There is no need to tell her, but at the time, I would have eaten dirt before I would have set foot in Wedding Tree again. "I met my husband in Dallas—he was an orthopedic surgeon, did you know that? He sent some of his patients to the rehabilitation center where Daddy stayed, and we met the week after we arrived. We were engaged within three months, and married just five months later. He was afraid I'd slip away if he didn't marry me fast. He was so smitten with me! He couldn't believe that a man would choose another woman over me. He said Jack must be crazy."

Amélie smiles. "That is exactly how a husband should feel."

"He was very sought after. All the nurses used to just swoon when he came by. Orthopedic surgeons make a lot of money, you know, and he knew how to invest—in oil and computers and things that really took off after the war. Anyway . . . his practice was in Dallas, so of course we lived there. Mother discovered she just loved living in a city, and she and Daddy wanted to be close to me, so they stayed. As for the packing and moving—well, Daddy couldn't do it and it was too much for Mother, and Hugh—that was my husband's name, Hugh—well, Hugh just had money to burn, so he arranged it all."

"That's wonderful."

"Yes." We fall silent for a moment, and the flakes of memory settle in my brain. One piece continues to float and hover. "What about the babies on the ship? Did Jack ever believe you about that?"

Amélie nods. "Once he realized that he knew me—really knew me, knew my heart and my motives—he knew I wouldn't have lied about a thing like that. And then it came to light that it had happened again! Another group of war brides sailed on the *Zebulon B. Vance* from England—some were English, of course, but others were French, Italian, and German—and the same thing happened. The staff took the formula and mixed it for the mothers, and seven babies died. The army tried to blame it on the mothers, saying it was their lack of hygiene." Amélie paused. "Jack had tears in his eyes when he told me of it." Her voice softened. "He was such a dear, dear man."

I feel a scratch of the old envy. I try to batten it down by remembering an old Spanish proverb my hospice counselor had told me: *Envy is thin because it bites but never eats.* "So you and Jack—you were happy?"

"Oh, yes. We made each other feel loved and accepted and treasured. I think that is all one can ask for in this life."

"Yes." Hugh had made me feel that way. I'm not sure I had fully reciprocated. I hope I had. I hope he believed I had.

"So," Amélie says. "Did you get the answers you came for?"

"I'm not sure," I say. "I'm not sure I asked the right questions."

Again, Amélie gives that appreciative laugh. "Is anyone, ever? And yet the right questions might be more important than the answers."

"You didn't really give me a chance. You insisted on telling the story your way."

She lifts her shoulders in that little French shrug. "It's my life. I have the right to tell it my own way, as long as I'm the one doing the telling." She gives a smile. "Now that I have, you are welcome to ask me anything you like."

"I think I have heard enough," I say.

Once again, she laughs, as if I have said something witty. She glances at her watch and rises to her feet. I reach for my cane and do the same.

"Well, Kat, it has been good seeing you."

"I thought you'd resolved to quit lying."

Once more, I make her laugh. "I wasn't so thrilled at first, but you're like fine wine, Kat. You've improved with age."

Really? I thought age had brought nothing but decline. It cheers me to hear her say otherwise, although I don't quite believe it.

She stands with her hand on the doorknob. "Now that you've heard my whole story, do you think that you can forgive me?"

"I hope so." My hospice counselor tells me it is necessary for my peace of mind; my religion tells me it is required for the good of my immortal soul. "I will try."

"Then you will succeed." She opens the door and holds out her hand.

I impulsively lean in, and awkwardly give her a kiss on both cheeks. It rattles me, doing something so out of character. I straighten my dress and put my purse on my arm.

She pats my shoulder and gives a little wave. "Au revoir, Kat." She turns and heads back into her apartment.

"Good-bye," I say, and reach to close the door.

"Oh, please leave it open," she calls.

I walk away, oddly unsettled by the thought of a still-open door between us.

AUTHOR'S NOTE

*T*his is a work of fiction, but I've tried to describe the historical events as accurately as possible.

One of those events was the Rafle du Vélodrome d'Hiver, a massive roundup of Jews by the French police that took place July 16 and 17, 1942. Tragically, 13,152 Jews were arrested, including 5,802 women and 4,051 children. They were held at the Vélodrome d'Hiver, an indoor bicycle racetrack and stadium, with almost no water, food, or restroom facilities. They were then transported in cattle cars to Auschwitz, where they were murdered.

The roundup accounted for more than a quarter of the 42,000 Jews sent from France to Auschwitz in 1942. At the end of the war, only 811 returned to France. In 1995, French president Jacques Chirac issued an apology for the complicit role the French police served in the raid.

Another event the novel describes is *l'épuration sauvage à la libération*, or the savage purge during the liberation—the way the French turned on their own citizens who had collaborated with the Germans during the occupation. An estimated 10,000 men were killed without a trial after the Allied landing, and many more were beaten. Women accused of sleeping with the enemy were publicly humiliated. Throughout France, approximately 20,000 women had their heads shaved. Known as *les femmes tondues*, these "shorn women" were stripped of all or most of their clothing and paraded throughout town to be pelted by garbage, spat upon, cursed, kicked, and beaten.

On a happier note, the U.S. War Bride Act enabled an estimated total of 100,000 foreign brides to come to the United States from the time it was enacted on December 28, 1945, until it expired in December 1948. These women were given non-immigrant status, bypassing stringent immigration quotas.

The Red Cross assisted the military and the State Department in getting foreign brides to America. The organization ran assembly centers, taught courses on life in America, and accompanied the brides on requisitioned ships.

Unfortunately, there were, indeed, baby deaths on board the *Zebulon B. Vance* as depicted in my novel. Two voyages with fatalities from widespread intestinal infections are documented: one sailing from Le Havre, France, on May 2, and the other sailing from Southampton, England, on June 24. To fit the timeline of my story, I changed the sailing date and created a fictional trip, but I tried to depict the actual conditions of the ship as accurately as possible based on historic accounts.

Although initially the military tried to blame the deaths on poor hygiene of the mothers, the problem was found to be a lack of sanitation on the ship.

THE

French War Bride

ROBIN WELLS

DISCUSSION QUESTIONS

1. Amélie told Jack, "In war, the concept of 'right' stands on its head." Is there a different moral code during times of war? Where does one draw the line?

2. In Chapter 21, Yvette said, "[Guilt] is the price we pay for being alive during this terrible time." What does she mean? Do you believe in survivor's guilt?

3. Amélie learned to lie and keep secrets to help free her country. Is lying always wrong, or are there exceptions? Would it be hard to "turn off" such learned behavior?

4. Pierre thought the Nazis would win the war. Is it human nature to want to align with the winners, or to stand with your fellow countrymen? Why or why not?

5. What was behind Yvette's decision to become the mistress of a high-ranking German? What do you think of her decision?

6. What do you think of the statement, "In war, we must use everything we have at our disposal. Nothing done to save France would be unholy."

7. Kat said that her father had never talked about his time during the First World War. Why do think that was? Why did many Second World War veterans not talk about the war once they came home?

8. Do you think Jack would have married Kat as planned if he hadn't met Amélie? Why or why not?

9. How did it affect the characters in the story to learn that the French government had fled Paris, then surrendered? Can you imagine how it would feel to have your own country overtaken and occupied by a foreign army?

10. Why do you think the French treated the collaborators so cruelly after the war?

11. In Chapter 16, when Amélie doubted that she was serving a useful purpose, Joshua told her that this was not for her to know; she must just believe she was and keep going. How did this advice impact her? Was it wise? Is this advice applicable to your life?

12. All of the women on the bride boats were leaving their families behind and traveling to a foreign land, not knowing when or even if they'd ever see them again. Can you imagine doing this? Why or why not?

13. In what ways does the book illustrate the era's attitudes toward women?

14. Describe Amélie's faith journey. Did Kat grow and change? What about Jack?